KIRSTEN KRUEGER

WHITE MATTER

AN AFFINITIES NOVELLA

WHITE MATTER: An Affinities Novella

ISBN: 978-1-7347664-0-0 paperback
ISBN: 978-1-7347664-1-7 ebook

Cover and Interior Art by: Ilona Parttimaa

AFFINITIES NOVELS
Blood
Nerve
Chromosome

AFFINITIES NOVELLAS
The Pixie Prince
Nero's Dominion
White Matter

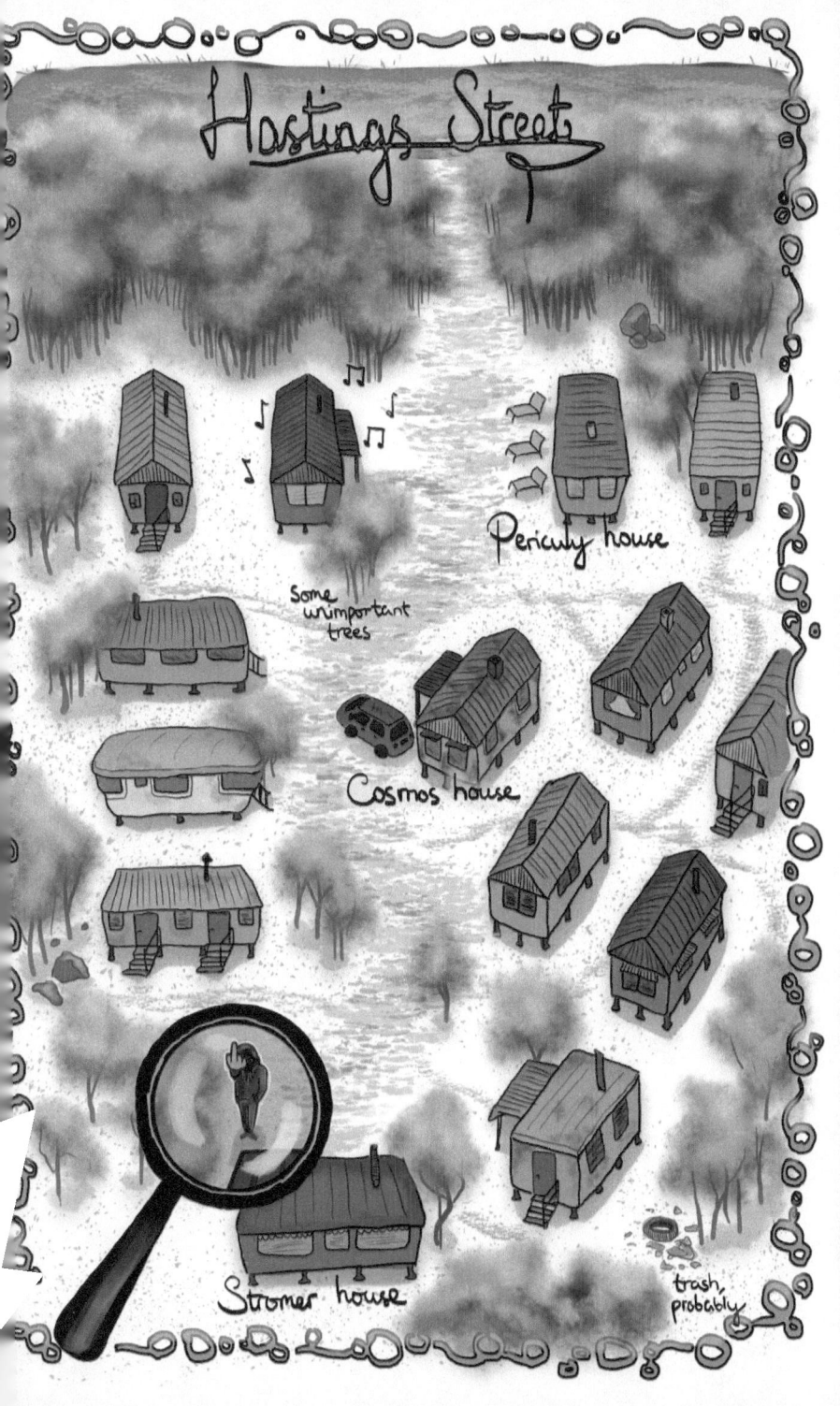

Part 1

The Manipulator and The Manipulated

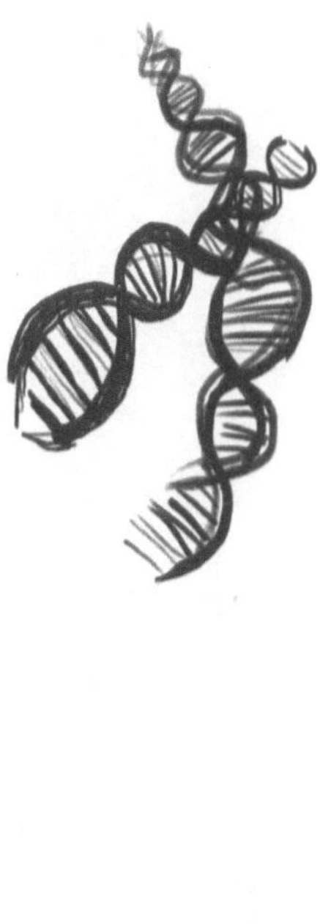

1

The Art of Beliefs

Tension coursed through the car as they drove home from school. Olalla Cosmos was young, only a first-grader, but she recognized the rage wafting from the driver's seat. It always felt this way before her mother lashed out.

"I shouldn't be in trouble," Olalla complained, arms crossed tightly over her chest. Her mother slammed hard on the brakes but didn't glance over her shoulder. "Tyler put his hand under the water by himself. I didn't make him."

Beside Olalla in the backseat, Artemis kicked her lightly in warning. *Shut up*, her older sister seemed to say with those colorlessly dark eyes. They were identical to Olalla's, but Olalla had never seen her sister's eyes when she gazed in the mirror. Artemis's eyes held a flat expanse of sternness while Olalla's were a deep well of cunning.

Still, Artemis had always looked out for her sister, and so Olalla kept her mouth closed for the remainder of the car ride.

When they arrived home, however, there was no stopping her tongue.

"I didn't do anything wrong," she insisted the moment they crossed through the front threshold. Her father sat on the couch in the living room, all the drapes closed, the television light blaring color across his face. As usual, a beer bottle hung lazily between his fingers, and dozens more were scattered on the stained rug, suffusing the air with the stench of alcohol. His wife didn't scold him, but she did scold Olalla.

Two steps into the kitchen—barely enough time for the girl to get a whiff of the food rotting in the sink—her mother whirled and slammed a palm against her vulnerable cheek.

The action was predictable enough that Olalla only staggered back a step before regaining her balance. Her face stung, and water welled in her eyes, but she resisted the urge to cradle her cheek or allow the tears to flow. Any other six-year-old would have. Artemis, at the age of seven, would have. But the slap of her mother's hand had become so routine that Olalla was almost numb to it.

Almost.

"Stop *lying*," her mother hissed through gritted teeth. Where Artemis's dark eyes were stern and Olalla's dark eyes were cunning, their mother's dark eyes were soulless and cruel, brimming with hate. Strands of lusterless hair hung around her face as she bent to sneer at Olalla's level, and the girl barely resisted the urge to yank on them.

"I'm not *lying!*"

Her mother yanked on Olalla's hair, which made her regret her restraint. "You manipulated a boy into putting his hand under scalding water. He *burned* his hand, because of *you*. You are a demon child."

"Don't start with that again." Her father took a swig of his beer. "Demons don't exist. Give the girl a spanking, make her do the dishes, and call it a day."

Disregarding her husband, Olalla's mother pulled at her hair and seethed, "Do not embarrass our family again. If I get another call from your teacher, you will not like the consequences."

Before Olalla could acquiesce or spit in her face, the woman flung her into the refrigerator. Her head hit the chipped turquoise door with such force that she lost her senses for a second and plummeted to the ground. Dazed, Olalla squinted up to see her mother storm out of the house while Artemis scurried to crouch beside her.

"Ollie, are you okay?" she whispered, a cry laced in her voice. Gently, she brushed Olalla's hair from her forehead and surveyed her face. "You can't talk back to Mother. You know it only worsens her temper."

"I know." Olalla glared at the door that their mother had disappeared through. Provoking her was almost as fun as convincing that stupid boy *Tyler* to burn his hand in the water. She would just have to find a way to evade the consequences from both—or the consequences from everything.

Perhaps Olalla should have been nervous to return home that day after school, but it was difficult to feel nervous about violence that she'd learned to expect—that she'd learned to accept.

A few years after the incident with Tyler, Olalla's mother had acquired a new job, for which she worked too late to pick up the girls from school. Their three mile walk back to the dilapidated ranch the Cosmoses barely afforded to rent had Artemis complaining for a full hour, but Olalla didn't mind it. She liked to watch people milling about the small town, then watch animals in the fields and forests. Sometimes, she told squirrels to hop from one tree to the next. Sometimes, they listened.

Today, she didn't have time to talk to squirrels. Today, she and Artemis ran.

Shortly after the two began their daily treks home, Olalla had noticed something strange whenever they walked past a certain house on Streamview Street: giggles, giddy and girlish, emanating from beyond the closed windows. Artemis hadn't acknowledged it, but her younger sister recognized the way her shoulders tensed.

When springtime had come, the laughter's volume amplified with the open windows, and by early summer, a group of three girls began sitting on the front porch of the house to openly mock Artemis.

"It's my glasses," she muttered once they'd passed. "It's stupid. Ignore them."

It was stupid, but Olalla did not like being told what to do, so she did not ignore them. Rather, she observed them with her shrewd eyes, watching how the center girl initiated the derision while the other two played along.

Until today, she'd let it slide, hoping after nearly four years the girls would *finally* move on, but they never did. This had become a daily ritual for them—a hobby. Well, Olalla had formed a hobby, as well, and she'd become quite adept at commanding squirrels to hop from one tree to the next.

"Stop," she ordered as soon as the giggling began. Startled, the girls stopped, and Olalla felt a swell of satisfaction in her gut. "Never make fun of my sister again."

The center girl stood and crossed her arms over her plaid sweater. "You can't tell me what to do."

That was true. Whenever Olalla told the squirrels, "Jump there!" they rarely listened. But if she encouraged them with,

"You want to jump over there!" they always did.

"You don't want to make fun of my sister."

Though the girl's brown eyebrows creased together, she didn't refute this statement. The thrill in Olalla resumed; she'd never commanded a *person* before. With Tyler, she'd spent ten minutes convincing him to place his hand under the scalding water, and even then, she'd physically nudged him into it. He had never been under the impression he *wanted* to burn himself. With this girl, Olalla had altered her desires.

She wanted more.

"You want to lay on the sidewalk, don't you?"

The girl began to shake her head, but then her blue eyes drifted to the concrete, and she nodded, descending the porch steps toward it. Her friends jumped up and gawked as she lowered to the ground and sprawled her body on the sidewalk, green bell-bottoms flaring around her ankles.

A smirk broke onto Olalla's lips, which she hid as she paced closer to the girl and crouched beside her head. "This is peaceful; you don't want to move."

In response, the girl closed her eyes, as if falling asleep. Her friends protested, and Olalla heard Artemis voice her dissent from behind. She knew commandeering them all at once was an impossible feat since she'd tried it numerous times with the squirrels, to no avail. Instead, she funneled all of her focus into the brunette girl, exuding a calming energy even as she reached into the bed of pebbles lining the walk to the porch.

To Olalla, the pebble beds had always seemed silly. Every time she passed them, she kicked a few and thought of how much nicer the yard would look had these beds been filled with mulch and flowers—perhaps some purple pansies. It was a relief to finally give them a purpose.

"You want to open your mouth," Olalla cooed, gently pushing the girl's chin with one finger, prying her lips apart. With the same patience, she dropped one pebble into the girl's mouth, muttering more encouragement when she coughed.

The other girls shrieked, and one demanded, "What are you doing?" while the other wailed, "I'm calling Mother!"

That was Olalla's cue to hurry.

Dumping a handful into the girl's mouth, she sprung up and said, "Open your eyes—open your eyes and *try* to mock my sister."

The girl did open her eyes, and then she tried to scream. Rocks clogged her throat, muffling her cry, and her eyes bulged with tears of panic.

Now, as Olalla and Artemis sprinted home, she could still hear the choking grunts, could still taste the sweet, sweet fear. At the memory, her smirk resurfaced. She'd only been granted a few brief seconds of satisfaction before her sister had hauled her away, too shocked to mumble more than, "Oh no, what if she dies?"

Olalla was tempted to say, "Then the problem is solved," but she felt that might cross a line with Artemis—or anyone. She had learned early on that most people did not view situations through the same lens she did.

When they arrived home, their father sat on the orange and brown striped couch, a beer bottle dangling in his hand, but he wasn't watching the television. His normally-groggy eyes were acutely set on the girls, terse with disbelief, probably because his wife stood in the kitchen doorway, simmering.

In their haste, the girls hadn't noticed their mother's car parked beside the house, home too early. If they had, Artemis might have insisted they agree on some false story. Now, Olalla knew she would do nothing to save her younger sister.

"Jennifer's mother called." Their mother took a step closer, arms wound tightly against her chest. "Jennifer's father was one of my bosses, you know."

That *was* hung in the air, an accusation and a threat. In the time it had taken them to sprint home, their mother had been *fired*.

When dropping pebbles into Jennifer's mouth, Olalla hadn't felt she was doing anything wrong—she still didn't believe she had. There was no guilt, even for costing her mother her job, but there was a nagging sensation of regret, like maybe she could have found a way to torture Jennifer without harming her own family.

There was also, embarrassingly, the smallest hint of dread as her mother advanced through the hall toward her.

"Y-you don't want to hit me," Olalla managed, but it was much less confident than her tone had been with Jennifer. No one believed a stuttered, spineless statement.

The hand against her cheek threw her into the nearest lamp, knocking it to the floor. Glass shattered around her, drowning out her father's annoyed protests. If she had to guess, the collision had probably almost destroyed his precious television. She didn't see any other reason why he would intervene.

Blood oozed from her broken lip, her bitten tongue. She tried to push herself off the grungy orange carpet, but shards bit at her skin. Artemis sniffled quietly by the front door, but their mother had yet to stalk out, as she normally did. This time, she marched into the living room and hauled Olalla up by her braids, the same black as the wisps splayed around the woman's face, adding to her aura of fury.

Olalla opened her mouth, prepared to vocally instill another desire, only the throbbing of her swollen tongue prevented coherent words. Her mother gripped her chin, thwarting any last hope of speech, and she braced her body for the pain surely to come.

You don't want to hurt me, Olalla thought, more a wish than a command. In her ten years of life, she'd learned wishing never worked. She either had to take what she wanted or make someone give it to her. With more force, she thought, *You don't want to hurt me.*

Her mother blinked, the rage bleeding from her expression, leaving it blank. Gradually, she released Olalla's hair and stepped back to regard her with hostility. The resentment festering in her pitiless eyes assured Olalla this wasn't the last time the woman would resort to violence, but it was the last time the girl would accept it. Like with the squirrels, she doubted her methods of defense would always work without flaw, but she would master the manipulation.

Her mother stalked out of the house, her father resumed watching his television, and Artemis studied her in a curious way that, for once, made the quality of her dark eyes reflect Olalla's.

Foolishly, Olalla had hoped the notion she'd planted in Jennifer's head would last, but a week later, after the shock of nearly choking to death on rocks abated, the girls were at it again. Every day Olalla had to tell them they didn't want to mock Artemis, and every day she felt her sister's unease grow.

Artemis never said anything about it, nor did she ever bring up the way Olalla sometimes compelled her mother not to hit her with nothing but a fierce look. Perhaps the many times the manipulation didn't work and she suffered bruises to the face made her older sister feel too guilty to inquire about what type of dark witchcraft Olalla had dabbled in.

As time progressed and their mother's violence became unnaturally scarce, Artemis's suspicion increased. Especially when Olalla's dark hair and eyes began to harbor a tinge of purple.

Frequently, her sister would vaguely question Olalla's abilities, and equally as frequently, Olalla would give her vague non-answers. Never did she attempt to use her manipulation on her sister, though; never *would* she. Artemis was the one person who always naturally acted exactly as Olalla hoped and expected her to.

One spring day, five years after the pebble incident, Olalla awoke to her mother yelling profanities. This wasn't particularly uncommon, but for the woman to storm into the girls' shared room and drag Olalla out of bed was an act reserved only for the gravest of occasions. Stumbling on bare feet, Olalla allowed her mother to drag her out of the ranch to the driveway, where their family's rusty car sat. The tires were slashed.

"You did this," her mother snarled, shoving the girl's face into the gravel beside one of the flattened tires.

Now at the age of fifteen, Olalla *could* have physically fought off the older woman, but she had to admit, she did often deserve her mother's anger. Not for this, though. She hadn't done this. As she parted her lips to say so, rock dust coated her tongue. Spitting, she hastily projected, *Olalla didn't do this.*

For the briefest second, her mother's grip on her hair loosened, but then a voice, feeble and quavering, said, "I-it was her. I saw her do it."

Olalla craned her neck as far as possible toward the house. Artemis stood in the doorway, wearing her favorite Fleetwood Mac t-shirt and flannel pajama pants. Though her voice had sounded scared, reluctant, her face was a mask of stone, remorseless.

"Of course," her mother sneered, tightening her fingers in Olalla's hair. "Of course you'd want me to be late for the first day of my new job—as if I'm not the one providing for you."

Olalla shook her head, but it barely moved. Gritting her teeth against the pain, she cast a notion toward Artemis: *You want to tell her it wasn't Olalla.*

Her sister's face didn't change. If anything, the severity of her gaze intensified from distaste to hatred, as if she knew Olalla had wiggled false desires into her brain.

After her mother beat her and stormed inside to call her mechanic friend, Artemis approached Olalla where she lay in the gravel, too dazed to feel properly enraged. With her unkempt hair and unfeeling eyes, Artemis looked like the true witch.

"There's something wrong with you—something evil."

Olalla smiled with dust-filled teeth. "And you thought prompting this beating would purge it from me? What's so evil about stopping your tormentors—or mine?"

Artemis's spine stiffened at the mention of those girls. Their taunting on the porch steps had dwindled to almost never, especially once they entered high school, but Olalla noticed the days Artemis didn't wear her glasses to school, even though she was practically blind without them.

"It's unnatural," she insisted in her toughest voice. Olalla barely restrained a sigh of pity. "You're unnatural, Ollie."

"Am I, Artie?" She narrowed her eyes at her sister, wondering what beliefs she might weave into that immalleable consciousness. Though she'd never prodded at Artemis's brain, she had sensed its presence, a bland blob. Part of her had wanted to coddle her mind, transform it into something unique, but the time for change had long since passed for Artemis Cosmos. The girl was set in her rigid ways—so rigid she would willingly frame her sister in order to conform that sister to her tasteless worldview.

Olalla did not enjoy being on the receiving end of someone else's manipulations.

"Yes, you are," Artemis declared, and she stuck to that belief, no matter how hard Olalla tried to alter it.

Their dynamic went on like that for months: Artemis purposely blaming Olalla, Olalla combatting her mother's attempts at brutality. She had to admit, it was good practice. But sometimes her ability didn't work, and she counted every slap from her mother's hand as a slap from Artemis.

Until one day she decided to pay her sister back. By mentally prompting Jennifer to pour milk on Artemis's head in the cafeteria.

It was so easy that Olalla couldn't prevent herself from laughing when it happened. Her volume was loud enough to turn a few heads; Artemis had friends, but Olalla had always sat alone, always refused to do more than give someone a patronizing smile if they dared talk to her. To cackle at her sister's distress must have solidified her classmates' unfavorable thoughts of her.

Not that it mattered. For that night, Artemis convinced their parents to *move*.

With milk-crusted hair, she screamed and wailed about her embarrassment, topping it off with a quiet, hissed, "You want us to move."

And then, apparently, they did.

Olalla was, to say the least, offended. Not only had she spent weeks calculating the best method to ruin her sister's reputation, but to ruin all that rumination, her sister had used *her* tactic. Did that mean anyone could master this ability, or were her parents' brains so worn from her years of manipulation that anyone could persuade them now?

None of it mattered. With a screaming fit and a simple phrase, Artemis had forced the Cosmoses to *move*. All of the silly little beliefs she'd planted throughout the people in this town over the years would be left behind. Jonathan, who she'd taught to eat yogurt with his middle fingers; Susan, who she'd convinced to sing Beatles songs every time a teacher called on her; Michael, who she'd practiced kissing techniques on until she became so frustrated that she made his lips bleed (and then made him forget it was her and not his girlfriend).

She felt like she was leaving a town full of half-painted canvases behind—*her* half-painted canvases.

Within a week, the Cosmoses had packed all their measly belongings. Within a week, they were bound for a town two hours away. They were bound for a tiny trailer park called Hastings Street.

2

<u>Walnuts and Witches</u>

Angor Periculy had lived on Hastings Street since the moment of his conception. Literally, his mother had screwed a random man in the bed she still slept in and then birthed him in their disease-ridden bathtub nine months later. It was a story he heard quite often, and it was a story he despised. No one successful ever grew up in a deteriorating mobile home.

That was why he couldn't wait until he transferred to a new high school in a few months. The foundation of his previous school, Lamerton High, had finally crumbled, so he and the seventy-eight other students in his small town would be relocated to a larger, more structurally sound establishment: East Mintle High School.

New town, new environment, new classmates—he would become a new man. The problem was his hair and eyes were pink, and no one looked upon someone kindly when their hair and eyes were pink.

Pink was an over-exaggeration, he supposed. Both his hair and eyes were still brown, but they'd faded over the years into a much lighter color that now harbored a reddish hue. To be accurate, his features could be described as medium-well cooked meat, which was only slightly more normal than his friend, whose hair and irises appeared as if they'd been mixed with blood.

"It's peculiar that the dye never sticks," Angor said one summer afternoon as he and his friend sat outside their mobile home in lawn chairs they'd stolen from the dump. From their vantage point, they could barely see the main road through the thick forest surrounding the trailer park. Despite the excessively loud rock-and-roll music blaring from the blue home across the dirt path, Hastings Street was quite peaceful.

"It's possible we've chosen bad dyes and a more expensive brand might work."

"Ever the optimist, Aethelred," Angor mused while gracefully cracking open a walnut with a rusty knife. After extracting the halves from their shells, he handed one to his friend and then studied the other, admiring the design. To some, walnuts were a snack; to others, they were the cause of severe allergic reactions; to Angor, they were a window into the mind.

Cracking open a walnut shell was the closest he would ever come to studying the human brain, and whenever he stared at the similar shape of the nut, he contemplated his deepest inquiries: how do thoughts form, how do beliefs form, how does pain manifest in one's consciousness? Modern science had only recently begun to delve into the mysteries of the mind, but Angor wanted to know *everything*. He wanted to hold a brain in his hands and uncover the function of every cell.

Though he and Aethelred had formed a brotherly friendship over the past five years, this was their one disconnect: Aethelred's lack of understanding when it came to Angor's love for science. His friend had always preferred the arts, like music and plays, and while Angor appreciated these things, he couldn't *enjoy* them. Every time they snuck into a theater, he spent the entire show wondering at the artist's process instead of admiring the talent displayed before him. How did the ideas for this show form? Where did creativity come from?

Aethelred simply liked to nod along to the music, to gasp and laugh and sniffle at all the proper times. Then he liked to flee the theater before the curtain was closed, lest he accidentally brush against another human. Unfortunately for Angor, his best friend had a phobia of physical contact. He hadn't let Angor dye his hair the multiple times they'd tried, even though the process would have been much quicker had he opted for assistance.

"Should we try bleach next?" Angor proposed before popping the walnut into his mouth.

Aethelred's unnaturally red eyes cut toward him with skepticism. "You'd rather be bald?"

"We won't be bald; we'll be blond. We'll be beach babes."

His friend choked on a walnut. "You've never been any-where *near* a beach."

"One of my mother's *friends* once drove us past Lake Erie. I suspect it was to purchase drugs from a dealer in Cleveland, but that's *semantics*, Certior. I've seen a large body of water, and that's what counts."

Mildly amused, Aethelred took the next walnut from Angor, careful not to let their fingers touch. Halfway to his mouth, his hand paused, and his eyes widened, resembling two plump cherries. Curious but not alarmed, Angor followed his gaze toward the trailer park's entrance, where an old sedan bumbled down the dirt road. The car's shabby appearance was on par for Hastings Street, but it was rare that an unknown vehicle tread on their territory. Frankly, it was rare Hastings Street hosted any cars at all. Not many residents in the park had enough cash to acquire a vehicle by legal means.

The boys watched, tense and prepped for action, as the car bumped along the unkempt path. As it passed the Periculys' ramshackle home, Angor noticed the occupants were a family, the parents in the front and two teenage girls in the back. One of the girls stared rigidly at the seat before her while the other peered out the window, glaring at everything in sight—including the boys. When their eyes met, Angor slowly allowed an eyebrow to inch beneath the unruly hair sweeping his forehead.

She didn't blush or look away. Rather, she maintained their shared gaze until the distance prevented it.

Angor waited for the car to make a U-turn at the dead end, but instead it stopped only one door down from theirs, at the moss-covered home that had been vacant since old Mr. Samson died two years prior.

Shifting in his seat for a better angle, he saw the car park before the front door, and the engine immediately began to smoke. The driver's door flew open for a middle-aged woman, whose dark hair was arranged in a ridiculous bun. Her skin was tanner than Angor's pale complexion would be even if he did live near a beach, and he suspected she hailed from a southern European nation, but he was never particularly keen on geography or anthropology. The accent of her voice confirmed she hadn't been born in the middle of Ohio.

Her volume was enough to rival the rock-and-roll jam across the street. On the other side of the car, her husband—balding, with an oversized gut that did not match the thinner structure of his face—emerged, visibly unfazed.

Despite his obvious lack of care, the woman would not stop lamenting about how shitty her car was and if, perhaps, her husband would stop drinking so much beer and acquire himself a job, they could afford a new one. To this, the man took a swig from his beer bottle, and the woman rounded the hood of the car in an attempt to take a swing at him. The familial brawl, which was not a particularly uncommon event on Hastings Street, was thwarted when the car's back left door opened, and a witch stepped out.

Angor did not think she was a witch in a derogatory sense. Firstly, he had always possessed a fascination with the occult. He did not think such things truly existed, per se, but growing up the last five years with Aethelred, who'd been raised amongst those who claimed to be oracles and magicians, had certainly opened his mind to the possibility of forces outside the human norm. He would not have minded studying the brain of a person who seriously believed in such fantasies.

Secondly, although witches had often been portrayed as evil in history and media, Angor found the concept of a woman with mystical powers and mysterious motives rather alluring. That was why this girl—the glaring girl—struck him as a witch. Her dark, ragged clothing merely added to the pleasantly eerie façade, and when the light filtering through the treetops hit her hair, it shimmered purple.

Stalking around the car, she approached her parents but stopped far enough that she wouldn't be caught in an attack. With a glare as assertive as the one she'd fixed on Angor, her attention drifted between her parents, and within a matter of seconds, the tension defused.

Angor might not have thought it strange had the mother looked at her daughter, but her back had been to the witch the entire time. It was as if the girl had nonverbally compelled her mother to desist.

Grumbling but not nearly as heated, the mother hauled a few bags from the crooked trunk and stalked into the white mobile home. For a moment, Angor wondered if they were legally renting or illegally squatting, but then he sensed a pair of poisonous eyes on him. A chill wracked down his spine as he met the witch's gaze once more. This time, her scowl wasn't one of judgement, but one that said, *Stay away.*

As the witch marched into the home after her mother, Angor slowly slid his focus in Aethelred's direction. His friend munched nervously on a walnut, peeking between the newcomers and his hands at rapid intervals.

"Please, try and tell me you *don't* want to touch her."

Aethelred stiffened at his friend's quiet but casual tone. "You know I most certainly *do not.*"

Angor snorted somewhat absently as he watched the second girl scramble from the car, giving the boys a panicked, embarrassed look before scurrying into her new home. "I didn't mean *sexually.* I meant, don't you want to run your fingers through her hair and determine if it's a wig? If it's not, you must be curious as to how she managed to dye her hair so effectively. You could definitely use some pointers there."

After opening and closing his mouth several times, Aethelred finally said, in a whisper, "You think she dyed her hair?"

No, Angor did not. He would have if his own had not changed so drastically, but after seeing his hair and his friend's hair shift to such unusual shades, he had to question if others experienced the same phenomenon. Though a hypothesis budded in the depths of his mind, he did not want to consciously think it, nor did he plan to ever speak it aloud.

Once he decided something, he became very adamant on maintaining that decision, and he did not have the resources to research the connection between the alteration of one's hair and the strange…*abilities* he and Aethelred often displayed.

Contrary to his own desires, he decided, "We'll have to see her eyes before we come to a conclusion."

Initially, Olalla had been mightily displeased with Hastings Street. It was a step down from the farm ranch, an even more derelict location for their increasingly derelict family. The closest civilized shopping center was over five miles away, and her new high school would be nearly eight. Walking home every day would be substantially more miserable than before, especially since she and Artemis were not on speaking terms, to put it mildly.

Luckily, she'd acquired a bicycle from the backyard of one of the abandoned mobile homes, which allowed her to commute into town for a summer job at the record shop. With her first little wad of cash, she bought a bike lock so she would be able to safely ride her stolen bicycle to school in the fall and avoid the walks with Artemis altogether. With her second little wad, she bought binoculars. How else was she expected to spy on the boys next door?

It was creepy—of this, she was aware—but any time spent in her bedroom was time spent peering out her window, trying to catch a glimpse of movement beyond the glass panes of the red trailer. Almost always, the sheer curtain was closed, but she'd often witnessed the boys' silhouettes, sometimes chatting, sometimes laughing, but never remotely close to touching.

This debunked her preliminary assumption that they were lovers.

Upon watching them spend many afternoons in their lawn chairs, consuming a ridiculous amount of what appeared to be *walnuts*, the nature of their friendship developed in Olalla's mind. Though they acted like it, they weren't brothers—at least, she didn't think they were. The red-haired boy was much taller and ganglier, while the other boy was shorter and built lean, like a runner. Where the red-haired boy's features were soft and innocent, the other boy's were sharp and enigmatic, like the shards of a broken mirror.

She wished, quite often, that she hadn't compelled him to stay away.

Enraged over her mother's embarrassing display of violence, Olalla had proceeded to project warning sentiments in every direction possible. In the moment, she'd wanted nothing more than to flee and be entirely alone, but as the day wore on, her desire to meet the boys progressed. Unfortunately, her warnings had engrained too deeply in their minds, and if they happened to spot her on her way to work, they did nothing more than creepily watch her depart.

Equally unfortunately, she refused to stoop low enough to greet them like a friendly neighbor. She was not friendly, and she did not want them to consider her a neighbor. Her ambitions rested exclusively in determining how their oddly-colored hair might be connected to her own.

One midsummer evening after work, Olalla hopped on her stolen bicycle to return to Hastings Street when she noticed two figures in the alley between the bank and the typewriter shop across the street. Pedaling a few blocks ahead, she crossed the road and discreetly rolled toward the bank, hoping the boys faced the other direction. She didn't want to *talk* to them; she merely wanted to observe—to determine if they were trustworthy, if they were mature.

They were not, she decided, based solely on the fact that they were currently spray painting graffiti on the typewriter shop's brick wall.

Olalla stopped her bike beside the front window of the bank, thankful it was closed. She inched toward the corner, hoping to catch a glimpse of the boys' illicit art, but then the sharp one spoke, his voice too close for her to risk peering around.

"You're a poor artist, you know." He sounded like he was chewing something, and Olalla had a fair idea of what. "I hope you didn't sign up for an art class at our new school."

"Angor," the other boy sighed in frustration. For a second, Olalla thought he'd said "anger" with a strange accent, but the word was so out of context that she quickly surmised it was the sharp boy's name. "My depiction is terrible because I don't stare at my stolen biology textbooks all day."

"And *that's* because you don't have any stolen biology textbooks." Olalla wasn't sure what enticed her more: the smirk in his voice or the fact that he'd gone out of his way to *steal* biology textbooks. "Your double helix looks like squiggly lines, Aethelred. It's a disgrace to Rosalind Franklin's memory."

"I thought those two guys discovered DNA—Watson and Crick?"

Olalla thought so, as well, therefore she was slightly surprised when Angor said, "Ah, but without Franklin's work, they never would have. It's always important to credit those whose work yours is based off of. And the fact you didn't know about Franklin—despite the picture of her I taped on our bedroom wall—is exactly why you've been subjected to spray painting the DNA double helix. I won't be able to associate with you if you fail biology this year, Aethelred. You're lucky I haven't asked you to spray paint the entire history of DNA, or the processes of transcription and translation."

"I don't know what either of those are," Aethelred mumbled before the hiss of the spray paint resumed. Olalla wasn't even tempted to peek at his depiction; her mind was still buzzing about Rosalind Franklin, a scientist she'd somehow never heard of. Olalla made it her business to at least know the names of recent prominent scientists, especially those in the fields of biology or psychology. For this *Angor* to know something she didn't unsettled her. Living in the Cosmos household, she'd grown accustomed to being the smartest person in the vicinity.

So wrapped in her thoughts, she almost didn't notice the man ambling down the sidewalk toward her. As not to look like a creep, she crouched beside her bicycle and busied herself with the wheels, as if fixing the chain. When the man's pace slowed in her periphery, she swore internally, knowing he'd probably stop to offer assistance. Why did people have to be so *nice*?

"Hey."

Olalla gritted her teeth and stood, prepared to hop on her bike and speed off before the boys saw her, but when she spared a glance upward, the man wasn't hovering near her. His attention was aimed inside the alley, where the hiss of spray paint had ceased. She knew exactly why Aethelred had stopped: The man was a police officer.

"What are you two punks doing?" he asked, though he didn't sound particularly angry about it. More annoyed and mildly curious. "Is that a penis?"

"It's not supposed to be." Angor continued chewing, unfazed by the authority figure. "I wouldn't put it past my friend for his mind to be in such places, though."

Aethelred's humiliation radiated from his voice. "I didn't—I'm not—it's a double helix."

"Is that a drug?" the officer asked, eyes scrunched as he tried to decipher whatever squiggles stained the wall. "Never mind—I don't wanna know. Look, I'd usually let you off with a warning, but I know Larry will be pissed you've drawn paraphernalia on the side of his shop. I've gotta take you—"

"You don't *have* to do anything." Olalla stepped beside the man, placing herself in the mouth of the alley. Though she tried to keep her focus on him, her vision was tempted in the boys' direction. Aethelred had the spray can hidden behind his back rather conspicuously, cheeks nearly as red as his hair, while Angor's mouth had fallen open mid-chew. Composing himself, he fixed her with an intent, probing gaze, and she struggled to mask her satisfaction as she turned back to the officer.

"You certainly don't *want* to arrest these boys, do you?" Olalla felt his mind thaw as his brows furrowed. "Oh, think of all the paperwork and wasted time. You'll probably have to learn what a double helix is—imagine the horror!"

The officer did appear a bit horrified at that notion. Still, she hadn't woven her desires into his brain the way she had with her parents, and he managed to object. "Miss, I appreciate your sympathy, but I really should—"

"Oh, aren't you sick of all the things you *should* do—of everyone telling you what you should do?" Usually, she liked to remain calm when planting ideas, but agitation seeped into her tone. How embarrassing would it be if she didn't successfully compel this man? The boys would think her a fool. "Wouldn't it be easiest just to clean up this mess and move on—avoid all the headache?"

She dug these last sentiments into his brain, attempting to induce an actual headache. Grimacing, the officer nodded. "I do hate paperwork... I'll go get a bucket of water."

Olalla had not expected the "clean up this mess" part to work. After he departed, she pivoted toward the boys, and their expressions mirrored her bafflement. Angor studied her with his peculiarly-colored eyes and concluded, "I could have handled that."

This she had expected. Simply from observing him over the past few weeks, she had deduced he was the leader of their duo. His pride radiated for miles, and this indignant reaction was precisely why she'd opted to intervene.

She hummed, tapping her pointer finger to her chin. "I don't think you could have."

A crease appeared between his pinkish eyebrows, but he instantly shook his head, immune to her attempted manipulations. His mind would be her most difficult challenge yet.

Too exhausted from the officer to attempt it now, she directed her attention to Aethelred's double helix. Since she'd never seen a penis, she couldn't accurately compare this to one, but it definitely did not look like the drawings of DNA strands she'd studied vigorously over the past few years.

"That looks more like some demon-invoking symbol than a double helix." Olalla crossed her arms and surveyed the boy's dark, tattered clothing and blood-red eyes. "Are you Satan?"

Aethelred's shoulders slumped, allowing the spray can to wilt at his side. "Why do people always think I'm evil?"

"Could have something to do with your hair. What kind of dye do you use?" she questioned in a way that said, "*I know you don't dye your hair.*"

Angor's eyebrows disappeared beneath his shaggy hair. "We could ask you the same." Before she could conjure a sly retort, he extracted an unshelled walnut from the pocket of his jeans and presented it to her. "For your services."

Olalla contemplated denying the pathetic payment for her superior talents, but she knew a walnut was not just a walnut to this boy. Graciously, she accepted the gift and popped it into her mouth. It barely tasted like anything. "Why do you *always* eat walnuts?"

A wry smirk surfaced on his lips, and she realized her error. She had, essentially, admitted to him that she'd been watching them.

After allowing that humiliating realization to settle, he shrugged. "They're nutritious—and they're shaped like brains."

Her heart swelled with everything she'd always wanted: a boy who knew what a brain looked like.

"I'm Olalla Cosmos," she introduced, suddenly the friendly neighbor she never wanted to be.

Angor spun toward his friend with raw excitement. "Ha! I knew they were Greek!"

For a second, she was shocked, but then a grin curled onto her lips. Apparently, the boys had been watching her, too.

Part 2

The Assailant and The Assailed

3

Trees, and Other Imaginary Things

Olalla's disdain for Hastings Street slowly degenerated into admiration throughout the summer. The boys quickly learned her work schedule and rode with her into town before every shift, waiting around the shops and often engaging in devious acts until she finished, upon which they would ride back to the trailer park with her. She attempted to remain aloof and detached, attempted to treat them more like test subjects than friends, but Aethelred was too innocently sweet and Angor was too attractively witty.

The day before school started, Olalla and the boys found themselves eating walnuts in their lawn chairs, as was their nightly routine. She wasn't sure where Angor had acquired the third, but its sudden appearance the day after she'd saved them from the cop brought her more joy than any bouquet of flowers ever would. The worn plastic felt more like home than the prison next door, and a few nights she'd convinced the boys to sleep outside with her to avoid Artemis's judgmental glares and her mother's incessant wrath. Waking up with bug bites was worth it.

That evening, Olalla intended to return home earlier than usual to prepare her backpack for the following day, but before she could remove herself from the chair, the sound of a door squeaking open halted them all. Apprehensive, the three pivoted toward the pine green trailer at the very end of Hastings Street, which Olalla had always assumed vacant.

The boy jogging down the front steps, as though he'd done it every day, quashed that assumption.

With anyone else, she would have continued about her business; people came and went throughout the trailer park at all hours. But this boy she'd never seen before, and this boy had dark green hair.

He approached them with a languid gait, gradually extracting a cigarette and a lighter from his pocket as he went. By the time he reached them, stopping only a few paces from the feet of their lawn chairs, the stick was lit and between his teeth. He spoke smoothly around it as he said, "Figured it was time I introduced myself to you losers."

Per usual, Angor's brow was wrinkled as though calculating a problem. "Have you been squatting there?"

The boy's green eyes didn't bother to follow Angor's toward the trailer at the end of the street. "Understandable supposition, but no, my parents rent it—have rented it for the past month."

Aethelred shifted in his chair. "We've never seen you."

"By design." The boy appraised Aethelred's worn t-shirt and fraying khakis, which, compared to his leather jacket and sleek jeans, looked particularly mangy. Olalla crossed her arms to hide her stained tank top, but the green-haired boy didn't remove his gaze from the red-haired boy as he puffed a cloud of smoke. "I've been that tree."

Tilting his head back, he indicated to the cluster of trees across the street. For a moment, Olalla wondered which tree he was referring to, but then she registered what he'd said and couldn't form a logical question.

"What do—how—what tree?" Aethelred managed to ask.

The boy took another drag of his cigarette before sauntering to the trees and planting himself among them. Olalla couldn't imagine he'd stood there for weeks, unnoticed. Countless evenings sitting in these chairs, staring at the forest as they contemplated complex concepts, had familiarized her with the layout of the trees, and there *had* always been one where the boy now stood.

In the blink of an eye, the tree was there again, and the boy was gone.

The three remaining teens scrambled from their chairs to gawk. An endless minute passed, and then Olalla and Angor hesitantly made eye contact. Though he'd never said so explicitly, she was aware that Angor, like herself, had a theory about the connection between their oddly-colored hair.

"You can shapeshift," he concluded, speaking to the tree.

A disembodied laugh echoed through Hastings Street. "What kind of fantasy are you living in?"

Olalla stepped forward, and the boy abruptly reappeared. A roguish smile curved his lips as he strolled toward them. "Did you not just shapeshift into a tree?" she asked, though the notion *did* sound outrageous. More outrageous than sewing desires into others' brains, even.

"How the hell d'you think I'd manage that?" The boy almost chuckled again, but he maintained poise by stuffing his cigarette between his lips. "I knew you three were freaks."

Aethelred's voice was quiet but deadly as he said, "We're not."

In all their evenings of chatting, Olalla had not uncovered the mystery behind Aethelred's sensitivity. She had once jokingly called him a freak, and he'd given the same terse response: *"I'm not."* About most things, he was calmly exasperated, but being called a freak rattled him to the core. Clearly, Angor understood the reasoning, but Olalla knew he would never betray his friend's trust by telling her.

"No need to get all hot-headed, Red." The boy pointed his cigarette in Aethelred's direction in mock castigation, and the red-haired boy stiffened at the nickname.

"How did you—"

"Your hair is red, idiot. But I do know your name, *Aethelred.*" After licking his lips a bit too seductively, the boy resumed smoking. "Weird, if you ask me."

Olalla had never seen Aethelred so flustered. "Well…" He stared at the leaf-ridden ground for a solid minute before stubbornly retorting, "What's your name?"

"Casimir."

"That's weird."

"No, it's not." To avoid further argument from Aethelred, Casimir blew smoke into his face and then barely suppressed a grin when the red-haired boy began coughing.

Angor, pensive and unfazed, said, "We've come to accept we're weird, and anyone who associates with us is weird by default. Weird breeds weird."

"True," Casimir agreed with a shrug. "So, what *weird* things can you freaks do?"

This was obviously meant to rile Aethelred, but he must have summoned some of Angor's stoicism, because he didn't react.

"You never confirmed what weird things *you* can do," Olalla pointed out. If he didn't willingly divulge the information, could she compel him to? Commanding her mother had become as routine as brushing her teeth, but she still had little effect on Artemis and no effect on Angor. Admittedly, she hadn't really *tried* with Aethelred. Not because she felt *guilty*, but because he never said or did anything to irk her.

Casimir released a dramatic, smoke-filled sigh. "Fine, Cosmos—"

"Don't call me that." The interjection had been immediate and shamefully defensive. She hoped she had enough control over her emotions to prevent her cheeks from reddening. With less vigor, she stated, "That's not my name."

"He calls you that." Casimir nodded in Angor's direction.

"*He* likes to piss me off."

Angor tilted his head to give her a lazy side-eye. "It's not particularly *hard*."

The briefest urge to playfully punch him surfaced, but she hastily stifled it. Though she and Angor teased Aethelred for his aversion to physical contact, she was equally as disinclined to touch others. The last person to touch her had been her mother, and she'd ensured that would never happen again. To touch Angor would open the gate to him touching her back, and she wasn't sure she wanted that.

"I've noticed," Casimir drawled, "because I've been that tree, as I told you. I guess I wasn't *actually* the tree, though; I only made you *think* I was the tree."

The last of Olalla's good humor faded with that admission. She did not like the prospect of someone else being able to alter others' thoughts. That ability was *hers*.

"I can make people see things that aren't there," he elaborated when none of them spoke. "*Hallucinations*, you could say."

Angor tapped a finger to his chin, intrigued. "So, you

warped our perception to make us believe there was an extra tree over there...in order to *spy* on us? Well, that makes Olalla's binocular-stalking seem a little less creepy."

Her lips parted in disbelief. He'd *known* about the binoculars, yet in their weeks of spending every day together, he'd never mentioned it. This time, she didn't refrain from verbally assaulting him with a few vulgar murmurings.

Casimir's sly smirk widened with each one. "It's lame, I know. Not the stalking, but the tree, I mean. The complexity of my hallucinations isn't too advanced unless I'm touching the person whose mind I'm altering. Wanna see?"

In one fluid motion, he reached for Aethelred, and Aethelred recoiled.

"No! Don't touch me."

With his hand suspended in midair, Casimir scrutinized the other boy, searching his guarded expression. "You're *not* a freak?" he asked as he finally dropped his arm. Aethelred's posture relaxed slightly but his eyes still screamed *run—flee.* "Right," Casimir huffed, pushing his messy green hair back from his forehead, "and I can *actually* turn myself into a tree."

"I don't like the idea of someone creeping into my mind so easily," Angor said, eyes fixed on the trailer across the street. "Cosmos can never manage it."

Olalla lifted her chin defiantly. "That's because I never try."

His eyes shifted back into focus solely for the purpose of shooting her a triumphant, knowing look. "Oh, I know you try. It's a very distinct feeling—your talons trying to wiggle into my white matter."

"Don't pretend you know anything about white matter. Most neuroscientists don't know anything about white matter."

Casimir arched his greenish eyebrows at Aethelred. "Do *you* know anything about white matter? Because I sure as hell don't."

A hint of the red-haired boy's passive exasperation returned. "You can't hang out with Angor and expect not to learn every scientific term."

"No one knows *exactly* what white matter does," Angor explained, resuming his deep-in-thought face. "It's a network of tissue in the brain that's believed to have no purpose since its existence has been known for centuries but we lack the technology to study it in a living human brain. I know it has a purpose, though. I know it's the secret behind our weirdness."

This was the first theory Olalla had ever heard from him. She knew he had many—she always sensed him *thinking*—but he rarely voiced hypotheses, rarely displayed such passion for an idea. It made her want to harness her ability to a finer extent, to see if she might be able to uncover brain functions through weaving thoughts.

"You lost me pretty quick there." Casimir chucked his cigarette butt into the dirt and snuffed it with his shoe. "You're making me wish I'd remained a tree."

"We could use *him* as your human experiment," Aethelred suggested to Angor.

Olalla pressed her smiling lips together as Casimir burst out laughing. He didn't stop, not even when Angor muttered, "We *could*. If I can concentrate well enough, he won't feel a thing."

Aethelred Certior hated school. The classes themselves weren't bad, but traveling the hallways was like wading through a nightmare. Sometimes he would walk all the way around the building to evade the clogged masses. Sometimes he would hide in the bathroom until the bell rang and was then late for class. Always he wore long sleeves and long pants, even in the sweltering late August heat. In the winter, he would often don scarves and gloves, which made taking notes difficult—and warranted immense bullying. He didn't mind. Anything to avoid physical contact.

The few times he'd accidentally brushed against his peers, he'd puked for days. The headaches, the traumatic images, the feeling of his soul being utterly lost—all that kept him sane was Angor's constant presence, his mumblings of "…missing three days of school for you…have to make a note about researching the connection between sensory neurons and mental illness…I think you're experiencing alexithymia…or hysterical neurosis, dissociative type…you might make a good case study—don't go back to normal quite yet, Certior…"

At the time, Aethelred understood none of it. All he could process was the pain and the sorrow—and that he never wanted to touch anyone again.

It had not always been like this. In his early life, he'd lived in extremely tight quarters and he'd touched people, accidentally and intentionally, every day. But then the headaches progressed at the same rate that his hair changed from brown to red. Everything had changed then.

Now, Aethelred took every precaution to avoid contact, and he'd learned to act as normal as possible, despite his crazy hair, his "evil" eyes, and his inherently strange countenance. For the most part, his classmates had evolved to leave him alone, but the collapse of his previous school—

his small, familiar, manageable school—had thwarted his efforts. Perhaps his anxiety over the first day in this new hell was the reason he'd been so perturbed by *Casimir*.

Aethelred was not often so short with people. Years with stoic Angor had dulled most of his natural anxiety, but sometimes it flared, and Casimir seemed to be an expedient catalyst in the reaction.

That was why his dread spiked tenfold when he entered his first class on the first day—late, as usual—and spotted the green-haired boy lounging in the very back row, ratty black sneakers propped on his desk.

This school was quadruple the size of his old school, with so many classes that either one of them could have been in, but of course, they had to be in this one together.

With only one seat open, he was forced to plop into the desk diagonal from Casimir. Aethelred refused to turn around and witness the sly smirk that must have inched onto the wretched boy's face.

Luckily, the teacher didn't make a spectacle of his tardiness, probably because he looked like a *freak* in his thick striped sweater and dirt-stained khakis. That thought alone raised his temperature, but he kept his budding panic at bay—until a crumpled piece of paper hit the back of his head.

Mid-sentence in his note-taking about the American Civil War, Aethelred whipped around to find Casimir's pine green eyes directly on him, sparkling with a challenge. The boy dipped his chin toward the paper at the foot of Aethelred's chair, which he coldly ignored.

A few minutes passed, in which Aethelred meticulously jotted down every word the teacher said. History had always fascinated him. It was the only reason he could tolerate Angor recounting the lives of famous scientists for endless hours. He liked to see the sequence of minor incidents that led to a major event; he liked to dissect each and decide how they amounted into cataclysms like war, or how seemingly insignificant occurrences changed a person's entire perspective. Since he was young, he'd been particularly gifted at probing people's pasts and determining how it would affect their futures. That was why he had been selected for—

Another ball of paper hit his head, and he was certain it sliced a cut in his ear lobe. Though he was tempted to spin around and tell the perpetrator to quit it, he summoned Angor's poise and continued documenting his teacher's lecture, each letter carefully crafted. "We're only trailer trash if we allow ourselves to be," Angor always said. "Elegant penmanship is a necessary step toward sophistication." Considering he'd rarely used a pen before meeting his friend, this had not been an easy task for Aethelred.

Five minutes before the end of the period, another wad of paper sailed across the room, this time landing directly on his desk. Reluctantly, he allowed himself a reprieve from his notes. Perhaps if he provided Casimir with a curt response to whatever urgency the letter entailed, this nonsense would stop.

With as little noise as possible, Aethelred opened the crumpled paper, witnessed the crude sexual drawings on the page, and then neatly slipped it under his textbook. His cheeks must have blazed as red as his hair, but he couldn't prevent himself from stealing an incredulous look in Casimir's direction. This was, apparently, exactly what the boy had hoped for, because he leaned on the back two legs of his chair and cackled silently for the remainder of class.

At the very last minute, when the teacher began clearing the chalkboard, Aethelred heard the front two legs of

Casimir's chair clank against the linoleum floor. He assumed the boy would rebelliously waltz out of the classroom before the bell rang, but Casimir's green eyes were suddenly trained on the board, probably for the first time all hour. Tentatively, Aethelred followed his gaze and nearly suffered a heart attack. For on the blackboard, right where the teacher had just wiped the eraser, were the same lewd depictions that had been scrawled on the paper, now in chalk.

In his alarm, words from yesterday flitted through his mind: *I can make people see things that aren't there.* The drawings weren't real; Casimir only made Aethelred *think* they were. Momentarily, his terror abated, but then the rest of the class started giggling, and the teacher frantically scrubbed his eraser over the board to no avail. Casimir had imprinted this false reality in *everyone's* mind, and it should have been funny, but Aethelred felt immensely embarrassed, as if Casimir had added their names above the stick figures. The wink the boy shot him when he mistakenly glanced back made him wonder if in everyone else's minds he had.

Hastily gathering his books, Aethelred darted out of the classroom seconds before the bell rang. The hallway flooded with students, swarming him like angry hornets, and his eyes darted in all directions, seeking a bathroom or closet he could slip into. As his vision locked on the nearest unopened door, someone nudged his arm and then remained there, blocking his path to safety.

"Reddy, Reddy, Reddy," Casimir sang in exasperation, standing much too close. Luckily, he wore his leather jacket, and Aethelred's sweater was equally as impenetrable, but other students jostled around them, and one was bound to accidentally make contact. "You act like you've never seen a dick before. You do have your own, don't you?"

"I—must go to class," Aethelred managed, plowing ahead.

With an eye roll, Casimir followed, casually letting their shoulders bump. Though it wasn't skin-on-skin, it still sent a pang of nerves through Aethelred. The other boy didn't acknowledge this nervous energy or their proximity. "That face you made was priceless, but I was hoping you'd throw a fit and rip up the note. *That* would have earned an out-loud laugh."

"I don't think it's fair to call it a *note*," was the only rational response he could conjure. "Also…it would have made too much noise if I'd ripped it."

"Bullshit. You just liked it."

The words were spoken so nonchalantly that it took Aethelred a moment to appropriately react. "N-*no*."

Casimir clucked his tongue but didn't remove his attention from the slow-moving river of students before them. "What class are you going to next?"

This topic seemed safer than any other they'd engaged in thus far, so Aethelred fumbled with his papers, pointedly ignoring the wrinkled drawing. "English," he announced after reading his schedule.

"Ah yes, the class where they try to drill the slang outta us vagrants. If you sit next to me this time, maybe I'll draw you something more innocent."

"Sit next to you? You have English next, too?"

"Sure."

Aethelred searched the other boy for a sign of his schedule, but his hands were tucked into the pockets of his jacket. He didn't even have a backpack. "How do you know we're in the same room?"

Now Casimir's eyes slid toward him, half-lidded and

amused. "Because where else would I want to go?"

Angor had thought attending a new school would transform him into a new man, but it was impossible to feel like a *man* or any subcategory of adult when he had to eat meals in a dingy room scented with rotting beans and full of hormonal imbeciles.

From where he and Olalla sat, he had a perfect panoramic view of the cafeteria around them. A boy sitting in the corner, trying to balance a spoon on his nose. A girl seated beyond Olalla, fixing her makeup in the reflection of a different spoon. Angor wished the girl would ask a person to be her mirror. Any decent human would tell her neon green wasn't a flattering shade on anyone's eyelids.

All he could do was focus on his biology textbook and pretend his peers didn't exist. To think he'd worn his nicest polo and khakis to this pitiful excuse for an educational institution—he shook his head, and Olalla snorted across the table. When he glanced up, she smirked in that shrewd fashion that simultaneously excited and unnerved him.

"Do you disagree with the facts in your textbook, Periculy? Think you know better?"

He returned her grin, though it was more of a grimace. "I disagree with this culture. Look at that embarrassment to humanity." He motioned to a boy eating French fries with his hands at the end of their table, who heard him and blinked, expression turning cold. "Forks exist, you know."

At that, the other boy gathered his tray and found refuge at a different table. Angor wasn't remotely sad to see him go.

"Are you determined to insult every person you encounter?" Aethelred slipped into the seat beside him, weariness etched in his boyish features. Angor realized why when green-haired Casimir plopped into the empty chair next to Olalla's, smacking his tray on the table with enough force to spray vomit-colored soup in Aethelred's direction. Sighing, the red-haired boy daintily wiped it with a paper napkin.

"If they deserve insulting, yes." Leaning back, Angor gestured toward his textbook in frustration. "There isn't one sentence of information on the brain in here. Our curriculum will consist entirely of facts I already know."

"Boo-hoo for you," Casimir jeered before savagely shoving fries into his mouth. "We'll hold a funeral for your superior intellect, which will surely deteriorate in the presence of us inferior beings."

Olalla pursed her lips, which was the closest she would ever come to displaying sympathy. "We'll have to spend more time in the town library, then—when I'm not working..." This last part was a barely-audible grumble. Of them, she was the only one who held a real job. Aethelred sold hand-stitched decor of clichéd sayings to anyone brainless enough to buy them, and Angor engaged in more deviant methods of acquiring money—for the sole purpose of saving time to brood, obviously. He had no idea what Casimir did. Perhaps the boy's parents had enough money to support him, or perhaps his methods were even less moral than Angor's.

"Want some?" Casimir tilted his canned beverage at Aethelred.

When Angor read the label, he waved a dismissive hand. "We don't drink that garbage. I've studied its effects on my mother's health, and it isn't positive."

"Speaking of mothers"—Casimir paused to take a swig of his carbonated drink—"is Angor yours?" After a moment, Aethelred absorbed the jab and bristled. "It seems like he dictates your decisions."

His posture went straighter than Angor had ever seen. "I don't like pop."

With a cough, Casimir spat out the brown liquid. "*Pop*? God, I really am in the midwest now, aren't I? Pop! Fucking freaks…"

As usual, Aethelred squirmed at the vulgarity—or perhaps the word *freak*—but he composed himself quickly enough to ask, "Where are you from?"

"Another dimension, probably." Casimir shrugged and fixed the other boy with a challenging, dark green gaze. "Do you care?"

From the closer end of the table, a person coughed, and they all turned to find Artemis Cosmos standing there, a tray clutched in her thin fingers. Though her chin was raised as she glared down at them through the lenses of her glasses, she exuded far less sophistication than her younger sister. Her dark hair was always pulled into a suffocatingly tight bun, and without Olalla's tint of purple, it lacked originality.

"Ollie," she hissed, eyes darting around with apprehension. "Sit with me. I can't sit alone."

Olalla blinked, and Angor swore the violet sheen in her irises increased. "Oh? Are you afraid someone will pour milk on your head if I'm not there to protect you?" Angor pressed his lips together to suppress a smile. After only a few days of knowing Olalla, she had told them why the Cosmoses had moved to Hastings Street. That was the moment he'd truly deemed her someone he wanted as a friend. "Sit by yourself, *Artie*."

The girl's brows knitted with a combination of panic and loathing, but she didn't heed her sister's command, not like Angor had seen others do. He couldn't ignore the flush of red rising in Olalla's cheeks, so he intervened with a smooth, "You don't want to sit with us, Artemis. Our friend Casimir has...a horrible disease."

"HIV," the green-haired boy confirmed as though they'd planned this lie. Angor wondered, uncomfortably, if it wasn't a lie. The number of cases *had* been quietly increasing over the past few years, if his research was correct.

Aethelred choked on his sandwich and had to thump his chest in order to dislodge the half-chewed bread. Artemis's tan face paled, and Angor hoped the fib hadn't sent her into shock.

"It spreads *extremely* easily," Casimir continued, and this time Angor was fairly certain he was lying. "Just by breathing the same air as me, you've probably caught it. Hey, look—I think I see some on your hand."

Angor saw nothing, but he assumed Casimir must have used his strange ability to show Artemis something truly revolting, because her eyes bulged in dismay. He also assumed Artemis knew absolutely nothing about human immunodeficiency virus, because instead of dismissing the deceit, as anyone who knew HIV didn't physically manifest beyond flu-like symptoms or transfer through the air would, she flailed and threw her tray across the room.

The contents splashed the floor while the plastic hit a boy in the head. Unfortunately, this boy was one of the few who actually resembled a man. As tall as Aethelred and far more athletically built, the boy approached their table and towered over them with narrowed eyes. A bruise had yet to form, but Angor knew the boy's forehead throbbed from the blow.

"What's going on here?" he asked, not angrily but suspiciously.

Though Angor had never encountered him before, he assumed the boy to be a senior based on the way his dark gaze roved their group with an air of authority. He probably thought them silly, reckless *children*. Angor opened his mouth to give a smooth, sophisticated reply, but then Artemis, after hastily examining her hand once more, squealed, "H-he flipped my tray!"

Casimir, at whom her finger was pointed, shrugged and said, "I have HIV. It messes with your brain—makes you do shit. Best to stay away, bucko."

The boy's nose twitched in disbelief. He probably possessed more knowledge on the human immunodeficiency virus than Casimir did, which was not an impressive feat. After scrutinizing them—specifically their hair and eyes—he sneered, "You're a bunch of *freaks*. Don't let them bully you," he added to Artemis, placing a comforting hand on her back. "I'll buy you a new lunch. C'mon…"

Wrapping an arm around her shoulders, he guided her across the cafeteria, though not before glancing back and nodding to his table of jocks. These boys also had the bodies of men, but their demeanors screamed ravenous wolves. As one, they stood from their chairs and stalked around the mess of Artemis's lunch to swarm the underclassmen in a sea of mint green football jerseys.

Aethelred gripped the sides of his tray while Olalla's back stiffened, her purple-tinted eyes glowering at each upperclassman. Angor sincerely hoped she was compelling them to walk away; physical combat had never been a strength of his, at least not in the way *normal* people physically combatted.

"We're pretty popular, huh?" Casimir mused, pausing to take a sip of his beverage. "Got all these *cool* kids giving us attention. Nice to meet you fellas. I'm Casimir Stro—"

"You're *deserving of a beating*," snarled the one directly behind him. His nose was a bit too large for his face, as were his muscles for his body.

"*You deserve a beating* would sound more grammatically correct, but I appreciate your attempt at witticisms," Angor said, tapping his fingers to the metal knife on his tray. He'd hoped the boys would notice his discreet warning, but they were far less shrewd than their leader, and Angor's remark had shoved them over the edge.

First, the big-nosed one grabbed Casimir's leather jacket and yanked him out of his seat. Then, the freckled one behind Aethelred seized the back of his neck to shove him forward into his tray. This attempt failed the moment their skin made contact; the freckled boy startled, as if electrically shocked, and Aethelred doubled over of his own accord, retching in the space between his and Angor's seats.

Before he could help his friend, fingers snared in his pinkish hair. For the briefest second, Angor panicked, but then he remembered himself, and with his mental will, he forced the boy to release him by inducing immense pain in his hand.

Howling, the boy behind him staggered back, and the big-nosed boy's fist paused an inch from Casimir's face as he spun to see why his friend had yelled. The green-haired boy must have used this reprieve to produce an illusion, because Big Nose's vision fixed on nothing, and his grip slackened enough for Casimir to effectively elbow him in the gut. Angor mentally amplified the pain, as well as provoked an ache in the freckled boy's head that had him heaving beside Aethelred.

Throughout all of this, Olalla had remained rigid in her chair, glaring at their fourth assailant. This one was actually a girl—a massive girl who wore the same jersey as the boys. Seemingly, she'd been tasked with attacking the Olalla, but her brow was furrowed in confusion, as if she couldn't remember her purpose here. Dazed, the older girl finally shook her head and ambled off, mumbling incoherencies.

Olalla shifted her focus to the moaning boys, warping their agonized minds, forcing them to stagger away. Once they were out of earshot, she released a breath and rubbed her forehead. Casimir did the same as he plopped into his chair and straightened his jacket. After shaking out his curly locks, his vision settled on gagging Aethelred.

"Did he electrocute that guy?"

Angor grimaced at his friend, who he knew would remain in this sickened state for hours, perhaps days. His phobia was more of an allergy, Angor supposed. "It would have been better if he had."

He expected more questions—which he would not answer, to honor Aethelred's dignity—but he did not expect Casimir to demand, "What did *you* do to them? I didn't even see you move."

Blatantly ignoring him, Angor slid his gaze to Olalla, who'd stopped rubbing her forehead in favor of staring blankly into the distance. He wished he'd been gifted with the ability to read minds, that way he wouldn't have had to reveal how utterly her ability intrigued him. "What did you make them believe?"

She didn't look at him as she replied, "That we defeated them and they're ashamed."

Beautiful—her mind was beautiful. Not only had she thwarted their aggressors once, but she had thwarted them eternally.

The shame would deter them from hurting the underclassmen again, but, Angor realized as they departed the cafeteria, it did not deter them from less violent forms of attack. Because as the four left lunch, struggling to carry Aethelred without touching his skin, the football coach cornered them and—for "ruthlessly traumatizing his players"—issued an after school detention.

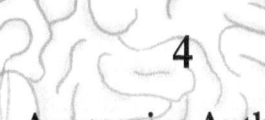

4

Aggressive Authority

"**Y**ou know what's really bullshit?" Casimir asked, his voice knocking on Aethelred's skull like a child wielding drumsticks. "That those wimps tattled on us by claiming *we* beat them up, and the coach is still on their side. I mean, c'mon—he should be begging us to join the team."

"Would you accept the offer?" countered Olalla's wry voice.

"Hell no. I'd do exactly what I already plan to do, which is attend every game and make those assholes hallucinate until they're crying in the grass."

"I don't know why you even asked, Cosmos," Angor said, a smirk evident in his tone. Aethelred wanted to tell them all to stop talking, but that would require lifting his head from where it was buried in the sleeves of his sweltering sweater.

After the fiasco at lunch, he'd spent the remainder of the school day in the nurse's office, puking into a trash can. His headache had yet to subside, but the nurse had deemed him well enough to attend detention.

Never before had Aethelred or Angor received formal punishment. At their old school, they were well-behaved students, beloved by every teacher they encountered: Angor for his smarts and Aethelred for his kindness. Now, his friend had accepted this punishment—even reveled in it. Aethelred could not comply with delinquency with such ease, though. He didn't want to be a rebel, but it seemed Casimir's presence had redetermined his fate.

The sudden sensation of fingers atop his head set his heart into a frenzy. He expected to lose all sense of reality, to spiral out of his own mind and into the past of another's, but his awareness didn't change. The sounds of Angor and Olalla bickering about biology still hit his ears, the stale scent of his sweater still invaded his nostrils, and those intrusive fingers still coiled through his hair.

Someone was touching him—continuously touching him—and he'd yet to vomit.

Apprehensive, Aethelred lifted his head. Olalla sat at the desk beside his, reciting lines from her biology textbook to prove that humans indeed have twenty-three chromosomes. Angor remained at the desk behind him, dismissing her every claim with "As far as we know." And Casimir lounged at the desk diagonal from him, too far to have touched him and then returned to his seat.

There was no one else near them. A few gossiping girls sat at the back of the classroom and a boy wearing a backwards baseball cap sat in the front row, but none seemed vaguely interested in their group. And, unless he'd gone crazy, Aethelred still felt someone coiling a finger through his hair.

Again he looked at Casimir, whose eyebrows shot upward. "Problem, Reddy?" he asked through the unlit cigarette between his grinning teeth.

There definitely was a problem, but he didn't want to voice it, especially not now that Olalla and Angor had paused their dispute to give him quizzical stares.

Shaking his head increased his headache, but he didn't grimace as he turned toward the front, where the teacher graded papers at her desk. The fingers had disappeared from his hair, but the headache had not gone with it. He rubbed his eyes to dispel his grogginess—and then felt a finger on his cheek, trailing from his temple toward his chin. It ran along his bottom lip, so languid and slow that he'd jolted in his chair before it reached the opposite corner.

From behind, Casimir snorted, but when Aethelred whirled toward the aisle, he wasn't standing there. He still reclined at his desk, twirling his cigarette between his fingers. "Are you having a seizure over there, or what?"

"I'm just—" Aethelred cut himself short when the other boy brought his cigarette to his mouth and ran the end over his own bottom lip, the same lazy motion Aethelred had just experienced. His eyes slivered, and he finished with a curt, "I'm fine."

"I never denied that." Before Aethelred could process the insinuation, Casimir kicked Olalla's textbook. "What are we gonna do about your sister?"

"What do you mean?" she demanded, almost automatically. "I can make her stay away from us."

"I would ask if you're actually capable, but that would probably offend you, and it's not relevant anyway. I meant, aren't we gonna dole out some revenge? Half the school's gonna think I have HIV now."

Angor's eyes slid toward him, amused. "For that, you have only yourself to blame."

"*You* were the one who claimed I had a disease."

"Other diseases exist, you know. You didn't have to pick one of the worst ones."

"Oh, what does it matter if people think you have HIV?"

Olalla drawled, slamming her textbook shut. "No one would have wanted to sleep with you anyway."

Casimir opened his mouth and then closed it. "I deserved that for questioning your abilities."

Angor crossed his arms, suspicious eyes boring into her. "I think we should make a formal pact not to use our abilities on one another."

She scoffed in offense. "I didn't plant that truth in his head. You think so little of me, Periculy."

"No, he thinks so little of me," Casimir said. "I do have common sense, you know. A jab for a jab."

"Is that how we're going to play it?" Angor's quiet tone wiped the smirks from their faces. "You sneak beliefs into his mind and then you force hallucinations into hers? Our trust for one another will deteriorate very quickly, don't you think?"

Olalla and Casimir exchanged a brief glance before staring in opposite directions. A long moment passed, and then Aethelred said, "*I* don't think we should trust him at all." Casimir blinked at the accusation before granting Aethelred a bland look. "We don't even know where you came from."

"Washington D.C."

Aethelred bristled, not at the place but at the direct answer. He almost didn't want to know more—he hated demanding information from people because he hated when people demanded information from him—but part of him was curious. "Why'd you move here?"

Casimir held his gaze, steady and intense, and Aethelred's mistake immediately became apparent to him; *a jab for a jab* could easily be translated to *a truth for a truth*, and he knew the green-haired boy would not forget revealing his.

"My dad lost his job—got hooked on some drugs again

shortly afterward."

Again dredged up enough questions, but *drugs...* hallucinogenic drugs? Aethelred's time spent with Angor had adjusted his brain to instantly form theories, but he did not want to know the truth—could not let himself know. Not only would Casimir use this as leverage to dig into his past, but Aethelred's mind would recreate the tale as vividly as if the other boy actually had touched him. His imagination had grown too wild.

"Surprise, his parents are as shitty as the rest of ours," Olalla droned before shooting Aethelred a smirk. "Can he be part of our gang now?"

"There will be no *gang* unless we can agree on some terms," Angor said as if they were in a business meeting, not high school detention. "We tell no one of our abilities."

Casimir rolled his eyes. "Well, of course—wouldn't want the church coming after us."

"I was thinking more of the government, but I suppose the church *would* think us devils."

"More like *know*." Black horns sprouted from Casimir's forehead, and with his manic grin, he did pass as an evil creature. "Reddy doesn't even need the horns—he already looks like Satan."

Olalla let out a short snicker. "That's exactly what I thought."

"I would add *no insulting* to the list," Angor said, "but then I fear the group would consist only of Aethelred."

"Oh, don't act like he's an angel," Casimir retorted with a dramatic air. "He called my name *weird*. I cried for nights!"

"I'm glad," Aethelred mumbled, but they all heard it, and Casimir's laughter boomed through the classroom. From the front, the teacher hissed an ineffective *"Shush"* and didn't resume grading papers until the boy finally stopped a minute later.

"Well, now that we've all been banned from our own gang, can we form a new one under new leadership?" Olalla proposed, crossing her legs in a formal pose. "Mine, preferably."

"And what rules would you enact, Cosmos?" Angor challenged, almost mockingly. "We all must conform to your plans and beliefs, and if we don't, you'll make sure we do?"

Her jaw shifted in displeasure. "No, I just…don't like how you've assumed this *authority* position. We should all be equals—that should be a rule."

He dipped his chin. "I agree."

Then the two of them stared at each other for a long minute, Angor with placidity and Olalla with fury. Casimir finally broke the silence by saying, "What are you two doing—having a mental make-out session? Can we at least conclude the meeting first?"

"Of course." Angor simpered, eyes still glued to Olalla. "Let's all take turns listing the rest of the rules and then each of us can close the meeting in turns. We'll draw straws to decide the order."

Aethelred recognized this was about to become a very passive aggressive ordeal. Angor and Olalla were both too assertive; they'd never been meant to join the same group.

"We won't use our abilities on one another," Aethelred chimed in, hoping his wariness didn't show. Then, glancing at each of them, he asked, "Is there anything else?"

Angor raised his hand in mock timidity. "I think I might have a suggestion, should the whole group consent to the sound of my voice."

"I do not consent to the sound of your voice," Olalla said

with a tart smile. "But I would like to hear your suggestion—perhaps you can whisper it to Aethelred and he can speak?"

Graciously, Angor leaned over his desk to divulge the rule into Aethelred's ear. With a sigh, the red-haired boy recited, "We agree to discover the source of our abilities and all concepts of biology, chemistry, and physics associated."

Casimir smacked his lips together to make a popping sound. "That sounds like a *you* thing." He pointed between Angor and Olalla with his cigarette.

"I have no qualm with splitting the group," Olalla said, arching her eyebrows at Angor. "Periculy and I can conduct scientific research while you two..." Her words faltered as she struggled to contrive a task for them. Aethelred certainly thought of nothing he and the rebellious boy could successfully accomplish together.

"We'll find something to do," Casimir assured her before gifting Aethelred with a wink that provoked uncomfortable heat in his body. "It'll likely include sabotaging your sister's life and giving that asshole jock a mental disorder."

Olalla barely stifled a laugh. "Sounds like fine work to me."

"As to me," Angor piped up before pivoting to Aethelred. "And to you?"

He pressed his lips together, pointedly ignoring the way Casimir's eyebrows wiggled in his direction. The only reason he didn't shun them and return his face to the nook of his elbow was because, mysteriously, his headache had subsided. "And to me."

As far as Casimir was aware, Angor had avoided allowing

anyone other than Aethelred into the crumbling walls of the Periculys' mobile home. Casimir knew the guy was embarrassed—although he couldn't deduce *why*, considering their entire gang lived in deteriorating mobile homes. Even so, he was mildly surprised when, after that first day of detention, Angor didn't stop him from following the other two boys through the front door.

To be fair, Angor hadn't *realized* Casimir was following until they were practically through the threshold. When they'd arrived on Hastings Street, the others riding their bikes while Casimir cruised on his skateboard, Olalla had continued toward her moss-ridden house, and Casimir had made them all see a false version of himself headed for his home. The real version of himself had waltzed to the Periculys' behind the boys, fully visible but somehow undetected. By the time Angor noticed him, Casimir was already shutting the door.

With a stiff spine, the pink-haired boy faced him, eyes darting with more nerves than Casimir had seen from him thus far. "Is there something you require?"

He shrugged, glancing around at the stained walls with glowing red roots weaving in and out of the vinyl. Though he was certain the roots were a hallucination, the mountain of empty beer cans in the corner beyond the couch seemed realistic since a sour stench permeated the air. Other than that, minimal clutter littered the area, which was a shock. He'd expected the place to be brimming with test tubes and possibly human subjects.

"Just wanted to check out the scene. Your place is bigger than mine," he added after peering into one of the two doors on the right. "We only have one bedroom."

Angor's mouth flopped open, but for once he didn't conjure a witty reply. Rather, he tautly said, "We'll see you in school tomorrow, I'm sure."

"Oh, I'm sure, too." Casimir jumped his eyebrows at Aethelred, whose cheeks were as pink as the drapes. His blood red hair was tousled from biking, and Casimir was tempted to actually coil his fingers through it—just to irk the kid, obviously. "And you'll see me now, since I'm not gonna leave."

With this statement, he strolled between the boys and plopped into the nearest armchair. The fraying fabric smelled like moldy pizza, but it was comfortable, and the armrests featured some drawings that looked delightfully in-appropriate.

"This your chair, Reddy?" Casimir asked, gesturing toward the art.

Aethelred peered over and blanched at the sight of it. "I didn't—Angor was trying to teach me to draw DNA."

"What does that stand for? Dicks 'n Ass?"

Angor coughed a laugh into his hand while Aethelred's face drooped like he might melt into a puddle of shame. Casimir would gladly pay a daily tithe to continuously see that expression.

"You should really go," Angor advised, maintaining his perpetual politeness. "We don't have much food, and I have a lot of homework to do."

"Mm, and I have a lot of homework I need you to do for me—probably." Casimir glanced at his back, where he should have worn a backpack like the other two but didn't. "I wouldn't know, and I really don't care."

Angor pinched the bridge of his nose and sighed. "Fine, but we need to remain quiet. I don't want to wake—"

"*Angor!*" a voice screeched from beyond the closed door. A moment later, it burst open to reveal a hunched, frail lady waving a beer can. The lines of her face were as sharp as Angor's but far less flattering, giving her a gaunt appearance rather than an austere one. Bags surrounded her eyes, nearly as purple as Olalla's hair, and her tattered clothes barely concealed the parts Casimir would rather not see.

All at once, he understood the embarrassment. This was what Angor did not want him to see. But, strangely, the state of this woman almost made him *like* the guy. Over the past few weeks of spying, he'd assumed the boy was a pretentious asswipe trying to be better than everyone, when in reality he only wanted to be better than this bedraggled slob.

"You woke me from my nap!" she wailed, shaking the beer around as if it were proof of her accusation. Casimir wondered if she actually held anything at all. He'd outgrown most of his susceptibility to hallucinations, but new settings often confused him, especially since his perception on what was *normal* had skewed over the years.

"I apologize, Mo—"

The woman threw her arms about as she sing-complained, "*Ring ring ring*—the phone was ringing and ringing and ringing and *finally* I got up, and guess who it was? *The school!*"

Angor's throat bobbed. "I can explain the detention."

"I don't give a shit about that—they *woke me up!*" To her, this offense seemed worthy of chucking her beer at her son, which is exactly what she did. The throw was pathetic, in Casimir's opinion, but at least the spray of liquid drenching Angor's khakis was proof that the can wasn't an illusion.

"You are so insolent," he grumbled. Pulling out a handkerchief—a fucking *handkerchief*—from his pocket, he dabbed at his pants until his mother stomped through the kitchen on bare feet and gripped his hair.

His body went motionless, his mouth clamping shut as she snarled, "What did you say?" He didn't answer before she released his hair and slapped his face. Casimir hadn't anticipated aggression—especially not *effective* aggression—from such a sickly woman, but the boy's pale cheek throbbed as red as Aethelred's eyes.

Violence didn't really faze Casimir, but injustice unsettled him. He shifted to the edge of the armchair, prepared to intervene, but then he realized something immensely more unnerving: Angor had not flinched. Angor had not moved at all. His head had turned, his body had swayed with the impact, but his expression had not faltered from its typical impassivity. The lack of reaction made Casimir question if it had even happened.

Carefully, he angled his attention toward the woman's bedroom and envisioned an unappealing pair of female undergarments on the floor. With disgust that was not at all an act, he said, "Yo, are those your *panties* lying out in the open? How *humiliating.*"

Angor's mother jolted and spun to see the exact image Casimir forced in her brain. Panicked, she scurried into her room, and he followed in order to slam the door behind her. The lock was on the inside, but he swiftly found a chair to jam under the handle, trapping her within.

After a long, tense moment of Casimir and Aethelred exchanging wary glances and Angor staring at the door, the broody boy finally said, "I'm surprised your trick worked. I wasn't under the impression she wore undergarments at all."

"You've thought about your own mother's undergarments?" Casimir questioned, ignoring the jostling of the doorknob behind him. "Weird, dude."

Angor's reaction to this was the same as his reaction to

the slap: nonexistent. It made Casimir regret entering the Periculys' home, and Casimir was not one to regret things.

With a pointed look at Aethelred, he retreated to his chair, and luckily, the other kid caught the hint and settled on the couch, awkwardly tucking his backpack beneath the dented coffee table. By the time Angor joined them, primly lowering onto the cushion farthest from Aethelred's, the red-haired boy had extracted his erratically organized folders and was tapping the pencil eraser to his chin. Momentarily, Casimir forgot Angor existed.

Then the asswipe spoke. "I suppose we can work together on the biology homework, since I know neither of you have a clue as to the definition of homeostasis."

Casimir could have utilized this opportunity to point out he hadn't collected any of his homework, nor would he have any intention of completing it regardless, but instead he casually asked, "So, are we gonna talk about her, or what?"

"Obviously," Angor sighed, running a hand through his long hair. It was the wildest part about him, yet it gave him the aura of an ancient leader or—with the pinkish hue—some elvish king. "She's such a pain."

Dully, Casimir raised an eyebrow. "I was gonna say she's an abusive bitch, but I guess we can put it lightly."

"I don't know if I would go that far. She still…entices me."

Casimir's face gradually contorted—worried, disturbed, and intrigued all at once. "I thought fantasizing about your mom's panties was weird, but now it's starting to add up. This is some Freudian shit, man."

Angor straightened with surprise. "You've heard of Freud? Not to offend, but—"

"Don't try to derail this conversation, you sicko. I can't

believe... You put up with this?" he demanded of Aethelred, who now wore his exasperated face instead of his ashamed one.

"You're talking about different people."

Angor ripped his brooding focus from the window to fix Casimir with puzzled eyes. "Who are you talking about?"

"Your mom."

A muscle twitched in Angor's jaw, but he didn't succumb to emotion. "We don't talk about her. I was talking about Olalla."

"Ah, that's reassuring." Casimir relaxed into the armchair and tapped his foot on the carpet. "I do feel like Olalla's got the potential to be an abusive bitch, by the way. But I don't think she will be. She respects us...somewhat."

"Of course she does," Angor said, frustrated, as he sprang from the couch and began pacing through the living room. "But of course she doesn't. She respects us as friends, but she does not respect us as humans."

Casimir pursed his lips. "That doesn't make any freakin' sense, Periculy."

"It makes perfect sense. We're her friends, but somewhere in the back of her mind, she'll always be aware that she's superior to us."

"*Is* she superior to us?"

"She can reshape our entire psyches, Stromer. Of course she's superior. I simultaneously want to destroy her and praise her, and the worst part is I don't know if she's purposely planted these sentiments in my consciousness."

Casimir lit a cigarette, hoping it would help the complexity of their predicament sink in. "I thought you said you could *feel her talons* or some poetic bullshit? I thought she didn't affect you?"

"I *can* feel her, and I *do* think I've fortified myself against her, but…how would I truly know?"

Aethelred fidgeted on the couch, eyes flitting briefly in Casimir's direction, as if he wasn't sure he wanted to voice this inquiry in the hallucinator's presence. "She agreed not to use her ability on us. What reason would she have to betray our trust?"

"It's not betrayal I'm worried about; it's unintentional usage. She's ambitious, and although it seems we have the same goals, we might not always have the same methods. We disagreed today, and you saw how adamant she was to sway us—how she *expected* us to alter our perceptions to hers."

Casimir puffed smoke in Angor's direction when he paced past the armchair. "Sounds like someone's bitter about their self-assumed leadership being revoked."

"I'm not *bitter*," he insisted, waving smoke away from his face. "I'm concerned she might conform all our brains into one without anyone—herself included—noticing. Without mental diversity, how will we determine if an idea is a bad one? How will we have individual identities? Why will we exist?"

Casimir had a sarcastic comment about Angor's dramatic existential crisis on his tongue, but it was interrupted by a knock on the front door, louder than the faint banging of Angor's mother in the bedroom.

Although he was closest to the door, Casimir didn't move, nor did he turn until Angor opened it and Olalla's piqued voice said, "You'll never *believe*—Did you piss your pants?"

"Yes," Casimir said, smirking at them around the back of the armchair. Olalla's gaze narrowed on Angor's crotch while the boy tried not to let her see too far into the house.

"Irrelevant," dismissed the pants-pisser. "Have you discovered something of value?"

"No, but—"

She paused at the faint wail of Angor's mother beyond the bedroom door. Casimir thought she said, "I need more beer!" but his mind sometimes altered reality into the most ridiculous possibilities.

"Do you have a hostage?" Olalla questioned, trying to peek her head through the threshold.

Angor's hold on the door was firm. "Technically speaking, yes."

Her confusion morphed into a mild but manic interest. "Are you experimenting on her?"

"Glad I'm not the only one to assume Angor's an evil scientist." Casimir blew smoke toward the doorway, and Olalla scrunched her nose. "Although, when I assumed it, I was *much* less excited."

She pursed her lips, as though he was the one deserving of judgment. "We have a problem."

"You couldn't have called about it?" Angor asked with the same courteously tense tone he'd used when Casimir first entered his home. "I gave you my telephone number for a reason."

Twisting to drape his legs over the armrest, Casimir sideglanced in Aethelred's direction as he suggested, "For phone sex?" Though the red-haired boy was not the target of the question, he coughed as if he'd never before heard the word "sex" uttered aloud.

"I couldn't use the phone," Olalla said, sadly disregarding the joke. "I had to get out of there."

Despite Casimir's temptation to quip about how "Phone sex wasn't good enough, eh?" he kept his mouth shut. Even in his weeks as a tree, he hadn't heard the girl mention anything about her home life except for her ardent hatred of Artemis, and he wondered if her rapid departure had anything to do with the parents she intentionally neglected to talk about.

"He's at my house," she said, which was not at all what Casimir had anticipated.

"Who?" Angor asked cautiously.

"William."

"Who's *William*?" Casimir sneered, trying to make the name sound more unusual than Olalla or Angor or Aethelred or even his own.

"William Ross."

Casimir sighed loudly. "Still don't know—"

"The asshole who's—apparently, after one measly afternoon—dating my sister." Angor's face tightened, Aethelred dropped his pencil, and Casimir accidentally singed the armchair with his cigarette. None needed her to, but still she clarified, "The asshole who set his friends upon us."

5

The Aftermath of Atrocious Acts

Angor never thought his nemesis would have a name as boring and generic as *William Ross*. He almost resisted their rivalry because of it. Part of him wished Casimir had ended up as his adversary just because his name was more menacing. The fact that, over the next few weeks, this clean-cut *William* progressed into their enemy made Angor wonder if perhaps *they* were the villains in this scenario.

Many at East Mintle certainly acted like they were. As William's animosity for them grew, their classmates began to take notice of their oddly-colored features, thus deeming them the "freaks" of the school. This did not faze Angor; he would not allow his inconsequential peers to deter his rise to greatness. Aethelred couldn't cope quite as easily, though. While Angor, Casimir, and Olalla utilized their skills to thwart attacks, their red-haired friend's ability was more of a hindrance than a strength. Some days he cut class to avoid students' verbal and physical harassment, and some days he received detention for skipping.

Fortunately for him, these punishments were not endured alone. Artemis's new gang of jocks provoked enough fights with Olalla to earn the younger Cosmos as many detentions, and for defending her, Angor was roped into these penalties. Since the upperclassmen didn't hate Casimir as intensely, he had to purposely obtain detention by smoking in class or riding his skateboard through the halls, a mad grin plastered on his face throughout.

At the end of September, during one of these after school punishments, Angor read something in a library-borrowed book on genetics that sparked his interest: a recently invented technique that would detect which genes were expressed in a specific cell.

"Have you heard of the Northern blotting technique?" he asked Olalla, whose nose was stuffed in a book on neurons. Her hair was like a curtain of purple pansies, and he couldn't help but think the hue had brightened since their first encounter.

From where she sat diagonally before him, she glanced back with quizzical and slightly envious eyes. If Angor had learned anything about her over the past few months, it was that she did not like when others possessed information she did not. "Should I have?"

He recognized her question as an attempt to belittle his discovery, so he countered with, "Only if you're up to date with current methods used to study genetics."

She frowned at the book on his desk. "Well, what is it?"

"You're aware that every cell in your body contains every one of your genes, yet each cell does not express every gene?"

"Of course," Casimir jumped in. His legs were propped atop his desk as he drew crude depictions on his ripped jeans. One drawing, Angor feared, was an exact replication of Aethelred's hideously inaccurate DNA diagram. "That's kindergarten-level shit, Periculy. Tell me something I don't know."

Olalla rolled her eyes, but Angor was grateful for their friend's sarcastic comment. Casimir and Aethelred were, somehow, the glue holding the group together. Without the boys' inferior intellect, Angor and Olalla might have forgotten how far ahead of their age they were—how much they needed each other's brains to accomplish their goals.

"Not all cells utilize all genes," Angor reiterated, this time for Casimir and Aethelred, who'd paused his English essay to listen. "If they did, every tissue in your body would serve the same purpose—there would be no difference between your brain and your heart. Our genes make us human, but they also differentiate us from other humans. To put it simply, I believe the four of us might possess a gene that differentiates us from other humans—but I would need to determine the amino acid sequence, then use this Northern blotting technique on samples of our cells...preferably neurons...or brain tissue..."

Casimir leaned away. "Don't look at me like that, dude. I can literally *see* the scalpel in your hands. I don't want you cracking my skull open like one of your walnuts."

Shaking out of his thoughts, Angor looked solemnly at Olalla. "I fear the technology isn't where we need it to be... Nevertheless, we should continue to study proteins and genes—see if we can find any cases of abnormal gene functions. First, I believe we should study my cells...my cutaneous nociceptors, to be precise."

"What the *hell* is that?"

Angor glanced toward Casimir, who'd recoiled in horror. Perhaps he should have let the kid remain ignorant, but he would need to start learning terminology if he was to be of any use to their mission. "The nerves in my skin that detect painful stimuli."

The green-haired boy dropped his legs from the desk, stomping his feet on the ground loud enough to earn a hiss from the teacher. "I fucking *knew it*," he whispered so the other students wouldn't hear. "You don't feel pain, do you? That's why you didn't flinch when—"

To Angor's immense relief, Casimir stopped himself before recounting what happened within the Periculys' house a few weeks prior. Forest green eyes darting briefly toward Olalla, he added, "That's how you scare the jocks away, isn't it? You *make* them feel pain."

"I activate their nociceptors, yes," he admitted uncomfortably. "It causes them no real harm; their brains only believe they're in pain."

"Huh, seems like we've all mastered the art of altering minds." Casimir lounged in his chair once again and jumped his eyebrows at Aethelred. "Except you, Red. No one knows what the hell you do. Maybe you're like our balancer—our atoner."

The other boy's brow furrowed. "What does that mean?"

"Well, the rest of us are out here engaging in intensely immoral acts—altering beliefs, inducing hallucinations, inflicting pain—and *you're* paying for it with your headaches and anxiety. You balance our wrongdoings by suffering our penance."

"Don't say that, Cas," Olalla mock pouted. "You're making me feel guilty. Our poor Aethelred."

He looked at the ground, avoiding her gaze even when she playfully nudged his shoe with hers. Knowing Aethelred, he would believe in absurdity like *karma*.

Angor puffed out an agitated breath. "There is no higher power punishing you for our sins," he assured his friend.

"And he wouldn't be paying for our sins, anyway. The headaches are a result of his unwillingness to improve."

Casimir's eyes slivered like pine needles, but he didn't press the subject. Angor assumed he'd badgered Aethelred enough about it to have learned he would never receive a straight answer. Even Angor had yet to understand the nature of his oldest friend's ailment.

"After school tomorrow—should we evade another one of these glorious detentions—we'll sneak into the science labs and steal one of the microscopes," Angor said quietly, speaking to Olalla.

"You think the school's microscopes are advanced enough to view neurons? I thought you had common sense, Periculy."

"We can use it for other things," he dismissed, returning his focus to the book in his lap. "Meet me outside the lab after our last period. Casimir, Aethelred, distract Mrs. Bishop for us. She's usually in there at that time."

"Only if you want to," Olalla added with false consideration. "We wouldn't demand anything of you two, would we, Angor?"

"Oh, we'll distract her." Casimir threw his legs atop the desk again and resumed his drawings. "I have a ploy that'll make her flee the room entirely. As long as Reddy consents."

Aethelred released a long exhale. "I suppose someone will have to ensure you don't kill the head of the science department."

"That's the...spirit..." Casimir's voice trailed off, and a moment later a pencil landed on Angor's genetics book. "Pst, that creep is looking at us again."

Angor knew who *that creep* was even before glancing toward the front corner of the room. The boy with the backwards baseball cap had quietly but indiscreetly observed them during every detention thus far. Seemingly, the boy spent every afternoon in this classroom, probably because he always refused to remove his hat.

This time, Angor didn't hesitate to meet the boy's eyes. He hoped the intensity of the eye contact would frighten him, but it didn't. With eyes as bright as limes, he stared back, a challenge written on his curious face. Angor sincerely hoped he hadn't heard their plans of theft. Although, he supposed, at this point a few more detentions wouldn't hurt his already deteriorating record.

"I failed first grade twice," Casimir said as he and Aethelred slowly strolled through the empty hallways after their last period the next day. Somehow, the two boys had ended up with the same exact class schedule. Aethelred had questioned it until Casimir began using his illusions to scare people off, successfully preventing unwanted physical contact. Now, even though he could have easily walked on the opposite side of the hall, he remained beside the hallucinator, so close their sweater- and leather-clad shoulders sometimes brushed.

"Me and reading don't jive," Casimir continued before purposely puffing smoke toward the detectors on the ceiling. That they didn't spray water in response was not very reassuring. "Letters always used to turn to monsters on the page. They finally let me pass because they were sick of me saying 'That's not an *M*—that's a dragon, you idiots.'"

Aethelred barely contained a chuckle. "I didn't ask you if you failed first grade."

"I know. I'm offering the information. Is that a problem?"

Aethelred peeked at the other boy, whose green eyebrows were arched. "It's just...not many people like to talk about the embarrassments of their pasts."

"Embarrassment? Bitch, I was *bragging*. Those old hags didn't know what to do with me. It was hilarious."

This time, Aethelred was unable to stop his cough of laughter. "Of course. How dare I equate you with a normal person."

"Your turn, Red," he prompted after a drag of his cigarette. "Brag about how wonderfully you aggravated someone in your youth."

Aethelred's instinctive reaction was to decline. The past five years had been spent blocking memories of his childhood. But he did have many fond memories that often slipped through the cracks.

"I tried to ride a tiger when I was six."

Casimir spat his cigarette onto the floor. It singed the linoleum, but he was too busy gawking at Aethelred to address the fire hazard. "You *what?*"

"I...tried to ride a tiger. It wasn't as crazy or reckless as you think—the tiger and I were friends. The...adults weren't very happy about it, though."

"Hold up." Casimir jumped in front and held out a hand to stop him. "You were *friends* with a tiger? You're gonna need to give me more context here, Reddy."

"I..." Aethelred cast an anxious glance toward the mint green lockers. "I think I've said enough. Can we continue to the science lab, please?"

For a long moment, the other boy surveyed him. "I'm not gonna be able to sleep without the full story. I'm gonna lay in my bed in the dark and think about you riding a tiger. Do you really want that?"

Aethelred's lips parted, but he was spared when a purple head poked around a row of lockers ahead.

"Can you two conduct your little distraction before I'm forced to compel you to?"

"That's against the rules, Cosmos," Casimir called to her without glancing over his shoulder. She and Angor hid between two sections of lockers across from the science lab, which was not the most inconspicuous location. Aethelred hoped whatever distraction Casimir had in mind would completely envelope Mrs. Bishop's attention.

"We're having a serious conversation about tigers over here," he added before finally retrieving his cigarette. The scent of burning rubber permeated the air until he exhaled another cloud of smoke.

"Have it with Mrs. Bishop once you've removed her from the lab," Angor suggested in a way that wasn't really a suggestion at all. That was his method of mind control: patronize others into compliance.

Mumbling an impersonation of Angor, Casimir trudged to the door and yanked it open. When Aethelred scurried behind him, he found old Mrs. Bishop at one of the lab stations amidst a chemistry experiment. She removed her safety goggles to squint at them.

"Mr. Stromer...Mr. Certior—I never expected to see either of you here outside of class."

Casimir clutched his chest. "I'm wounded, Mary. I thought you knew about my crush on you."

Aethelred's head bobbled in disbelief, and the teacher appeared equally as befuddled. Though Casimir didn't move, the woman's eyes protruded a second later, as if viewing something truly horrifying. Then, with a grin, he taunted, "If you want me, you'll have to catch me."

"I don't—" she began, but Casimir had already grabbed Aethelred's sleeve to pull him down the hall. The boys broke into a sprint, and Mrs. Bishop rushed from the room after them, shouting variations of their names that echoed through the halls. Casimir's laughter rivaled her wails, like a hyena loosed after years of captivity.

The woman's frail bones must have hindered her chase, because the boys soon reached the library, where the faint sound of her calls was swallowed by the silence within.

"What—" Aethelred panted, but Casimir tugged him along before he could form a coherent sentence. They disappeared into the maze of bookshelves, submerging in the scent of old leather encyclopedias. Once they reached a vacant aisle, Casimir released him and threw his head back against the books.

"I should probably stop smoking before I run. Or maybe just never run again."

Aethelred ignored his laments and hissed, "What did you make her see?"

"Us," Casimir huffed, regarding him with playfully slivered eyes. "Naked."

Abruptly, Aethelred stopped panting—stopped breathing entirely. "How—how did you…form that image in her mind if you've never…"

"Seen you naked? I made an educated guess." Casimir's dark gaze trailed the entire length of his body, and Aethelred wondered if he'd neglected to remove the hallucination from his own mind. "C'mon," he beckoned, pushing off the bookshelf. "Let's go look like we're studying so she'll think she's gone insane when she finds us."

"I wonder if the run will kill her," Angor said, his focus trained on Mrs. Bishop as she struggled to catch up with the boys. "If so, I hope she's opted to donate her body to science."

Olalla removed herself from between the lockers. Close quarters didn't bother her, but being squished against Angor for twenty minutes had made her strangely nervous. "I don't think her withering flesh will contribute much to our cause. After whatever Stromer planted in her mind, I won't be surprised if her brain goes completely senile."

"Whatever happens, let's hope she doesn't return." He eyed the corner around which the teacher had disappeared and then started toward the lab.

Olalla followed, eager to enter the science sanctuary without adult supervision. In class, their experiments were always controlled, always predictable, always manufactured to teach but not discover. She wanted to mix unknown chemicals and dissect unstudied flesh.

"It appears Mrs. Bishop was measuring the amount of acetic acid in vinegar," Angor concluded after observing the active work station. A long, slender buret was clamped above a beaker filled with fuchsia liquid, which would have overflowed had he not stopped the titration. "She passed the endpoint—a shame. Perhaps we should redo it for her."

"Perhaps we should complete our theft first." Abandoning the chemistry demonstration, Olalla approached the cabinet of microscopes and opened the doors to admire them. Her old school had only a few, but East Mintle had more than twenty, each shiny and pristine.

"Most teens dream of a new car," Angor said as he positioned himself beside her. "We dream of new microscopes."

"Weird breeds weird," she muttered, extracting one from a shelf. She'd brought a few old t-shirts to wrap it in, but she still feared it would break in her backpack on the ride home. "Grab us a few petri dishes and slides."

Angor obeyed without complaint, which was unusual enough for her to wonder if she'd unintentionally forced him to.

"I'm acting of my own will." He paused rummaging through the drawers to shoot her a wry look. "I have no qualm with listening to your commands when they fit my own interests."

Her face flushed, and she refused to meet his eyes. She hated how easily he read her, but there was no way to avoid it; their minds functioned on the same wavelength—the selfishly, ambitiously, greedily curious wavelength.

"Do you remember when you were questioning if humans actually have twenty-three chromosome pairs?" she asked while meticulously swaddling the microscope.

"You mean when I was trying to irk you?" he countered from where he squatted beside an open drawer. Even crouched as a thief, he exuded the elegance she'd always strived for. "How could I forget?"

She could have smirked—could have surrendered to the banter—but this was a theory she'd pondered for weeks, one crazier yet more serious than she'd ever dared to believe. "I was thinking…what if *we* don't have twenty-three pairs? What if we have twenty-four?"

Angor didn't hesitate in saying, "I think it's much more likely we have a few altered genes. To possess extra chromosomes would make us entirely different creatures—a new species."

"What if we are a new species?" she replied, quiet but fervent. "A better species."

Pivoting on his toes, he studied her like he might study a chart of data, attempting to decipher the correlations. "I don't know that we are better. More advanced, maybe, but not *better*. What we can do…it helps no one but ourselves. That makes us worse."

"Morally." His face settled into a sterner expression, so she added a lighthearted smirk to her next statement. "You know I don't care for morals."

He tapped his fingers on the wooden drawer. "Perhaps you wouldn't hate me, then, if…"

"If?" she prompted when he didn't finish.

His eyes snapped to hers, chilling and ominous despite their warm, innocent hue. "If I told you how I acquire my funds. If I told you how I inflict pain on passing strangers and then snatch their wallets as they writhe in agony."

Olalla's hand trembled on the half-wrapped microscope, not with fear but with excitement. She had fantasized about robbing stores and banks—she *had* actually stolen from kids at her old school, just to see if it was possible. Convincing others they *wanted* to depart with their money was not a simple task, but she had improved since her last attempt. The only reason she hadn't abandoned her stupid job at the record store was because she'd assumed Angor would find burglary deplorable.

"It's not something I'm proud of," he continued, wincing at his own confession. "My mother stopped working when I was young—too young to obtain a job of my own. I stole so we could eat, and now that I'm old enough to earn money by legal means…I have no desire to."

"Why did you wait so long to tell me?"

"I…did not want to fall out of your favor."

"Periculy—" She snorted. "You've only just fallen *into* my favor."

He perked up again, confused but hopeful. "You will not shun me for this?"

Sinking to the floor, she leaned her back against the lab station drawers, facing him. "I can *control minds* and you haven't shunned me. Of course I won't judge you."

Like an animal approaching a trap, he tentatively lowered himself to the ground and stretched his legs to run parallel to hers. They didn't touch, but they didn't need to; they were creatures of thought and mind, for whom the touch of words transcended the touch of bodies.

After a moment of twiddling his thumbs, Angor said, "We are still in the middle of a heist, you know."

Olalla dismissed this with a wave. "I'll compel Bishop to leave should she return."

His eyebrows inched up beneath his shaggy hair. "You didn't want to try that earlier? You might have saved the woman's life."

"Casimir and Aethelred needed a purpose in this mission. Imagine what chaos Stromer would cause if left to his own devices."

"Would it be worse than inadvertently killing Mrs. Bishop?"

"You don't have a very vast imagination, do you?"

Angor pursed his lips, failing to suppress a smile. "I was never encouraged to imagine. I was always forced to accept life as it is and adapt."

"Adapt..." Olalla picked at a loose thread on her jeans, ruminating. "Who hurt you, Angor?"

He stiffened, vision fixed on the wall. "Why would anyone have hurt me?"

"I don't know, but I do know you had to adapt, and your adaptation is clear: the ability to block or trigger pain."

"You think our abilities are an adaptation?" She opened her mouth but he lifted a hand to interrupt. "Who hurt *you*, Olalla? Or rather, who *tried* to?"

Her teeth clamped the inside of her cheek as she recognized she'd unintentionally invited this line of questioning. "You think anyone can hurt me?"

Angor released a breath sown with impatience. "I was seven years and five months when my ability first manifested—"

"If you think telling me your tragic backstory will prompt me to reveal mine, you're wrong."

His lips quirked to one side. "Well, you just revealed you have one, didn't you?" She scowled but didn't inhibit him from continuing. "I was seven years and five months when my ability first manifested, but I was younger when my mother morphed from a passive drunk to a violent drunk. I didn't understand at the time, but I believe one of her frequent lovers had become abusive, and she then turned that aggression on me.

"I was raised not to expect maternal love, so the violence did not affect me emotionally; it was the pain that bothered me, the sting in the moment and the bruises that lasted days afterward. I wanted to be numb, and then one day I was. One day, she struck me, and I felt nothing. The bruise existed, but it was inconsequential. I was ecstatic—especially when my mother began wincing and rubbing her own arm in the exact spot I should have felt pain. The pattern persisted, and though I didn't know *how* it was happening, I knew *what* was happening. I just never…"

With a shake of his head, he broke out of his reminiscence. "You believe we possess a certain gene that rapidly evolves to suit our needs?"

"Or desires. I always needed to control others, and I always *wanted* to control others. Too many act in ways they shouldn't."

"And *you're* the one who dictates *should* and *shouldn't*? Sounds like you're playing god, Cosmos. Don't you fear Zeus will strike you down with lightning?"

Olalla rolled her eyes and considered kicking his elbow, but he wouldn't feel it if he didn't wish to. "I would if he were real. Lightning would certainly be a formidable power. Do you think anyone has the ability to control it, as we have the ability to control parts of the nervous system?"

"That sounds like fantasy. And if your theory is correct, one would need to have suffered electrocution to adapt in that fashion."

She did not voice her following thought—her dark, villainous thought—that she would have liked to electrocute someone and see if such an ability developed. If Angor's theory was correct, however, they would need to possess a special gene in order to evolve. If Olalla's wilder theory was correct, they would need to be an entirely new species.

As they stood, Olalla faced away from him and softly said, "My mother hit me, too. She was the first person I wanted to control, and the first person I did control."

Even though she busied herself with wrapping the microscope, she felt his gaze on her. "I always thought it made me weak," he said.

"Funny," she mused without humor. "I always thought it made me strong."

He actually did laugh, a rare but precious sound. "Your ego knows no bounds."

Considering Angor was the most pompous boy she knew, a retort would have been easy, but the door opened before she could voice one. Her mind readied to impose beliefs on Mrs. Bishop, but it was not Mrs. Bishop standing in the doorway: it was the boy with the backwards baseball cap.

"Are you burning rubber?" he asked, nose scrunched. Likely, he smelled the charred linoleum from when Casimir idiotically dropped his cigarette. The boy's face contorted further when he inhaled a whiff of the vinegar. "Or…acid?"

"Titration," Angor said, rising as casually as he could. Olalla, who had studied the fluidity of his motions for months, noticed how stilted his movements were now. "The acid is being measured via titration."

The boy did not care about the experiment, though, not after he spotted their backpacks and the lump of t-shirts beside Olalla's. "What are you doing?"

Though she had been prepared to alter the teacher's mind, snaking into this boy's daunted her. Not only did his neurons feel more strongly connected than the elderly woman's, but his will was as firm as Angor's, and she did not want to embarrass herself in front of either. Her skill with mentally weaving beliefs had improved, but for this, she required the added influence of spoken words.

"We aren't doing anything you care about," she said, lacing each syllable with absolute conviction.

The boy's brows furrowed as the intensity of her forced truth cascaded through his brain. Despite his apparent confusion, he retreated for the door and disappeared, only to pop his head back in a moment later. "I want to be in your gang—with you and those other boys," he declared with a ferocity that made Olalla wonder if he'd observed her manipulations and was attempting one of his own. "Your weird hair gang."

"Sorry," she replied without any remorse. "I don't think you do."

He didn't necessarily look convinced, but he did look annoyed as he glared between them and then stormed out. Angor released a sigh, but Olalla's muscles remained tight, her fists trembling. Something about the boy's vibrant green eyes unnerved her—perhaps the fact that those eyes had watched them intently enough to know their plans. It was only a matter of time before he realized the motives behind their after school exploration.

Angor slipped the petri dishes and glass slides into his backpack. "How long do you think that will last?"

"I'll have to reinforce it," Olalla lied; she would have to *enforce* it, since she doubted her supernatural persuasion had influenced the boy at all. She despised the sense of uselessness—the sense that her months of development were unraveling due to one fortified mind. Once they uncovered the biology behind their powers, she would find a way to use that knowledge to advance her capacity. She would find a way to make every mind bow to her will.

6

Bookcases, and Other Inconsequential Things

Casimir "studying" was actually Casimir smoking a new cigarette while creepily watching Aethelred complete his algebra homework from across the table. Aethelred was not typically a fan of studying, but to this definition of the word, he was particularly impartial.

Mrs. Bishop had darted into the library fifteen minutes prior, bemoaning through labored breaths about two students running around naked. The librarian had led her to them and then had advised her colleague to speak with a counselor about the possibility of dementia. Mr. Stromer and Mr. Certior weren't naked, after all; they sat quietly in a secluded corner, diligently working.

The ruse had evaporated the moment the women retreated down the aisle. Casimir had thrown his randomly-picked encyclopedia onto the carpet, disturbing a few nearby students, and extracted a new stick to light.

"The sign says no smoking," Aethelred informed him, nodding toward the plaque above the window.

"Oh, well, what does my cigarette say?" Casimir blew smoke in his direction, prompting coughs. "I don't care."

Scowling, Aethelred dropped his attention to the math problems, but most were unanswered. He'd spent the majority of the time staring out the window, watching students joke in the courtyard, imagining the histories that had brought them to this exact moment. The blond boy had a scar on his arm—how had he acquired it? The brunette girl wouldn't stop wringing her hands—why was she so nervous?

"*So,*" Casimir began, drawing him out of his imagination. "How did you and Angor end up living together if you're not brothers?"

"How do you know we're not brothers?" Aethelred asked, which was a very stupid thing to ask. Not only were their last names different, but they'd explained to Casimir and Olalla that they'd only known each other for five years.

Casimir pointed neither of these out, though; coolly, he drawled, "Because you're the whitest of all white boys and Angor's—I don't know—a fucking *warlock*?" A blink was all Aethelred managed, at which the other boy groaned. "Why do you have to be one of *those* people?"

"Wh-what people?"

"The people I need to *inform* when I'm joking."

Aethelred picked at the pages of his algebra textbook. "Well...I just always thought Angor was paler than me."

Casimir's laughter boomed through the silent room, wending between the aisles and causing one girl to poke her head around a bookcase to glare at them through her glasses. The bawdiness embarrassed Aethelred—it was one of the main reasons he couldn't stand Casimir's presence—but he also found it difficult to look away while the boy cackled in his seat.

"All right," he said once his amusement subsided, "explain me this: are you two dating?"

This time, Aethelred's coughs were what spurred the grumpy girl's virulent glare. "Dating? Why would we be dating?"

"Right." Casimir leaned deeper in his chair. "That answers my question—all of my questions."

"What were your other questions?" he inquired, even though he wasn't quite sure he wanted to know. Luckily, or perhaps unluckily, Casimir's only response was a smirk before he took a pull of his cigarette.

"I could show you things, you know—what you want to see, what you don't want to see." His eyebrows jumped as he flicked some ash onto the table. "But you're too weird about being touched."

"If you touch me," Aethelred began, emphasizing each word, "all of your memories will involuntarily transfer to my brain."

Casimir's expression did not alter as he processed this information, but the quiet stillness was enough for Aethelred to know he'd shocked the boy. Frankly, Aethelred had shocked himself. He had never intended to tell anyone of this truth—not even Angor.

The green-haired boy splayed his arms on the table, an open gesture. "I have nothing to hide."

With caution, Aethelred eyed the glowing cigarette, the calloused palms. His headaches would be unbearable, and he would probably vomit on the library floor, but Casimir had already seen him in such a state, and he knew the boy found more pleasure in personally humiliating him than ragging on his uncontrollable ailments.

When he did nothing but stare at Casimir's hands, the boy closed them and sat forward, reaching across the table. Aethelred started to recoil, but his reflexes were too slow; fingers hovered beside his cheek before he could remove himself from the chair, as petrifying as a blade held to his throat.

"Are you scared of my touch?" Casimir murmured at a volume that was, for once, actually appropriate for the library. He was merely threatening to poke Aethelred's cheek, but with the knowledge he'd been given, it was much more than that; it was consent to every secret, every sin, every moment he'd ever endured.

"Yes," Aethelred admitted.

"Good." A crooked grin slashed across Casimir's face. "You should be." Then he ran his finger down Aethelred's temple, just as he'd made him feel in detention last month. This time, he didn't sense the finger trail all the way to his lips; his mind snapped out of the present to process the last seventeen years of Casimir Stromer's life.

The memories were more agonizing than Aethelred had ever experienced, not because of the content of the boy's past but because of the vastness of his cognizance. Throughout his life, Casimir saw and tasted and smelled things Aethelred never would have dreamed about—partially because of his prudence and partially because he didn't have a hallucinogenic mind. Neon-colored creatures and decadently-flavored sweets and fragrances of the finest colognes—all clashing with opposites of themselves in a jumble of hypocrisy.

Much of Casimir's childhood was characterized by these contradictory sensations and the headaches they produced. Aethelred understood that, at least. He did not understand, however, why the Stromer parents had given their five-year-old child magic mushrooms.

The only reason Aethelred recognized the psilocybin was because Casimir did—and because the result of its consumption was definitely *magical*. A sense of disembodiment overcame him, accompanied by self-reflection too deep for a five-year-old's maturity. Then the images arose, the same ones that plagued Casimir's mind for the remainder of his life, striking his sanity until it warped into something unnatural.

As the scenes unfolded, Aethelred came to the conclusion that the Stromers were not evil, nor did they intend to scar their son; they wanted to *enlighten* him with a spiritual experience. In that sense, they were nearly as eccentric as Aethelred's childhood guardians, but their public appearance was not indicative of their recreational habits. In their community, Mr. Stromer was a respected businessman and Mrs. Stromer was a popular personality. In their home, Mrs. Stromer engaged in daily hallucinogenic experiences and Mr. Stromer dabbled in more dangerous drugs, eventually forming an addiction to cocaine.

While his parents neglected him for fleeting pleasures, Casimir struggled with his mental affliction and acted out in an attempt to gain their attention. Nights were spent running around shady neighborhoods, losing himself in the maze of alleyways that appeared as an enchanted forest in his mind. Days were spent skipping school in favor of experimentally inducing hallucinations on whoever was unfortunate enough to come across him.

If Aethelred retained the information correctly, this year was the only one in which Casimir had actually attended all his classes. Even in this state of mental turbulence, he had to wonder if Casimir's sudden attendance had something to do with their shared class schedule.

At the age of thirteen, Casimir had snuck into his father's cocaine stash, after which Mr. Stromer tried to break his addiction. The craving returned after he lost his job, which, as

Casimir had explained, resulted in their move from Washington D.C. to Ohio.

Witnessing the hallucinator spy on their group from his guise as a tree was a surreal experience. Aethelred was amused by the witch and warlock ensemble Casimir's mind had draped over Olalla and Angor. Then he was frazzled by how frequently Casimir ignored them to simply stare at *him*. Though not every specific thought transferred to Aethelred's brain, he was aware of the impression he'd had on Casimir and how it amplified with every interaction over the ensuing weeks.

When he finally returned to his own consciousness, he felt uncomfortably warm in uncomfortable places. He also felt a sense of incompletion, as if parts of the history had been omitted.

He also felt a finger dragging his lower lip downward before pulling away.

Rubbing his eyes, Aethelred focused on Casimir, who'd resumed lounging in his chair, a bored expression on his face.

"Okay, great. You know what my shitty parents are like— cool." He threw his cigarette on the floor and snuffed it with his shoe. Usually, Aethelred might admonish him for ruining the carpet, but the absence of a headache dazed him. With the intensity of Casimir's past, he would have thought he'd pass out completely, but he felt normal, as if he hadn't been touched at all. The tingle on his lower lip confirmed he had. "Now can I use my Affinity on you?"

Aethelred stared at their hands on the table, only a few inches apart. "I know your entire past."

"Yup, and it's in the past, so can we move on?"

"But you know nothing about me."

"I know you suck at algebra." Casimir flicked his math

homework off the table. "We have that in common. I know you have a weird aversion to lettuce, of all fucking things. The fact you don't like tasteless things should flatter me, but you don't like pepperoni either, and that's just a crime. I know you hate the word *freak*. Your reaction to it gives me hope for a better future, one in which I might actually start to feel emotions—imagine that. Oh, and I know you shiver when I touch you."

"You don't know that," Aethelred blurted without fully thinking. This list of known *facts* had rattled him, mostly because he hadn't realized Casimir watched him *eat*. With a little more conviction, he added, "Because it's not true."

Casimir's eye roll was so dramatic that his head rolled with it. "Fine, you don't shiver—you spasm. Better?"

It was not better, but Aethelred had grown tired of always being the flustered one. Hesitantly, he met the other boy's pine green gaze and said, "You don't know I grew up in a traveling circus."

He did not think Casimir's constantly half-lidded eyes were capable of popping so wide. "You *what*?"

Aethelred cleared his throat and sat a little straighter, trying to summon some of Angor's poise. "I don't know how you find that more ridiculous than my ability to absorb your entire past."

"I just…didn't know circuses were still a thing." Casimir's shock mollified, but there was a hint of suspicion to his expression. "Sounds like some 1920s shit."

"It's not as popular as it used to be, but our circus managed to survive. We traveled all throughout the United States. I don't even know what state I was born in."

"Hm, it's unfortunate they abandoned you in a state as boring as Ohio… Or did the whole circus disband?"

Since he was not quite ready to explain his departure from the circus, he said, "I like Ohio. It's calm—not so many people as on the coasts."

"How did you grow up in a *circus* and end up as the living embodiment of lettuce—and not even *like* lettuce? You're a conundrum, Red."

"Maybe I'm bland *because* I grew up in such craziness," he suggested, unable to prevent his lips from curving. "I never knew a normal life until I met Angor. For as long as I can remember, we were on the road, doing shows four nights a week. I wasn't actually *in* the shows—I worked in the outside tents with the psychics."

"The *psychics*? Maybe I assessed the situation completely wrong—maybe *you're* the warlock and Angor's the whitest of all white boys. So, you told people their pasts, then? What use is that? Did you dredge up people's suppressed memories or some cruel shit?"

Aethelred bit his lip, but oddly, revealing his former life to Casimir was not as intimidating as he would have guessed. "I helped the psychics determine people's pasts so they could predict the future more accurately. There might have been some witchcraft involved, but I was too young to really know. All I knew was that my assessments of the past were always correct, and the psychics loved me for it."

Casimir snorted into his hand. Then he burst out into maddened laughter. For the first time all afternoon, Aethelred didn't fear the librarian's reprimand. He might have been bold enough to tell her to go away should she approach them. "You—at a circus! I'm imagining a bird trying to swim through the ocean."

"Penguins exist."

This apparently warranted more laughter. "All right, all

right… I've never had a fascination with penguins, but you've really opened my mind today, Reddy. I need to see this."

"See…me as a penguin?"

"No, you in your natural habitat." With an impish grin, Casimir hopped to his feet and extended his hand. "Let's go to the fucking circus."

Casimir liked to think Aethelred's ensuing spasm was because he'd touched him, but it very well might have been because as they touched, red fabric spread over his torso, each thread weaving together until a shimmering jacket covered his sweater. With gold embroidered pants to match, he suited the insult *freak* perfectly.

"Devilish," Casimir commented after languidly appraising the apparel. Aethelred, now standing, gawked down at himself before his widened eyes trailed over Casimir's matching green suit.

"You really are a tree," he said, which was about as close to a joke as Aethelred would ever manage. A laugh shook through Casimir, and he was reminded of his finger barely brushing the other boy's hand. That centimeter of contact was all that kept the illusion around them—the illusion of a three-ring circus.

"How…" Aethelred began, but he didn't form a coherent question as his ruby eyes digested the magnificence of the tent around them. Chaos abounded within the red- and white-striped walls—elephants stomping throughout one ring, bears unicycling around another, and a tiger prowling in the center. Above, acrobats tiptoed on tightropes and flipped through metal rings, bending in unnatural poses. Clowns ran around the perimeter, white-painted faces flashing in the dim light. Casimir jumped when one darted past them, all rainbow curls and crazy eyes.

"I understand why you're so skittish now," he said, but Aethelred didn't appear nearly as anxious here as he did in the school hallways. His brow was creased in confusion, not discomfort. "This is the full force of my ability," Casimir explained, at which the red-haired boy finally tore his gaze from the madness to look at him. "From a distance, I can only imprint my own imagination, but with physical contact, I can expand on another's imagination—or in this case, memories. Guess we're both invasive with our touch, aren't we?"

Aethelred's discomfort surfaced when he glanced down at the finger on his hand. "I suppose so."

"Shall we take a look around?" Casimir proposed, gesturing grandly to the tent.

"We're still in the library...aren't we?"

"Yeah. So?"

"So...won't we bump into bookcases...or people?"

"Probably." Casimir kicked what appeared to be empty air, and his shoe hit the leg of the table they'd sat at. "I'm not sure if you've gathered this about me yet, but I don't really give a shit." Aethelred's lips parted, probably to object, but then Casimir shifted his hand, intertwining their fingers. "Must I drag you through your own memories?" he questioned, tugging him along.

Aethelred stumbled one step before planting his feet and refusing to move—well, except to try prising his hand from Casimir's grasp. For that purpose, he had no problem jerking his arm like a fool.

"What's the problem, Certior?" he demanded, tightening

his grip. "You've already seen my past—no reason to fear my touch now."

Red didn't speak, but he didn't relent his frantic struggles, either.

With a sigh, Casimir stepped closer and bent sideways in an attempt to fall in Aethelred's downcast line of sight. "Red," he said slowly, as if consoling a child, and waited until the boy surrendered to eye contact. "What's the problem?"

"We can't see anyone, but they'll see us. All the other students—they'll see—"

"Are you a homophobe?"

Aethelred stopped squirming to grimace. "Not exactly…"

Casimir licked his lips into a grin. "Worried people will think you're gay?" In response, his red eyes darted away. With renewed glee, Casimir crept closer until their bodies nearly touched. Aethelred stood a few inches taller, so the shorter boy rose on his toes and whispered directly into his ear, "Worried people will *know* you're gay?"

Sucking in a dramatic breath, Aethelred staggered back, so far their hands almost yanked apart. Casimir maintained his hold and pulled him toward the tent's exit. "Show me your psychics. I want you to convince me you aren't a warlock."

Aethelred swallowed. "I don't know if I can. I don't know what I am."

"You're like me." Casimir winked. "A freak."

Contrary to what he'd expected, this comment actually prompted the boy to comply. Hand-in-hand, the two strolled through the tent flaps, where darkness awaited them. Compared to the vibrant colors in the tent, the black haze was a shock, but it gave Casimir the opportunity to focus on the few distinguishable sights: cotton candy and popcorn booths, face-painting stations, and a small tent as violet as Olalla's hair, labeled *Psychics* in fancy letters.

"I don't remember any of the locations we stopped at, really. They all blurred together," Aethelred said, staring at the void beyond the circus. "But this"—he gestured with his free hand toward the striped monstrosity—"was my home."

Casimir sucked on a tooth and then clucked his tongue. "You already know it's nicer than mine was."

The other boy tilted his head in contemplation. "In some ways, perhaps. In other ways, perhaps not. I never got to make friends—never got to be alone. Never got to go to school."

"You say that like it's a bad thing."

Casimir felt Aethelred's fingers twitch and grow clammy. "I was quite behind when I finally started classes. Angor spent countless hours tutoring me. I feel bad because...it all seems for naught. I've never excelled in school—I can barely pay attention half the time. I think Angor began teaching me in the hope I'd become his science sidekick, or something. He's replaced me with Olalla rather quickly."

"You're still claiming you *don't* have a crush on Angor?" Casimir asked, since he wasn't sure what else to say. Emotions had bled from his brain a long time ago, but Aethelred's dejection rallied a droplet from a well that had run dry. "I mean, you're jealous of Olalla, and we all know what's goin' on between *them*."

The poor kid looked genuinely befuddled. "Angor doesn't like Olalla—not like that, at least. He thinks romance is a waste of time."

Casimir snorted. "That is a very Angorian sentiment to have... Are you dawdling because you don't want me to see the psychics?"

"I'm dawdling because I don't know what we'll see." He eyed the purple canvas with unease. "I have many memories from within that tent, and I don't like them all."

"If you're waiting for me to console you, I'm not going to. However, if you tell me you'll start weeping if we go in there, I'll say let's get the hell out of here. I'm allergic to tears."

Aethelred squared his shoulders, glaring at the tent as if facing off a dragon. "I'll be fine."

Casimir shrugged, and they started toward the entrance, bumping into a few bookshelves on the way. By the time they parted the imaginary strings of beads in the tent's threshold, Casimir had two stubbed toes and Aethelred wouldn't stop rubbing his injured nose. The former planned to voice a quip until he beheld the scene before them.

Beneath hanging lanterns and dreamcatchers rested a round table, upon which a crystal ball sat. This, along with the two psychics in their layers of fabrics and necklaces, Casimir had expected. He had not expected to witness a young version of Aethelred, seated between the two women, wearing the same metallic red costume as his older self.

Although he was probably only eight years old, young Aethelred exuded the same anxiety as his aged counterpart. Steel blue eyes flashed in every direction, and his fists trembled atop the patterned tablecloth. Oddly, Casimir found comfort in the familiar panic. The ordinary brown hair was what disconcerted him; it didn't suit the Aethelred he'd come to know.

"You mustn't fret, child," one of the psychics said, clasping the boy's fist in her ringed fingers. He winced and recoiled as if she'd burned him. "It's normal to feel this way when immersing in others' minds. The touch is necessary to channel the memories, and the past is the key to the future."

Young Aethelred gritted his teeth as the other psychic snatched his hand. While the first had a pleasant face with kind brown eyes and smiling lips, the second fit the definition of a witch with her hooked nose and wrinkly cheeks.

"You must continue to work, child," the witchy one said with a voice like crinkling paper. "Otherwise, what use will we have for you?"

Child and teenage Aethelred gulped at the same time, and Casimir felt the tension growing in the air. He also felt the urge to kick the wrinkled lady, though he knew his foot would go right through the illusion of her—and possibly hit a bookshelf in the process.

The one thing he could do—which he did do—was sweep the hallucination from their minds. As their perception shifted back to the reality of the library, Casimir probably should have offered to let Aethelred spill his grievances, but what the hell would he even say when the boy blubbered about how his psychic mothers had been abusive creeps? "*Yup, I know, sorry, man?*" And although he couldn't complain about their still-entwined hands, Casimir wasn't much into consolation via touch, either. He wasn't an "I'll rub you on the back 'til you're okay" kinda guy. He was an "I'll thump you on the back until you stop crying in favor of attacking me" kinda guy, and he didn't think this kid was the type to attack no matter how many times someone hit him first.

Despite his curiosity over Aethelred's past, part of him regretted his access to it. He wasn't interested in the intimacy its aftermath would produce—wasn't interested in long conversations about their shitty pasts that would result in offering or receiving empathy. He was, however, very interested in their current predicament, for during their meandering through the circus, they'd arrived at an entirely different part of the library, one in which more than twenty students sat at clusters of tables, staring at them.

While their peers should have been disturbed by the two ambling aimlessly through the library, ogling invisible objects, every single one of them gawked only at the boys' entangled hands.

Casimir rolled his eyes but didn't release Aethelred. "*Relax*, normies. We don't have HIV, all right? And even if we did, we'd keep it amongst ourselves—*trust me.*"

A few jaws dropped, and Aethelred stiffened as if warding off his brain's implosion. Casimir cackled, pulling him from the library and showing off their interlaced hands to everyone they encountered, reveling in any discomfort that was not his own.

7

Crafters of Nightmares

For twenty minutes, Olalla waited outside the school with Angor in comfortable silence, both processing what they'd learned and hypothesized in the science lab. When their two friends finally met up with them, Aethelred looked like he'd puked on a teacher, or something equally horrendous, and Casimir looked like he'd won a prize by immoral means, or something equally delightful. Neither boy asked how the lab raid went, and neither Olalla nor Angor offered any information. The four rode to Hastings Street in silence, each lost in their own thoughts.

Olalla could not discern what discomfited her about the boy with the backwards baseball cap, other than the fact that she'd been unable to infiltrate his mind. Her frustration over her incompetence failed to ebb, especially when the gang arrived at the trailer park and she spotted William Ross's car parked before her house.

Its black exterior matched the dark ambience of the forest, but nothing about the brand new vehicle belonged on Hastings Street. In this dilapidated place, it was a gleaming reminder of what they all wanted but would never have.

Well, unless she and Angor discovered something truly monumental. Or if Olalla unlocked the potential to alter all minds, thus commanding anything they wanted from anyone, always.

Fraught with anticipation, Angor didn't notice their enemy's car as he collected the microscope from Olalla and locked himself and Aethelred within their home. She didn't have the energy to insist on following; all mental functions were trained on dispelling her dread.

Before Casimir could continue to ride roughly along the gravel on his skateboard, Olalla grabbed the sleeve of his leather jacket. "Come over and hang out with me for the afternoon."

He glanced at the Periculys' from the corner of his eye. "You're a smart girl, Cosmos. Do I really need to explain this to you?"

"I'm not asking you on a date," she said through her teeth. Then, a bit too aggressively, she parked her bicycle beside her home and cocked her head toward William's car.

"You're afraid to confront Ross alone?" he questioned, kicking his skateboard to rest beside her bike.

She hoped her shrug seemed nonchalant. "I just figured you might want to practice your *ability* on this fine afternoon."

"Of course," he conceded, but his smirk implied he didn't believe her. She didn't press the issue. As long as he said nothing to Angor, she didn't care what Casimir thought of her. He was wrong about his guess, anyway; it was not William she feared.

The only lights illuminating the inside of her family's mobile home came from the television, which her father idly watched, and from above the stove, upon which Artemis and her boyfriend cooked fajitas. Whenever Olalla tried cooking, a burnt scent corrupted the air, but Artemis was as rigidly perfect with the preparation of her food as with everything else. Every plate, knife, and chopped pepper was arranged neatly on the small countertop, and the finished product would look like it'd been cut out of a cooking magazine. William stood dutifully at her side, obeying every clipped command.

"Chopped onions—count them. We need exactly one fourth in each fajita."

William counted the tiny pieces of onion as if it were totally normal. Perhaps for upstanding citizens, it was.

That's silly, Olalla made him think. *I should just dump them all on one fajita.*

William eyed the bowl of chopped onions for a moment, then emptied it onto the melted cheese of the fajita in the pan.

Artemis gasped and then whirled around to glare at her sister where she stood near the front door with Casimir. Olalla's momentary elation over her success waned. She'd hoped it would spark an argument between the couple, but her sister knew her tricks too well.

"You ruined Mom's fajita," she seethed.

"I'll eat it if you add some pepperoni," Casimir offered as he peered toward the stove.

William stared at the pile of onions as if it were a body he'd murdered. "I-I'm sorry. I didn't mean—"

"It wasn't your fault," Artemis interjected, finally tearing her attention from her sister. "We'll fix it."

As she returned to cooking, her movements even stiffer than before, William set the bowl on the counter and turned to Olalla and Casimir, guilt evaporating.

"Hello," he greeted without warmth.

Olalla simpered. "Don't you have a football practice to be

at?"

"It ended, so I came over to help Artemis with dinner."

"How generous of you," Olalla said aloud, while in her head she thought of a very specific way in which he could help his girlfriend. With both hands, he cupped the hot sides of the pan and flung it across the living room.

Everyone except Olalla screamed—William in pain, Artemis in horror, her father in surprise, and Casimir in amusement. The cheesy fajita clung to the window, slowly oozing down the glass, but Olalla was more interested in William's blistered hands. He gaped at the welts forming on his palms, panting.

"Oh, that wasn't very helpful," Olalla mock pouted.

Artemis didn't bother to inspect her boyfriend's injuries. Grabbing the metal spatula, she charged toward her sister, only to stop abruptly and whack her own head with the utensil. The weapon wasn't very effective, but it did cut her forehead. Tears sprung in her eyes, tears not from pain but frustration.

"You're unnatural," Artemis snarled, angling the spatula for an attack.

"I know," Olalla said. Though she didn't alter her sister's mind in that moment, Casimir must have shown her something monstrous, because she staggered back into the stove, alighting her shirt with the open flame.

Again she screamed, and William hastened to quench the fire by smacking it with a dish towel. Olalla was tempted to make him stop—to make him believe he didn't care if his girlfriend burned to ash—but instead she took the opportunity to drag Casimir into her and Artemis's shared bedroom, slamming the door behind them.

She flattened herself against it, hoping her friend could

not tell how rapidly her heart beat. She could barely explain to herself why the thought of Artemis injured panicked her—after all, her sister never cared about *her* injuries. Explaining this unwanted reaction to Casimir was not something she wished to attempt.

Luckily, he scanned the room rather than her, examining the bunk bed and the two starkly different halves on either side of it. Artemis's, organized and pristine; Olalla's, brimming with textbooks and scribbled notes.

"Your house is bigger than mine, too," he said, extracting a pack of cigarettes from his pocket.

"Too?" she echoed, since she could think of nothing better to say.

"Angor's place is the same as yours, just a little less...discordant." He paused to light a cigarette, then toed the carpeted floor. "I'm guessing there's not actually a huge chasm in the middle of this room?"

She swallowed; the symbolism was not lost on her. "No. What else do you see?"

"Your mom looked like a monster in the family portrait on the kitchen wall."

"That's real enough."

He tapped his knuckles on her desk. "I see a drawing of you and Angor smooching among your science bullshit."

She straightened, fairly certain none such drawing existed, though not *entirely* certain. When deep in thought, she sometimes doodled unwittingly. "You do not."

Smirking, he leaned on the desk to block her view. After taking a drag of his cigarette, he said, "There's a mountain of beer cans in the living room."

"Real."

He nodded, unperturbed. "Angor's mom had one, too.

Guess she's an alcoholic like your dad."

Olalla kept her lips sealed. Given what Angor had admitted, it wasn't a shocking revelation, but she felt weird knowing this when the information had not come directly from him. She also felt weird about Casimir knowing, after merely one glance, what her father was.

"My dad's a cocaine addict," he said through a laugh and a puff of smoke. "You and Periculy are so hung up on your pride, but neither of you think your pride is your own. Fuck our parents—we'll be better than them. Or worse, but in a better way."

She understood exactly what that meant. Her parents, Angor's parents, Casimir's parents, even Aethelred's parents—they'd all destroyed their children's lives in one way or another, but with their abilities, the four broken children could cause the destruction of so many more. It would not be so they could waste away on a couch, glued to a television, though; it would be so they could conquer hearts, conquer minds, conquer the world.

"Can your sister do what you do?" Casimir asked, eyeing the clean side of the room as if he wished to casually light it aflame.

"No," Olalla answered automatically, although she often wondered the same. As sisters, they shared many genes; it was possible they shared this, as well. "I don't know... Have you felt her try?"

"Nah, but it just seems...fishy that Ross is so wrapped around her finger. I didn't think all that *love at first sight* bullshit was real, but they started dating *immediately*."

"William Ross's mind is a simple place. He is neither very good nor very bad, and it makes him easy to manipulate. I imagine my sister can do it with ease, even without the aid of supernatural force."

"And your sister—she's not easy for you to manipulate?"

Olalla thought of the years she'd avoided altering Artemis's mind—the years her sister had acted exactly how she'd expected. Then she thought of the past few months, in which Artemis had acted unpredictably, in which Olalla had practiced worming into her thoughts. Moments ago, she had made her sister want to hit herself in the head with a spatula, but the effort had exhausted her. She did not think she would even be able to influence someone as simple as William after that feat.

"Not as easily as I would like."

The day after they stole from the science lab, Olalla quit her job at the record shop. This shocked Angor—until she asked if he wanted to rob that same record shop together. A coy smile inched onto his lips, as if she'd asked him on a date. Perhaps she had. The two had more fun manipulating money from her former boss than they would have had at any restaurant or cinema.

With their newly acquired funds and free time, they began researching their own biology, taking blood samples to study under the microscope. Poor Aethelred was squeamish about this, and since he wouldn't allow the others to touch him, he had to cut his finger and drop blood onto the slides without anyone to steady his trembling hand. Perhaps Olalla should have felt a little guilty, but they would all need to suffer for the sake of science.

Unfortunately, the blood samples did not yield ground-breaking discoveries. In order to study their genes, they would need an electron microscope, and even the entire net wealth of East Mintle wouldn't have been enough to buy one. Still, Olalla and Angor took notes on their cells, searching for some difference between their own and a regular person's. For this comparison, Olalla extracted some of her father's blood while he was passed out drunk on the sofa. Other than his enlarged blood cells from over-consumption of alcohol, they didn't find any apparent differences.

After two weeks of little progress, the weird hair gang decided to shift their focus back to the harnessing of their abilities. With Angor's permission, Olalla attempted to infiltrate his mind, always to no avail. Whether his thoughts were naturally fortified or he built the walls himself, the impenetrable shield aggravated her. She wanted to be able to morph anyone's mind, and anyone included Angor Periculy.

Casimir's and Aethelred's brains warped like fresh clay, so she didn't bother with them. The former was too busy making the latter envision falsities that brought a blush to his cheeks, anyway.

In the two weeks since they'd raided the science lab, the hallucinator's capabilities had flourished to the point he could simultaneously change the perceptions of everyone in the school cafeteria. One day, he'd made everyone see Artemis with a unibrow and buck teeth, for which Olalla nearly told the boy she loved him. The only reason she refrained was because she did not exactly know what love felt like, but she imagined the joy swelling in her gut over her sister's shame was pretty damn close.

After that stunt, Casimir declared himself ready for a "truly spectacular spectacle." To this, Aethelred had said, "That's redundant." Olalla assumed the hallucinator then imprinted something rather lewd on the prude boy's mind, because Casimir's grin stretched too wide and Aethelred's cheeks burned too red.

For this divine demonstration, Casimir instructed them to accompany him to the football game that Friday evening. Angor protested even as he hopped on his bike and rode eight miles to the school alongside them. They had *work* to do, he claimed, and although Olalla couldn't disagree, she also couldn't suppress the schemes forming in her mind. Only when she informed Angor of her plan did his complaints cease, replaced with a small, evil smile that might have made her flail off her bike in glee if she were more easily influenced by her own emotions.

Surprisingly, Aethelred didn't fret about their venture to a public event, perhaps since the brisk October weather allowed him to wear his usual sweater with a hat, scarf, and gloves. Only his eyes and the bridge of his nose were visible as they locked their bikes in front of the school and trekked around the perimeter toward the football field.

"Why would anyone willingly come to this place after school hours?" Casimir questioned, eyeing the brick building with disgust. He'd lit a cigarette the moment he'd jumped off his skateboard, and his sweatshirt's hood covered his green curls, almost making him look like a normally deviant boy.

"We're here willingly," Aethelred pointed out as he kicked a few pebbles on the gravel drive. Ahead, stadium lights illuminated the darkened sky, and the raucous cheers of overenthusiastic teens echoed into the fields beyond. The game had already begun, but they weren't here for the game; they were here to settle the score.

William Ross had vowed to destroy them the day they'd first assaulted his innocent Artemis. He never said so, of course—he was too cool, cultured, and kind for proclamations of revenge. But he always found a way to twist their interactions, to pin the freaks with the oddly-colored hair as the bad guys. Olalla could warp his mind temporarily, but it never lasted more than a day. His righteous contempt for them ran too deep.

The burns didn't help. Though Olalla had repeatedly assured his mind that she'd had nothing to do with the injuries, Artemis always convinced him otherwise. The fact that their star quarterback had been forced to sit out a full game because of his bandaged palms had enraged the entire football team, and due to Artemis's influence, they knew exactly which weirdos to unleash their anger on.

Earlier that week, one of William's groupies had shoved Aethelred into a locker with such force the metal dented. In her spurt of wrath, Olalla compelled the boy to eat a pencil. He'd chewed half of it before William rounded the corner and intervened. The boy went home vomiting but returned the day after, unharmed. She would remember next time to increase his urgency. Or have him swallow the object whole.

Since then, the rivalry had exploded. The pencil-eater stabbed Olalla's arm with a pen yesterday and ran away before she could retaliate. The giant girl kicked Angor in the shin this morning, and then she promptly fled in fear when he didn't react to the pain. Casimir miraculously evaded torment—possibly they saw him as a literal demon—but behind his blithe grins, Olalla noticed the twitch of fury in his eyes during each of these assaults.

"We're here because it's our duty to sabotage this game," he corrected Aethelred, hopping atop the stones lining the road. His skipping resembled the movements of a child, but his eyes narrowed with a shrewdness beyond his years as they finally reached the stadium.

A sea of mint green consumed the home bleachers, where boys shouted in frustration and girls swooned in awe. Across the field, the few spectators for the Criglodge Crows were nearly indistinguishable in their black and dark blue garb, which Casimir had purposely dressed to match. Angor didn't own any black clothing—nor did he allow Aethelred to— since it was *too punk*, and Olalla only had one beige coat to choose from, but all three had deftly avoided any shades nearing mint green.

"People are painfully predictable," Angor sighed, wincing as he absorbed the scene on the bleachers. Olalla cared not for her mindless peers; her gaze settled specifically on Artemis, who stood within a group of rambunctious fans, all wielding signs they believed would affect the game but in reality had no consequence.

"How the hell did *she* become popular?" Casimir wondered, which was a good question. Olalla's sister held a sign for William—*ROSS #56* written in bold letters—but she didn't smile or laugh like the rest of her friends. Even when East Mintle scored, she remained as rigid as a statue.

"She fears for him," Olalla realized.

"Hm?" Angor prompted as the four plopped onto an empty spot near the edge of the bleachers.

"My sister fears for Ross's safety. She's worried he'll injure himself in the game."

Slowly, Angor angled his head to look at her with incredulity. "You read her mind?"

"No." Her lips quirked to one side. "People are just painfully predictable."

The briefest satisfaction flitted over his face, but a shadow of rumination dimmed it. Provoking a smile from Angor was usually a tricky task, but the past two weeks had amplified the difficulty; their lack of progress had consumed him.

She should have been stressed, too, but most of her mental energy had been exhausted by her constantly renewed hatred for Artemis and William. The couple spent most days in the Cosmoses' mobile home, cleaning up after her drunken father or cooking dinner for her nasty mother like the suck-ups they were. Their relationship was disgustingly well-mannered.

"Well, I guess that means we have to ensure Ross injures himself in the game." Casimir dropped his cigarette on the metal bleachers and smothered it with his shoe. "We exist to make fears come true, after all."

"Don't tempt me to change our gang slogan," Angor said wryly. "I'm too fond of *weird breeds weird.*"

"I won't make you part with your beloved phrase, Periculy," Casimir assured with heavy sarcasm. Inching to the edge of his seat, he honed his focus on the field below. Olalla didn't know much about football, but it had been impossible for her to ignore William's frequent humble brags of, "Oh, I'm just the quarterback," upon which her mother would fawn over how wonderful Artemis was for finding such a talented boyfriend.

Now, William exuded pure cockiness as he hopped around with the ball, preparing to throw it to his teammates. Olalla wished she could literally force his muscles to stop functioning. But then something more marvelous happened: unprompted, he dove to the side, slamming his shoulder into the grass and dropping the ball.

As her sister sucked in an alarmed breath, Olalla let out a confused but delighted laugh. "What did you—"

"Gorilla," Casimir answered before she could finish, triumph shimmering in his eyes. Olalla's cackles were uncontainable, especially when William staggered to his feet and spun in frantic circles, searching for the beast. Since Casimir had only planted the image in his mind, he appeared utterly mad.

Shaking his head, William composed himself and resumed his position, ignoring his teammates' cautious demeanors. Seemingly, the next play went as planned, but Casimir wasn't finished. Seconds before East Mintle could score their first touchdown, the hallucinator induced an image at which the player threw the ball and sprinted off the field, shrieking.

Cries of disappointment erupted throughout the stands, masking Olalla's and Casimir's snickers. Angor was not prone to laughter, but he did snort and hide a smile behind his hand. Aethelred's eyes protruded, stunned but sheepishly amused.

"What did you make *him* see?" he asked Casimir.

"Giant bat. What should I do next, Red—a black- and orange-striped feline that six-year-old children ride like ponies?"

Casimir must have taken Aethelred's startled expression as an affirmative, because when the game began again, several East Mintle players darted off the field in terror, screaming what sounded like "TIGER!" Olalla didn't understand the part about six-year-old children, but she knew the fear filled her with a spike of mirthful adrenaline.

That was not the best of it, though. As the coach stomped onto the grass to confront his crazed players, a few more dropped to their knees with wails of lament. When their coach demanded an explanation, they each claimed their dead mother lay before them.

Aethelred fixed Casimir with a troubled glare. "Isn't that a bit cruel?"

"Don't interrupt me," the other boy commanded, holding up a hand to silence him. "I'm turning nightmares into reality."

And he did. Within minutes, every player including William had collapsed, crying in the grass, just as Casimir had once promised.

The Criglodge Crows removed their helmets to gawk at their felled opponents while East Mintle's coach attempted to haul his players to their feet. Many in the crowd shouted encouragement, but many others in the crowd were annoyed, therefore it was not particularly difficult for Olalla to bend their minds farther in that direction, prompting them to rip their signs and shout profanities at their own classmates.

"Phew," Casimir sighed, sprawling against Aethelred as he closed his eyes. "That's taxing work."

Olalla expected their skittish friend to squirm away, so when Aethelred didn't move, she shot an inquisitive glance at Angor, who blinked uncomprehendingly. Knowing she wouldn't coax an explanation out of Aethelred if even Angor was shocked, she nudged him and muttered, "Ready for the killing blow, Periculy?"

He nodded and robotically pivoted his attention to the students protesting the game's result. Without any display of exertion, he inflicted sharp, quick spurts of pain. In a wave, each person around Artemis jerked an arm, which Olalla made them believe her sister had pinched.

One by one, they spun on her. A half hour ago, they might have affably asked her why she'd pinched them all, but now, after her quarterback boyfriend had lost East Mintle the game, they barraged her with a slew of curses. One boy was angry enough to snatch her sign and tear it to shreds.

Olalla encouraged their agitation, feeding their brains nasty sentiments. Artemis's flustered mortification lasted until one boy exclaimed, "You betrayed your sister!"

Instantly, he seemed befuddled by his own statement, but Artemis understood it. As the rest of her friends continued to castigate her, she settled her stern gaze on her sister, radiating stone cold enmity.

Olalla had not meant to project that belief on the boy. Frankly, it was embarrassing she still thought of the rift that had severed their relationship. She wanted Artemis to believe she didn't care—and she didn't want to care. But a pathetic part of her still clung to the idea of her and her older sister on the same team, braving their mother's barbarity together.

That pathetic part needed to die.

Never had she wished she could use her ability on her own mind, but it would have helped to have a supernatural force reshape her beliefs, erase any lingering attachment to her sister. Instead, she had to slice it with a smile, one sadistic enough to crack Artemis's rigid resolve.

For every blow you deliver, Olalla will deliver one worse, she wove through her sister's thoughts. It mixed like soap in warm water, bubbling with truth and popping with implications. Artemis's dismay was apparent, but Olalla didn't crave dismay; she craved war.

You want to fight her, and you want to win, she added. She did not add her own silent vow: *And, Artie, you will lose.*

"Well," Angor huffed, feeling drained after spending all evening with such imbeciles, "I'm glad that silliness is over with. Now we need to focus on what really matters: our origin and our future."

Casimir rolled his eyes as he juggled a striped hat between his hands, which he'd snatched off a red head of hair a few minutes prior. Aethelred had made one attempt to retrieve it and then succumbed to his defeat. It seemed Angor would have to begin drilling assertive sentiments into the boy's mind again, as he had when they were younger.

Their group hadn't left the stadium until every last person departed, wanting to bask in their conquest. Casimir and Olalla wanted to, at least. Aethelred had watched each tear-stained player trudge off the field with a guilty wince. Angor hadn't watched anything at all; he'd stared into the darkness, trying to puzzle out how they might acquire an electron microscope and then the equipment for a Northern blot test.

He had so many theories. Perhaps they each possessed a polypeptide sequence never seen before, or perhaps their genes underwent different modifications in the Golgi apparatus—or perhaps their abilities were due to something completely undiscovered, something beyond their realm of understanding. None of this could be proven or disproven—at least not by someone as young and impoverished as he—and that irritated him to no end.

"Relax," Casimir droned, pulling Aethelred's knit hat over his own head. "You have the rest of your life to remove the stain of your mother from your legacy."

Angor stiffened, sensing Olalla's attention from his other side. He knew she was likely imagining said stain of a mother hitting him, as he had stupidly confessed she did.

Although the girl saw their capacity to endure as a strength, he had not lied when he claimed the abuse was his weakness. He did not like being out of control, and he did not like the prospect of Olalla knowing there were moments when he was out of control. Perhaps he feared she would utilize those fragile moments to her advantage, or perhaps he feared she would abandon him simply for having fragile moments at all.

"That *spectacle* of yours might seem important tonight," Angor said, "but in a few years, when we leave this place, no one will remember; no one will care. They *will* care what we make of ourselves, though—what we discover. The best way to defame William Ross is to outshine him. His popularity will die at this high school, whereas we will transcend this inconsequential hierarchy to earn respect and prestige. We won this battle, but it has no impact on the true war."

Casimir scoffed as they turned toward the school. The night air was hollow without cheers to fill it, and their path was nearly indistinguishable without the distant stadium lights to illuminate it. Since no one was around, they chose to cut through the alley between the main building and the sports locker rooms, a shorter route to their three bicycles and Casimir's skateboard.

"We will have that war eventually, Periculy," Olalla said, gazing up at the starry sky. "For now, we have this petty one with which to practice our abilities. Do you deny it's helped us advance?"

Angor pursed his lips. He did not want to give her the satisfaction of being correct, but she was. After weeks of warding off William's lackeys, he'd gained the strength to inflict pain on multiple people at once. He could envision every microscopic nociceptor in a person's body and trigger specific ones. He could induce and inhibit headaches, which was a complicated endeavor he'd never accomplished before. Perhaps these little battles were silly, but they were not purposeless.

"I simply question whether our advancement will yield true progress. Will it matter if you can convince everyone we've discovered a new gene if we have not?"

Olalla's face morphed into a dark scowl, but she was unable to retort before they reached the end of the alleyway, where a group of silhouettes blocked their path.

Though their faces were shadowed, Angor knew by their girth that they were football players. Every bruise, scrape, and sore muscle they'd obtained during the game was apparent to him. Admittedly, he could amplify their pain much easier than he could mollify it. His time with Olalla and Casimir had inclined him toward his more vile impulses.

"We don't know how, but we know you sabotaged the game," William said, his voice less composed than usual. Normally, he was the embodiment of a charming athlete, but Casimir's hallucinations seemed to have shaken him.

"So you plan to beat us up?" Angor surmised while silently taking inventory of their opponents. The same four who'd attacked them in the cafeteria after their first encounter with William were present, as was Artemis. She stood beside her boyfriend, her authoritarian air not at all diminished by her shortness. "If I recall, fights never end particularly well for you."

"No." William stepped out of the shadows, into the moonlight. His expression was not one of malice but of self-righteousness. "We plan to apprehend you and bring you to the police. They'll make sure justice is served—they'll make sure you never hurt anyone again."

Olalla laughed, sashaying toward him. "Oh, William, you can't even prove we've done anything. Besides, do you want your sweet Artemis to be related to a convicted *criminal?* That will not reflect well on her."

"You deserve this, Ollie," her sister sneered, surging forward. At that, Angor hastily joined Olalla's side, as if this small girl posed a greater threat than her muscled boyfriend. Her attack was only verbal, but Angor knew it affected Olalla deeper than a slap would have. "You've deserved punishment since you almost made that girl choke to death on rocks."

Olalla's nose twitched, but she refused to match her sister's snarl. "That was for *you*."

"Well, this is for everyone else. You'll kill someone if I don't stop you."

"Then stop me, Artie," she whispered, eyes glowing a brighter shade of purple. For a moment, her sister seemed confused, but then she crouched and gathered a fistful of rocks from the gravel path.

Angor had not been aware that Olalla once compelled a girl to eat rocks. Though he admired her ruthlessness, he did not think it was something he wanted to witness for himself. That was why he was mildly relieved when William slapped his girlfriend's hand before it reached her mouth, spraying the dusty pebbles on her sweater.

Artemis's shock over what she'd almost done dissipated as quickly as it had arrived. With newfound fury, she met her sister's gaze and said, "We already have stopped you."

As one, William's gang moved into the light, revealing what Angor had not seen before: three bicycles and a skateboard, mutilated.

The bikes' metal frames were bent beyond repair, and Casimir's skateboard was snapped in half. They must have used tools to cause such damage, and Angor was grateful they hadn't brought those same tools to exact their *justice*. Still, without any mode of transportation to flee to should they escape, they would have to outrun William's car on foot.

"And you think *we're* the criminals?" Casimir stepped beside Olalla, his demeanor lax but his eyes brimming with hate. "I'll show you criminal."

He didn't move, but a ghost of him shot forward, pulling free a knife to slash across the closest boy's neck. The football players cried out in horror as transparent blood oozed from the illusion of a wound. Angor knew Casimir made their enemies see the gore in full. To them, the tang of fresh blood scented the air as their friend gurgled for breath. He clutched his throat as if he truly was dying, and Angor ensured he felt the pain and the panic of death.

The boy dropped to the ground, passed out from the intensity of the agony, and Angor hoped his "death" would deter his friends from further conflict.

Perhaps it would have if not for Artemis.

By now, she must have guessed Casimir's ability or thought her sister had forced the belief of the boy's death into their brains. Her dark, hardened gaze trained on each of them before she commanded, "Apprehend them. Apprehend these *murderers*."

William stayed behind, squatting to examine his "dead" friend, as the three brutes advanced: Big Nose, the freckled one, and the giant girl. Angor sighed and, without much effort, activated the nociceptors in each of their knees.

All three collapsed, howling. Casimir—as his real self, not a phantom—took the opportunity to thrust his foot into Big Nose's face, and the crack of bone echoed through the alleyway.

Olalla must have made the giant girl believe her freckled friend had doled the blow, because she rolled over and began pummeling him. The two grappled as the injured boy spat out the blood dripping from his big nose into his mouth.

Casimir advanced to deliver another kick, but he froze when a yelp sounded from behind them. Whipping around, Angor found William's hand wound in Aethelred's hair as his friend's face scrunched in pain. Distracted by the brawl, none had noticed William slip around to take innocent Aethelred hostage.

For once, his strange ability was actually effective; the harmless static shock surprised William into releasing Aethelred. As their enemy stumbled back, Angor prepared to activate his nociceptors as he had with the others, but interference proved unnecessary. Another had snuck up behind William to smash a watermelon on his head.

The attack was so unexpected, Angor actually balked, unable to magnify the ache blossoming on William's scalp. The juice and fruit drenching his face looked like thinned blood and torn tissue. He coughed when it entered his mouth, but there was no way to avoid it stinging his eyes.

"Let's...go." He stumbled blindly toward his friends, who'd stopped wrestling to gawk, dumbfounded. Angor wouldn't have been surprised if Casimir had shown them actual blood and gore coating William's head, or if Olalla had made them believe that was what it was.

As the disoriented leader staggered past, Casimir moved to trip him, but Angor gripped his friend's shoulder to stop him. As much as he would have enjoyed watching William face-plant in the gravel, their enemies were retreating; to disrespect that choice would make *them* the villains.

"I'm telling Mom," Artemis sneered as the muscle behind her malice retired. Without the football players, she was nothing more than a petty child. Not even her threats to tattle held weight. Once, Angor supposed Olalla feared the consequences of her sister's words, but his heart swelled to see a smile slip onto her lips now, her confidence completely unaffected.

"Tell her whatever you like, Artie. I know what she'll *believe*."

With that, the defeated Cosmos turned and stomped over the wreckage of the bicycles to follow her boyfriend's posse. They'd carried their "dead" friend, who would wake shortly and make them all wonder what the hell was wrong with their perception. Perhaps that would be their real downfall—the insanity they slowly slipped into after so many dissonant memories.

Appearing more peevish than Angor had ever seen him, Casimir stalked to his skateboard to examine the broken pieces. None of the others moved; Aethelred kept touching his hair where William had grasped it, a little dazed, while Angor and Olalla fixed their attention on the one who'd felled their enemy, standing amid the guts of the watermelon: the boy with the backwards baseball cap.

"Never pegged you guys as the type to get into brawls with the jocks," the boy said, nudging the watermelon remains with the toe of his shoe.

"We aren't," Olalla replied curtly, "but if you've been watching us so keenly, you know we've never been given a choice."

"I'm all about that—choice." The boy pulled a banana from behind his back, and Angor wondered if he had a whole backpack full of fruit. After examining it for a moment, he tossed it to Aethelred, who fumbled to catch it. "I like to choose what I do, who I am, what I *believe*." He glared at Olalla for that last part. "Like, when I've seen my peers stealing from the science lab and a little voice in my head says, 'That can't have happened,' I choose to say, 'No, I think it did.' Life's fun when you refuse to pretend away the ridiculous shit."

"Amen to that," Casimir chimed in, though his tone was dull as he continued to appraise his broken skateboard. He abandoned it when the boy with the backwards baseball cap chucked a banana at his back.

"We can't always get what we choose," Olalla countered, fists clenched at her sides. "Sometimes our choices are made for us."

"Ah, but they shouldn't be." The boy extracted another banana and tossed it to her. "Everyone should make their own decisions, even if they're stupid."

That was a road Angor was not sure he could take—one where people were granted unlimited freedom. As he had observed, many were not intelligent enough for such privilege. Of course, to say so would sound quite pretentious, so he let Olalla say, "I think you have too much faith in humanity—and I think you should leave. You've been most helpful, but you aren't interested in us."

Angor sensed the shift in the air with those last words. The boy must have felt it, as well, because his brow furrowed, as if trying to ward off her influence. He even lifted his hand, like he might physically deflect her mind control, but Angor soon realized that wasn't his intention at all. Before their very eyes, an object grew from the boy's palm, crawling out of his flesh until it was its own entity: a peach.

With a complacent smile, the boy removed his backwards baseball cap and revealed a head of short, lime green hair. "Can I join your weird hair gang now?"

Angor's jaw dropped, but he couldn't formulate a word. He barely caught the peach when the boy threw it to him. It was real—fuzzy, ripe, tangible. This was beyond anything they'd witnessed, anything they'd fathomed. Olalla had mused about harnessing electricity, but elemental powers seemed too fantastical for Angor. Now they had observed a human conjure fruit from his skin, and fantastical seemed possible.

Another peach materialized from the boy's hand, and he held it up like a toast. "Consider this my initiation gift."

Casimir sniffed his banana. "Is it poisoned?"

Angor's gaze flitted from his peach to the boy's—the same fruit, as if the boy thought he and Angor were on the same level. Perhaps he did not want to join their group but to *lead* their group. Olalla had denied Angor the title of leader, but even from afar this boy had recognized the inherent authority, and he now wanted to match it. "I'd rather like to know the symbolism of these fruits," Angor decided, narrowing his eyes at the boy.

His eyebrows, which he'd somehow darkened, arched. "You and I are the only two who don't prefer dicks."

Casimir glanced at his banana and then burst out laughing. Aethelred looked like he wished someone had knocked him out during the skirmish. Olalla side-eyed Angor, a little sly, a little seductive.

"You're not just making us think these are real, are you?" Casimir asked the boy once his chortles had subsided.

"How would I do that?" he countered, cocking his head in a way that implied he assumed Casimir knew exactly how one might do that.

"I'd show you, but I don't want Red to get jealous." Casimir winked at Aethelred, who instantly shook his head. "Oh, c'mon—don't deny there's a reason you've yet to throw that banana in disgust."

"I don't want to *waste* it…"

"I can make plenty more," the boy assured him, "and I can drive you guys home, unless you'd rather walk."

"You have a car—and you can drive?" Casimir questioned, incredulous. "Aren't you a freshman?"

The boy smirked. "My parents are rich assholes, so I always steal their cars—and I don't mind breaking the law. I'm Ephraim Mayer, by the way."

Angor didn't care about his name, but he *did* care about his power—his unnatural ability to conjure natural objects. When he peeked at Olalla, she wore the same scheming face, likely thinking of the knowledge they might uncover with a few of his cells.

"You can join our group—temporarily, at least," she said, turning the banana methodically in her hands. "I have an idea."

8

Drowning in Decay

Olalla's idea involved sabotaging the football team's locker room. The only problem was they had no means with which to enter the football team's locker room.

"Good thing I was gifted the perfect tool to break a window," Casimir said, brandishing one half of his broken skateboard. That was when Aethelred decided he had to tell them he knew exactly where to acquire the key.

Casimir, of course, was not surprised to hear Aethelred had absorbed every memory when William grabbed his hair, but he still gave a peculiar look when the story was told. Olalla responded with an almost manic excitement, demanding to know their enemy's every weakness and fear. Ephraim took the revelation well for having just joined their group, but then again, he could produce fruit from his skin, so nothing should have seemed outlandish to him.

Angor reacted the worst; he stared at his oldest friend with vacant eyes, as if the news had stolen his soul. In some way, perhaps it had, for when they'd first met, Angor had unwittingly touched Aethelred, thus exposing him to all the horrors and truths of his childhood he'd always purposely omitted—his unloving mother, her physically abusive lovers, and all the people Angor had hurt and cheated to survive. All things Aethelred had no right to know, yet he did.

"You know where the Rosses live?" Ephraim asked as he extracted a set of fancy BMW keys from his pocket. "I'll drive you there."

"Unfortunately, I know the way," Aethelred admitted with a sigh. He felt Angor scrutinizing him but could not bring himself to fully glance in his friend's direction. "And I know they leave the back door unlocked. The keys should be hanging on the inside wall unless, in his stupor, William forgot to hang them."

"Even if we have to pry them from his clenched fist, it won't be a problem." Casimir chucked his ruined skateboard aside, which granted Aethelred the tiniest sense of relief. "I can make him see us as monsters instead of men."

"Perhaps we are monsters…"

Casimir cupped a hand around his ear. "What's that, Red?"

"Nothing," he said through another weary exhale. To Olalla, he added, "Must we really do this? Haven't we won enough for tonight?"

"There can never be *enough* winning." With that, she shot a deliberate look at Angor, but upon noticing his blank expression, her humor waned. "I'll wait here with Periculy. You three retrieve the key."

A grin split Casimir's lips. "With pleasure."

Aethelred was hesitant to leave his friend in such a nonplussed state, but he did not wish their inevitable conversation to happen in front of the others, either. So he followed the other boys to the parking lot, where Ephraim's parents' BMW waited.

Casimir whistled and ran a hand along the white hood,

slow and sensual. "This is real—an E23? Fuck me."

"I hope you're talking to the car, not me," Ephraim said as he unlocked the driver's door and slid into the seat. As he unlocked the other doors, Casimir tilted his head at Aethelred.

"Who were *you* hoping I was talking to?"

By now, Aethelred had caught onto the purpose of Casimir's games—that he sought a flustered reaction. Typically, Aethelred unintentionally fulfilled that desire, but he wasn't in the mood, not after the anxiety of the fight and the mild headache William's touch had induced.

"The car," he replied blandly before rounding the vehicle to claim the seat behind Ephraim's.

To Aethelred's delight, Casimir seemed a little agitated when he plopped into the passenger's seat. "Sure you don't want me to drive, kiddo?" he asked Ephraim as the younger boy backed the vehicle out of its parking spot.

"Have you ever *driven* a car before?"

"No, but it can't be that hard. Olalla's mom does it."

Aethelred snorted. "Too bad Olalla's not here to hear you say that."

"Olalla's the girl with the purple hair?" Ephraim asked as he stopped at the school's entrance. Aethelred told him to turn right, and he did.

Casimir stopped tracing probably-inappropriate depictions on the window to say, "Yeah, and don't say she's hot or any of the other lewd remarks you planned to say. She's Angor's girl—we've all accepted and respect that."

"So I was wrong when I guessed you two are gay?"

Aethelred averted his eyes when Ephraim tried to meet his gaze in the rearview mirror. He busied himself with counting the apples piled on the floor at his feet until he heard Casimir's seat squeak. By some extravagant mechanism, he'd made it recline so he was practically lying down, head extending into the backseat.

"That's to be seen, my friend," he said, winking at Aethelred before he closed his eyes. "So, Mayer, tell us—how'd your rents get so rich?"

"I'd rather like to know how you made your eyebrows dark," Aethelred piped up, mostly to stop himself from staring at the way Casimir's green curls poked from beneath the knit hat he'd stolen.

Ephraim grinned at him through the mirror. "Do you always emulate the pink-haired guy?"

"Mostly," Casimir confirmed before Aethelred could deny. "Though I can't say *always*, since I don't *always* find Angor attractive."

It took Aethelred a minute to comprehend the insinuation, and by then Ephraim was already laughing. "Okay, okay—I use my mom's cosmetics to darken my eyebrows. I have to do it every day; dyes don't work, as you probably know. And my rents are rich 'cus my dad's the CEO of some research company. He's a mega douche, and my mom's a dirty gold digger. Hence why I always steal their shit."

"Then you'll probably be disappointed to know we're all douches and gold diggers and, on top of that, trailer trash," Casimir said.

"Speak for yourself," Aethelred grumbled. "I wouldn't marry a woman for money."

"That's because you wouldn't marry a woman *period.*" Though his eyes were still closed, Casimir smiled as if he saw the blush creeping onto the other boy's cheeks.

"Turn left here," Aethelred mumbled, and luckily,

Ephraim heard him over his own snickers.

They decided to leave the car at a park down the street from the Rosses' and walk the remainder of the way. Ephraim then declared he'd stay in his parents' stolen car, lest someone else come and steal it. Considering it was nearly midnight and the Rosses lived in a quiet neighborhood, Aethelred didn't think that should have been a concern, but he lost the will to argue when Ephraim conjured a banana and tauntingly began eating it as if it were…something else.

"That kid's fun—more fun than the rest of you." Casimir bumped into Aethelred as they walked down the road but didn't acknowledge the contact before lighting a cigarette.

"Why don't you turn him into the new victim of your pestering, then?"

With the cigarette halfway to his mouth, Casimir paused to perk his eyebrows. "I said he was *fun*, Red. That doesn't mean I wanna date him."

"You wouldn't be able to even if you wanted to." This was said too gravely, too bitterly, but Casimir didn't call him out, nor did he disagree. Perhaps Ephraim was right about what they were, but it didn't matter, because in a few years they would have to marry women and start families, as was expected of them.

"So," Casimir started through an exhale of smoke, "you didn't puke when Ross touched you."

Aethelred stared at the darkened houses along the street, then at the starry sky above, contemplating the entirety of William's past and how it had barely affected him. A mild migraine had formed at the center of his head, but it was nothing compared to the crippling nausea he'd previously experienced.

Then he considered the tone of Casimir's statement and

frowned. "If you're implying William and I are romantically involved—"

Casimir spit out his cigarette and barely caught it. Even though the smoldering tip singed his palm, he didn't react, likely because his hands contained so many burn marks already. "I was *not* implying that, but please tell me if I should have."

"Of course not!"

"Okay, good. I was *actually* implying you've improved your ability—or adapted better, or whatever bullshit Periculy spews all the time. You've improved, and there must be a *reason...*"

All at once, Aethelred understood. Over the past few weeks, Casimir had accidentally brushed against him almost every day. Each time, Aethelred glimpsed what had occurred in the other boy's life since they'd last touched, and each time the absorption of memories felt more normal.

Perhaps *accidentally* wasn't the right description.

"You..."

A smirk slithered onto his lips. "Yes?"

"You've been helping me..."

"Yes?"

"I've grown more immune to the effects because..."

"Because what? Because I touch you?" He ran his pinkie carelessly along Aethelred's jaw, nearly burning him with the cigarette.

The immediate imprint of memories prevented him from panicking. Aethelred re-experienced the whole day through a new point-of-view, from when Casimir intentionally grazed his hand while passing a note in math class to when Casimir's pinkie caressed his face now.

Most prominent was the horror of the football game, the

grotesque, harrowing images the hallucinator had forced upon the players. Bones breaking, flesh bleeding, people dying—it all transpired upon that field, at least in their minds, and in Casimir's, too. He imagined it all, witnessed it all, and then slumped against Aethelred as if he'd done nothing more than an intense workout.

The second most prominent memory—and the one Aethelred almost wished to have seen less—happened in the car, when he'd thought Casimir's eyes were closed. As Aethelred had avoided the other boys' gazes, however, Casimir's eyes had peeked open, just to watch the way the moonlight gleamed off his red hair.

Then something unreal happened: Aethelred turned, timidity in his eyes. Casimir didn't move, even as he inched closer. If anything, Casimir stiffened, unsure whether to trust his senses when the other boy leaned down and whispered, "It wasn't the car I hoped you were talking to. It was me."

A blink, and Aethelred found himself on the Rosses' street again, walking alongside Casimir. He took a drag of his cigarette and said nothing about what he thought happened in the car. *Did* he think it had happened, or did he know it had been an illusion? Was anything real to him?

"I-I think you should stop."

Casimir didn't even look at him. "Uh huh. Why—afraid of progress?"

"I don't want to live in your head," he insisted, hoping his voice didn't waver, "and I don't want a version of myself to live in your head, either. You act like I'm one of your hallucinations—something you can manipulate—and maybe I am. Maybe I'm not who you think I am."

Now Casimir did look at him, calm rage etched in his glare. "You've seen all my memories and you really think that? You're a fucking idiot. This the one?"

The subject change was so abrupt that Aethelred would have been utterly lost if Casimir hadn't nodded toward the house to their right—the Rosses' house.

"How'd you know?" he managed.

"Willy's car." Casimir pointed to the black Cadillac Seville with his cigarette before dropping it and snuffing it with his shoe. His demeanor had shifted so rapidly, Aethelred wondered if the angered version of him had been an unintentional mental projection of some kind—something Casimir had wanted to say but hadn't; only, in his emotive state, his mind had shown it to Aethelred anyway.

Feeling more awkward and unsure than ever, he led Casimir around the two-story house to the back door. As anticipated, it remained unlocked, granting easy access to the rack of keys hanging within. Aethelred did not enjoy thieving at all, but he did enjoy it more than trying to articulate his convoluted emotions.

Before he closed the door, Casimir poked his body in and grabbed another set of keys.

"These are the ones," Aethelred hissed, holding up the keys he'd extracted.

"I know." With a wink, Casimir sauntered around the house, leaving Aethelred to hastily but quietly close the door and scurry after him.

"What are you doing?" he demanded once he'd caught up, aiming to keep his voice low.

"Taking one step out of the trailer trash can," Casimir said as he unlocked the door to William's car. Halfway into the driver's seat, he paused to add, "I have a car now, Red. Does that turn you on?"

Open-mouthed and utterly baffled, Aethelred said

nothing before the other boy slipped within the vehicle. A moment later, the window rolled down, allowing him to call, "Oh *right*—you're not a gold digger. Too bad. Have fun walking back to Eph's car."

"Wait," Aethelred squeaked, hurrying to the passenger's side. He yanked on the door handle, but it wouldn't open. With a villainous grin, Casimir dipped his chin in farewell and then peeled out of the driveway.

Lights flickered on within the Rosses' house. Alarmed, Aethelred dashed into the street, sprinting toward the park where Ephraim waited as quickly as his body would allow. His long legs gave him great strides, but he'd never been inherently athletic, and his knees kept clonking together. He was ready to give up and accept he would probably be caught when he ran into a solid object: William's car.

Due to the momentum, his torso doubled over the trunk, and he groaned as pain laced through his limbs. In his haze of panic, he hadn't noticed it at all. He *would* have seen it if the lights had been on, but Casimir had turned them off and shifted the car into park. As with the frequent touching, there was nothing accidental about this.

The driver's window rolled down again. Casimir snaked his body out to witness Aethelred in his groaning glory. "Get in, loser."

"Periculy." Olalla threw another pebble at him. This one hit his arm, but he refused to stop pacing, to stop stroking his chin, to stop fretting like the over-thinker he was.

At least thirty minutes had passed since the boys departed, and Angor had yet to utter a word beyond his quiet mutterings; Olalla's presence had been forgotten. After demanding his attention numerous times, she finally succumbed to sitting cross-legged in the gravel and pelting rocks at him as he paced from one side of the alleyway to the other. Most times, she missed. Sometimes, she hit the remains of their bikes, the stone clinking against the warped metal.

Artemis would pay for that. She would pay for *everything*.

William and his friends might have been the weapon, but Artemis was the wielder—the true villain. Olalla vowed to tear her apart, cell by cell, until she was less than dust.

Her hatred for her sister was all that kept her from slumping against the school's outer walls and drifting to sleep. Midnight had surely passed, and her brain ached from such exertion. Now was her only moment of reprieve; when the boys returned, they would have work to do, and when she arrived home...she did not like to think of how her mother would react to whatever exaggerations Artemis had spewed.

"Periculy," she tried again, this time chucking a stray piece of brick that had chipped off the wall. It landed in his path, and he actually halted.

Slowly, his head pivoted, eyes grave as they met hers. "Aethelred knows everything I've done."

Olalla gnawed on the inside of her lip for a moment before saying, "When was the last time you touched him?"

Sighing, Angor plopped to the ground and mirrored her sitting posture. "When we first met, almost six years ago. I was in town one afternoon...thieving...when a boy with bright red hair sprinted straight for me. Aethelred is not a talented runner, might I add—he looks like a crippled lamb."

She tried very hard not to laugh, and she failed. "Okay, go on."

Likely to avoid her eyes, Angor began drawing circles in the gravel with his finger. "Well, I was inclined to simply step out of the way and let him continue on, but then I noticed two women chasing him. They looked like witches—dark makeup and baggy dresses and crystals weighing down their ears. They were not particularly fast, but neither was Aethelred, so I knew they'd catch him. Without really thinking, I induced pain in one's foot and she toppled. The other stopped to aid her, and I took that moment to grab Aethelred and pull him into the nearest shop.

"Naturally, the static shock when we touched surprised me, so I clutched his shirt to drag him along. We escaped through the back of the shop and rode to Hastings Street on my bicycle. Aethelred did *not* enjoy sitting on the handlebars—he was shaking too hard to balance."

"I can imagine. He's not very talented at riding a bike normally."

"Well, that's because I had to teach him at the age of eleven. Before that, he'd never ridden one. '*But I did try a unicycle once*,'" Angor added in an accurate imitation of Aethelred's bashful voice.

"A unicycle?" Olalla repeated, bemused.

He stopped drawing to challenge her with quizzical eyes. "You haven't guessed? I thought you were perceptive, Cosmos. Aethelred grew up in a circus."

Her mouth opened and closed a few times before she managed, "How would I have *guessed* that?"

"He's hinted at it enough—always accidentally mentioning all the cities he's been to or making references to the *tiger* that was his only childhood friend."

Olalla thought for a moment and then winced. "I don't really listen when Aethelred rambles."

Angor's lips curved slightly as he leaned back on his hands and stretched his legs to cross his ankles. His fancy loafers, now coated in dust, rested only an inch from her. "Too busy daydreaming about me?"

"More likely about microscopes."

His grin broadened as he nodded. "That's probably a better thing to daydream about."

She pursed her lips in an attempt to resist his charm. "So, what did you do as a child that you don't want Aethelred to know about?"

For this, Angor resumed his cross-legged position and played with the hem of his khakis. "I might have once killed my mother's lover."

"You...you *killed* someone?"

Her expression must have been one of true dismay, because Angor shifted uncomfortably and avoided her gaze. "Oh dear... If you're having this adverse of a reaction, I can't imagine how much Aethelred must despise me."

"No, no, I just...never thought you were capable of such...brutality."

He huffed out a breath, rubbing his forehead. "I am capable of many things I wish I were not. My mother's lover—well, one of my mother's many lovers—was unbearable. Most were cruel men, but this one used and abused her in every way.

"I didn't care about that so much—by then, I was nine, and I'd already experienced her abuse, already gained my ability. But this man included me as his victim, hissing slurs at me, stabbing me with his cigarettes, forcing me to comply in his drug runs. One day, I'd had enough. As we were jaywalking across a street in Cleveland, I made him crumple in pain. He sprawled on the road, moaning, unaware of the car that was unaware of him."

Olalla remained silent for a moment. Then she flicked some dust at him. "That was disappointing. I thought you'd stabbed him."

A weary smile emerged. "The gore would have amused you?"

"No, the actual *act* of murder would have. You didn't kill him. If he hadn't been such a wuss, he would have continued through the pain. His demise was his own."

Angor shook his head. "Nevertheless, I reveled in his death—I *smiled* at his mangled body, Olalla. I'm sick; I've always been sick. And I didn't want Aethelred to know the extent of my illness. He's too pure for such derangement."

Olalla bit her lip but didn't console him. His words were an echo of her own thoughts, though his tone was much more remorseful than hers ever would be. "Remind me never to let Aethelred touch me," she said, thinking of that kid, Michael, and his bloody lips. Kissing someone and making them forget about it wasn't quite as heinous as murdering someone, but she didn't think innocent Aethelred would appreciate it, either.

Before Angor could confess to any other crimes, headlights appeared at the end of the alleyway, blinding Olalla. She squinted until they turned off, but neither she nor Angor moved, even when she realized it was William's car. Though it would be draining, she could deter him once more.

"What kinda freaky ritual are you two engaging in?" Casimir's voice demanded as the driver's door flew open. Aethelred extracted himself from the passenger's seat with far less flare, but Olalla still gawked, because that was *definitely* William Ross's car.

"You stole his car?" she questioned, scrambling to her

feet. "Where's the other boy?"

"The other boy has a name," Ephraim said as he hopped over the hood of William's car to enter the alley. Aethelred followed with clumsily while Casimir had parked at an angle that allowed him to slip between the building and the vehicle with ease. "And what do you care if I'm here? That one has the keys."

That one proved to be Aethelred, who fumbled with the keys before tossing them to Angor. As he unlocked the locker rooms' entrance, Olalla simpered at Ephraim. "Because *you* are the key to our sabotage."

9

Drenched in Decay

"Aethelred," Casimir prompted, since he'd used every other variation of the kid's name without success. "What are you trying to do?"

With his hands splayed on the window, Aethelred turned and coughed at the smoke wafting toward his side of the car. "I'm trying to pull down the window so I don't suffocate by smoke inhalation. There's no crank…"

Casimir glanced in his direction to display a grin and, consequently, nearly drove them off the road. Perhaps it was for the best Ephraim hadn't given him control of the BMW.

Shortly after arriving at the school to deliver the locker room keys, Casimir had slipped back into his newly stolen car, declaring he had to repaint it and scavenge for replacement license plates. He'd also declared Aethelred as his companion for these tasks, and though the red-haired boy had looked exhausted, he hadn't complained. Before they departed, Angor had advised they hide the car, since even William wasn't stupid enough to be fooled by a half-assed paint-job, but Casimir had merely flipped him off before inexpertly peeling out and destroying the school's lawn.

Now, as they drove down the empty road toward the outskirts of East Mintle, he'd lit a cigarette in an attempt to eradicate the scent of jock itch and cologne from the leather seats. As with most things, this displeased Aethelred.

"You know there's a button, right?" Casimir asked when the kid resumed his attempts to lower the window with his fingers.

"A button?"

"To roll down the window automatically."

Aethelred removed his hands from the glass to shoot Casimir a befuddled look. "That exists?"

"We're in a luxury car, Red—a button exists for everything. I'm not showing you how to do it, though. I need to rid this thing of Ross's stench," he said before puffing more smoke. He would have preferred for Aethelred's scent to fill the space, but his fragrance of mild florals and musk wasn't strong enough to reach Casimir's nostrils unless they were extremely close, like when he'd leaned on Aethelred during the football game. After their conversation while walking down Ross's street earlier, he doubted they'd touch again for a long, long time.

"How did you make the football players see their worst fears if you weren't touching them?" Aethelred managed to ask after dramatically clearing his throat. "I thought you could only impose hallucinations from others' imaginations with physical contact?"

Drumming his fingers on the steering wheel, he admitted, "I've been studying them—determining what might scare each one most."

"I didn't realize you were so…observant."

Casimir shifted his focus to the passenger's seat and dragged his eyes up and down Aethelred's tense form. "I am very observant."

Red eyes flew wide, not because of the suggestive

comment but because, in the moment his attention wasn't on the road, Casimir almost swerved off it.

Hastily, he jerked the wheel to correct their course, and his shoulder collided with the window. A laugh bubbled in his throat, partly from the panic of the almost-accident and partly from the exaggerated dismay on Aethelred's face.

"I wonder…what will kill me first," he panted, clinging to the door handle. "Smoke inhalation or your erratic driving."

"Hey, that was the first time we've swerved in the past mile, okay? We're fine."

In his periphery, Casimir noticed the boy gradually relax until he sat in the seat like a normal human. "I will admit," he finally said, his tone a bit too astute, "for someone who's never driven a car, you're not *too* terrible."

Casimir's driving hand tightened on the wheel as his other hand fought not to crush his cigarette. Having seen his entire past, Aethelred knew the hallucinator had indeed driven before—that he'd lied to Ephraim. Now he was calling Casimir out on that lie in the most childish, condescending way.

Instead of retorting, Casimir remained uncharacteristically silent. For the rest of the ride, Aethelred's periodic coughs were the only noise beyond the hum of the engine. Casimir had forced him to tag along so they could talk, but now he had no interest in speaking, nor did he know what to say. How could he explain the mangled meat of his mind? How could he explain his irrational insecurities?

How could he suture the tear that had formed between them when Aethelred had seen the hallucination of himself? Casimir couldn't *suture* it—that was the answer. If he tried to mend it, it would become an indistinguishable mess of band-aids and insincere well-wishes; he'd never possessed the capacity to do anything *neatly*. He didn't have the patience to explain that his hallucinations of Aethelred were involuntary—or that he always knew they weren't real. But he *always* knew, because this kid didn't have the balls to flirt so blatantly, and because, frankly, he wouldn't have wanted him to.

He liked the way Aethelred concealed his emotions, often to the point that Casimir couldn't detect what the boy felt at all.

After fifteen minutes of speeding down straight roads and colliding with cows that turned out to be Casimir's imagination, they arrived at the junkyard: a fenced area teeming with ancient cars. Though most piles consisted of automotive parts, a few contained random crap people had probably illegally dumped. Parking William Ross's pristine vehicle before the gates seemed like blasphemy, but otherwise, Casimir felt comfortable. This was the kind of place he would probably live in after graduation—if he graduated.

As soon as he turned off the car, Aethelred stumbled out the passenger's side and doubled over to hack into the dirt. Rolling his eyes, Casimir slid out the driver's side and snuffed his cigarette. According to the signs, the scrapyard wasn't open to the public, but the gate was unlocked, and to him that was as good as an invitation.

He didn't check if Aethelred followed as he entered and began his search for a license plate that looked like it belonged on a 1977 Cadillac Seville. In a literal dump, that was a task easier said than done. He had to climb a mountain of cars to uncover the newest one, and then he had to use a rusty screwdriver to remove it. Engrossed in his quest, he almost fell off the pile when Aethelred's voice suddenly sounded from below.

"This is where Angor and I found our lawn chairs."

Casimir gripped the nearest bumper and hoped the entire mound wouldn't avalanche. Once he'd determined it wouldn't, he peered down at Aethelred, a ruby amid a sea of trash. Casimir was fairly certain his mind accentuated the glow of his hair, because the moon was not nearly potent enough to make it *that* bright.

"I'm kinda offended I haven't received my own lawn chair yet." Casimir shot the other boy an accusatory look before sticking the license plate between his teeth and beginning his careful descent from the car mountain. Upon reaching solid ground, he removed the plate and spat the taste of metal and grease from his mouth.

Aethelred scrunched his nose at the saliva. "Why don't you find one now—or just imagine one for yourself?"

The last part was added with heavy sarcasm, so Casimir countered with, "I think I'll just share yours."

Apparently, the kid had grown a spine since their earlier altercation, because instead of blushing, he frowned. "Won't the police know this plate isn't registered for the car—or possibly not at all?"

"You should know by now that what people *think* matters very little to me. Besides, I'd have to get pulled over for them to check, and I have no intention of getting pulled over."

"Of course you'll get pulled over—you drive like you're blind."

"That's offensive to blind people, Red. How dare you—"

"Why did you lie to Ephraim about never driving?" he interjected, his voice too stern for condemnation of such a trivial fib.

"Why didn't I tell him I had to teach myself to drive

when I was eleven and my dad was too high to get us home safely? Gee, I wonder."

Flustered, Aethelred averted his gaze to the nearest pile of junk. "I just mean...it just makes me question what else you've been lying about."

"Nothing to you." Casimir spat again, though not aggressively enough to reveal his true agitation. "You *know* I don't lie to you."

"I can see what's happened to you, but I can't see how you feel about it. Maybe you loved teaching yourself to drive."

Casimir arched an eyebrow. "I didn't. It scared the shit out of me. Happy?"

A sigh escaped his mouth, but his arguing stamina must have reached its limit. "I found paint," he said, holding up a rusted bucket with dark paint smeared on the label. When the moonlight hit, it shimmered pine green. "Can we go now?"

"Cranky tonight, Certior. Yeah, we can—"

Casimir cut himself short when a growl emanated from behind. Slowly, he spun to find a massive German shepherd prowling toward them, crouched low, its brown and black fur blending with the darkness. The dog bared its teeth, and Aethelred audibly gulped.

"Hey, doggy," Casimir greeted warily. "We're just—"

Before he could utter another word, the animal lurched forward. Casimir hooked his free hand in Aethelred's sweater to yank him along, and the two sprinted through the maze of garbage toward the exit.

"I need to stop running after I smoke!" Casimir shouted through labored breaths. "Was there a dog here last time?"

"No! We came during the day!"

"Figures," he exhaled right before Aethelred tripped on a

stray car bumper. Casimir grabbed his arm to prevent him from face-planting, and then he snatched the paint can to prevent him from dropping it. The open gates were within sight, and he didn't want to have to return here, not even to acquire his own fancy lawn chair.

Although, with the dog a few short paces behind them, he might not have the choice to return.

Casimir had never used his ability on an animal before, but when he locked onto the dog's mind, he found it more malleable than the football players', which was, frankly, surprising. Since the scrapyard was full of cars, he induced a hallucination of one in the dog's brain, and when the animal tried jumping on the hood, it hit empty air.

Thrown off balance, it rolled through the dirt but didn't surrender. Despite its slowed pace, the dog still managed to catch up and tackle Aethelred to the ground.

Casimir skidded to a halt and whirled around, unsure of how he would wrestle this snarling monster but determined to do so. Only, the dog wasn't snarling; it had plopped atop squirming Aethelred to smother his face in kisses.

"Huh." Casimir cocked his head, trying to find concern in how the boy writhed and wailed beneath the creature but coughing out a laugh instead. "Never thought I'd be jealous of a *dog*. Save some for me, will ya?"

The dog continued licking Aethelred until Casimir finally decided to pry him off, after which the dog nuzzled into his ripped jeans.

"Should we bring it home? It can just be a one night stand if you're not up for the commitment."

Scowling, Aethelred wiped his face with the sleeve of his sweater and pushed to his feet. "It's…kind of cute," he conceded, awkwardly patting the animal on the head. "But it's not my type."

"Why?" Casimir asked dryly. "Because it's not human?"

"No." A small smile played on Aethelred's lips as he retrieved the paint can from Casimir and started toward the exit. "It's a female."

"You want me to cover this place in fruit? Why don't I get one of my guns and shoot holes into the lockers instead?"

Angor glanced at Ephraim through the dimness of the football locker room. Only the moonlight from the small windows above the mint green lockers illuminated his bright eyes and backwards baseball cap. "You have guns?"

"Of course I have guns." Ephraim removed a helmet from where it hung on the wall and conjured a handful of blueberries to smash on the interior. "My superpower is lame as shit. That watermelon trick only works as a surprise attack."

"Do you attack people often?"

"No, but I want to be prepared."

That was a precaution Angor could admire. He always wanted to be prepared, as well, but he'd never expected to find himself in a conflict so grave it involved *guns*. He was glad Casimir wasn't around to hear such deadly weapons were within their reach.

As Ephraim squished blueberries into the rest of the helmets and Olalla ran her fingers over the lockers in a way too cunning for anyone's comfort, Angor contemplated all the reasons their hand in this mischief might be discovered...and how it didn't quite matter. If Artemis publicly blamed them, Olalla would ensure no one believed her. If William recognized his car, Olalla could make him believe he'd never had a car at all.

She multiplied life's possibilities by infinity.

Shaking out of his thoughts, Angor watched a peach sprout from Ephraim's hand. Other than for the instance of this sabotage, his ability wasn't very useful, but Angor had to appreciate the sheer novelty of it. He could grow fruit—*food*—out of nothing. This could change everything.

It could also ruin everything—not for the world as a whole, but for Ephraim as a person. If the government or a large corporation were to realize his ability, would they use him as a slave to produce food for the hungry? Helping those in need *seemed* noble, and perhaps he *should* sacrifice his freedom to aid the greater good, but was that fair?

Angor understood Ephraim's freedom argument, at least a little, when he then considered what atrocities a government or powerful group might force him or Olalla or Casimir to commit with their abilities.

"You called it a *superpower*," Angor said as the peach rapidly rotted in Ephraim's hand.

The boy chucked it at one of the lockers before raising his dark brows. "I did."

"Do you think that's what it is—a superpower?"

Another peach materialized in his hand. "How else would you describe it?"

"We've been calling them *our abilities*," Olalla jeered at Angor, as if it were his fault they'd organically named it such. He knew by her smirk that she enjoyed the term *superpower* a little too much.

"Same thing," Ephraim dismissed as he threw the now-rotten peach at the next locker.

"*Superpower* makes us sound like comic book characters," Angor said. "We need to pick a formal term for what we can do—for what we are. Something that doesn't provoke an image of us running around in tights and capes, saving innocents."

"Oh, of course"—Ephraim hurled another peach—"we wouldn't want anyone to suspect us of saving innocents."

Olalla leaned against an empty wall and pouted her lower lip. "You don't want to see me in tights, Periculy? I'm offended."

Angor pursed his lips but didn't reply. The image his mind created wasn't unpleasant.

"So, we won't call ourselves superheroes because we don't like saving innocents," Ephraim said, "and we won't call ourselves supervillains because we don't like wearing tights. What does that leave us—superneutrals?"

Angor ignored his jest and stared at the floor, ruminating. His vision snagged on the East Mintle logo painted on the tiles. "Mintle...Mental—that's what binds us all: the mind."

Olalla jabbed her thumb at Ephraim, who'd just thrown a peach at the last locker. "Except him. His power is more...nature-oriented."

"Then he can be Natural," Angor concluded.

Ephraim rolled his eyes as he paced back toward them. "I don't like labels."

"I like it," Olalla said, which Angor hadn't expected. So far, she'd vetoed every one of his ideas simply to irritate him. "*Mental...* Makes us sound as unhinged as we are."

"Should I design something inappropriate with bananas?" Ephraim asked as he crouched to arrange a few bananas on the tiles.

Angor wasn't particularly interested in what he might

design. He *was* interested to know if the boy could conjure walnuts. When he posed this query, Olalla tipped her head back to cackle. Mildly embarrassed—since it had been a serious question—Angor didn't wait for the answer before changing the subject. "How do you do it—without even a seed or *anything*? Matter cannot be created, but you defy that rule."

Ephraim shrugged as he added more bananas to his arrangement. "At first I thought it was literal magic, but now I think the fruit expands from my dead skin cells. It's always easier when my skin's dry."

"Gross," Olalla stated, almost absently. After a moment, she asked, "When did you first discover this *superpower*?"

"Well, I used to be allergic to most fruits, but my parents would force me to eat them. They'd make my throat itch and my eyes water. One night, after I'd been force-fed an apple, I woke up without any of my usual symptoms and found my bed brimming with apples. I was five, so I screamed. My mom came in and scolded me for always refusing to eat apples when, clearly, I loved them so much I'd stolen a ton from the kitchen. The same thing happened every night with whatever fruit I'd eaten that day. Eventually I learned I could control their production. I haven't had an adverse reaction to any fruit since."

Ephraim finished his banana display and stood, but neither Angor nor Olalla looked at it; rather, they stared at each other from the corners of their eyes, sharing a moment of realization. Olalla's adaptation hypothesis had some validity, it seemed.

Conjuring an apple, Ephraim reached above the lockers and rested it there, far enough out of sight that the football team wouldn't notice until it caused an infestation of ants. As he did, his sweatshirt lifted to reveal a splotch of ink on his abdomen. Angor stepped forward, squinting through the poor lighting, to find it was a tattoo of a hand protruding from a graphically bloody wound, holding a gun.

"That's…eccentric," Angor commented before he could stop himself.

Ephraim blinked and then lifted his sweatshirt to reveal the tattoo in its full, gruesome splendor. "My parents *hate* it," he said with a manic grin.

Angor refrained from saying he, too, hated it. "Don't show Casimir—he'll get too many ideas."

"Are you his mother?"

"Oh yes," Olalla chimed in, jumping her eyebrows in Angor's direction. "Periculy likes to think himself the leader, but he's really the mother hen of the group."

Ephraim laughed and spent the remainder of the time clucking or making "Why'd the chicken cross the road" jokes. Angor began to wonder if this boy was some sick figment of Casimir's imagination come to life.

Once their mission was complete, the locker room's scent of sweat had been replaced with that of overripe fruit. They exited the building without being arrested, which was nice, and Ephraim drove them to Hastings Street, which saved a considerable amount of time and energy. The problem was that, when they arrived at the trailer park, Angor could not decide whether their new acquaintance should be trusted— whether Angor *wanted* to trust him. The weird hair gang had become a smoothly functioning machine over the past few months, and the addition of a new cog might throw off their entire rhythm.

As Angor and Olalla exited the car, Ephraim said, "See you in detention Monday," which was probably an accurate statement. If they didn't receive detention for sabotaging the game or ruining the locker room, William and his crew would ensure they did some other way.

Olalla shut the passenger's side door and nodded to the boy before he drove away, dirt clouding in his wake.

"What did you make him believe?" Angor asked her as Ephraim disappeared and Hastings Street succumbed to desolate silence.

"Nothing. Why should I have altered his mind? He's one of us."

Angor eyed the tire marks Ephraim's fancy BMW had left on the jagged dirt road. "In some way, perhaps, but I do believe he differs from us biologically. Regardless, I would like to study his genes."

"What are friends for?" Her playful simper faltered when she glanced over her shoulder at the Cosmoses' home. The windows were dark except for one, beyond which the light of a television flashed. Angor hadn't yet stepped into her house, but from the outside, he had observed that the television never seemed to turn off.

He cleared his throat. "If you'd like—"

"Yo, you guys didn't get arrested," Casimir's voice called from behind. "That's nice."

Angor turned to see him and Aethelred approaching from the far end of Hastings Street, where the Stromers' home resided. "Neither did you."

Aethelred rubbed his forehead, swaying as if on the verge of collapse. "It was a near thing."

With an eye roll, Casimir said, "We were *fine*. A junkyard dog almost mauled us to death, but—semantics. The good news: I think Reddy grew muscles from running *twice* tonight, and who would've thought that'd be possible?"

"Everyone *has* muscles," Angor said. "Some just have less muscle mass than others."

Casimir threw his head back and stared at the sky. "If I tell you we hid the car like you asked, will you refrain from being a know-it-all for five seconds?"

"Where'd you hide it?" Olalla asked.

"Behind my house. We covered it in leaves—super stealthy."

Aethelred winced as if the stupidity of Casimir's idea physically pained him. "Perhaps we can search for a tarp tomorrow."

"You should keep the car hidden for a few weeks," Angor advised. "William will be less likely to suspect—"

Casimir barked out a laugh. "I *want* him to suspect—I want to rub it in his face that I stole his car and there's nothing he can do about it."

"There are several things he can do about it, and the majority of them result with us in jail," Aethelred mumbled.

The hallucinator dismissed this by pushing through the group toward the Periculys' house. "Are we going in, or what?"

Angor had foolishly thought to invite Olalla into his home, but he did not want Casimir to enter again, not after what he'd witnessed last time. "Well—"

"Oh *c'mon*. We're not gonna make our girl go home to those she-devils and that lazy blob, are we?"

Their girl did not react to this; Olalla's expression remained carefully neutral, but Angor detected a twitch in her eyelid, akin to his own discomfort whenever his home life was mentioned.

"Actually, I was going to make *you* go home," Angor countered, provoking another eye roll from Casimir before he continued onward and quietly barged into the Periculys' house.

Olalla shot Angor a questioning look, which he answered with a nod. Tentatively, she trailed Casimir through the front door, but before Aethelred could follow, Angor grabbed his sleeve.

"I wanted to—"

"Angor, I'm sorry," he blurted out, features pinched with remorse. "I should have told you the truth of my ability sooner, but I feared you would kick me out if you knew the violation I committed."

"*Violation*—Aethelred...you discovered I *murdered* someone—"

"And I didn't leave," he said with a tired smile. "That should say as much about me as it does about you."

Angor pressed his lips together. He was not sure how to proceed with this conversation—how to tell Aethelred that he had been a better friend than someone as cold and heartless as Angor deserved.

"Uh, guys," Casimir prompted from within the house, mercifully ending their awkward exchange. "Problem."

Sighing, Angor trudged through the open doorway, expecting a prank. Surely, the hallucination of a crude image would invade his living room upon his entrance, and Casimir would revel in Aethelred's discomfort.

Stepping into the warm but putrid air of his unfortunate dwelling, Angor found that a crude image indeed occupied the living room, but it was not an illusion; his mother sat on the couch, draped in a blanket of empty beer cans, nostrils flaring at the sight of them.

10

Memories and Mirages

As the frail woman stood, beer cans cascaded to the floor with an unpleasant jingle. Alcohol stained her threadbare garments, and the stench saturated the air, as potent as the Cosmoses' house. Olalla assumed this hunched, scowling creature to be Angor's mother—a disturbing combination of her own parents.

With her thin limbs, it was quite possible *she* didn't have muscles, but Olalla knew the lack of strength didn't affect the severity of her abuse—not to Angor, at least. For him, the issue was his pride, and Olalla understood why being demoralized by this wretch would wear on his esteem.

"I waited up for you," the woman hissed, stepping forward and crushing a can with her bare foot. She stumbled but caught herself on the coffee table, pushing a few of Angor's textbooks to the floor in the process.

He didn't look at them; his stare fixed on the wall, detached and slightly befuddled. "Why?"

"Because our neighbor stopped by and said you killed someone!"

The scene flashed bitterly in Olalla's mind: Artemis coming here, knowing they hadn't killed that football player but telling his crazy mother so, anyway. She wondered if her sister had gone to the Stromers', as well. Based on Casimir's descriptions of his parents, they wouldn't give a damn, but Angor's mother gave enough damns for all their horrid parents.

"And now," she went on, each word a dramatic slur of syllables, "you and your gang think you can show up here so, what, I can save you from the feds?"

Angor finally met her gaze as she kicked cans to form a path for herself. "Mother..." His tone was patient, but not the condescending patient he used with Olalla when she was stubborn; caution laced this patience—and fear.

A beer can flew through the air, colliding with his sweater. One at a time, the woman retrieved more from her pile, throwing them slowly enough for Angor to dodge. He didn't, though; he barely flinched. His only acknowledgement of the attack was a mild wince as he beheld the liquid splattered on his khakis. Olalla realized then why his pants had been wet the last time she'd knocked on his door.

From the corner of her eye, she glanced at Casimir, who glanced at her in return. Either of them could have stopped this, but neither would. Olalla had solved the problem of her mother, and Angor would have to solve the problem of his, too.

Except he wasn't solving it; without moving a muscle, he could have made her drop to her knees in pain, but he accepted each blow from the aluminum cans as if he deserved them.

Gritting her teeth, Olalla honed her attention on the woman and projected, *You're tired; moving is a burden. Stop.*

Angor's mother froze mid-throw. Though convincing her of her laziness hadn't been particularly difficult, Olalla knew her arm would soon grow fatigued from holding that position, and she would likely snap out of the daze. Once she refocused on her son, the assault would resume, and in many ways, it would never end. As long as Angor lived here, he would have to deal with the abuse, and he would.

Olalla couldn't tolerate the thought. After so many years of her own mother's mistreatment, watching Angor accept it enraged her. She whipped toward him, and with a quiet, deadly tone, she said, "I can make her disappear."

Angor broke out of his stupor to blink at her. "What?"

"I've been practicing something."

"What?" he repeated as if it were the only word his tongue remembered how to form.

"You don't remember…because I've been blocking your memories."

Casimir's eyes narrowed. "I thought we agreed not to use our powers on each other?"

"Have you two been following that rule?" Olalla arched her eyebrows and looked between him and Aethelred, whose cheeks reddened. Although she didn't know the extent to which they practiced on one another, the two spent a suspicious amount of time together, and Casimir, at least, had improved his ability. "I've been practicing for a time like this—to help *us*. Angor, I can make her forget this place, her life, her past—*you*. I can make her leave and never come back."

For a long moment, he picked at his lip in rumination. "If I say no, will you do it anyway and make me forget her?"

With the aggravation building in Olalla's core, she probably would. "I don't think you should forget her," she said instead, which was also the truth. "I think you need to remember how small she made you feel and how it inspired you to grow."

His lower lip began to bleed, but he didn't stop picking at it. "How will you enforce this forgetting if she's gone?"

Olalla shrugged. "I don't need to. The memory blocks are different than warping beliefs—it's more like a wall than a seed. The plant of belief can be uprooted for another or wither from neglect, but the wall is more permanent. It can be broken, but only by extreme force. I don't think your mother is that strong."

The taste of blood must have hit his tongue, because he lowered his fingers. His eyes darted in her direction, feverish with the desire to eradicate his mother but hesitant about the method. Their trust had fortified over the months of their friendship, and Olalla didn't think her admission to practicing on him had put a dent in it; his arrogance prevented him from accepting aid.

"Let me help you," she whispered, so low the other boys didn't hear. Since she couldn't compel him with her ability, she compelled him with her expression, infusing desperation and empathy into her features. When he swallowed and nodded, her smile was genuine, albeit wicked.

First, she had his mother drop her arm. The beer can fell with it and rolled across the room to hit Angor's loafers. Then, Olalla closed her eyes and traversed through the web of the woman's mind, spinning cocoons around any memory that involved Angor or Hastings Street. She much preferred this aspect of her ability; nurturing beliefs was tedious, endless work, but stifling memories was like patching holes in a cracked bathtub. The result was ugly, but the sap of her influence was less likely to ooze out. With nowhere to go, it would congeal and eventually harden. To break it, one risked shattering the brain entirely.

When Olalla opened her eyes, Angor's mother was

blinking in confusion. "You want to walk to the nearest bus station," she told the woman. "You want to take a bus across the country, somewhere warm where you can live without a care. You won't want to turn around—why would you? This place has nothing for you."

The spoken words weren't necessary for Olalla's ability; in fact, they contradicted the beliefs she truly implanted. *You want to walk until your joints ache and your feet bleed. When you can walk no farther, you'll jump in front of a car or off a bridge or whatever is most convenient for you to end your life. Death is your only desire.*

The spoken words *were* necessary for Angor's sake; he had to believe his mother had departed for a better place, no longer his responsibility or burden. He might have hated her, but he would mourn her, and a mournful Angor would not achieve the accomplishments they'd strived for.

After his mother staggered out the door, more zombie than human, Casimir slammed it, Aethelred retrieved a napkin, and Olalla watched Angor's dead expression. He ignored the napkin when offered to him in favor of striding to the front window.

"The hell did you do to him?" Casimir growled, his glare more severe than she'd ever seen.

"Nothing," she murmured, troubled. Perhaps she would have to block his memories, after all.

"I can't believe she's really gone." Angor's voice filled the room, haunting in its emptiness.

Olalla's hands clenched into fists at her sides. "Do you want me to bring her back?"

His head pivoted toward them, a smile blooming on his lips. "No, no. I've never felt so…free."

Reverently, he paced through the room to pick up his fallen textbooks. After neatly placing them on the coffee table, he began to collect garbage, depositing each article in the trash can, one at a time.

Upon exchanging uncertain looks, the other three joined him, copying his weirdly ritualistic method in silence. They cleaned the living room, the kitchen, even his mother's filthy bedroom, until everything was pristine. By the time they finished, the crooked clock on the wall—which Angor gently righted—indicated it was past two in the morning.

Olalla's body felt exhausted, but her mind was invigorated. She hoped her victim would walk far from East Mintle before succumbing to death, but with Angor's newfound energy, perhaps he wouldn't care to hear of his mother's death. It would be an accident, of course; Olalla had told her to start a new life, not end hers.

With bright, meat-pink eyes, Angor surveyed the house— *his* house—and gave a satisfied nod. As he kicked off his shoes, Olalla realized she'd never witnessed him barefoot before. He wore socks, but the lack of shoes—the lack of formality—felt oddly intimate.

"Well," he said as he plopped onto the couch. They'd vacuumed it, and Aethelred had cleaned the fresh beer stains with his napkin, but it still looked far too shabby for someone as regal as Angor. He'd placed an oversized bowl of walnuts amid his array of textbooks on the coffee table, and now he cracked one open with his rusty knife. "Make yourselves at home."

Almost nervous, Olalla lowered herself onto the opposite side of the couch, so far the other two boys could have fit with ease. Aethelred moved to occupy the spot, but Casimir grabbed his sweater before he reached the coffee table.

"C'mon, Red," he said, eyeing the two on the couch with mischievous eyes. "Let's go to bed."

Aethelred's shoulders slumped, as if that comment alone was more tiring than hours of labor. "Was that meant to rhyme?"

Casimir jumped his eyebrows at the other two before dragging Aethelred along. They disappeared into the room Olalla hadn't entered—the boys' bedroom.

"Do you think they're actually gay?" she whispered, hoping they wouldn't hear through the thin walls.

"Oh, obviously." Angor popped half a walnut into his mouth and offered the other to Olalla.

Amused, she received and chewed it before drawling, "Why *obviously*?"

"Because neither of them have even *attempted* to approach me with the question of what we should do about you." With a smug arch of his eyebrows, he leaned back into the couch and rested his hands behind his head, annoyingly casual.

"What you should do about me?" she repeated, though she was too shrewd not to know exactly what he meant.

"You know, which one of us *gets the girl*."

Olalla barked out a sarcastic laugh and pulled one knee to her chest in an attempt to mimic his too-cool demeanor. "What makes you think any of you will?"

"Well, I suppose the *getting* is entirely your choice, but the pursuit falls to one of us—me, apparently, considering our friends have no interest in you."

Her insides coiled at his words, but not in the right way. For a few moments, she'd been giddy with his insinuations—until the last bit, which gnawed on her esteem. Perhaps Casimir and Aethelred were gay and infatuated with one another, but that didn't stop her from feeling bothered by the prospect that they had no interest in her. She wanted everyone to have *some* interest; people were more easily manipulated when interested.

Could she make them want her? Could she twist their natural instincts? The questions elevated her heart rate with an intoxicating sense of power. She had forced that kid, Michael, to kiss her, but he'd preferred girls to begin with.

He also hadn't possessed knowledge of her ability. He also hadn't been her *friend*. She shouldn't have thought about how to sexually manipulate her friends—nor should she have delighted in the possibility. A long time had passed since Olalla had done what she *should* have, though.

Cracking open another walnut, Angor swung his legs onto the couch and stretched them toward her, so close his scandalously sock-covered feet nearly brushed her. She locked eyes with him and discarded any thoughts of other boys. If Angor could look at her like that—like he was in total control when *she* was the mind controller—then she had no need for anyone else.

In fact, the complacent, almost impish curve of his lips stirred nervousness in her gut. She'd never met anyone who was her equal, but Angor was in so many ways. Their brains worked on the same wavelength, after all.

Remembering that made her wonder if he'd guessed the unethical questions she'd thought and if his sly eyes now mocked her for them.

"When did you realize you could erase memories?" he asked, which was the last thing she'd expected or wanted him to say.

Her face soured. "It's not *erasing*—it's *blocking*."

"You're avoiding the question."

Embarrassed, she pretended to find interest in the dirt on her high tops. "I…received a lower grade than you on our biology test a few weeks ago. You mocked me for it, naturally, and I was so annoyed that I wanted you to forget completely. Strangely, you did."

She figured he would recall the incident and mock her once more, but his face scrunched pensively as he flipped a walnut between his fingers. "Do you think your ability adapted again? Do you think you're...*evolving?*"

"Perhaps," she said, since she would never admit she didn't know. "Or perhaps the blocking of memories is a facet of the ability I've already formed—although, I suppose the uncovering of this ability could be considered the evolution of my skill. I hope I'll continue to evolve—I hope we all will."

Angor was too deep in meditation to notice her amend her selfish sentiments. "Have you discovered any other facets I should know about?"

Ah, there was the anger over her violation. She'd assumed he would not be pleased to know she'd broken their pact, but this passive-aggressive tactic was almost worse than outright reprimand.

"No," she answered honestly. "I'd planned to tell you, you know. I wanted to improve first, though. I wanted to... impress you."

He met her gaze, his eyes simultaneously intense but soft. "You almost always do."

Her stomach coiled again, this time in the right way. Still, she was not quite sure how she would react if he crawled across the couch to show her how impressed he was. She hadn't kissed anyone since Michael, and though she'd learned the mechanics of it, she didn't understand physical passion— she didn't like the thought of surrendering control, of giving in to primal desires, of becoming more physical than mental.

But an innate part of her *wanted* Angor. She wanted to

taste him. To inhale his scent of old books and coffee and walnuts. To meld their minds.

Instead, she broke eye contact to stare at the front window. "The rest of my ability is painfully pathetic. I can only plant one belief in one person's mind at a time. I fear I'll never be able to commandeer a whole crowd at once."

"You will," Angor said, though he didn't sound particularly thrilled about it.

She ignored the hint of warning in his tone. "The bigger problem is the reinforcement. It would be so much easier if my beliefs *stuck*."

"Perhaps once we've studied it more, we could devise something to enhance your ability."

"Yes," she said, hoping her voice didn't betray her feverishness. "Perhaps. Perhaps we should first look for more people like us—Mentals, Naturals, whatever you'd like to call us. It's too coincidental that all five of us ended up in East Mintle and there's no one anywhere else with powers."

Angor fetched another walnut, the couch shifting with him. "And what would we do with these people?"

"Hang out? Eat walnuts?"

Suspicion entered his eyes. "As tempting as that sounds, it wouldn't be very productive."

"We could expand our gang—form a community. We could build a town where none of us would be outsiders. Weird Hair Land!"

He snorted and tossed half a walnut to her. "That's interesting…definitely something to consider. Would this be a trailer park community?"

"Of course not," she scoffed. "We'd build a magnificent city—white buildings and ridiculously tall towers. It would be like heaven, and we would be its gods."

Angor lifted one eyebrow. "And what would Aethelred and Casimir be?"

"Where there's a god, there's a devil."

His snort sounded more like a laugh this time. "All right. You've convinced me, Cosmos. I'll dream on it." Then he reached behind his head to turn off the lamp. Drenched in darkness, Olalla felt even more aware of their proximity.

She cleared her throat. "I should return home, I suppose."

"You shouldn't." His tone was as black as the air between them. "Artemis has a vendetta against us now, and who knows what she told your mother. I won't risk losing you to their malice."

"Because I'm the only intelligent mind beneath this roof?"

"Because what would the King of the Weird be without a queen?"

She hoped the darkness hid her smirk. "I'm not sleeping in your mother's disease-ridden bed."

"I wouldn't expect you to."

Her vision had adjusted enough for her to see him close his eyes and nestle into the cushions. Despite his implied invitation, she tried her hardest not to touch his legs as she relaxed against the armrest and propped her feet atop the back of the couch. A normal girl might have draped her legs over his and siphoned his warmth, but Olalla was Queen of the Weird, and she'd been born for the cold.

"I don't think all three of us will fit," Aethelred said before Casimir had even slammed the door behind them. He and

Angor kept the bedroom free of clutter, but he still felt self-conscious about the hallucinator scrutinizing his unmade bed and the scribbled notes splayed on his desk.

"All *three*? Are we inviting Angor? Or does the King get his own room and Olalla's stuck with us?"

"Oh—well, I mean…I thought the boys would all share one room and Olalla would have her own."

Casimir chuckled sarcastically as he approached Angor's side of the room. The stolen microscope sat atop the pedestal of his nightstand like a holy relic. Textbooks towered from his desk toward the ceiling, and the plaid purple sheets were perfectly tucked into the bed, displaying stains and discoloration from years of use. "Then you don't know your oldest friend as well as you thought you did. You think he'll forfeit this opportunity to sleep with her?"

Heat crawled into Aethelred's cheeks at the thought of Angor and Olalla *together*. "You think she'll want to?"

Casimir threw a mocking glance over his shoulder. "Have you *seen* Angor? She'll want to."

The blush extended toward his throat as he recalled all the times he'd seen more of Angor than he probably should have considering his friend would never quite look at him the same. "I, um, had a bit of a…crush on him when we first met," Aethelred admitted.

"Tell me something I don't know." Casimir slumped onto Angor's bed and leaned on the pillows, crossing his legs. Despite the droning tone, curiosity sparked in his green eyes.

"He…saved me. I admired him a little too much for it, I guess. There were…same sex couples in the circus, so I didn't realize how taboo it was until I went to public school."

Casimir extracted one of Angor's many tomes from the pile beside the bed and examined the spine. "Did you ever try to kiss him?"

"No, I—you *know* I didn't," he decided when a wry smirk split onto the other boy's lips. Of course Casimir knew; Aethelred had made his aversion to touching wildly clear. "I'm trying to be honest with you, and you're messing with me."

"Don't know what you expected from me." Carelessly, he dropped Angor's book atop the pile and cocked his head. "It's obvious you're a sexual prude. Guess it should bother me, especially considering you're two years younger than me, but—what can I say? I love all kinds of fags."

He extracted a cigarette from its pack and flourished it in the air, the punch line to his little joke. Aethelred nearly laughed, not in amusement but in amazement. He'd never experienced an attack of homophobic slurs—probably because he possessed much more obvious characteristics for people to deride—but the insulting connotation of the word discomfited him. Yet, somehow, Casimir always found a way to take that which ought to be offensive and flip it in his favor.

Still, he didn't look as satisfied with his pun as he normally would have, nor did he light his cigarette. It twirled between his fingers in an almost anxious manner. "I kissed a boy once," he said, startling Aethelred. "I was twelve; he was older—not sure how much older, but definitely older. Didn't really know him, but he was attractive enough, and I was...*curious*—not about him but about *me*. I knew I was *supposed* to like girls, but I never had much interest in them. I let them claim me as their boyfriend in grade school and used them as a shield of straightness so I could stare at boys and be thought of as *creepy*, not gay."

Swallowing, Aethelred slowly lowered himself onto his

own bed, facing Casimir. "I...know—about the girls," he added, realizing his statement was unclear. "When I first glimpsed your memories and all your childhood *girlfriends*, I thought..."

"You thought I was straight?" He coughed out a laugh. "That was my intention, dear Aethelred. Couldn't have you catchin' on too soon."

"But I...I didn't see you kiss a boy. You're *lying*."

"Not lying," he said, tilting his head back to stare at the ceiling. "I just hid it from you. I buried it so deep you'd never find it—so deep I never find it, except in moments like this, when I *think* too much."

So, that was what had felt as if it'd been omitted. Aethelred hadn't been aware anyone could hide a memory like that—although he should have been, since he had many memories of his own that he'd locked in a coffin and thrown into a sea of forgetting.

"I kissed him and I hated it," Casimir practically spat. "Probably because he was straight and almost ran off to the fucking *cops*. I used a hallucination to make him think I was a girl."

Aethelred's whole body cringed. "Oh...I see."

"Yeah. After that encounter, I decided I was straight. Then I met you—or rather, spied on you in the form of a tree."

That was his cue to laugh, but Aethelred couldn't think past the confession. He'd foolishly admitted at the junkyard that he wasn't attracted to females, but now that felt less *foolish* and more *dangerous*. A small fascination had expanded within him over the past weeks, one that begged to know what romance might be like with Casimir Stromer, but his rational brain knew the possibility was nonexistent.

Dazed, Aethelred reclined on his own bed and stared at the peeling walls. The quiet extended so long he was certain Casimir had fallen asleep, but when he glanced at the green-haired boy, he was studying his cigarette like he didn't see ones exactly like it thirty times a day.

The realization that Aethelred knew how often Casimir smoked increased his lightheadedness.

"Are you…hallucinating about me right now?" he asked in what he hoped was a steady voice.

Casimir shot him an irritated look. "You think I hallucinate every time I shut up for more than a few seconds?"

"I don't see any other reason for why you'd refrain from gracing the vicinity with your intellectual thoughts."

Casimir laughed so hard he nearly retched onto the floor. "Okay, okay, you're right—I was hallucinating. I think I still am. I'm talking to myself right now, aren't I?"

Brow furrowed, Aethelred studied him intently. "What do you mean?"

"I *mean*, you walked out." He nodded toward the door. "There's no way in hell you stayed in here with me. You hate being alone with me to begin with, and after the dumb shit I just said… The real Aethelred probably awkwardly stumbled out of here to go share the room with Olalla for the night, since that's less scandalous, somehow."

Aethelred wiped his suddenly clammy palms on his rumpled sheets. Casimir didn't think this was real; Aethelred could essentially do anything he wanted right now and the hallucinator would believe it was an illusion. It would be immoral, and he didn't really have the guts to do it, but he did wonder what would happen if he approached Casimir now. If he joined him on Angor's bed, if he curled up against him, if he fell asleep to the scent of pine and smoke in his nostrils.

It would lead to nothing, Aethelred rationalized. He could wake up early, as he usually did, and pretend he'd slept on the couch. Casimir would never know, and they could go on as they always had.

But the wrongness of it unnerved him. He'd told Casimir he didn't want to be one of his hallucinations, and he didn't want their relationship to be, either. If Aethelred was going to succumb to his feelings, he didn't want the honest part of him to live only inside Casimir's head.

"I am here," he said boldly. "There's nowhere I'd rather be."

Casimir rolled his eyes. "God, my head is a cheesy place."

Panic seeped into Aethelred's sweaty pores. He didn't know how to convince Casimir he was really there. What must it have been like for the boy to never know reality—to always wonder if the world was a lie?

There was one way he might convince him, and it involved the fantasy of his deception without the actual deceiving.

Shaking, Aethelred stood from his bed and approached Angor's. Awkwardness characterized every movement as he lowered his lanky body onto the mattress, squishing against Casimir, who flailed like a wounded seal in response.

"Can you not—" He stopped squirming to rub his temples. "I'm not—I don't want—"

"I-I can move." Aethelred threw one leg off the bed, too stunned by the adverse reaction to completely remove himself. "I didn't mean—"

Casimir's suspiciously slivered eyes halted his babbling. "It is you, isn't it?"

"Yes," he breathed, heart beating too fast.

"Then you're welcome." Casimir scooted against the wall, allowing Aethelred to share the tiny bed with him. Carefully, he swung his leg up, aware of all the inches where their clothing touched.

"The hallucination of me isn't?" he managed to ask.

"Of course not. That asshole is too forward. If I liked that version of you, don't you think you would've found me kissing the air in Ephraim's car? I like the you that doesn't know where to put his hands when he sits"—Casimir glanced at his hands, which fidgeted uncomfortably in his lap—"and doesn't know how to hold eye contact." In response, Aethelred tried to hold eye contact but found it extremely difficult and ultimately looked away. He sensed Casimir grinning. "A minute ago, when I thought you were a hallucination, I was gonna say I don't want you to live in my head. I want you to be real. Sometimes I wonder if I've imagined you entirely."

"I...suppose I am weird enough to have been born from your imagination. I don't know who my parents are, so it's possible."

"Now *you're* messing with me." Casimir elbowed him before shifting to rest his head on Aethelred's shoulder. It was less *cuddling* and more like the boy thought him a convenient pillow, but Aethelred didn't imagine his bony shoulder would be worth the convenience. Pulling out his lighter, Casimir waved the cigarette and grunted, "This gonna bother you?"

Aethelred stared at the ceiling he'd spent so many nights staring at while stressing over nothing. Now, a small smile inched onto his lips. He closed his eyes, inhaling cool pine and fresh smoke. "Not at all."

11

Blinding Brightness

After his horrendous loss to the Criglodge Crows and his humiliating surrender to watermelon innards, William Ross was defeated; he and his band of jocks no longer harassed the weird hair gang. Even upon discovering their "dead" friend was not truly dead, they shied away from the underclassmen whenever they crossed paths in the halls, and they took the blame for the fruit in their locker room, which soon led to an infestation of rats. Angor supposed their apprehension could have been Casimir's doing, but regardless, they had won.

"*For now*," Angor reminded his peers whenever they became particularly cocky about their victory. "We're playing the long game, here. We have to succeed in life, not just in school."

Although she agreed, Olalla would roll her eyes at this proclamation. Then Casimir would conjure a caricature of Angor that spewed over-exaggerated declarations of world domination, and even Aethelred would giggle into the sleeve of his sweater.

Between the quelling of their enemy and the eradication of his mother, Angor felt like a new man. The little mobile home on Hastings Street was not where he planned to stay forever, but for the time being, it was *his*. Most teens would have utilized this opportunity to throw parties and litter the house with beer cans, but Angor had lived a life littered with beer cans, and he had no intention of returning to that life. Instead, his dwelling brimmed with science textbooks, stolen microscopes, and, of course, walnuts.

Casimir slept over most nights, claiming the doodle-covered armchair as his bed, but Olalla only stayed if she happened to fall asleep while examining tissue samples in a microscope. Angor knew she liked the space and their company, and sometimes he ventured to think she might like *him*, but still, she felt obligated to return home.

Perhaps she didn't want Artemis to think she'd successfully driven her younger sister out. Perhaps she didn't want her mother to think she'd successfully driven her youngest daughter out. Perhaps she didn't want that to be the truth—that they'd driven her out—and she maintained her position in her family home merely to reassure herself of her own control.

Angor didn't know if any of the Cosmoses had punished Olalla after the football game, but if they had, she never spoke of it. His nature was not to feel guilt or empathy, but after she'd saved him from his own mother, he owed her a debt. If he could give her the same peace and satisfaction she'd given him, he would.

The opportunity never arose, however. As the school year wore on, Angor and Olalla fell into an endless pit of research, and the matter of their human deterrents became overshadowed with the need to uncover the mystery of their abilities. They immersed their minds in information on genetics, neurons, and white matter. One of the three held the key to their *superpowers*, and if their assumption was correct—if other Mentals or Naturals or even *Physicals* existed—Angor did not want anyone else to discover the science first.

By the time spring arrived, they had little to show for their efforts. Angor could block pain better than ever before, but he didn't understand *how*. Did his mind tamper with the pain receptors themselves or the current as it ran along the axons or the actual perception of pain within the brain? Without the proper equipment, he might never know.

"Periculy," Olalla prompted one evening in late May. She sat cross legged on the floor, three textbooks open around her in preparation for their final exams next week. On the opposite side of the coffee table, Angor slumped on the couch, mindlessly poking his skin with a needle. "You're bleeding."

Unfazed, he glanced at his left arm, riddled with tiny punctures, some of which dripped onto the couch. The blood didn't affect the already-stained pink cushions. "Indeed," was all he said.

She lifted an eyebrow, which had brightened into pure purple over the past few months. Likewise, his features had settled into a color more akin to human muscle than well-done meat—another anomaly that's cause plagued his thoughts.

"We've been studying nonstop," she said, flipping a book closed. "We should go out—just the two of us," she added when Casimir dropped one leg to the floor behind her. He lounged in his typical position: head reclined on one armrest, legs draped over the other, bottom sagging in the middle.

At her addition, he threw his leg back onto the armchair and puckered his lips sassily. "That's rude."

"I'm asking you on a date, Periculy," Olalla said through her teeth, eyes fixed acutely on him. He refused to meet hers directly; he'd learned her mind control worked best with eye contact. "Will you deny me in front of everyone?"

Aethelred, washing dishes in the adjacent kitchen, dropped a plate in the sink and shot Angor an anxious look before retrieving it.

"Would you *let* him deny you?" Casimir asked as he chucked his green yo-yo in the air and caught it effortlessly. Months ago, Angor had first seen the boy playing with it the day after he'd attempted to draw on Aethelred's pants, since his were completely covered with ink depictions now. Since Aethelred had asked Angor to accompany him to the toy store the evening before that—and he did not particularly like marks on his clothing—the origin and purpose of the yo-yo were clear.

"Of course." Olalla slapped another textbook shut. "If Periculy has no natural interest in me, my natural interest in him will die very easily."

Angor rolled his needle onto the table between his bowl of walnuts and Casimir's ashtray. Since the night they'd slept on the couch together, nothing *romantic* had blossomed between him and Olalla, but the tension had magnified, as if they both knew the option was there yet neither wished to grasp it. This was her attempt to test a hypothesis they'd both thought but never spoken.

"Where should we go? The Dittrick Museum of Medical History in Cleveland, perhaps?"

Her face lit at his proposal, probably more because of the museum than who she would attend it with. "Yes!" She closed the last textbook and jumped to her feet, facing Casimir. "You'll drive us."

"To a *medical museum?* Fuck no. You'll have to warp my mind, Cosmos."

Olalla peered over her shoulder at Angor—for *permission*, he realized.

Rather than granting it, he shifted his gaze meaningfully in Aethelred's direction. Engrossed in his task of tidying the kitchen, the red-haired boy didn't notice their attention, nor did he notice the grin snaking onto Casimir's lips as he processed the implication.

"Fine," the hallucinator said, "we'll go to the museum— on a *double date.*"

This time, Aethelred dropped a plate to the floor. For once, Angor appreciated his mother's tasteless plastic dishes.

"That sounds nice," Aethelred managed after picking up the soapy plate, "but you don't have a date."

Casimir opened his mouth, but Olalla cut him off by saying to Angor, "We'll have to stay local, then."

He would have expected her to fight for the museum, but surprisingly, her soft spot for Aethelred swelled larger than her scientific interest. Intrigued by the fact that Olalla Cosmos had some semblance of a heart, Angor tapped a finger to his chin. "Hm…all right. What do normal people do in East Mintle?"

"Eat at a diner, or"—Olalla cringed—"roller skate?"

"Sounds delightfully mundane. Let's roller skate. It'll be the perfect place to cause a little chaos."

"I'll drop you off," Casimir offered, "but only if Red comes." Gently, Aethelred set the clean plate on the counter and prepared to object, but the other boy rolled off his recliner and held up a hand to stop him. "We aren't going *in*, okay? I wouldn't be caught dead *roller* skating."

And thus it was settled. The four piled into Casimir's car,

Angor and Olalla assuming the backseat, and Aethelred reluctantly riding shotgun, as usual. Since the unlawful transfer of ownership, the car had always smelled of fresh cigarette smoke and fast food. Wrappers decorated the floor, and the once pristine beige leather seats now adorned mythical creatures and cartoons of Aethelred associating with said mythical creatures. On the way to or from school, Olalla sometimes used a pen to weave Angor into these sagas, and though he refrained from smiling, the drawn versions of himself never failed to amuse.

As promised, Casimir and Aethelred remained in the car when they arrived at the roller rink. Neon lights illuminated the steps to the entrance, where teens flowed in waves of bell-bottoms and belly shirts. In his khakis and button up and Olalla's cutoff jeans and striped t-shirt, they would stand out as nerds more than ever.

"This is not our scene," she muttered as Casimir sped off, smoke billowing from the driver's window. Angor agreed, but they entered anyway, submerging in a world of laughter, lights, and disco balls. The sight of their peers—the popular ones, the preppy ones, the ones who chose a life of debauchery and meaninglessness over science—solidified this idea as a bad one.

Angor's desire to depart exponentially increased until a new variable altered the equation. Behind the counter, framed by rows of roller skates, stood William Ross. He smiled at a group of girls as they collected their skates, but as soon as they left the counter, giggling, his demeanor turned dejected.

This was the William they had known since the harrowing football game. Because of that loss, their team didn't make it to the state championships, and because of that failure, his popularity had waned. Only his closest allies bothered with him now, Artemis included.

Angor was grateful for her absence in this moment. The animosity between the Cosmos sisters had burgeoned over the months, like a malignant tumor suffocating all in the vicinity. Olalla acted noticeably nastier on days she encountered her sister, and Angor wasn't sure how to feel about the venom that sparked in her eyes at the mere mention of Artemis.

Her reaction to William was less menacing, but she still held the posture of a predator as she prowled through the group of giggling girls to approach him.

"William Ross," she greeted as if they were old friends. He straightened and eyed them with unease. Everything about him was predictable and boring, from his generic side-combed hair to the football jersey he wore instead of a work uniform. Angor didn't think it worth their time to harass him, even after all he'd done to torment them. Nor did he think roller skating was a more advantageous utilization of time, though, so he said nothing. "You *work* here? How embarrassing."

His jaw hardened. "I have to save for a new car, since mine was stolen, and for college, since I haven't been offered a scholarship."

Both of which were their fault, he did not add. He'd never confronted Casimir about the car, but as soon as he saw a Cadillac Seville outside the Stromers' mobile home with a messy paint-job and rusted plates, his glare for the boy became ever-present.

A simper enveloped Olalla's face as she cupped her cheek in mock sympathy. "How sad. It's probably for the best, though. You would've flunked out, anyway."

"My grades are fine—better than they used to be."

"Better since you met my sister, you mean? She can be so dull sometimes, but I know intelligence runs from *somewhere* in our bloodline. She's been tutoring you, hasn't she? I bet she filled out all your college applications, too, hm? I shouldn't have expected otherwise—you're nothing without Artemis."

William's dark eyes narrowed, but he didn't protest. "You have an affinity for being a real bitch, you know that?"

"I do know that."

Perhaps Angor should have injected himself into this conversation—either to encourage or discourage Olalla's cruelty—but his mind snagged on that word: *affinity*.

"That's it," he said aloud, interrupting Olalla's demoralization of William's character. "That's what we have—*Affinities!*"

She fixed him with a questioning look but refrained from furthering their conversation in favor of compelling the defamed football player to bring them two pairs of roller skates for free. Angor might have wondered how Olalla knew his shoe size, but his mind was too enamored with the fact that they now had an official name for their anomaly.

After trading his loafers for clunky skates, he guided her away from the counter, whispering, "We don't have to use the dreaded term *superpowers*. We have *Affinities*, Olalla."

"That doesn't change the term for what we *are*. We still have to be *superheroes*—or, if we listen to Ephraim, *superneutrals*. I suppose we could remain the weird hair gang..."

"No, no—we *have* Affinities and we *are* Affinities. That'll be our all-encompassing name."

Olalla cocked her head, considering, and then a dark grin formed on her lips. "Oh, William, you've inspired us more than you'll ever know."

Angor agreed, and he did share her enthusiasm, but her treatment of William bothered him. Though the boy had tormented them in numerous ways, they had defeated him—for now, at least—and it was not in Angor's moral code to attack the loser. Even if he saw his mother now, he would wish nothing ill toward her. He had not quite forgiven her, nor had he quite forgiven William, but he did not believe in reopening old wounds.

"Has William mistreated you in your home?" Angor asked without preamble as they entered the rink. Teens rolled along the wooden floor, some with leisure, others spinning or crouching or dancing. Olalla, whose skating skills far surpassed his, nearly stumbled into the wall.

"Why would you think that?"

Angor shot her an impatient look as the majority of his focus lay in remaining upright on these wobbly skates. Aethelred's opposition to this activity now made absolute sense, especially when one of their school's jocks whizzed past them.

"Although you may not care about him anymore," Olalla said once they'd both gained balance, her tone calm but cold, "he is still on my sister's side, and that war has not ended. I don't believe it ever will."

Angor frowned, partly because of her statement and partly because a young child had just sped past them at an ego-diminishing speed. "Won't it end when you move out?" He contemplated formally asking her to move in with him, but instead said, "We won't live on Hastings Street forever. Every storm passes."

"Oh, we're getting philosophical, Periculy? Then you should know it's always raining somewhere; wherever we go, we'll face hardships. I intend to end one predicament before involving myself in another."

Angor knew what that meant; she would not leave her family until she could seamlessly manipulate them all. Considering she'd yet to do more than erase a few of Angor's memories, her goal would not be easily achieved.

The sounds of disco music and laughter reigned for a few minutes before she added, "I suppose *this* is a predicament, though."

"What?" A crooked smile was her only reply, and he knew he needed to make at least one educated guess before she would grant him an answer. "Our relationship?"

"What relationship?" she countered almost mockingly. "I was referring to our ineptitude at roller skating."

"Ah," he said in a way that he hoped didn't betray his embarrassment. "Well, the only way to solve that is to improve, and I don't believe either of us have any intention of returning here."

"Perhaps not, but *good* is only a comparison to *bad*, and both are subjective. One way to pull ourselves up is to pull others down—bring them to their knees."

Angor didn't particularly like the ethics of that method. That didn't stop him from smirking when one of the jocks dropped to his knees on the wood before them. To anyone else, it appeared an accident, but nothing accidental happened in their sphere of life.

"That was cruel," he commented.

She rolled her eyes and elbowed his arm. "You liked it."

"I prefer more of a challenge."

Her mouth opened, but she didn't voice her inquiry before Angor slid his foot into the path of the next boy to pass them. Flailing, he landed not far from his friend and whipped his head up to find the perpetrator. Angor pretended he hadn't noticed as he said to Olalla, "I agree the film was awful," as if they'd been in conversation the entire time.

She refused to play along, hissing, "Now they're onto us. You've made it a hundred times harder."

He flashed a smile as they followed the rounded corner and caught a glimpse of the glaring boys. "In the challenge lies the fun, Cosmos."

Since October, Aethelred had mastered the laborious skill of rolling down the passenger's window. At first, Casimir had disliked this for two reasons: One, it removed his cigarette smoke, dulling the scent in the car and alleviating Aethelred's hilariously dramatic coughs, and two, Ohio winters were freaking *cold*. Once the spring air had thawed, he'd minded the wind flow a *little* less, especially when Aethelred began instinctively closing his eyes to the balmy breeze, relaxing for the first time maybe ever.

That was how it had been for the first few miles after they dropped Angor and Olalla at the roller rink. Then Aethelred opened his eyes and ruined everything.

"What are you doing?" he demanded, bracing his hands on the door and the dashboard. His head whipped around, drinking in the scene. They'd driven in the opposite direction of Hastings Street, past the high school to a park where the traveling circus had erected their festivities.

The sun had nearly set, but the circus lights flashed across the grass and trees, illuminating the grand striped tent that had swallowed the soccer field. Families skipped across the lawn to the entrance, their laughter flitting through the open windows as Casimir parked his car in the packed gravel lot.

He hadn't *known* this was the same circus Aethelred had grown up with, but the expression on the boy's face confirmed it.

"No—no, no, no," he repeated, gawking at the threatening array of bright colors and sniffing at the intimidating scent of buttered popcorn. Casimir snorted, though he did have to admit the clowns greeting the children were mildly terrifying. He also had to admit that while Aethelred's reactions often seemed over-exaggerated, they were genuine—and warranted.

Aethelred never said much about his time at the circus, but Casimir had noticed how ill he looked on days the cafeteria's popcorn machine was functional or how he'd spent the majority of Halloween hiding in the bathroom after the football team decided to dress as clowns. The circus had traumatized Aethelred, and bringing him directly to it was heartless…but also necessary.

"Look, I don't know exactly what went down with you and this circus, and it's none of my business, but I *do* know you'll never get over it if you don't face it. So, we're here to face your demons, Red," Casimir announced before exiting the car. By the time he lit a new cigarette and rounded the vehicle, he expected Aethelred to have removed himself, too, but he still sat paralyzed in shock.

With an eye roll, Casimir yanked open the door. "Yo, the problem?"

Aethelred blinked, a gesture too innocent for the sinister hue of his irises. "I-I can't…"

"Obviously," Casimir droned, grabbing his striped sweater to haul him from the vehicle. The knitting was too suffocating for even the evening air, but Casimir knew the perspiration beading on his forehead wasn't from the heat.

Warmth, Aethelred had grown used to; the circus, it seemed, he never would. "Which is why I'm here—to make sure you *can*."

With that, he kicked shut the door and dragged the other boy toward the field. Aethelred tried digging his heels into the gravel, and the trek became so arduous that before they reached the grass, Casimir halted completely, whirling to glare at him. "You really wanna turn around—be a coward?"

"Yes," Aethelred said without hesitation.

Casimir released the sweater to rub his forehead in exasperation. "Tell me why, and I'll drive you straight back to Hastings Street. What did they do to you?" As expected, the boy said nothing. "Aethelred," he prompted and then paused, considering. "Is that even your real name?"

"I…don't know. It's what they always called me. I never knew my parents. Certior was a name Angor made up because he thought it sounded sophisticated."

"Figures." Casimir took a drag of his cigarette and, for once, blew the smoke away from Aethelred. "So, what are we doing?"

Swallowing, the boy cast his gaze toward his old home as if it were a graveyard, not a scene teeming with laughter and life. "Let's…check it out."

A smirk inched onto Casimir's lips as he snuffed his cigarette in the gravel to do just that.

Together, they strolled onto the grass, soaking in the sights of face-painted kids and cotton candy machines. It wasn't quite as grand or psychedelic as the carnivals Casimir had attended in Washington D.C., but perhaps that wasn't because of the lack of ferris wheels and silly games but because he'd mastered his ability enough to see what was real—mostly. The glowing sign above the tent had to be an illusion.

"*The Wickedly Wicked Cirque*," Casimir read, over-exaggerating a French accent with the last word. "That's not sketchy at all."

Aethelred said nothing; he continued onward like a ghost returning to his grave.

The obnoxiously high-pitched tone of the circus piano grew louder with every step, and the density of the crowd thickened until they walked not of their own volition but with the wave funneling into the entrance. Aethelred ducked his head and shrunk into Casimir's side as they passed the clowns. Belatedly, the hallucinator realized why: as children and teens passed, the clowns snatched them from the throng to take *pictures*. Parents shouted and smiled, delighted to snap photos of their kids in the creepy embrace of these white-faced, red-nosed freaks. Casimir cast an illusion to all within range, making them believe he and Aethelred didn't exist at all.

Only once the horde fanned into the tent, giving the boys room to disentangle and stagger to a cooler, emptier spot beneath the metal bleachers, did Casimir let out a breath, spewing, "This place is a nightmare. As bad as my childhood hallucinations, maybe."

"Now you understand my desire to leave," Aethelred huffed, brushing his ruffled red hair from his forehead.

"Still wish you trusted me enough to talk about it," Casimir muttered. He hadn't intended for the other boy to hear, but the bashful aversion of his eyes confirmed he had. "Let's play a game of truth for truth, shall we? I'll explain a memory I've omitted from your awareness, and you tell me exactly why you fled this circus. Other than the clowns, because we all know that was reason number one."

Aethelred's cheek twitched, but he didn't smile. "You already told me about the memory...of the boy..."

The boy Casimir had kissed—yeah, he still tried suppressing that one, even after he'd confessed it while lying in Angor's bed months ago. There was another truth he'd smothered, though, one that affected his everyday life, one that, even in this moment, he didn't quite want to believe.

"You don't know why I started smoking."

Aethelred's brow creased. "Some guy offered you a cigarette when you were ambling around the city one day... You were ten."

"Yeah, and why'd I take it? Because I'm a freak, like you. Because I'm nervous—*anxious*—all the fucking time. Because I can't sit still; I need to be moving. And I'm paranoid—I'm *scared*, okay? Cigarettes keep me grounded. They're the only things I know are real. The nasty smell, the suffocating feeling—it's all that's familiar to me. I'm a mess, and I don't like to admit it, because I don't know how to fix me, and I wouldn't want to if I could."

Aethelred's mouth flopped open, and even when someone bumped into him from behind, the shock didn't fade. "I didn't...I didn't know you face a similar mental ailment. You always seem so...nonchalant."

"Nonchalance is my coping mechanism. Gotta will the chill, you know? Well, I guess you don't know. Somehow you've embraced the anxiety like it's an endearing personality quirk."

The remorse in his red eyes implied he was about to apologize or empathize, either of which Casimir would have hastily dismissed. Instead, a half-wince, half-smile consumed his face. "I can't decide if this would make us a better or worse pair."

"Worse," Casimir said through a laugh, playfully kicking his shin. "Always worse. Now, tell me—"

But Aethelred's attention had shifted past him, eyes protruding at whatever lay behind Casimir. Slowly, he pivoted to find two figures approaching from beneath the bleachers. One swung from the metal framework like a monkey while the other contorted through the tighter latticework like smoke slithering through the cracks in his mobile home's walls.

Casimir prepared to induce horrifying hallucinations on the minds he assumed to be the psychics', but when the two landed before the boys, the light exposed them as a young man and woman, both sporting elated grins.

"Aethelred!" the woman exclaimed, lurching forward to envelop him in a hug. The puffs of turquoise feathers on her shoulders swallowed Aethelred's bemused face. "We never thought we'd see you again!"

After examining the woman's sequined attire to see her ass nearly falling out of her leotard, Casimir diverted his gaze to the man, who was the living embodiment of a Ken doll. Despite the physical exertion of using the bleachers as monkey bars, his golden hair remained perfectly sleek, and his muscles bulged beneath the tight fabric of his royal blue full-body leotard. Casimir didn't realize he was staring until the man clapped him on the shoulder and offered his other hand for a shake.

"Alistair. You?"

"I'm gay—I mean...Gary.... Casimir," he finally managed, shaking the man's hand.

"Gary Casimir," the man mused, and neither boy corrected him. Aethelred probably hadn't heard since he was too busy spitting bright feathers from his mouth. "You're dating our young lad, huh?"

Alistair moved to hug Aethelred, but the boy didn't return the gesture as he spluttered, "D-dating? Why would we be dating?"

The woman rolled her dark eyes. "Oh, please. We pegged you as gay the day you showed up at our circus, and you were barely two."

As Alistair pulled away, Aethelred grimaced and massaged his temples, probably trying to process the memories the two had unwillingly thrust upon him. Casimir smirked, partially because of the woman's comment and partially because Aethelred hadn't collapsed from the physical contact, a sign of progress that could be attributed fully to the hallucinator's efforts over the past eight months.

"We want to hear all about what you've been up to," the woman enthused. "When Agnes and Gwen told us you'd run away, we were all so worried, but they assured us you'd be okay. They knew you'd be here tonight, actually—they're the ones who told us to look for you."

The way Aethelred's face paled confirmed Casimir's guess that Agnes and Gwen were the creepy psychics who'd raised him.

"They're excited to finally see their oracle again," Alistair said with a wink. "We'll show you where—"

"Whoa, whoa, whoa," Casimir cut in when the man took Aethelred's elbow to guide him along. "We wanna see the show first."

"Oh, of course!" The woman clapped her hands together. "We should get in position, too. We can fetch you after; I'm sure Aggie and Gwen won't mind waiting. C'mon, we'll show you where the best seats are."

Looping her arm through Aethelred's, she escorted him

from beneath the bleachers. Casimir followed behind Alistair, since that position provided the optimal view. He almost didn't notice how much the crowd had dispersed until the woman led them to the third row of bleachers and he saw everyone had taken their seats. The lights on the perimeter of the tent had dimmed, brightening the center ring. Unlike the hallucination in the library, the circus now contained only one large ring, where a man in a shimmering red coat stood.

"Enjoy the show," the woman said before flipping off the side of the bleachers, landing lithely on the canvas below.

"Hey," Casimir called before Alistair could follow. The man paused and turned, blond eyebrows raised at the boy's lazy grin. "I turn eighteen next month."

Alistair's face looked perfect even when contorted in confusion. "Uh, happy birthday…almost?" Then, too dumb to comprehend Casimir's flirty connotation, the man flipped off the bleachers and jogged toward the center.

"You know he's twenty-six," Aethelred said flatly, his voice nearly drowned out by the ringleader announcing each member of the circus in a thick French accent. Clowns, jugglers, camels, and women in bikinis with feathers pluming from their heads all entered the ring and walked in a continuous circle. When the woman—"the incredible contortionist, Nathalia!"—and the man—"our lead acrobat, Alistair!"—jumped into the ring, Casimir cast a wry glance in Aethelred's direction.

"You know you're jealous."

The boy frowned but didn't try to deny it. "We need to leave. The psychics *know I'm here.*"

"We do need to leave, but we can't." Casimir angled his head toward the exit, where four clowns stood guard like bouncers at a club. The canvas threshold had closed, so unless they could squeeze beneath the tightly pegged bottoms of the tent, they were stuck. "Tell me what the hell is up with you and those psychics."

"First, we have the world's most intelligent elephants!" the ringleader declared before the music's volume increased.

Aethelred directed his attention toward the wrinkly gray beasts stomping into the ring and pursed his lips. "He can't know they're the *most* intelligent. They love to over-exaggerate and—"

"*Certior*," Casimir growled, grabbing the boy's sweater in his fist. Against his desires, Aethelred peeked at his companion. "Tell me *now*."

Swallowing, he aimed his red eyes at his feet. "Well, you already know the psychics weren't the nicest to me."

"Yup, and my parents aren't to me, either, but I don't tremble at the mere mention of them. What did they do to you?" Casimir demanded, enunciating each syllable. Angor would have prodded gently—or perhaps not at all—but *gentle* wasn't an adjective Casimir knew how to utilize.

"Look at that elephant go!" the ringleader shouted as an elephant rolled around the ring atop a ball.

Though the act was impressive, they didn't have time for Aethelred to ogle it. Casimir grasped his chin, ignoring the tingle in his fingers as his memories transferred from his nervous system to another's.

"They hit you, didn't they?"

Unable to rotate his head, Aethelred was forced to meet his eyes at last. "No, they didn't. They just wanted to use me when they realized my power."

Casimir released him with the aggression meant for the two women he'd never met. "So they did abuse you—they knew how physically sick your ability made you and they forced you to use it anyway."

"Yes," Aethelred conceded slowly. Below, the ringleader called for applause, and the crowd obliged as the elephants lumbered out of sight. "But it was more than that. When they realized how accurate my ability to perceive memories was, they wanted me to use it on the ringleader."

Together, they examined the man from afar, now introducing a shirtless performer who dragged a trampoline into the circle with him.

"They believed—"

"Pause one sec." Casimir held up a finger, eyes trained on the shirtless performer, whose pants were as tight as his abs. Aethelred waited a moment, expectant, but when the man simply flipped on the trampoline, the red-haired boy rolled his eyes.

"They believed the ringleader was abusing his wife," Aethelred explained, drawing Casimir's focus away from the performance. "They wanted me to use my ability to uncover the truth and testify against him."

"Did you?"

"No. Well, I did witness the ringleader's past. He never abused his wife. I told the psychics, and they wanted me to lie about it—to use it as blackmail against the ringleader to convince him to sell the circus to them."

Cheers from the crowd overpowered Casimir's low whistle. The fine specimen on the trampoline had done a triple flip, but Casimir wasn't really interested in that anymore. "Damn, that's corrupt."

"Indeed. The worst part is that when I refused, they decided they wanted my power for themselves. The best way to acquire it, they thought, was to mix my blood into a potion."

"What?" Casimir blurted out loudly enough to attract a few stares. He ignored them. "Did they cut you?"

"No, that was when I ran away. They'll try to cut me if they find us, though."

"God—I can't believe people bring their *children* to this place. Creepy clowns, psycho psychics—"

"I don't think *all* psychics are psychos. I was, in some ways, a psychic myself, and the practice is quite... intriguing..." Aethelred's voice trailed off when the trampoline hottie left the ring, making way for a new act.

"Let's welcome our *mystical* psychics, Agnes and Gwen!" Skipping to the side, the ringleader waved his arm toward the darkness, from which two figures emerged.

Draped in fancy fabrics and glittering jewels, the psychics stepped into the ring and swept the crowd with mischievous smirks. In the hallucination of the psychic tent, Casimir had thought the younger one more humane, but after Aethelred's tale, he knew they were both as wicked as witches. The Wickedly Wicked Cirque, indeed.

"You seein' this?"

Aethelred nodded nervously. "Unfortunately. They were never given their own act in the show before. Perhaps they threatened the ringleader with their lies..."

As clapping subsided, the possibly blackmailed man proclaimed, "And welcome to the ring their magnificent pet, Hypnosia!"

Panic sparked in Casimir's gut, the same panic he felt whenever he navigated city alleyways and his mind obscured their angles and lengths to disorient him—the panic of an animal trapped by a predator. For a predator prowled into the spotlights, its black- and purple-striped fur provoking gasps from the spectators.

Casimir was more disturbed by the fact that the tiger's violet eyes cut through the entirety of the crowd to settle acutely on Aethelred.

"This's gotta be a hallucination—tell me I'm hallucinating."

"Not hallucinating," Aethelred choked out.

"Then tell me that tiger's your friend," Casimir hissed as the tiger crept around the ring to position itself between its masters.

"The tiger I befriended was blue, not *purple*!"

"Oh—*oh*, it was *blue*? Well, that's normal," Casimir said with heavy sarcasm. His vision darted toward the exit, where two more clowns had joined their comrades on guard duty. They each held patterned juggler's clubs now, and despite the smiles painted on their faces, they oozed malevolence.

At the center of the tent, the psychics beamed delightedly at the audience's awe before raising their ringed fingers to silence the murmurs. "Hypnosia is not an ordinary tigress!" the younger woman declared. "She has been granted special abilities!"

"Indeed, she has!" the older woman chimed in, her crinkly voice echoing through the tent. "Hypnosia will select one lucky person from the crowd to *hypnotize*!"

Some inhaled sharply, some laughed anxiously, and some, like Casimir and Aethelred, sat utterly paralyzed, especially when the tigress leapt beyond the ring to ascend the bleachers.

Casimir wasn't surprised the beast chose them; surely that had been the psychics' design. Still, he found himself unable to move, unable to use even his mind as a defense when the predator halted before Aethelred and pinned him with those glowing eyes.

The animal's scent was oddly pleasant, a calming blend of lavender and vanilla. Casimir would have expected a wild creature to reek, but the psychics had groomed this tigress into something unnatural. Perhaps they'd extracted some other unfortunate kid's blood and fed it to Hypnosia when she was a cub—if the transferring of powers via blood was even possible. He'd have to ask Angor and Olalla if he didn't die in this tent of a heart attack first.

"Hypnosia has chosen her victim!" The elder psychic's tone was one of merry theatrics, but Casimir knew this wasn't an act. These psychos would find a way to let the tigress devour Aethelred and convince the witnesses it was all an illusion.

As the beast's purple irises began spinning like a whirlpool, Aethelred became transfixed in her gaze, immune to Casimir's nudges. This was his fault—Aethelred was about to fall into the clutches of two blood-thirsty maniacs and the blame rested solely on Casimir's shoulders. He tried weaving his hallucinations into the tigress's mind, but her fortified brain resisted. Besides, even if he found the strength to infiltrate her barriers, what the hell would he show her? Nothing his brain could conjure would scare a *tiger*.

"Rise, chosen one!" the young psychic called from below. In the clutches of the creature's hypnosis, Aethelred stood, face devoid of its typical apprehension.

"Fuck this," Casimir grumbled, shoving the red-haired boy aside. The family on the other side of the aisle yelped when he landed in their laps, but Casimir didn't glimpse their outrage. He'd assumed Aethelred's spot, standing before the tigress, his vision locked on the entrancing pools of her eyes.

The last thing he heard was Aethelred's appalled, "No!" before his mind sunk into a world of blurry violet.

12

Deafening Darkness

Olalla and Angor spent the remainder of their time at the roller rink tripping anyone within range. They had to resort to using their Affinities after too many eyes began watching their feet, and their game quickly became a competition of who could assail more victims. Once they'd felled everyone—and fallen quite a few times themselves—they decided to return their skates and journey back to Hastings Street.

After Olalla tied her sneakers and Angor secured his loafers, they hobbled through the exit, both wobbly from an hour of physical and mental exertion. In her exhaustion, she collapsed against the front steps' railing when he merely tapped her arm.

"I've discovered why Aethelred feared going out tonight." Angor nodded toward the fliers tacked on either side of the front doors. Most were for local businesses, but one stood out with vibrant colors and depictions of elephants, acrobats, and clowns.

"*The Wickedly Wicked Cirque,*" she read. "That's not sketchy at all."

"It's at the park tonight," Angor said, almost absently.

"He's probably facing an internal panic attack. I hope Casimir's keeping him company."

"That's a cruel thing to wish upon our poor Aethelred." The statement was meant to be a joke, but she did worry for their innocent friend's mental health. His anxiety had lessened over the months—an improvement credited mostly to his friendship with Casimir—but Olalla knew the hallucinator could alleviate one's stress as easily as he could induce it.

To prolong their devious streak, they *persuaded* two preppy girls to forfeit their bikes. Angor had suggested they call Casimir via payphone, but Olalla had effortlessly convinced him that stealing was more convenient. She hadn't even had to use her Affinity on him.

Thirty minutes later, they rode their sparkly pink bicycles into the darkened trailer park. Rock music blared from the blue house, as always, and flashing television lights illuminated the windows of the Cosmoses' home, as usual. Blackness filled Angor's windows, likely because Aethelred had already gone to sleep and Casimir didn't need light to smoke and draw hideous depictions on the walls.

The two discarded their stolen bikes near the front door. Olalla paused for a moment, assessing the predicament that's existence she'd previously denied: their *relationship*. Perhaps they had gone on their first real date...or perhaps Angor had taken her proposal as a jest between two friends, not a sincere inquiry from a potential romantic interest. Although they'd enjoyed their time at the roller rink, she detected a disconnect between them, a difference in their values gnawing at the string between their consciousnesses.

So many months she'd spent trying to impress him—now his disapproval over her treatment of William dredged up an unfamiliar shame that stirred anger in her core. The rational option was to confront him about their disagreement, but to what end? Angor possessed an admirable amount of ambition, but he often lacked the aggression to attain his goals. His methods were passive, patient; he would never understand Olalla's cutthroat techniques, nor her desire to utterly eviscerate her enemies.

"Goodnight, Periculy," she said, civil but terse. When she turned to trek toward the den of her demons, his thin hand grasped her wrist. Though she halted, she didn't pivot to face him. Her gaze remained focused on the Stromers' mobile home as she attempted to wrangle her pathetic emotions.

"You don't have to," his soft voice sounded from behind her.

"I do," she gritted out.

"You're sixteen now—you can emancipate. You know none of us will let them hurt you. I know Aethelred cares for you, and Casimir at least respects you. If he didn't, I suspect that by now he would have tried to seduce me into whatever romance he and Aethelred have going on."

Olalla snorted—then considered he might have actually been serious. Fractionally, she rotated her head in his direction. "Does that mean you're *mine*?"

He dropped her wrist as if disgusted by the idea, but she refused to fully glimpse his expression. "You and I are the same."

"Yes," she admitted, "and I never wish to be owned."

"Then there's your answer."

Finally, she succumbed to facing him. Disgust was not evident in his features; if anything, he seemed open—hopeful. If their brains operated on the same wavelength, he felt as ambivalent about the possibility of their romance as she did, but he still thought about it. He still dreamed about what it would be like to grab not only her wrist but her waist, her head, her lips, her heart.

And he was also aware of the problem: Olalla might not have a heart. Possibly she had not been born with one, or possibly it had shriveled at such a young age that she couldn't conceive what it meant to be human. The difference in their values was that she did not have any beyond her own self interest, and that was what would sever the thread between them.

Despite that fact, the boys had summoned qualities in Olalla that she had locked in an impenetrable casket: loyalty, which had once tethered her fiercely to Artemis; the need for companionship, which her sister's betrayal had shattered. She had learned to depend on the boys, and they had learned to depend on her. If Angor said he would protect her, he would, not because he wanted anything from her but because he cared for her beyond what her friendship might gain him. Until now, she hadn't realized it, but she cared for him beyond the promise of their shared aspirations, too.

"I'm not like you," she whispered, avoiding his eyes. "I can't walk away from my problems, and I can't let them walk away from me. I can't *forgive*, and I'll definitely never *forget*. My mother and Artemis still…own me. They'll always be reminders of what I once was—weak and powerless. If I leave…if I don't face them now…they'll come back again and again, as physical or metaphorical barriers. I can't…"

She ran a hand through her hair, frustrated with the ability she'd spent months harnessing yet often felt like she had no control over. For brief instances, she could compel her mother or Artemis, but their brains would never belong to her in the way hers had developed to belong to them.

Angor's eyes flickered toward her mossy home and

hardened with determination. "Let's end the war tonight, then—together."

Olalla had no idea what she would say to her mother to put an end to their cold war; she didn't even know if her mother would entertain a conversation. If she wasn't cooing over Artemis and William or berating Olalla's life choices, she locked herself in her bedroom and refused to be a parent. The mere thought of the woman aggravated Olalla to a point of mental turbulence too intense for her Affinity to function.

Angor would be with her, though; he would anchor her to the objective.

"Okay," she said lamely before leading him to her family's home. He matched her pace, striding with purpose. The expression he wore deemed anyone who disagreed with him an utter fool, which was unfortunate, considering Olalla typically went out of her way to disagree with him. For him, she probably was a fool.

The smell of alcohol hit their nostrils the moment they stepped through the front doorway. Angor scrunched his nose as if he hadn't dwelled in the same stench for sixteen years. Olalla supposed his immunity to it had vanished; his house now smelled of Casimir's cigarette smoke and Aethelred's vegetable casserole since walnuts didn't have a scent. She'd never imagined loving cigarettes or vegetables, but the sight of her father passed out drunk on the couch was far less preferable to Aethelred clumsily cooking or Casimir smoking in the most obnoxious fashion possible.

With the television set on the highest volume, Olalla might not have heard her mother rummaging through the refrigerator if she hadn't snapped, "You're home past curfew" without glancing over her shoulder. Judging by the tone, she knew which daughter she spoke to.

Scanning the area, Olalla noticed the door to her room was open, revealing her sister's absence. "Artemis isn't here, either."

"Your sister is out with her friends. She *asked*, unlike—" The woman cut herself short when she spun and spotted Angor. Her face was dark with only the dim stove light at her back, but when the television brightened enough to illuminate her features, they were twisted with ire. "This is the devil Artemis always talks about, isn't it?"

Angor, ever smooth, replied with a cordial, "It's likely she was referring to one of our other friends—or perhaps several of our other friends. Aethelred looks the part, but Casimir and Ephraim both possess the qualities."

Her nostrils flared, magnifying her brutish idiocy. "You aren't welcome under our roof."

Olalla was tempted to snarl, but Angor's fingers brushed against hers, reminding her to stay calm. After a deep breath, she managed, "Yes, Mother, *our* roof. I live here, too, and I invited him. Don't worry—we won't be here long. We only need to collect my belongings."

Suspicion replaced her mother's wrath. "Collect your belongings? Where the hell do you think you're going?"

Olalla could have used her Affinity to prevent the inevitable screaming argument, but would that be a true victory? Her mother had to accept her departure with a conviction that wouldn't blow away in the wind of her absence.

"I'm moving out," she declared, shoulders squared. "It's clear I'm unwanted here. This will be easier for all of us."

"*Easier*? Your rent is the only reason we can afford to live in this hovel!"

Olalla smiled with all the coldness in her core. "Have

Artemis contribute. She's the reason you decided to move here in the first place."

"You act this way in front of your friends, do you? Disgraceful," her mother scoffed before resuming her search through the fridge.

"At least I don't act like you."

The woman's hand curled around the fridge door's handle, knuckles whitening. "Go to your room, you ungrateful brat. And *you*," she sneered at Angor, "leave before I call the cops."

He leaned against the doorframe and crossed his ankles. "The cops will have little effect on this situation."

Her dark eyes narrowed. "Is that a threat?"

"Do you feel threatened?"

Angor must have uttered the question a bit too maniacally, because in one swift motion, the woman reached into the fridge and threw something at them. Olalla didn't realize what it was until the plate shattered at Angor's feet, the ceramic remnants littered with slices of pepperoni and cheese.

His pink eyes slid from the failed attack to the attacker. "Casimir will be displeased to know you've wasted this."

Olalla tilted her head back and forth in consideration. "He'll probably eat it even if it's been on the floor."

"But if it's been in your mother's hands?"

"Mm, you're right—probably not."

Her mother responded to this insult in the only way she knew how: by throwing *food* at them. Loaves of bread, bottles of condiments, the leftover tacos Artemis had cooked the night before but refused to let Olalla eat—it all flew toward them in uncoordinated arcs. Most hit the wall or the floor. Only an apple managed to pelt Olalla, and it was so rotten she barely felt it.

Angor, still lounging against the doorframe, snorted when ketchup hit the door and painted it with a streak of red. "This is really what we're doing—a food fight?"

"I thought you were short on money, Mother," Olalla taunted as she retrieved a bag of bread and surveyed it for mold. If it wasn't stale, she'd keep it. "And now you're wasting all this food? How brainless of you—although, I suppose everything you do is brainless. Maybe that's why I've never been able to fully control your mind: you don't have one."

The fridge was barren now, but her mother's rage wasn't appeased. Through her seething breaths, she didn't appear to have heard Olalla's jab at all. She scoured the metal box for more food, and when she found none, she shifted her attention to the counter and grabbed the first object in sight: a chef's knife.

If this house only belonged to her parents, Olalla wouldn't have been concerned; neither of them cooked, and the knife would have been as dull now as the day they'd bought it. Artemis sharpened the knife religiously, though—she liked everything to be perfectly effective, and because of her diligence, the blade would effortlessly cut meat, including human meat.

"Get...*out*," the woman panted, aiming the tip in Angor's direction. She stood far enough that he wasn't in immediate danger, but he still straightened and braced his body for a fight.

"You're not going to use that," Olalla said, but she didn't lace the words with her Affinity. Part of her wanted to see if she had the strength to handle this situation without her supernatural ability. A bigger part of her was afraid her supernatural ability wouldn't work and her worst fear would be actualized: she would have no control, nor a backup plan of control.

"Should we ensure she doesn't?" Angor muttered, eyeing the knife.

Before Olalla could answer, her mother lifted the blade higher, but not more than one step was taken before the weapon dropped from her hand, clattering to the floor.

She stared at her palm, face contorted in pain. Angor's expression tightened as he prepared to use his power again, but Olalla held up a hand to halt him.

"Let me do this," she hissed in annoyance. She didn't want him to see her fail—she didn't want to see *herself* fail—but her mother's thoughts were too frantic to catch, like a fish bolting through murky waters. Olalla watched the woman crouch to seize the knife once more, and she knew the time for her backup plan had arrived. "You want to let me leave," she said, emphasizing each word with the persuasion of her Affinity. "I'll never be your problem again. Artemis will be your only child, like you've always wanted."

She dug into every meadow of her mother's mind and filled them each with the cement of this belief, but none would harden. The woman's deranged thoughts burned all invading ideas to ash.

"It's not my fault," her mother whispered and then, louder, shouted, "It's not my fault they died!"

Instinctively, Olalla and Angor shared a puzzled look. In the living room, her father coughed and stirred on the couch but didn't rouse.

"Who?" Olalla asked, eyes darting toward her bedroom, wondering if the darkness hid bodies. She couldn't imagine her mother had murdered precious Artemis or William, but in this crazed state, the woman might commit any kind of atrocity.

"You know who." Her mother retrieved the knife, lips curling in feral resentment. "My sisters—the one whose deaths you blamed me for! If I hadn't brought home the flu virus, they never would have died, you always said."

"What is she talking about?" Angor questioned through the side of his mouth.

"Her sisters—my aunts," Olalla murmured, raking her recollection for any relevant information. "They died of the flu when they were young. She's never spoken about it, though—I only know because my father once mentioned it…before his alcoholism progressed."

"It wasn't my fault!" her mother screamed. Olalla had not heard that pitch since she was young—since before she'd begun to stave off her mother's violence. The memories that tone dredged up were not pleasant.

"If I agree," Olalla said through her budding headache, "can we end this, please?"

With a guttural cry, the woman charged through the tiny kitchen, slamming her daughter into the food-splattered wall. The bag of bread fell from Olalla's hand, and she barely processed what had happened before metal nipped at the base of her throat.

"I didn't kill them, but I should have killed you," her mother hissed, breath hot on Olalla's face. She didn't squirm under the threatening hold, but her blood rushed through her veins at a pace far beyond her control.

Beside her, Angor's tension and shock wafted at a palpable frequency. "Can I intervene now?"

"No," Olalla breathed, refusing to break eye contact with her mother. Fiery rage pulsed from the woman's bottomless irises. Olalla had always respected her own insanity, but her mother's was of an entirely new realm. How was she to rationalize with such madness? She had stopped her mother's abuse in the past, but then the weapon had been fists, not a giant *knife*. Even thwarting the slaps had drained all her mental energy.

She'd tamed the woman as much as one could tame a wild bull; in the end, she was no match for those vicious horns.

What bothered her about this scenario was that the aggression wasn't actually aimed at *her*. She had always expected to die at her mother's hand, probably over something silly that Artemis had blamed on her, but she didn't like the thought of dying in the place of someone whose identity she didn't even know.

"Who do you think I am?" she demanded, moving her throat as little as possible. At that question, her mother blinked and then balked, her newfound focus prompting her grip to slacken.

"You...look just like her..."

"*Who?*"

Perhaps Olalla had spoken too harshly, because her mother pressed the blade harder again, this time breaking flesh. "My *mother*. You've always looked like her, and you've always acted like her, too—cold, selfish, manipulative."

Despite the tang of her own blood in her nostrils, Olalla smirked. "It must run in the family."

The knife trembled. Until now, she had assumed her mother never gave a second thought to her innate belligerence, but now she understood her mother didn't *want* to hit her; she *wanted* to suppress her fears and demons in the same way Olalla had always wanted to suppress her fears and demons. Without the evolution Olalla's genetics had granted her, Dimitra Cosmos had resorted to physical domination.

Olalla did not like to think what she might have resorted to had her Affinity never developed.

"I can't let you leave here, can I?" her mother whispered, voice quaking as tears spilled down her cheeks. "This won't end tonight—you'll return here to ruin me once you have the means."

"Funny," Olalla said tonelessly. "I thought the same about you."

The knife bit deeper, but the alarm had diffused from Olalla's awareness. She let the coolness of the metal fuel the frozen atoms of her soul.

"You're right," the woman croaked, the words nearly unintelligible. "I have always wanted Artemis to be my only daughter."

This did not surprise Olalla, nor did it affect her. She felt like an actress in a play with a shittily written script. Her voice lacked inflection as she recited, "Too bad I don't have an Affinity for granting wishes."

Bemusement flashed over her mother's face, and Olalla used that moment of uncertainty to snake into the simplistic maze of her mind. With far less exertion than her younger self had employed, Olalla compelled her mother to cease the assault. Pacified, the woman stepped backward and stared blankly at the wall, a robot awaiting commands.

And oh, did Olalla have commands.

As Angor loosed a breath of relief over a conflict averted, Olalla convinced her mother to change the angle of the knife. The woman didn't notice until the tip plunged into the right illiac region of her abdomen.

"Olalla," Angor gasped, probably without meaning to.

She didn't hear him; her mind pictured the diagrams of anatomy they'd studied over the months, and she frowned.

"That won't do quite enough damage," she concluded, even as her mother choked out a petrified cough at the blood staining her pale blue blouse. If Olalla was lucky, the knife had punctured her mother's large intestine, but still, that could be mended if Angor decided to virtuously call an ambulance.

Again, she ordered, this time forcing the blade into the right hypochondrium quadrant. In a state of shock, her mother's aim was sloppy, and she'd likely further wounded her large intestine instead of her liver.

Again. Her mother yelped when the knife slid into the left hypochondrium, possibly slicing her stomach in half.

"Have fun eating Artemis's perfect food now," Olalla sneered, but the taunt fell on deaf ears. The tears had stopped flowing from her mother's eyes, but the blood gushed in waterfalls of red, pooling on the linoleum at their feet.

"*Again*," Olalla commanded aloud, blowing this one like a kiss. The final stab perforated the epigastric region, sinking in and then up to slice the vital organs beneath her sternum, piercing her heart.

For her last conscious act, Olalla made her mother yank the knife from her chest, allowing the blood to leak from all four crevices. The weapon remained in her hand even when she collapsed—Olalla ensured it. There could be no question this was a suicide when the cops inevitably arrived.

A few silent moments passed, in which only the faint sounds of the television wove through the air. The woman's chest stopped heaving, and her blood stopped gushing, but Olalla couldn't believe it was real—she couldn't believe her mother was dead.

With staggering steps, she approached the body and dropped to her knees beside it. The bruises from roller skating shot pain through her legs, and the thick pool of blood seeped into her jeans, but physical sensation lay outside her current comprehension. Her mother's stern, unyielding face was now frozen in horror, eyes staring absently into a world she no longer inhabited.

Tentatively, Olalla ran her fingers over the clean slices in the corpse's abdomen, hands trembling at the reality of what she had done. *She* had done this. She'd killed her mother.

For the first time she could recall, her eyes burned with tears. One after another, they dripped off her cheeks, mixing with the blood on the floor, the blood on her hands. Distantly, she was aware of Angor lowering to his knees beside her, drenching his favorite khakis in blood. He didn't touch her, didn't comfort her. He was probably calculating the best way to subdue her before she decided to kill all witnesses.

The thought dragged a laugh up her throat. She wouldn't kill Angor—she would never kill Angor. Even if he called the police, she wouldn't have the strength to kill him. He was the reason she'd had the strength to do *this*, after all. He was the reason that, after years of suffering under her mother's hand, she had finally ended the predicament.

She had also ended a life. It should have bothered her— the human part of her acknowledged that—yet it didn't in the slightest. She would do it again without hesitation. She would kill every person who hurt her, every person who stepped in her way, and she would laugh like she was laughing now.

The joy was so foreign it was almost painful, like a ball of gnarled thorns expanding in her thoracic cavity. She had never laughed this hard or this long. The cackles poured from her mouth like the blood had poured from her mother's wounds. Dimitra Cosmos had died of exsanguination, and Olalla Cosmos would die of debilitating laughter. Her immune system had never equipped her with the antibodies to ward off such invasive ecstasy.

"I've...always wanted to do that," she managed through heavy breaths. "I just imagined *I'd* be the one holding the knife. This method presented much less resistance." When no answer came, she curbed her emotions and faced Angor. He wouldn't even look at her; all of his focus lay on the slowly cooling corpse. She tried to gauge his expression, but as usual, his slightly pensive face was unreadable. "Say something, Periculy."

His pink eyebrows twitched toward one another. "I...don't..."

"Tell me I'm an abomination—a monster. Tell me you're appalled."

"I...don't think I am," he said, each word meticulously spoken. His head slanted in her direction, eyes squinted in rumination. "I'm sick, remember? You've ended the conflict in a way that cancels out all future possibilities of the conflict resurfacing. I understand your relief—your satisfaction. A mirror to my own after my first kill."

"Your first? Are there others you haven't told me about?" she asked, lips quirking to one side. She hated how much she needed his approval, but she loved having it—loved that he hadn't stormed out in revulsion or deemed her unfit for existence. She considered that if she loved anyone—if she *could* love anyone—it would be him.

"Well, I'd say I was an accomplice in this one," he mused in that cocky yet sophisticated way of his.

"Don't try to take the credit," she admonished, playfully

backhanding his arm. Blood smeared on his white sleeve, but he didn't even glance at it. His vision fixed on her face, scanning her wet eyelashes, her tear-stained cheeks, her stupidly grinning lips. The disconnect evaporated, allowing the string between them to tighten until the pull was too strong to resist.

Without meaning to, Olalla leaned toward him, pausing only when their shoulders touched. She had been this close to him physically but never this close to him mentally, morally, emotionally. She had not thought she possessed emotions like these—the kinds that made her want to lose control.

You want to kiss Olalla, she projected, spinning that belief until it coated even the most automatic and visceral parts of his brain in a web of longing. His face inched toward hers, eyelids fluttering shut, until their lips brushed.

It wasn't quite a kiss; it lacked the passion she'd seen between others. She feared her intimacy with Angor would be as mechanical as her kissing practice on Michael—a side effect of her Affinity—but then she realized the restraint was deliberate. Angor had stopped with their lips barely touching so he could whisper, "You don't have to tell me I want to" before consuming her bemusedly parted lips with his.

The moment their mouths melded, Olalla relinquished all self-control, giving free reign to her hands. One gripped his face, printing a bloody palm on his cheek, and the other dug into his hair, pulling at the absurdly long, absurdly *soft* locks. He cupped the back of her neck in return, his thumb caressing her ear in a way that shot heat through her core. She wanted to push him into the puddle of her mother's congealing blood, soak him in her sins, and then devour every inch of him.

That unorthodox fantasy died when the door opened

behind her and a wail shook the cracking foundation of the Cosmos house.

First Olalla's attention snagged on the living room, where her father had finally jolted out of sleep. Then she followed his bleary gaze to the front doorway, where Artemis and William stood, eyes protruding above the hands shielding their fallen jaws.

Olalla had gone from victor to villain in a matter of seconds, and she wasn't sure which of her new opponents to address first.

Luckily, Angor recovered quicker, jumping to his feet and subduing Olalla's gradually rising father with a dose of pain to his legs. He crumpled into the couch once more, moaning and oblivious, as always.

"What did you *do*?" Artemis cried, not at Angor but at Olalla. The girl's eyes had not left their mother's supine body, framed in glittering red.

Containing her agitation, Olalla indicated toward the corpse with a blood-stained hand. "She killed herself—can't you see?"

"You—*murderer*! You aren't even human," she concluded as she watched Olalla's smile grow. "You're unnatural."

The younger Cosmos sister stood and tapped a bloody finger to her lower lip. "No, I'm *supernatural*."

William convulsed like he might vomit or faint. Sadly, Olalla didn't witness him do either before his girlfriend lunged, tackling her to the ground.

Though blood splattered Artemis's face at the impact, it didn't deter her from clawing any inch of her sister's exposed skin. This was not at all how Olalla had imagined rolling in her mother's blood, but with Artemis yanking chunks of her hair out, she couldn't concentrate well enough to end the fight mentally.

Instead, she relied on physical instincts: a knee to her sister's side, spit in her sister's face, thumbs threatening to gouge her sister's eyes. None of the moves were very successful, but neither were Artemis's.

After numerous fruitless counters and minutes of uncoordinated grappling, Olalla gained the momentum to roll atop her sister, claiming the dominant position. From here, she could have easily pummeled Artemis's face or retrieved the bloody chef's knife to end this conflict as brutally as the last, but...that wasn't true, was it? She *couldn't* easily end Artemis's life, a fact which added new layers to their already oversized dilemma.

For a while, she'd hoped things might return to the way they once had been: Olalla and Artemis, a team. But her sister—despite functioning on a different wavelength—was of the same breed, the breed that didn't forgive or forget. The only way to end this was death.

Or forgetting.

Olalla stared down at her sister, remembering all the days they'd played as children, all the nights they'd danced together in their room, all the times they'd stuck up for each other. Mostly, Olalla had been the one to defend Artemis, but she'd never regretted it, even now. She would have to make her sister forget all of it; she would have to weave a tightly knit blanket over the very existence of herself in Artemis's mind. Because if her sister pulled one stray thread in that cover, the entire truth would unravel.

The crafting of this mental block required such precision that Olalla figured it might take as much time as knitting an actual blanket. She wasn't sure for how long she stayed there, pinning her sister down, resculpting her mind. At some point, her eyes drifted closed, and when she opened them, Artemis's face and body had slackened, her chest rising and falling in peaceful sleep. The rewiring of her cognizance had apparently been too much for her conscious brain to handle.

"Thanks," Angor's voice sounded when Olalla finally attuned her mind to the outside world. Standing, she spun and found him leaning against the kitchen counter, one set of fingers placing the phone on the receiver and the other undulating in open air. She realized why when a second noise hit her ears: William groaning as he writhed on the ground.

"Oh, good, you're finished." Angor pushed away from the counter and stopped creepily twirling his hand, but William didn't stop moaning.

Olalla eyed the telephone warily. "Did you call the cops?"

"Ephraim," he said, not even offended that she'd assumed the worst of him.

"Why?"

Angor arched an eyebrow at the crime scene between them. "We need a car."

"Why wouldn't we just use Casimir's?"

At that, he looked genuinely befuddled. "Didn't you notice Casimir's car wasn't parked in front of my house? They must have gone out somewhere."

Olalla had not noticed that. She'd been too consumed with dread. Now, that dread seemed silly; she'd curtailed the problem with grace. Keeping that confidence in mind, she crossed the room to thrashing William and set to work on his mind. Not only was his consciousness easier to mold, but it required less molding. In less than two minutes, Olalla had tampered with his every memory of the Cosmoses to make him believe what he needed to believe.

Still, between the reconfiguring of his brain, the intensity of Angor's pain Affinity, and the trauma of witnessing a dead body, William's feeble brain shut down, succumbing him to the same peaceful sleep as Artemis.

That left only her father to deal with. For him, she would merely alter a few things. Any authorities would assume his claims to be the crazed ramblings of a deranged alcoholic, anyway.

"What reality did you plant in them?" Angor asked once she'd finished.

Olalla strolled toward the kitchen, careful not to leave bloody handprints on the counter as she rested against it. "Artemis Cosmos never had a sister, and her mother was always suicidal. She'll remember this scene"—she motioned toward the corpse—"but not as it actually happened. When she wakes, she'll want to get far away from this place. She and William will settle somewhere across the country and hopefully become low lives since neither acquired a proper high school diploma."

Angor pressed his lips together before saying, "That's actually quite generous of you. I'd expected something…crueler."

Olalla shrugged but refused to answer the implied question: *why*? *Why* was she letting Artemis live? Why didn't she just off her whole damn family?

"I'll write a suicide note," she told him as she rinsed her hands in the sink, "since my father will probably call the police when he wakes in the morning. I should practice my 'emotional daughter' act in case they want to interrogate me… You'll be my alibi, won't you?"

"Of course," he agreed without hesitation. She granted him a brief, coy smile, still incredulous that he hadn't fled the premises at the first drop of blood.

As she constructed her mother's suicide note, Angor bound Artemis's and William's hands and feet. Normally, one remained unconscious for only a few seconds or minutes before rousing, but they had no idea what to expect with this unnaturally induced sleep. As a precaution, he also gagged them. Olalla had never seen a more beautiful sight.

"Whoa," was what Ephraim blurted when he stepped through the open doorway. His lime green eyes popped as if he needed more than the pupils and irises to fully see.

"Get over it, Mayer," Olalla said as she slapped the suicide note onto the counter. Her hands were still red, but the note had remained mercifully stain-free. She frowned at the marks her scuffle with Artemis had left on the floor, clear signs that someone other than her father had been here. "We need you to throw these two in your trunk."

His jaw slackened when she nodded toward the gagged and bound couple that he hadn't noticed beyond the death and blood. "You should have told me you wanted to murder your mom. One of my guns would've been much less bloody than this mess. Good luck cleaning the linoleum."

"Too bad we don't know anyone with a cleaning Affinity," Angor mumbled, lips pursing at his ruined clothes.

"Affinity?" Ephraim echoed.

"We vetoed the term superneutrals," Angor informed him. "Apologies."

The green-haired boy blew out a sigh as if that slight was as egregious as the murder. Still, he helped Angor carry Artemis and William out to his car and deposit them in the trunk.

Olalla lingered in the house a moment, knowing she would never willingly return. Perhaps the authorities would drag her here to witness the crime, but otherwise, she would avoid it. Her family, her childhood, even her belongings she'd come to retrieve—none of it would weigh her down any longer. Like Angor had become a new man in his mother's absence, Olalla would become a new woman now. These people had controlled her, but never again. She would control her own destiny, even if it meant controlling everyone and everything else in the process.

"I keep a body bag in my car." Olalla startled at the voice. She hadn't noticed Ephraim appear in the doorway beside her to survey the corpse contemplatively. "Just in case."

"Where would you put it—the body?"

"There's an incinerator in one of my dad's labs. No one will notice since it always smells like shit in there."

"I'm glad Casimir's never around when you mention these things," Angor said, materializing between them.

"Judging by this crime scene, Cosmos is the one we need to be cautious around," Ephraim joked. Angor snorted, but Olalla barely managed a smile.

"We'll leave her as she is," she decided, finally turning her back on her mother for the last time. "Better they think her death a suicide than suspect it was a murder."

Ephraim nodded in understanding, and Angor closed the door behind them before the three entered their getaway vehicle.

"Where *is* Casimir?" Ephraim asked as he started the car. "And his boyfriend?"

Angor shifted where he lay on the backseat. "They dropped us off at the roller rink but never came back, it seems."

"The roller rink? Did you go there to trip innocent children?"

"And adults," Olalla added, resting her head against the

passenger's window. "Although, I don't think *innocent* fits any grown person."

Ephraim gifted her with a wry smirk. "Clearly not."

As the car crept up bumpy Hastings Street, Angor fell off the backseat with uncharacteristic clumsiness. Olalla opened her mouth to tease him, but then his hand clapped her seat and she spotted his terrified expression in the rearview mirror.

"Oh *no*."

"What?" Olalla demanded as Ephraim slammed on the brakes.

"No, no, keep going—we need to keep going," he urged, and the driver rolled his eyes before continuing toward the main road. "I know exactly where the boys are."

Aethelred watched in horror as Casimir followed the hypnotic tiger down the steps toward the ring, his usual swagger reduced to robotic strides.

At the realization that the wrong boy had fallen into their trap, Gwen's face twisted in annoyance. As the younger of the two psychics, Gwen had always acted like Aethelred's mother, instructing him to eat his vegetables, brush his teeth, or wash his clothes, and then shooting him that same irritated look whenever his scattered brain forgot. Though she hadn't loved him like a mother would have, she had at least cared for him.

Agnes had cared for nothing except their rising greatness—their power.

Hate wasn't a word young Aethelred had comprehended,

but older Aethelred understood it was the clawing sensation in his gut when he gazed upon Agnes. Her partner's agitation had no effect on her; she grinned like a hungry snake emerging from a pile of sparkly fabrics. The manic delight was a direct result of witnessing Aethelred's dismay. His inability to conceal his emotions had revealed to them how much Casimir meant to him—how they could use the hypnotized boy against him.

Agnes's excitement spread to Gwen when the tiger and the boy stepped into the spotlight and Casimir's hood fell, revealing his unnaturally green hair.

"What a pleasant turn of events."

Agnes didn't speak into the microphone, but it was close enough to catch and magnify her words. The crowd murmured at Casimir's odd appearance, and one kid exclaimed, "I want green hair!"

The hallucinator probably would have shouted a cocky or profane comment at the child if he weren't in an utter trance. Hypnosia's stare had leached every quirk from his demeanor, leaving a blank, Casimir-shaped vessel behind.

It still *was* Casimir, though. Beyond the idle eyes, his mind remained, and Aethelred couldn't bear to watch the psychics circle him like two sharks waiting to chomp.

"When I snap my fingers, you'll bow to our lovely crowd!" Gwen proclaimed, and the spectators cheered as she gestured around the tent. Once the enthusiasm ebbed, she snapped, and Casimir sunk into a low, rigid bow that seemed inorganic to his typically languid limbs. Aethelred covered his mouth to stop himself from gagging, but even if he'd vomited, no one would have noticed; everyone was as transfixed on Casimir as he was on the tiger.

"When *I* snap my fingers," Agnes said, leaning so close

she almost kissed his ear, "you'll take Gwen in your arms and waltz around the ring!"

Without waiting for the audience's reaction, the old woman snapped her ringed fingers. An eerily fluid grace overtook Casimir's body as he lurched toward Gwen and trapped her in a perfect embrace. They spun along the perimeter of the ring, her skirt twirling and fanning over his drawing-defaced jeans.

Aethelred shook his head in an attempt to ward off his nausea. Bowing and dancing were docile tasks the psychics had strategically employed to accustom the crowd to the thought of a boy being unwillingly manipulated. Soon the commands would turn embarrassing, then cruel, then deadly.

This was Olalla's ability but *worse* because the manipulator was a *tiger*, and although Aethelred probably wouldn't have stood much of a chance against Olalla in a physical brawl, he *definitely* wouldn't stand a chance against a *tiger*.

When the waltz ceased, Gwen stumbled breathlessly into Agnes while Casimir resumed his spot before Hypnosia, standing, breathing, and staring as if he hadn't moved at all.

"This time," Gwen began once she'd stopped panting, "when I snap my fingers, you'll give our beautiful Agnes a kiss on the cheek!"

The spectators *aw*-ed as the boy planted a mechanical kiss on her wrinkly flesh. Aethelred cringed with his entire body. Casimir, if he'd retained any awareness, had to be internally retching at this point.

"Now that you've seen Hypnosia's talents," Agnes said, cheeks still flushed from her overdramatic reaction to the kiss, "we shall show you ours!"

"Oh no no no no," Aetherled moaned, squishing his face between his hands.

From his left, a kid's voice jeered, "What's wrong with you?"

He didn't even glance at the child as he covered his eyes. "*Everything.*"

"For our first mystical act, we must draw a drop of blood!" Agnes proclaimed, pulling a silver dagger from the many folds of her dress. The crowd *ooh*-ed as though she hadn't extracted a lethal weapon with which she planned to *cut* Casimir.

The thought yanked Aethelred from his immobilized state of panic. He jumped to his feet, voice carrying through the tent with a definitive, "*No!*"

Anticipation lulled into scornful whispers. Gwen's eyes protruded in genuine surprise, but Agnes's dropped jaw was an act. The malicious intent was clear in her eyes; she *wanted* Aethelred to intervene. If he descended to the ring, he would step right into her scheme, giving her *two* supernaturals on whom to perform her creepy blood ritual.

If Casimir could have spoken, he would've told Aethelred to *sit the hell down*, and he probably would've used a worse swear word, too. Interfering now would nullify Casimir's sacrifice; he'd *saved* Aethelred, and the best way to honor that would be to watch and do nothing.

Beside him, the child who'd mocked him scoffed and threw popcorn at his feet. "*Freak!*"

Rage trickled into Aethelred's blood, not because the word insulted him but because *freak* wasn't even the worst adjective the boy could have sneered. *Weak, fearful, pathetic*— any one of those would have accurately described Aethelred in this moment, letting Casimir suffer the fate that should have been his. The anger he felt now was a long and slowly brewed mixture of shame and self-loathing that he'd finally swallowed and couldn't stomach. He should have dealt with the problem of the psychics when he was ten. He should have told the ringleader the truth instead of running away. He should have revealed the entirety of his past to Casimir instead of hiding his cowardice.

Using his rare spurt of adrenaline, Aethelred stormed down the steps, grabbing the mocking boy's popcorn bucket on the way. The kid shouted in outrage, but Aethelred simply emptied the popcorn into his lap before plowing onward. With the empty cardboard bucket and a pointy plastic cotton candy stick he'd stolen from a small girl, he descended into the ring.

Agnes cocked her head and Gwen almost laughed when Aethelred placed the bucket on his head as a helmet and pointed the cotton candy stick as a sword. A few childish giggles flitted through the air, but no one complained about this interruption to the show. They probably assumed it was part of the act; Aethelred had always looked like he belonged in the circus, because he always *had* belonged in the circus.

"Do not draw his blood!" he commanded in the strongest voice he could muster. In his ears he sounded like a bratty child, and in their eyes he probably still looked like a meek ten-year-old.

Agnes, certainly, was not intimidated. "And why shouldn't we?" she challenged, angling the knife toward Casimir. Aethelred would have to dart past that weapon to grab him, and then he would have to contend with the swirly-eyed tiger. Either way, these crazy women would acquire blood, but Aethelred didn't really care as long as it was *his* blood, not Casimir's.

"Because it's me you want!" he declared, stepping into a fighting stance. "And I won't come quietly!"

As if on cue, the music's volume increased and Hypnosia prowled around Casimir to assess her new target. A few gasps sounded when the tiger exposed her teeth in a snarl, and Aethelred swore he peed his pants a little.

Still, he didn't falter—until a chuckle echoed from above.

The psychics whipped their heads upward in the same moment Aethelred did. On the metal beams sat a boy, legs swinging, lime green hair hidden beneath his backwards baseball cap.

"You should have joined the drama club, Certior! I hope your boyfriend's lucid enough to remember this."

Ironically, Aethelred had been hoping the entire time that Casimir would *not* remember this. This was the most ridiculous and brash thing he'd ever done. For once, he wouldn't have minded if someone called him a freak. The assessment would have been correct.

"What are you doing up there?" Aethelred called, nonplussed.

Instead of answering, Ephraim yelled, "Eat melons, motherfuckers!" before showering the tent in fruit.

He must have stationed them throughout the rafters, because they dropped from every corner. On the bleachers, softer fruits fell, like strawberries and grapes, but in the center ring, a torrent of cantaloupes and honeydew melons hailed.

Cheers erupted from the crowd, but the psychics shrieked and shielded their heads to protect from the boulder-like fruits. Though Aethelred's instinct was to flee, not one melon landed close to him, which he knew was Ephraim's design. He remained perfectly motionless until a watermelon slammed Gwen's head, startling him and knocking her unconscious.

"*Ohhh!*" Ephraim sang from above. "Bullseye!"

Aethelred found it impossible to share his enthusiasm when Agnes hadn't dropped the knife, nor had Hypnosia stopped pacing. As far as he'd seen, four melons had pelted the tiger without hindering her supple strides.

If Ephraim couldn't thwart the beast, Aethelred would have to. Her purple eyes continued to spin like whirlpools, and until they stopped, he doubted Casimir would snap out of the trance.

Aethelred sucked in a breath, wondering if he possessed even a fraction of the athleticism it would require to dodge a tiger's pounce. He'd just deduced the chances of success were slim when a hand grasped his shoulder.

Whirling, he arced his cardboard sword to stab his attacker. The tip bent on impact, but Angor didn't flinch at the blow.

"You look foolish," he said without actually looking at Aethelred. His pink eyes fixed on Agnes, who howled and released the knife to cradle her hand.

"He means you look adorable." Olalla winked before training her own focus on the psychic. With another howl, this one born from misery, she collapsed beside Gwen and sobbed into her shawl. "The classic *your friend is dead* trick. Works every time."

Aethelred wanted to spit out numerous questions, especially when he noticed they were both caked in *blood*—an ungodly amount of blood. A few scratches marred Olalla's face and arms, but neither seemed to have suffered major injuries.

"Let's get out of here," she said, nodding to the exit, now devoid of the creepy clowns.

"The t-tiger…hypnotized Casimir," Aethelred managed, pointing his crooked cardboard stick toward the center of the ring. The hallucinator stood there like a scarecrow amid a violent storm, and the animal circled him like a glacial hurricane, slow and taunting.

"That is a problem…" Angor tapped a finger to his chin twice before jolting as if electrically shocked. After rummaging through the pockets of his blood-stained khakis, he pulled out a handful of pepperoni. "Aha! Courtesy of your mother," he added to Olalla with a jump of his eyebrows.

She pursed her lips, unimpressed. "No offense, but I don't think that *tiger's* gonna give a shit about *pepperoni*."

"It's not for the tiger." Then, with Angor Periculy levels of sophisticated poise, he approached the creature holding only pepperoni as defense. The sight might have made Aethelred feel less pathetic about his own attempts if Angor didn't proceed to force the tiger to the ground with the sheer will of his mind.

"A hypnotic tiger," Olalla mused, watching impassively as Hypnosia jerked in pain. "How difficult would it be to bring it back to Hastings Street for testing?"

Aethelred didn't respond, for Angor had glided past the tiger to wave pepperoni in Casimir's face. The scent must have drawn him from the hypnosis, because his head shook violently before his green eyes honed on the greasy meat.

"Mayer," Angor prompted, and by only his surname, Ephraim knew to barrage the fallen tiger with as many fruits as he could produce. Preoccupied, the beast didn't notice the others scurry away, Olalla hauling Aethelred and Angor coaxing Casimir.

Not until they safely exited the ring was the hallucinator granted a handful of pepperoni. He inhaled it and demanded, "Why the hell did you have that?"

Shrugging, Angor opened the tent flap. "Figured I might

need a snack. Murder makes a person hungry."

Olalla elbowed him as they emerged into the cool nighttime air. "*I* did the murdering."

Casimir jabbed his thumb toward the pile of clowns not ten paces from the tent's entrance. "You killed the clowns?"

"We had a bit of a brawl," she replied breezily. "Then I made them all hit each other with their bats. I'm not sure how *none* were left standing. We didn't stick around to watch. Too busy saving your asses."

"Fucking felines," Casimir grunted, throwing a glare over his shoulder as they hurried across the park lawn. "Did you know that bitch, Cosmos—the tiger? Bet she's your long lost cousin. C'mon, Periculy, tell me humans and tigers were once part of the same species or some shit."

"Some actually believe humans and other mammals share significant DNA, but we won't know until the human genome has been sequenced. However, it's much more likely Olalla and the tiger suffered a similar event that forced their Affinities to evolve into—"

"Whoa, okay, you're throwing out way too many terms for me to follow. Come back when you have all the information and a condensed version for us simpletons." Green eyes slid sideways with that last comment. Even though Aethelred was relieved to know Casimir was unharmed and back in his right mind, he really wished the boy wouldn't look at him right now. They were *jogging*—or in Aethelred's case *stumbling*—and he hadn't had the wits to remove his popcorn bucket helmet. Casimir's whole body seemed to tremble with a steadily increasing build-up of derisive comments and barking laughter.

Upon reaching the Cadillac Seville, they piled into their usual spots, and in the front, the boys' shoulders bumped before they righted themselves in their respective seats. Aethelred was thankful their skin hadn't brushed in the process; he did not have the mental energy to relive that horrid experience through hypnotized eyes.

"What about Eph?" Casimir asked, checking his face in the rearview mirror. After wiping a splatter of watermelon from his cheek, he glanced at the backseat passengers.

"His car is here," Angor explained. "He'll catch up with us later. That was the plan—rendezvous at Hastings Street."

Casimir banged his curls against the headrest. "I hate when you speak French like we know what you're talking about."

"It means we'll meet up, Stromer. How do you know *rendezvous* is French but you don't know what it means?"

"I've been hypnotized tonight, Periculy. Can you keep the patronization to a minimum?" After shoving the keys into the ignition, Casimir paused and gave Angor another suspicious look through the mirror. "Why do you have a bloody handprint on your face?"

Aethelred had wondered the same, but now didn't seem the appropriate time to inquire. The circus show certainly would not continue after that fiasco, and soon the spectators would flood the parking lot, rendering their escape impossible.

He almost piped up until Angor wedged himself between the front seats to inspect his bloody cheek. "Do I? What a sentimental token of this night."

Olalla tugged him back to her side and rolled her eyes before resting her head on his shoulder.

Despite his previous urgency, Aethelred paused his panicked thoughts to share a long, confused glance with Casimir.

"That's new," the hallucinator noted.

"Oh, not that new. We all know Angor's been pining after me for months," Olalla droned sarcastically before shutting her eyes. "I had to kill my own mother to force a proclamation of love out of him."

Snorting, Casimir slapped his hand on the steering wheel and started the engine but then froze. "Hold on." His eyes darted to their blood-drenched knees, and he blanched. "No, you didn't—you killed your freakin' *mom*? We went on a circus date and you went on a murder date? Fuck. We should have done that." He scrunched his face at Aethelred, as if the direction of their "date" had been his fault. "We should have killed those bitches. At least we should have killed the tiger so it can't hypnotize anyone else."

Aethelred pressed his lips together. Maybe they *should* have killed them, but he was glad they hadn't. He didn't want to be a murderer; he didn't know what to think about sitting in the same vicinity as murderers.

Then again, he'd been rooming with a murderer for the past five years, and who knew how many people those psychics had killed in their *rituals*. As hard as he tried to maintain his innocence, the world was intent on corrupting him.

"So, are we on the run now?" Casimir asked, finally pulling out of the parking spot. "Do we need to flee the state?"

"No," Olalla sighed, "but I'm flattered you would for me. We framed it as a suicide."

Casimir coughed a laugh as they reached the park's exit, and he had to slam on the brakes to avoid colliding with a car whizzing down the main road. "You think the Queen of Righteousness is gonna believe that? I know you're powerful,

Cos, don't get me wrong—"

Angor cleared his throat. "Artemis and William are in your trunk."

Again, Casimir slammed on the brakes, this time halfway into the other side of the road. Luckily, the street was desolate, because he remained there for a solid minute, staring at the fields ahead.

"We'll probably take them over the Pennsylvania border if you're up for the drive," Angor added, oblivious to their shock. In his defense, Casimir and Aethelred were often overdramatic, and Aethelred hadn't really reacted to the knowledge of the bodies in the trunk, anyway. After the craziness at the circus and the casual confession that Olalla had murdered her mother, he'd become numb to everything.

"All right, sick," Casimir finally said, releasing the brake to press on the gas pedal. "I dig the idea of using Willy's car to deposit his corpse somewhere. Seems like a fun full-circle kinda deal. If anyone in this car tries to tell me there's some fucking literary device for that, I'll drive us all off a cliff."

Angor had already opened his mouth, but he snapped it closed at the threat. "They aren't dead. Olalla has decided they should start a new life elsewhere."

Casimir's eyebrows disappeared beneath his messy hair. "She *did*? What alternate universe did I wake up in?"

"Just focus on driving, Stromer," Olalla drawled, stretching to prop her legs atop Aethelred's seat. "I want them out of the state before the cops start investigating."

"All right, all right... How the hell'd you open my trunk, anyway? I thought I locked this thing."

Yawning, Angor tilted his head back. "I had a spare key made in the event that you lost yours."

"Fuck you for knowing me so well," Casimir barked, but

an exuberant grin had consumed his face. A moment of silence passed, and then he exploded with laughter, succumbing to complete hysteria.

Aethelred tried to keep himself rigid and vigilant, assuming he'd have to take the wheel at any second, but Casimir's unadulterated laughter elicited a degree of happiness he rarely let himself feel. Within a minute, his anxiety had crumbled into a fit of chortles that increased when his bucket helmet fell over his face and Casimir slapped the steering wheel until it honked.

"You guys are so *gay*," Olalla teased, tapping Aethelred's ear with her bloody sneakers.

"Only you would use a synonym for happy as an insult, Cosmos," Casimir returned through his dying chuckles. "You two are so *morose* back there. Lighten up, lovebirds. Your mom's gone, your mom's *dead*, and we just defeated Aethelred's psychic mothers and their freaking pet *tiger*. We're the winners!"

"I don't know." Olalla hummed and dropped her feet to the floor. "I think I regret it."

Angor didn't rub her arm or stroke her hair, but he did cast a sympathetic look on her, which was as much consolation as he would ever give anyone. "You shouldn't. She deserved it."

"No, not killing my mom—I mean sending Artemis away. I should have made her believe only the suicide so she could stay here." Angor's brow creased in concern when Olalla sat up and animatedly threw her hands in the air. "Who will we torment now?"

A wicked grin spread across his lips as he draped his arm over the seat behind her. "Whomever we like—or dislike, I should say."

Casimir started to announce they'd passed the Ohio-Pennsylvania border but paused after a glimpse of the couple snoozing in the backseat. They were hideous sleepers—Angor's mouth hanging open and drooling into Olalla's blood-crusted hair. Casimir supposed their relationship could be nothing other than dysfunctionally weird. They'd fallen in love in the throes of *matricide*, after all.

Smirking, he cast a discreet glance in Aethelred's direction. He was awake, red head leaning against the window, which he hadn't opened since Casimir hadn't extracted one cigarette in the past hour. The thought made him instinctively pull the pack from his pocket, but not in a normally needy way.

Their circus date—since that was, indeed, what Casimir had planned for it to be—had ended in a disastrous success. Yeah, he'd been hypnotized by a tiger and nearly chopped to ribbons by a deluded crone, but afterward Aethelred had *laughed* about it. He'd shed his skin of anxiety in an attempt to save Casimir, and even now, it hadn't regrown.

Of course Casimir's knight in shining armor would wear a fucking popcorn bucket helmet and run like a crippled lamb. If reality could become any stranger than his hallucinations, that was how.

Even stranger: the recollection of his hypnosis didn't faze him. Thinking of the tiger's giant maw or the crinkly witch's cheek on his lips didn't provoke the desire to light a stick—though, the latter did make him shudder. Serenity had characterized the entire trance, and maybe that was because those were the effects of hypnosis, but Casimir believed his tranquility had stemmed from the knowledge of Aethelred's safety. He wouldn't have given a shit about the psychics cutting him in half if it meant Aethelred remained untouched.

Which brought him back to his cigarettes. He turned the box in his hand, listlessly watching the empty highway ahead. Smoking wouldn't be an easy addiction to break, especially since Casimir had a naturally addictive personality, but there were better things to be addicted to, and he knew a certain something that would solve his problems rather than create more.

Releasing the wheel entirely, he cranked down the window.

Aethelred startled at the car drifting sideways and the wind flooding through the gap. "What are you doing?"

Casimir ignored him in favor of chucking his cigarettes out the window. They hit the pavement and disappeared from sight. "I don't need those anymore."

"*Tonight* made you recover from your paranoia?" he hissed upon realizing the other two were asleep in the back. "I've never felt so terrified in my life."

"Of course not," Casimir dismissed with an eye roll. "I just think I've found a better way to cope."

The innocent wrinkle of Aethelred's eyebrows solidified the decision Casimir should have made months ago. Abandoning his focus on the road, he leaned toward the passenger's seat to grip Aethelred's neck. "I crave you more than I crave cigarettes," he whispered onto his lips before plunging into them.

This wasn't like kissing that pansy in D.C., because this wasn't Casimir trying to figure out himself; this was Casimir learning *Aethelred*—learning which angles made him arch into the kiss, which position of Casimir's hand on his neck made him suck in a little gasp.

Unfortunately, there wasn't quite enough time for Casimir to study these details before the car drove off the road.

"God dammit—what are luxury cars for if the driver can't make out with his passenger and expect it to assume autopilot!" he griped while jerking the vehicle back onto the highway.

Aethelred slammed into his seat and choked out, "What are you doing!"

Casimir stomped on the brakes and parked the car in the middle of the road. "I don't know what I'm doing, but I know I wanna keep doing it," he said. Then he seized Aethelred's head with both hands and feasted on his face.

To Casimir's immense surprise, Aethelred didn't voice any inquiries after that, nor did he protest the illegal parking. Instead, he let Casimir explore his mouth and, after a few minutes, had the audacity to tentatively lace his fingers through pine green curls.

Not breaking lip contact, Casimir rose to climb into the passenger's seat when a cough sounded from behind. Reluctantly, he pulled away from Aethelred and fixed the wide-eyed couple with a scowl dark enough to nullify the fact that they were both murderers. "Yes, Periculy?"

"This is all very romantic," Angor croaked, still groggy from sleep, "but we do have two stowaways in the trunk."

"Yeah, and they're both gonna stay there a while longer," Casimir snapped before resuming his climb into Aethelred's lap.

Part 3

The Betrayer and The Betrayed

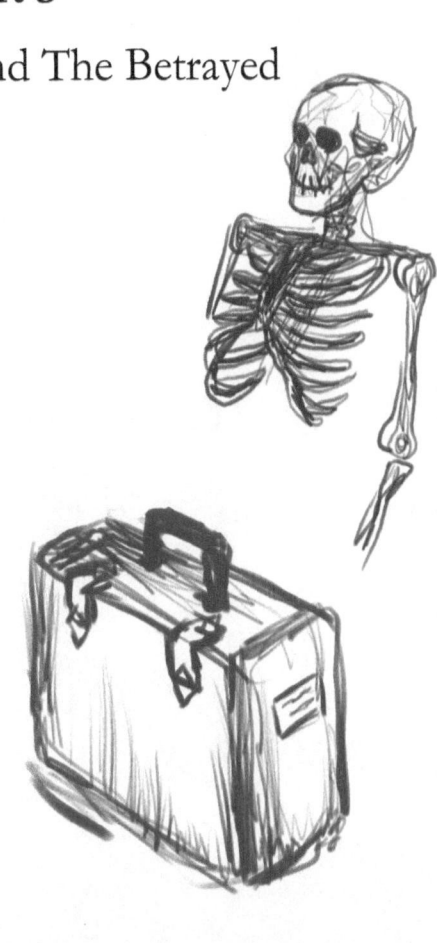

13

A Compound Fracture

The weird hair gang spent the next two years tormenting whomever they liked—or disliked.

Their victims mostly included teachers, police, and anyone who looked at them the wrong way. They never *murdered* anyone—other than those they'd already murdered—but their treatment of others wasn't exactly *humane*. At some point throughout their research and experimentation, Olalla had stopped considering other humans her equals—or perhaps she'd always thought that way because it was the objective truth. She was superior; all Affinities were.

When Olalla moved in with Angor, Casimir moved in with Aethelred, and the four became a true family overnight. At first, Angor insisted on giving Olalla her own room—his mother's former bedroom—while the three boys shared the other. That plan failed the first night when Angor retired to the room last, only to find the door locked.

"Get your own room!" Casimir yelled from within. "We're being gay in here!"

"No, we're not," followed Aethelred's exasperated voice. "I'm studying for the history exam."

"Like I said: *gay.*"

Angor didn't argue; he seemed content to sleep on the couch, cuddling his bowl of walnuts. For a week the pattern persisted, until one night he and Olalla fell asleep while reading a biology textbook in her bed. They woke in the morning with drool distorting the mitochondrion diagram, purple and pink hair tangled on the pillow.

Despite their mutual distress over a mitochondrion diagram gone to waste, they decided they didn't hate waking in the same bed. Thus began their slow acclimation to sharing, not just their physical space but their mental space. For two who had always been reserved, the easy exchange of thoughts and emotions took time, but within two years they'd adapted into more socially reliant creatures.

Over time, each member of the gang naturally assumed different responsibilities: Aethelred cooked delicious meals to the tune of Casimir heckling him from the armchair; Angor hoarded coupons to shop for groceries as if they couldn't acquire endless funds by altering a few thoughts or triggering a few nociceptors; Casimir cleaned any clutter or garbage, since it was always his; and Olalla—well, she didn't have a specific job other than to oversee everyone else's work. Some might have taken the term *bossy* as an insult, but whenever Casimir sneered it at her, she beamed with satisfaction.

The house was never a mess, no one ever yelled—beyond Casimir shouting vulgar compliments at Aethelred every time he walked into the living room—and pain was practically non-existent, partially due to Angor's Affinity but mostly due to the fact that none of them wished harm upon the others. Even Ephraim became like a weird cousin to them, showing up at the most random times to gift them with fruit baskets or show off his motorcycles or prompt Casimir to draw him new tattoo designs.

Through it all, Olalla almost started to understand the concept of love.

As for her blood relatives, her father was the only one she occasionally came in contact with. He lived alone in the mossy mobile home and received financial aid from the local church whose members also helped him with menial tasks. A few of the churchgoers once stopped by the Periculy house to see if one of its residents would like to check on Mr. Cosmos each night, as nice neighbors do. Olalla made them believe they were burning in hell.

After that Angor proclaimed himself the official door-opener and Casimir never drove past the church when she was in the car, lest she try to mentally attack them from afar. Olalla scoffed at how ridiculous the notion was—"What could I really do from that distance in the five seconds it takes to drive by?"—but in truth, she probably *would* have tried to mentally torment at least one of those assholes. Her father probably would have died from liver disease by now if they weren't so *nice*.

Dimitra Cosmos's *suicide* hadn't gained much press coverage, nor had the police conducted an investigation. Between the note and Olalla's sobbed testament to her mother's depression, they'd decided not to further upset the family by prolonging the process. Of course, they'd *wanted* to investigate until Olalla aligned their wants with her own. They'd also wanted to know what had happened to Artemis Cosmos until Olalla made them forget she existed.

If only she could erase her sister so easily from her own mind.

The question of Artemis's fate crept up on her at the most inopportune times: when she was taking a test and one of the football players walked by the classroom; when she was weaving through the hallways at school and saw a girl with a too-tight dark bun; when she was reading in the library and the word *unnatural* popped up on the page. Every time her whole body froze except her heart, which siphoned energy from the rest of her dormant cells to pound at an unhealthy rate.

She knew Angor noticed, but he never commented on her episodes. Surprisingly, *Aethelred* did.

"I know how you feel," he said one day when they returned from school to witness a pile of garbage outside the Cosmoses' house. Apparently, the churchgoers had helped her father clean out the girls' bedroom, for Artemis's notebooks and clothing lay among the trash bags. Due to a malfunction in her brain, Olalla stopped mid-stride and stared at the meaningless items until Aethelred appeared beside her, grimacing.

"You think I have feelings?" she joked, relaxing her posture. Angor would have played along for her sake, but the disconcertion didn't leave Aethelred's expression.

"I think about the circus often—too often." He sighed, red eyes fixed absently on the trash heap. "Sometimes the dodgeballs in PE make me think of the crystal balls. Sometimes your eyes remind me of the tiger's."

Olalla cocked her head to give him an admonishing look. "Red, you know I'd never use my Affinity on you."

"I know. We can't help what triggers thoughts in our minds, though… Well, you can, I suppose."

She chewed on the inside of her lip for a few moments before asking, "Do you want me to erase it—the circus? It'd make you happier."

"No, no, I wouldn't want that. It *would* make me happier,

but it wouldn't make me *me*."

Olalla pondered that for months. Though forgetting Artemis would have made her happier, it also would have made her naïve. She would trust anyone—she would depend on anyone. All the important lessons her sister had taught her about cynicism would disappear.

How altered was Artemis without any memory of her younger sister? Perhaps she was less spiteful—happy, even. Perhaps she was *dead*. After the incident, she'd never returned, and Olalla assumed she and William had started a life somewhere else, but it was possible their lives had ended entirely. She wasn't sure which alternative she preferred.

At first, she'd hoped the pair would degenerate into vagrants, but she knew ambition was sown into every one of her sister's genes. Artemis had likely weaseled her way into a prestigious college, not unlike how Olalla secured spots at an Ivy League school for herself and her friends.

The weird hair gang spent their last spring break driving along the east coast, interviewing at the most reputable educational institutions. Olalla and Angor impressed every person they spoke to, naturally, but Aethelred's awkwardness ruined his chances. After the first failed attempt, Olalla warped the interviewers' minds, subtly enough that Aethelred would never know he'd only gained admittance through her Affinity. She could have done the same for Casimir, but she didn't waste the energy. At every destination, he refused to accompany them and instead spent the hour scaring random students and vandalizing everything in sight.

In the end, Olalla, Angor, and Aethelred decided they would attend the same university while Casimir would stay in East Mintle until Ephraim graduated high school. This had caused tension between *the gays*, as Casimir insisted they be called, but the hallucinator had confessed to Olalla that his choice had nothing to do with Aethelred.

"I need a break from the obsessive science shit," he told her when the plans were made. "If Angor tries to explain mitosis to me one more time, I'll permanently transport my brain to another dimension."

Frankly, Olalla was offended that Angor had talked about genetics with Casimir at all. In her mind, that was equivalent to flirting with another girl.

Still, that wasn't the reason Olalla's desires began to drift from the concepts of science and the excitement of attending one of the world's best schools.

The week before they graduated high school, Ephraim slammed his tray on their lunch table, a haunted look in his lime green eyes. "Did you hear?"

"They've decided tomatoes are a fruit and you can conjure them now?" Casimir guessed as he plucked the uneaten salad from Aethelred's plate with his fingers.

"No, that's stupid—tomatoes are obviously vegetables. I'm talking about the group of kids with weird hair they found dead in New York City."

Olalla froze with her fork in her mouth, and Angor pushed his tray forward to lean his elbows on the table. "What are you talking about, Mayer?" he demanded.

"They won't talk about it in the papers, but my uncle's an officer in the city. Says the kids were frequent shoplifters and could do 'crazy' things. Won't say *what*, but it doesn't matter now. They were offed, and my uncle thinks it was a government job."

Slowly, Olalla lowered her fork to her plate. "The government murdered a group of Affinity children?"

"They were sixteen…but yeah, that's what it looks like."

A cold rage overcame Olalla, not because random children had been unlawfully murdered but because those random children could have easily been *them*. If the government deemed anyone with weird hair a threat, they *would* be next. She had lived most of her life in fear of an overarching authority, and she would not allow anything to take her mother's place now that she'd gained her freedom, not even an entity as powerful as the government.

The wrathful schemes running through her mind must have been apparent on her face, because Ephraim amended, "Maybe that's not the case—I don't know. Just…be careful on the east coast, yeah? Don't let anyone realize what you can do. And if you find others, warn them. Now that we know there *are* others, maybe I'll skip college and tour the country to find them all."

"I'm in," Casimir said, to which Aethelred fidgeted in his chair and refused to look up from his food. Casimir then proceeded to fantasize about how they would become a traveling circus of freaks, and after over-exaggerating the extent of this escapade, the entire idea became a joke, but Olalla didn't stop thinking about it, not that day—not even after graduation. The entire summer, her thoughts circled around how Affinities were bound to become a segregated class, if not an outright enemy of the public. The people in power would abuse them, as her mother had abused her, and the government's minions would ruin every facet of their lives, as Artemis had attempted to ruin hers.

It consumed Olalla more than their research. Their hypotheses were problems that might never be solved, but *this* was a real problem she knew she could solve. She had solved her mother, hadn't she?

The options in solving this dilemma would require more

strategy, but she considered the best method until their very last day on Hastings Street, when she finally came to her conclusion.

"Where are the other weirdos?" Casimir asked that afternoon, peeling her from her poisonous thoughts. The two sat in the living room, him in his armchair, a sketchpad in his lap, and her on the pink couch, which they'd never bothered to replace.

She'd been staring at the window, lost in her own mind, and it took her a minute to process who the *weirdos* were. Being the only girl, she could collectively call them "the boys," whereas Aethelred mostly referred to the group as the "others" and Angor often said "our fellow Affinities," since he was so turned on by the term. Since they'd declared themselves such, Casimir had refused to use the word, but he did spend a decent chunk of his free time contriving acronyms for A.F.F.I.N.I.T.I.E.S., most of which started with "Aethelred" and contained as many inappropriate words as possible.

"They went out to buy some last minute supplies for the trip tomorrow," she reminded him.

"I know, and they've been gone for two hours." Casimir dragged his pencil over the paper in an aggressive stroke and frowned at whatever he'd drawn. "I don't trust Angor driving my car. There's too much going on in that big brain of his for adequate concentration on the road. Just like there's too much going on in your brain for you to do more than ogle walls." With that addition, he arched his eyebrows at her. They'd never changed from pine green, but he had grown some facial hair over the years, a dusting of which coated his jaw now. "What are you thinking about, Cosmos? How much you wanna kiss Periculy when he gets home?"

"Remember when Ephraim talked about traveling the country to look for other Affinities?" she prompted, disregarding his taunts.

"And I annoyed Red so much he actually ate his salad just so I couldn't? Yeah, of course."

She rolled her eyes. "Well, I want to do that. I want to expand the weird hair gang—make a whole weird hair *town*. Become a force so grand the government can't kill us like they killed those kids in New York."

Casimir gnawed on the end of his pencil before scribbling more weirdness on the page. "It's not confirmed the government had anything to do with that. Besides, how do you know there're enough of us to form an entire town? And why would you even *want* a whole town of weirdos we have to take care of?"

"We would be a *community*; we would take care of each other."

"You mean they would stand between us and the government like a shield? I know how your twisted mind works, Cos."

She couldn't fully suppress her smirk. "A queen doesn't go into battle, does she?"

"You and Periculy, always thinking you're royalty." Casimir shook his head. "You know *he'd* run the town, don't you? C'mon, I know you two are *dating* or whatever, but Angor would never share that authority. He'd pretend, sure, but he's as greedy as you are."

"If we're both greedy, what makes you think he'd win the title of ruler?"

"Because he could make you writhe in pain for all eternity and you can't control his mind."

This was still true—as far as they knew, at least. After the night of her mother's murder, Olalla had not once tried to control Angor's mind, not even for practice or sport. Given the more intimate nature of their relationship, doing so felt like a violation of trust, and he was the only person she fully trusted. Yet she wondered if she could control him or if he was the one person she would never conquer.

Before she could attempt to defend herself, the front door opened, admitting Aethelred, who struggled to haul four bags of groceries. He hadn't even made it halfway across the short distance to the kitchen when Casimir jeered, "Leave, Red. You're distracting me with your sexiness."

Aethelred's cheeks, already flushed from the summer heat, deepened to the scarlet of his averted eyes. "I'm just *walking.*"

"*Exactly*," Casimir drawled, but the word was overpowered by Angor gently kicking the door to enter, carrying his own four bags of groceries with far more sophistication.

"Maybe your aversion to vegetables is the reason your Affinity is so strange," he proposed, clearly continuing a conversation they'd started in the car. "Think about it—your lack of nutrients could be why your brain waves refuse to connect to another's unless there's physical touch."

"It doesn't matter, Angor." Aethelred dropped his bags on the kitchen counter. "I probably could practice my ability to the point of reading anyone's past with sheer mental will, but I don't want that power."

"Wouldn't it be better if you could control it so you *didn't* read a person's past every time you touched them?"

Aethelred ignored his friend in favor of placing the food in the refrigerator. Considering a large portion of what they'd bought was walnuts and potato chips, the task didn't take very long. "I'm going to finish packing. We'll leave at six tomorrow morning?"

"As long as Cosmos doesn't keep me up all night whispering about how we probably have an extra chromosome," Angor teased before plopping a walnut into his mouth. Olalla didn't smile at him; she could barely look at him. She wanted him to leave now so she wouldn't have to deal with her own irrational emotions.

"I'll try not to oversleep," Aethelred mumbled, slightly amused, as he disappeared into his bedroom. Angor vanished into his a moment later, and Olalla cringed for a full minute before he finally beckoned for her to join him. His tone was light, but the fact that he used her first name implied his displeasure.

"Ooh, someone's in trouble," Casimir sang, not bothering to glance up from his doodling. Olalla presented him with her middle finger anyway.

The room that had once been littered in old lady panties and empty beer cans was now a nerd's utopia. Random notes with chemical equations and anatomical diagrams covered every inch of the peeling walls. Multiple stolen microscopes sat atop the dressers, accompanied by stolen petri dishes and stolen textbooks. The newest addition were two suitcases, one on Angor's side of the bed and one on Olalla's. He stood above hers, which was conspicuously empty.

"You haven't packed." The statement was an accusation, but his voice contained the hint of a question.

She lifted her chin, hoping to exude dignity. Though she and Angor had proven themselves equals over the years, times like these still made her feel like a student under a teacher's reprimand. His sleekly styled pink hair and endless supply of button up shirts did not mollify that feeling. "I've decided I won't go to college."

"Won't... Why?" he asked, attempting to hide his surprise with a cool expression.

"Do I need to?" she challenged a bit too defensively. "I can take any job I want by simply walking into the establishment."

"Olalla—we're about to have access to the technology we've lacked for years. We're about to uncover the knowledge we've sought—gain the accreditation we need to become respected members of the scientific community."

"I'll find other ways to gain access to it," she lied, knowing she would lose all of Angor's admiration if she admitted there were matters more important than science. "And I don't need a degree. Neither does Casimir; we can both make anyone believe any piece of paper is our diploma."

"I've always known Casimir wouldn't come to college. You..."

Olalla fiddled with a loop on her jeans to avoid his imploring gaze. She had expected anger from him—although, she wasn't sure *why* she'd expected that. Angor never caved to rage; his emotions ranged from tepidly content to wearily frustrated, but this gleam in his muscle-pink eyes was new: sorrowfully betrayed.

"I'll stay here with Casimir and Ephraim," she began, almost uncertainly. "We'll spend the year planning, and then we'll depart on our mission to gather all Affinities across the States. It's the only way to ensure our freedom, Angor—if we're all united as an immovable force. Any science you discover will be for naught if the government wipes you out the moment they realize you can supernaturally tamper with people's nerves."

"Nociceptors," he corrected. "I can't tamper with *all*

types of nerves."

She pinched her forehead. "That's not the point. The point is, this is important. You don't have to join me—I won't even ask you to—but you can't stop me. You *cannot*."

His parted lips snapped shut at the implication. He could not stop her because she would not *let* him. She would control him before she would let him control her.

"You've been plotting this with Casimir and Ephraim?" he questioned, annoyance surfacing. "For how long?"

"Not together, no, but I know they'll join me. You know neither of them are cut out for a studious life. They want to be in the action."

"Does there have to be *action*? Even if the government's after us—which is merely Ephraim's speculation—wouldn't it be easier to discover how our abilities came to be and exchange that knowledge with the government for our safety?"

"You think we'll be safe if the government learns the extent of what we are? We'll go from experimenters to experiments too quickly for any negotiation. We have to be the first to act; we have to assume the worst."

Angor pressed his lips together for a minute and then exhaled a defeated breath. "If that's what you desire, then fine, but I want no part in it. Aethelred and I will leave in the morning without you. I wish you the best."

Her jaw shifted, numerous retorts on her tongue, but she voiced none of them. This had gone smoother than she could have anticipated—no screaming, no emotional manipulation. Angor was letting her do exactly what she wanted without insults or pleas. She should have been relieved.

Instead she was unnerved by his calmness, his apathetic resignation to the fracturing of a relationship that had taken years to calcify. He retrieved his suitcase mechanically, acting as if he'd always expected her to make a decision this idiotic, as if she were a parasite he'd hoped his body could work symbiotically with but, after closer examination, he chose to remove.

As he exited their shared haven of scientific and emotional exploration, all progress they'd made over the years died.

"So, what should we do for your last night here?"

Normally, Aethelred jumped when Casimir snuck up to rest his chin on his shoulder, but now his mind felt too numb to react.

"Something romantic," Casimir murmured, "or, better, something *dangerous*? A little game of Dodge the Deer?"

Aethelred sighed. Dodge the Deer was Casimir's "fun" game in which he would make them see deer on the road and swerve to avoid the hallucinations, mostly in an attempt to give Aethelred a heart attack. Really, he did enjoy a bit of the thrill, but one time they'd hit an actual deer, and that had ruined the game for Aethelred. The deer had been fine, as had the Cadillac Seville, but he didn't believe the same miracle would occur twice.

"I'd just like to go to sleep," he said as he closed his suitcase and snapped the buckles shut. When he bent to place it beside his bed, he felt that Casimir no longer stood at his back.

"Okay, fine, we don't have to play DTD—happy? Wanna just go for a casual drive? No surprises."

Aethelred refused to turn and glimpse the earnestness

that must have characterized Casimir's face. It was a rare expression he'd grown to love, and he knew his resolve would collapse entirely if he beheld it. "I think it's best if we don't."

"Oh? Any particular reason?"

For weeks he'd dreaded this inevitable conversation. He'd put it off as long as possible, but he knew it must have shown in his behavior all summer—since he, Olalla, and Angor had accepted their spots at the college, at least. With another weary sigh, Aethelred pivoted to face his greatest fear.

Since their sophomore year, Casimir hadn't grown in height, but his face had lost much of its boyishness, now replaced with the harder features of a man. And he *was* a man—twenty years old now, even if he acted like he was five half the time. Aethelred wanted to watch him grow for the rest of their lives, but every day that notion became more of a cruel dream than a tangible reality.

"I don't want to make this any more painful than it has to be."

Casimir flicked his fingers, as he often did now without cigarettes to fiddle with. "So it'll be better that you're leaving if we don't spend our last night together, together?"

"Well, that's what it is, isn't it? Our last night together. We're done after this, aren't we?"

At that, he went oddly still. "What are you talking about, Red?"

Aethelred gestured helplessly between them. "This— whatever we are—can't last. We can barely stay together when we're together."

Rolling his eyes, Casimir lightly kicked his green yo-yo where it lay on a heap of clothes. It had darkened to a putrid color with its excessive use, and Aethelred wondered what would become of it after tonight. "Right, because I annoy the shit out of you."

No, because we shouldn't *be together,* Aethelred thought sullenly. *Because we're both men, and the only people who approve of us are all probably psychopaths, yourself included.* Aloud he said, "You decided to stay here. What did you think would happen?"

"I thought we'd call each other. Telephones exist. Plus, it's not like you're going to the moon. I can visit, and I'm sure I'll get so bored that I will."

"If life is so boring without me, why don't you rent an apartment near the campus?"

Casimir's face soured with agitation. "Because I know you don't want me to."

"I—" Aethelred rubbed his forehead, staring at the colony of empty chip bags in the corner of the room. "We haven't made an effort to hide our…relationship here, and that's been fine since everyone already thinks we're weird. At the university, though…how we're perceived will affect our futures."

"And your bright red hair and eyes won't automatically classify you as a freak?"

The term didn't bother him anymore, but he was unsure of how to deal with the building fury in Casimir's tone, an emotion rarer than his sincerity and never aimed in Aethelred's direction. "You know I'm not as smart as Angor. I have to seem as professional as possible, despite my odd features. That task will be made much harder if I'm seen as…deviant."

"Deviant, right, because I'm so obviously a low-life."

Aethelred's voice was tight as he ground out, "You know that's not the reason."

Casimir blew out a breath, fingers twitching at his pocket,

as if searching for his cigarettes. The habit of smoking had not been easily broken; even now Aethelred had to steer him away from buying packs at the store. He'd done it, though, for Aethelred, and now Aethelred couldn't muster the strength to maintain their secret relationship. He recognized his cowardice, a trait he would never overcome.

"Fine. If you don't wanna spend the night together—or be *together* at all—then get out." Casimir nodded to the door, his fierce green eyes trained on Aethelred. "Make this easier—take the easy fucking way out, why don't you? I'm not worth the stares and the whispers."

Aethelred's mouth flopped open, but he couldn't produce a sound. It wasn't true—Casimir *was* worth it—but Aethelred wasn't brave enough. With one last look at the room they'd shared, a physical manifestation of the time they'd shared, he collected his bags and departed.

In the living room, silence and darkness reigned. The sun had set, and only the light above the front door illuminated the couch, upon which Angor sat. His pink eyes rose, blank and emotionless.

"You aren't sleeping in there?" he asked as if he already knew the answer. As if he'd heard the entire argument, or was shrewd enough to know the boys' relationship could end no other way.

"You aren't sleeping in there?" Aethelred countered, gesturing toward the other bedroom. He knew the answer already, too. Olalla's distance over the past months was a mirror to his own; he had suspected she wouldn't join them since her purple eyes alit at the mention of those murdered Affinity kids.

"I suppose we'll switch," Angor concluded, standing to approach the room that had once been his. "Let's leave at five tomorrow morning. I don't intend to stay up much longer."

Aethelred didn't intend to, either, but he knew he would. He doubted he would have a truly peaceful night of sleep any time soon.

That night, Angor slept in Aethelred's bed. Casimir considered offering him his old bed back. Then he considered seducing him as a petty stab at Aethelred. In the end, he fell asleep with a less appealing hallucination of the red-haired boy lying beside him.

That night, Angor slept in Aethelred's bed. He considered cleaning up the dirty laundry and endless potato chip bags. Then he considered marching over to the other bedroom and demanding Olalla see reason. In the end, he squeezed his eyes shut and dispelled any thoughts except those of science, since that was all that mattered to him now.

That night, Aethelred slept in the same bed as Olalla. He considered building a barrier of pillows between them so he wouldn't accidentally brush her skin in the middle of the night. Then he considered wrapping himself in five layers of clothing, even with the humidity, to ensure there was no chance he'd glimpse her past. In the end, he decided it didn't matter; he wouldn't accidentally roll in his sleep because he wouldn't fall asleep at all.

That night, Aethelred slept in the same bed as Olalla. She considered saying something to him about how relieved she was to be done with Angor, hoping he would relay it to his friend the next day. Then she considered barging into the other room to relay those sentiments to Angor directly. In the end, she stared at the ceiling and contemplated all the ways she could manipulate the world to prove to Angor—and herself—that her decision was necessary, and that she hadn't thrown away the best part of her life for something far, far worse.

14

Clinically Constructed History

"And here we have a blood transfusion apparatus from 1934." Angor gestured toward the towering glass case, within which rested two tiny needles connected by a tube. There were more technical terms for the equipment, Aethelred knew, but he didn't particularly *want* to know anything about a blood transfusion apparatus. "The first successful human blood transfusion occurred in 1818, if I'm not mistaken."

Angor was never mistaken. He knew every little detail of medical history in this museum. That was the reason the Dittrick Museum of Medical History had hired him as their tour guide, in fact: because no one could outmatch his nerdiness.

"Before that, they tried animal blood!" Angor let out a weird laugh that he clearly thought was charismatic, and a few girls giggled near where Aethelred stood at the rear of the tour group. His job was to silence misbehavers and encourage laughter at Angor's strange sense of humor. Sometimes, his red eyes alone accomplished the former task, but the latter was an impossible feat. One time they'd had a man willingly engage with Angor's dramatics, but then he'd tried to steal the show and had mysteriously twisted his ankle while climbing the stairs.

The museum was much smaller than they'd expected. Only three floors housed historical medical equipment, and the main foyer consumed half of the first two floors with its grand windows and iron-railed staircases. Angor declared it a waste of space, but they did utilize the glossy white walls to hang old paintings and tools. The other rooms contained artifacts, diagrams, and anatomical models that Aethelred now knew far too well.

When he'd agreed to take an internship at Case Western Reserve University for their first summer after completing their undergraduate degrees, Aethelred had assumed he would shadow a psychologist and learn their practices. Instead, he'd found himself trailing Angor's every move, working with him at the university's museum and aiding his research on the human brain. The research wasn't really *his*; their internship was under a well known scientist who'd gifted them with more information on neurons and glia than Aethelred had ever wished to acquire. He supposed this might help his career aspirations, but mostly he felt like Angor's sidekick—his forever-shadow.

"Well, we can't think them too foolish, can we?" Angor mused as he guided the group from one of the upper rooms toward the gaudy stairs. "Their knowledge was quite primitive, but it paved the way for all we know today! Imagine—in fifty years they'll mock *us* for our practices. Someone will laugh at my thesis on white matter, I'm sure."

Though he stated this as a joke, Angor was very sensitive about his thesis on white matter and would probably hunt down anyone who dared question it, even if it was proven wrong when they were frail seventy-two-year-old men.

Angor walked backward down the stairs, his lab coat sleeves flapping about as he pointed toward the medical art lining the walls. Knowing each word of the speech, Aethelred began to daydream until they reached the bottom of the steps and a figure in a black cloak and beaked plague mask sprinted toward them.

Screams echoed toward the high ceiling as the ominous figure charged them. Two teenage girls cowered behind Aethelred, and for once, he was grateful for the bulky lab coat his friend insisted he wear.

"What are you doing?" Angor groaned as the plague doctor stopped before him. His hands were pressed to either side of his head, keeping the mask in place.

"I cannot work the buckles," the man said, voice muffled beyond the leather.

Angor pinched his forehead. "You've ruined the surprise, Than. You were supposed to scare them in the other room."

"Scare us?" One of the girls peeked her head out from behind Aethelred, appalled.

"Help me put it on, and I will hide again." Than shuffled closer to Angor, removing the creepy mask to reveal his tanned face. "Nothing to see here!" he said to the tour group, his accent distinct now without the leather inhibiting his voice. When they'd first met him at the start of the summer, they'd recognized it immediately: Greek.

Of course, Angor had been wary because of the last Greeks they'd encountered, but Aethelred persuaded him not to judge so shallowly. After all, if they compared all fathers to Mr. Cosmos, most men would be a lost cause; if they compared all mothers to Dimitra Cosmos, many women would be dead; if they compared all dark-haired girls to Artemis, a majority of the female population would be missing; and if they compared all Affinities to Olalla, they would have to call themselves "selfish, science-betraying control freaks."

This Greek, it turned out, was an Affinity himself. Than hadn't recognized the term, obviously, and he hadn't told them outright, but after confessing he had two PhDs when he looked to be no more than twenty-seven, Angor started to theorize and then confronted him about his ability to live longer than the average human. Apparently, he was two hundred sixty-eight years old.

He was also the most attractive man Aethelred had ever encountered. Straight nose, shapely jaw, and eyes like dark chocolate. His hair matched perfectly, which had been their second clue. Also, they'd deduced that no one with such looks could be a normal human.

The girls cowering behind Aethelred concluded the same. With wide eyes, they peered around him and mouthed variations of "He's so hot" at each other.

"Well, turn around," Angor prompted with a sigh. Than complied, allowing the slightly shorter man to strap the plague mask on his head.

"How do I look?" he asked upon spinning to face them.

"Handsome!" one of the girls called.

Than touched the beak. "That's concerning..."

A smirk budded on Aethelred's lips, but it died when he spotted a hint of color beyond the museum's glass front doors.

They knew a few Affinities who attended the university, and a few more who lived throughout Cleveland, but he would never mistake those pine green curls, shrouded in a cloud of cigarette smoke.

His first instinct was to run and hide behind one of the

plastic skeletons, but he overrode that urge to flee. He'd become adept at calming himself with the help of his therapist. At small intervals, Dr. Howard had exposed him to that which he feared until he'd gained the confidence to speak to strangers, to chuckle at the mention of his bright red hair, to attend a night at the circus without vomiting. The anxiety never *went away*, but he'd developed the bravery to embrace it.

His success had inspired him to study psychology for his undergraduate degree; he wanted to help people overcome their anxious ailments, too.

This, however, was the one anxiety he'd never tried to overcome. He avoided cigarette-smoking men—he avoided attractive men in general—and he certainly avoided all thoughts of Casimir Stromer.

"Angor," Aethelred beckoned, exuding poise despite his inner dread. "You might want to look outside."

"Is there a man in a plague mask waiting to tell us about the bubonic plague? If not—"

"I'm allowed to want to see the medical museum!" a voice bellowed from outside, drawing everyone's attention. Angor finally looked and blanched when he beheld Olalla Cosmos standing on the steps outside the doors, gesturing wildly toward the building. Besides her vibrant purple hair, she was unrecognizable. Distressed jean shorts hid beneath the length of her plaid shirt. Black knee socks blended with her dark combat boots. A giant purple *tattoo* stained her right thigh, which Aethelred realized was a depiction of a *microscope*, the design abstract and weird enough to have been drawn by Casimir. Some things never changed, he supposed.

"*Fuck* the medical museum!" her green-haired friend shouted before stalking away from her to press his face to the glass door. "Hear that? You're all a bunch of—"

The insult evaporated from his tongue when his eyes focused on the scene within the museum, on Aethelred standing closest to the doors. His cigarette dropped to the sidewalk as he stumbled backward, tripping against Olalla, who shoved him away and rolled her eyes.

"What, Stromer? Are they conducting a catheter demonstration in there?" Her voice was softer now, almost indistinguishable. She started toward the doors, but Angor beat her to it. After pushing through his befuddled tour group, he yanked open the glass, leaving only two feet of air between himself and his ex-girlfriend.

Her eyes protruded like two grapes. Neither said anything until Angor finally managed to call over his shoulder, "We'll resume the tour in a few minutes. Please follow the plague doctor to the plague room."

"That sounds murderous," Olalla observed, not disapprovingly. Angor didn't respond; rather, he pivoted to grab Aethelred's sleeve and pull him through the doorway.

The midsummer sun reflected off the white stairs, momentarily blinding Aethelred. He was accustomed to being too warm, so the perspiration forming on his skin didn't bother him, but it took a few moments for his eyes to adjust to the shift in lighting. Once his vision acclimated, he saw Casimir and Olalla were not alone. Three others stood with them: a woman in a tie dye sundress, a young boy in ratty black clothes, and Ephraim Mayer.

"Well, well, well, what a surprise. Who would've guessed the world's biggest nerds work at the medical museum." His chartreuse eyes examined their lab coats, amused. He must have hit a growth spurt once they'd left, because he now stood the tallest of them all, even lengthier than Aethelred. In the past four years, he hadn't ditched his backwards baseball cap, though he wore a new one now: black with the white words "Affinities for Freedom" etched above where a tuft of his green hair poked out. From the rolled up cuffs of his leather jacket, two dragon heads slid down his forearms, fused into the skin. Their open maws spewed neon green fire to his fingertips. Though Aethelred found them disturbing, he was also mildly impressed with the advancement of Casimir's drawing skills.

"Mayer," Angor greeted tautly. "Stromer."

Ephraim nodded in acknowledgement; there had been no hard feelings between him and them before they'd left East Mintle. For Casimir and Olalla, though, it appeared the hard feelings had irreversibly ossified.

"This is a sick joke, isn't it?" The hallucinator whirled on Ephraim, jabbing a finger in his face. Ink stained his hands, and a few tattoos escaped when the sleeve of his jean jacket drifted up his forearm. "You knew they worked here."

"I didn't *know*, but one of our Affinity friends *did* mention two boys with red and pink hair she often saw at this museum…"

Casimir spat at Ephraim's boots. "Bastard," he muttered before sneering at Aethelred's and Angor's lab coats. "These two *scholars* look like they have work to do, so let's get the hell out of here, hm?"

"Not quite yet," Olalla said, touching Casimir's hand in a way that was too familiar, too *normal*. In their three years of friendship, she hadn't succumbed to physical contact with anyone except Angor and, even then, never in public. Although she didn't *hold* Casimir's hand, the brush of skin was enough for coldness to consolidate in Aethelred's gut. "We should catch up with our old friends."

Angor appraised them, a puzzled gleam to his eyes when

they grazed the woman and child standing beside Ephraim. Ultimately, he reverted his gaze to Olalla. "It does appear much has changed since we last spoke. Nice makeup," he added without bothering to mask his disparagement. Her cosmetics were the most ostentatious: thick mascara and purple eyeshadow that made her look like she'd been punched in both eyes. Casimir and Ephraim both wore a light layer of eyeliner, and the new woman had rainbow glitter on her eyelids. What struck Aethelred as odd about her was her lack of oddness—her tawny hair and blue eyes. Whoever she was, she wasn't an Affinity.

"Nice ponytail," Olalla countered, sly eyes mocking the pink hair tied at the nape of Angor's neck.

"I know it looks ridiculous," he conceded, "but it's practical. I've always been more impressed with the mental than the physical, anyway."

Olalla pursed her lips but didn't relent. "I didn't realize you needed a degree to be a tour guide. How low you've fallen, Periculy. I thought you wanted to take over the world."

Angor glanced back at the building, feigning surprise. "You think this is the end for us, Cosmos? Is that because *this* is the end for you?" He inclined his head toward their punk attire. "How shameful. Aethelred and I are merely doing this on weekends for fun. During the week, we work with Dr. Earnest Carpenter, researching gray matter."

Judging by the sudden set of Olalla's jaw, she'd heard of Dr. Carpenter. "How predictable—you being an apprentice, basking in this institutionalized nonsense. This isn't the end for us, you know. This is just the beginning for us—for Affinities for Freedom."

Angor very obviously stopped himself from recoiling at the phrase. They had heard of Affinities for Freedom, a growing movement of "overzealous young people who are, basically, the antithesis of hippies," one reporter described. The media had characterized them as a harmless group that reveled in mild chaos and grunge culture, akin to anarchists, some said. They did not realize the power these radicals possessed, nor the atrocities they might commit to obtain their perception of freedom. The faint scar on Olalla's throat was a testament to their immoral capabilities.

So far, they hadn't *killed* anyone, but they'd run into enough scuffles with the police to earn scars on their faces and an unsavory reputation for all with strangely-colored hair and eyes, to Aethelred's chagrin.

"I thought you didn't like labels," Angor said to Ephraim.

Olalla flicked a bug off her shoulder. "He doesn't. I made it up. It gives our organization an air of professionalism."

"Ah, yes, very professional. All of my sophisticated, intellectual friends fight police officers in the streets."

"Hey, now, we're all friends here—we're all *Affinities*. Well, almost all," Ephraim amended with a grin back at the woman. She was crouched in a squat, muttering to the young boy, who was hacking at the sidewalk with a *knife*. "Chop! Chop! Chop!" he whispered as she tried mollifying his aggressive movements. When that proved fruitless, she redirected her focus to the adults.

"Are you mocking me, Ephraim?" The woman squinted up at him before fixing her playful scowl on Olalla. "Or was it you?"

"This is Sarah, my wife," Ephraim said, ruffling her hair. She swatted him away before finally snagging the knife from the boy, who, despite looking nothing like them, must have been their *son*. Aethelred blinked, unable to conceive that Ephraim, the youngest of them, was *married* with a *kid*.

"Started dating after you guys left, and we eloped on the day of graduation."

"*Instead* of going to graduation," Sarah clarified, cocking her head in lighthearted reprimand. "My parents were *not* happy."

"Neither were we," Olalla chimed in. "We couldn't believe Mayer would bring a Regg into our fold."

"Regg?" Angor repeated. "As in…*Regular*? Is that what you call non-Affinities?"

Sarah nodded. "It's the least offensive term they could come up with. Cas certainly had a few…creative ideas."

He held up his hands in surrender. "I won't say any now. I did promise you minimal swearing as a Hanukkah present last year."

Her brow furrowed, head shaking slightly, as she tucked the child's knife into her dress pocket. "You just cursed at everyone in the medical museum."

"I cursed at the medical museum, not the people in it."

She opened her mouth to retort, but then the little boy let out a wail, tugging at the pocket where his knife went. With a sigh, she extracted the weapon and returned it to him. As he resumed his sidewalk slicing, she grimaced. "This is Fraco. Don't mind him. He just really likes *chopping* things for some reason."

Ephraim's lips curled in displeasure as he watched the kid. "Sarah found him wandering around the city a few weeks ago and refused to bring him to the cops. We put up posters but no one's claimed him yet, and no fucking wonder. Look at him."

Fraco continued stabbing at the concrete like a broken machine. His erratic swings eventually landed the blade in Casimir's boot, and the man let out such a loud, long series of curses that every passerby gaped at him. Aethelred, who'd barely been exposed to any swearing since his last encounter with this crowd, blushed profusely.

"You motherfu—" Casimir cut himself off to dig through his jeans pocket. A moment later, he found his lighter and hastily dismantled it to pour the flammable fluid on the boy's head.

"No, no, no!" Fraco cried, allowing the oil to drip into his mouth.

Sarah gasped before rapidly gathering the boy into her arms. "Cas! That's so dangerous! He's going to be sick! And it could get in his eyes and give him a rash—"

"Sarah's very *nice*," Olalla cut in, glancing blandly at Aethelred and Angor, "which is annoying, but I let her stick around because it's interesting to have another girl in the group. Also, she never calls the cops on us. By the way, Sarah, this is the guy who helped me murder my mother."

Despite being *nice*, Sarah was not fazed by this admission, giving Angor a nod hello before resuming her attempts to wipe the oil off Fraco. For that, Aethelred felt a kinship with her— another innocent soul corrupted by these crazies.

"Thank you for telling her of all my dark deeds. Now she'll fear me forever," Angor droned.

"Does it matter what any of us think of you?" Olalla placed her hands on her hips, revealing the crop top beneath her open plaid shirt.

With a mixture of lust and distaste, Angor eyed her exposed stomach. "No, I suppose not. The next time I see you, I assume you'll be a corpse, and I'll be delivering the eulogy at your funeral."

She expelled a bitter laugh. "You think I'll let *you* write my eulogy? How ignorantly adorable."

"Why do you think we'll be dead?" Ephraim asked. Glancing between the two of them, his eyebrows creased, as if he'd just considered all this banter might not be good-natured.

"We've heard about the riots—the violence in the streets. It's only a matter of time before bullets find your heads."

"Or before we put bullets in other people's heads." A dazzling grin split Ephraim's lips. "I have a whole arsenal of weapons, my friend. Even those who have Mental Affinities or Useless Affinities"—he jumped his eyebrows with self-deprecating humor—"will hold up against the big boys. We haven't shown our might yet, but today's the day, brother. It's luck we found you, I think. We're employing our largest mass of Affinities *ever* today, and we're gonna take Cleveland as our own."

"You're going to *kill* the police?" Aethelred blurted out.

Casimir's lips hooked into a crooked grin. "We're gonna kill anyone who resists our authority."

"Civilians?" Angor clarified, unsurprised. "I suppose that's to be expected of you. What's your death count now, Cosmos? It was two last time I checked."

Olalla's purple eyebrows scrunched, but she didn't reply before Ephraim butted in with, "We aren't killing civilians unless it's absolutely necessary, 'kay? This is about destroying the government, not becoming the government. We won't be tyrants."

Frankly, Aethelred couldn't believe Olalla didn't instantly interject with her own conflicting ideas. That was how it had always been with her and Angor's co-leadership. Aethelred wondered, with unease, if Olalla had implanted this idea in Ephraim's head. She'd never promised not to use her power on him, nor had she ever expressed the inability to do so.

The manipulation should have bothered him, but what unnerved him more was that if his assumption was true, Olalla didn't want unnecessary death but Casimir *did*. He'd always been careless, but never *malicious*. In Aethelred's mind, the hallucinator had remained that nonchalant twenty-year-old, always sarcastic but never angry. The sloppy way Aethelred had ended their relationship seemed to have lit an endless fuse of aggression in him.

"By tonight, we'll be in charge of an entire city," Olalla gloated. "What have *you* done? Sat in a classroom? Taken a few tests?"

Angor straightened his lab coat. "I've engaged in quite a bit of research, actually. You'll be pleased to know your theory was right, Olalla. We have forty-eight chromosomes—twenty-four pairs."

Her eyes closed and reopened very gradually. After a full minute without movement, Aethelred began to worry she'd ceased breathing.

"Like monkeys?" Ephraim questioned. Angor gave him a bemused look, and he added, "I did pay attention sometimes in bio."

"You know this for certain?" Olalla managed, scanning him for signs of deceit.

Angor often explained how, if he ever encountered her again, he would rub it in her face that he'd discovered the truth—that *he'd* proven her hypothesis. Faced with that option now, his years of building spite were forgotten, replaced with remorse. "I used my own DNA in the experiments—and Aethelred's."

"Hold on," Casimir said, "let's go back to the monkey thing. *Are* we monkeys?"

Aethelred assumed this was meant to be a mockery of

their science, but Angor replied with a pensive, "We're… something—something not exactly *human*. At least, not in the sense we should be. We're…a different species."

"A superior species," Olalla murmured, hand over her mouth as she stared contemplatively at the museum.

"I don't believe we should take it *that* far. It's not—"

"It's *true*, Aethelred." Her purple eyes bolted to him, feverish. "Regular humans can't do what we do, and they'll never be able to."

His gaze flickered to Sarah, one of these *Regular* humans, but she was too busy drying Fraco with the skirt of her dress to care.

"Well, cool," Casimir barked as he lit a new cigarette with the lighter fluid he'd retained. "Periculy discovered we're a new species, like we always knew he would. What have *you* done?"

This question was directed at Aethelred, who balked at the vehemence in his tone.

"He's been hard at work," Angor defended, "studying the DSM-III."

"The psychology encyclopedia?" When Aethelred nodded, Casimir's jaw shifted with skepticism. "Isn't that the book that claims homosexuality is a mental disease?"

"They took homosexuality out of the last edition of the DSM in 1973," Aethelred said.

Ephraim wiggled his bright green eyebrows. "You know that fact well, don't you?"

A few years ago, the implication might have panicked Aethelred, but now he chose not to let his identity embarrass him, even though he would have preferred if it were a disease he could eradicate. "I try to absorb as much information as I can."

Casimir's expression soured further, likely because Aethelred had spoken too similarly to Angor, which the hallucinator had always hated. "Do you? Practicing your homosexuality then, are you? Going around kissing boys and absorbing as much information as possible?"

Aethelred couldn't stop himself from twitching at that. "I meant in the classroom. I'm going to school for a few more years so I can practice as a psychologist—a therapist."

A strange look of confusion crossed Casimir's face, as if this information conflicted with the younger, less developed version of Aethelred that had frozen in his mind.

Before the conversation could continue, one of the glass doors burst open behind them, from which Than emerged in his plague doctor's mask. Ephraim instinctively conjured a banana while Olalla and Casimir honed their focus on the new arrival, prepared to employ their Affinities. Than grappled with the leather straps for a minute before finally prying the mask from his face. Olalla and Ephraim relaxed but Casimir didn't.

"They are becoming riotous in there," Than breathed, wiping a thin layer of sweat from his forehead. "They think we plan to gas them with the Black Death!"

"Tell them we do," Angor said. "Make them feel the fear of those who suffered bubonic plague in the thirteen hundreds. It'll lead to a truly immersive experience. I'll be in shortly. I have to tie up some business first."

Than sighed but didn't even glance at the other Affinities before slipping on his mask and retreating into the museum.

"We really should finish this swiftly," Angor said, now to their old friends. "Olalla, could we have a moment?"

"And Red, could we have one?" Casimir arched an eyebrow but didn't wait for an answer before discarding his cigarette to clutch Aethelred's sleeve and haul him away, much like Angor had before. This time, he was dragged down the front steps to the side of the building, where a small park rested. He assumed they might have a nice walk through the grass and trees until Casimir pinned him to the museum's exterior.

"You asshole—pretending you aren't happy to see me." His fist twisted in the lab coat, pressing on Aethelred's chest. Though he *sounded* angry, his lips curved with a wry grin. "Did Angor engrain you with so much of his science-sexuality that you forgot you're attracted to me?"

Swallowing, Aethelred trailed his eyes from messy curls to dirty high-tops. Casimir's taste in clothes hadn't changed over the years—everything dark, everything ripped—but his lean muscle mass now filled them in a way Aethelred couldn't ignore. "I haven't forgotten. H-how have you been?"

The scent of smoke filled his nostrils as Casimir leaned closer. "Wanna find out?"

He did—he desperately did—but when the gap between their lips threatened to close, he found himself shoving Casimir away, so reckless and frantic their hands nearly brushed. "Stop," Aethelred panted, barely aware the fist had left his lab coat. "We shouldn't—we never should have done this—this…*couple* thing. It's going to make it so much harder when…"

"When *what?*"

"When we end up with other people."

"Like who—*who* are you gonna end up with? That sexy creeper in the mask?"

"*Than?*" Aethelred reeled back in bewilderment. "Than's a friend—he's here because he's working toward a PhD in marine biology. He's—he's *straight*. Most people are straight!"

"Ah," Casimir exhaled, nodding with false enthusiasm. "So that's why you bothered with me: there aren't many other options. Now that you've seen the world—seen men like that Greek god—I'm just trailer trash."

Aethelred folded his hands before him and summoned patience. "I'm talking about the fact that we'll have to marry *women*—if we want to marry anyone at all."

This earned an eye roll from Casimir. "Fuck conforming. Red...we're gonna take over the world, like Angor always said except a million times better. With Eph's vision, we'll be safe."

"Were you listening? It's not because we're Affinities—"

"I know, I know, it's because we're both *men*, but that doesn't matter. Ephraim wants freedom for *all*. We're gonna shatter all the norms. In a few years, no one's gonna give a shit that we have powers *or* that we both have dicks."

"Ephraim's vision...it's not the answer—violence is never the answer. Have you even *tried* diplomacy? Do they even *care* about Affinities, or is this some manic grab for power? And what will Cleveland look like when it's over? How will Affinities act when their powers are unchecked? You know how hard it was for us to tame Olalla into not using her powers on *us*. Imagine others like her who might deceive us without the threat of a government."

Casimir chewed on several parts of his lower lip before finally expelling a weary breath. "Okay, fine, *I don't know*. I'm not really involved in the planning; I just use my Affinity on whoever they tell me to and give tattoos to whoever joins the gang—"

"*Give* tattoos? You...actually..."

"Am a tattoo artist? Well, not legally, but that's the point, isn't it? Why should I have to pay for a license to do art?"

"Because you're putting ink in people's skin and they want to be assured they won't acquire an infection from it?"

"Okay, bad example—you know I'm not into politics. Most laws are outrageous, though. *Now* there aren't any restrictions against Affinities, but that's why we need to *act* now—before they decide using our powers is a crime. Before they throw us in jail simply *because* we have powers."

Aethelred couldn't completely argue; there was a level of paranoia he often felt, worrying someone might link their weird hair to their supernatural abilities, worrying the government might imprison them or *kill* them. The future of Affinities deserved to be discussed in an official manner, though, not determined by an outright assault on the police.

"You know what's going to happen, don't you?" Aethelred questioned. "Angor will launch his own plans and demand a diplomatic meeting with the Cleveland officials— or the *president*, knowing how far Angor likes to take things. If you both act at once, who do you think the government will favor?"

"We don't want the government's favor. We just want to be *free*. You won't accept this is the only way because you're *afraid*. You hate conflict; you hate confrontation. It's the reason you avoided the circus for five years."

"It was," Aethelred agreed, refusing to break eye contact, "but not anymore. I went back to the circus after my first year of college—The Wickedly Wicked Cirque. They renamed it The Moonlight Madness Cirque, since the fiasco with the psychics and the fruit gave them such a bad reputation. The ringleader fired the psychics that night, as one would expect. I...offered to testify against them in court, but they've seemingly disappeared. Hypnosia's still there, but she's under new ownership—a new psychic the ringleader hired. She's really nice—actually cares about the psychic practice and doesn't want to hurt people… Anyway, I work with the circus when they stop in Cleveland now. They're having a show next weekend, actually, if you…want to come."

Throughout the speech, Casimir wore a stunned expression, but the conclusion evoked childlike glee. "Now *that's* a reason not to plunge Cleveland into utter chaos tonight: a date at the circus with Aethelred Certior. Like the good old days."

"I'm not asking you on a *date*."

"Uh huh."

"I just—can't we be *friends*? Is that possible? I've…missed our group."

Casimir picked at a rip on his jacket sleeve. "I don't know why you're asking *me*. Cos and Periculy are the gang leaders."

"Do we need their permission to be friends?"

"I probably need to ask Ephraim," Casimir admitted, pine eyes glancing up with a grimace. "He's my freaking *master* now. Little brat gets a wife and thinks he's more mature than me all of a sudden."

A faint smile tugged at Aethelred's mouth. "Is he not?"

"Shut up." Casimir threw a thread from his jacket in a lame attack. It fluttered directly from his fingers toward the ground. "I'm twenty-four now, Red. I'm practically middle-aged."

"You think you'll die at fifty?"

He examined his jacket for more loose threads. "Sixty, if I'm lucky."

"You might live longer if you quit smoking."

Casimir froze as if he'd hoped Aethelred hadn't *noticed* he'd resumed the habit. Right, like he could ignore the acrid smell, the visible smoke, the way it made him seem younger, weaker. Aethelred didn't credit him for his anxiety, of course, but during his time away from smoking, he'd exuded a sense of determination that he now lacked. He seemed like an aimless ghost, wandering through the world without a body or purpose to anchor him.

"Does it matter how long I live?" Casimir asked, so low it was almost a whisper. "What am I living for? Ephraim and Olalla's dream of an Affinity utopia? Yeah, sounds worth living for."

He didn't agree with their plans, then—not entirely, not enough to feel passion. As far as Aethelred had seen, Casimir had only ever displayed passion for one thing, and it was making Aethelred squirm, or laugh, or talk, or cuddle in a tiny twin bed and stare collectively at the ceiling, quiet and calm and just *being* without anyone or anything to tell them not to be.

Unfortunately, a world existed beyond that bed—beyond them.

"Your hallucination haunted me, you know." Casimir kicked the grass. "Guess it's what I deserve. Guess I deserve everything this wonderful world has given me."

Aethelred stepped away from the wall, close enough to draw Casimir's vision upward. "That's not true. You deserve...happiness. To move on."

"Move on to *who*? If you suggest that Greek god, I'll punch you. If you suggest *anyone* I'll punch you. You're the only one I'll ever want."

Rubbing his hairline, Aethelred stepped back again. "You can't guilt me into dating you."

Casimir's lips parted with genuine shock. "I'm not—that's not what I'm trying to do—"

"Cas, let's go!"

They turned to see Ephraim waving with both arms on the sidewalk. They stood close enough to clearly see him, but perhaps the frantic gesture implied something had gone catastrophically wrong with Angor and Olalla's conversation.

Even so, Aethelred didn't want them to go—none of them, not even Ephraim's stranger of a wife. He wanted them to be the weird hair gang again, for Artemis and William to be their only problem, for things to be as simple as they had been in high school.

"Stay," he implored softly.

Casimir's eyes slivered, cautiously waiting for some prank to be revealed. "And if I stay? We'll...what?"

"Be friends," Aethelred offered, weaker than he'd intended.

"We'll be *friends*? Because you're too embarrassed to be anything more? Right." Casimir let out a bitter laugh before sticking his cigarette between his teeth. Taking a drag, he blew a suffocating cloud into Aethelred's face. "Later."

Angor had spent his first semester in college using his enthusiasm over the access to knowledge as a shield against all thoughts of Olalla Cosmos. Then he had spent his second semester in college watching that shield disintegrate until he was faced with the desperate longing for her companionship.

At the conclusion of their first year, he'd planned to drive straight back to Hastings Street, but one of his professors had invited him to partake in a science convention shortly after finals. Unable to say no, he had participated, which meant he and Aethelred returned to East Mintle two days after the high school's graduation.

They'd pulled into the trailer park in the Triumph TR7 Angor had bought earlier that year. Anywhere else, the vehicle was fairly inconspicuous, but almost any car attracted attention on Hastings Street. He'd expected Olalla and Casimir to hear the engine and run out to greet them. He'd expected the whole weird hair gang to reunite, all past squabbles forgotten. He'd expected his tales of endless science equipment to entice Olalla into abandoning her crazy dreams and return to their practical ones.

Instead, they'd found the Cadillac Seville absent and the Periculy trailer empty.

The space had been tidy—too tidy for the pair to have been out for only a short time. The refrigerator had been barren, and the bedrooms had been stripped of any possessions that didn't belong to Angor or Aethelred. Their other halves had left, and they'd had no intention of returning.

In place of the walnut bowl, a cluster of various merchandise had cluttered the coffee table. Pins, flyers, t-shirts—all printed with the words "Affinities for Freedom" above a depiction of a brain surrounded by shattered chains. Angor might have appreciated the design if all Affinities were Mentals.

Thwarted plans usually led to the formation of better plans for Angor, but in that moment, he had not been able to think past the fact that Olalla was gone and he had no idea *where* she'd gone. She could have been halfway across the country—she could have been in *another* country. With their slogan "Freedom for all," anywhere on the globe was viable.

Until that day, he had not realized how much he missed her questioning his every idea and decision, how much he missed her forming hypotheses and plans, how much he missed every facet of her mind. In that moment, she hadn't been close enough for him to excuse those sentiments as her influence. He supposed, with his practiced mental shields, nothing he had ever felt for her had been forcefully imposed.

After that, throughout all the summers Angor and Aethelred had spent in East Mintle, the rest of their gang had never returned to Hastings Street.

But now they were *here*, at the medical history museum, Casimir smoking again, Ephraim wearing a handgun on his hip, and Olalla looking like she just walked out of a punk rock concert. It was absurd.

Still, Angor was determined to restore Olalla to her previous self, hence why he asked for a private audience. If he could discuss his scientific discoveries with her away from the influence of the others, perhaps he could switch on the innately curious part of her brain and switch off the innately power-hungry part.

He guided her to the right side of the building, leaving a respectful distance between them. He did not grab her like Casimir had grabbed Aethelred; he had never been as comfortable with physical contact as Casimir was—nor as Olalla had become, apparently.

He'd noticed the way she touched the hallucinator's hand, and it had provoked an alarming amount of jealousy. Not because he thought the two were romantically involved; he didn't think there was one heterosexual cell in Casimir's body—or more accurately, one cell that wasn't completely obsessed with Aethelred.

Nevertheless, Angor envied that Casimir had maintained a relationship with Olalla, had grown a *stronger* relationship with her, even. At one point, Angor would have given up all his future romances for the chance to simply be Olalla's friend. Then he'd realized she was like a drug: bad for him, but he hadn't noticed until he'd gone through withdrawal. She was intoxicating, but debilitatingly so. She had made him believe he could do anything, and he had done anything, but most of anything consisted of the things he should not have been doing. Stealing, conning, killing—he'd engaged in all of it with her, and without her, his morals had shifted slightly toward the lighter end of the scale. *Slightly*.

"Well, Periculy, here's your moment," Olalla declared, crossing her arms as she stopped with her back to the building. The shade of surrounding trees shadowed most of her face, but a few beams of sunlight hit her hair, lightening it to the color of lilacs.

Angor cleared his throat and simpered. "Why have you convinced Ephraim to kill the fewest number of people possible—and why is he your puppet? Seems like more work than if you were to run the organization yourself."

Olalla rolled her eyes. "I'm not controlling him. We're friends, and we agree on this. Why should we kill random people? I'll kill those who've wronged me, but so far, none of the people in this city have. If they mutiny against us, that's a different story." A pause ensued, in which her defiance wavered. Her gaze darted toward the street, where a group of students walked by, laughing as the two of them might have if she'd chosen to join his studious adventure four years ago. "Who else do you think I killed?" she asked. "Did...did Artemis turn up dead somewhere?"

"No. My mother did."

Her attention snapped back to him. Apprehension filled her expression, but not shock, nor sympathy, nor guilt, nor any of the emotions she should have felt.

"Earlier this year, I began searching for her," he

explained, pacing back and forth in a short line as he recounted the tale. "I thought she might want to see my college graduation—I thought she might have changed for the better. But now I see people don't change for the better." Halting, he shot her an accusatory look. "In my search, I discovered from Pennsylvanian authorities that six years ago, she got off a bus and then got hit by that same bus—jumped in front of it, claims the bus driver."

Olalla said nothing. He'd hoped she might confess to it, might repent, but remorse was not a language she spoke.

"You made her kill herself," he said.

A moment passed, during which Olalla glared past him, breathing carefully. "Why are you upset?" she finally demanded. "You watched me kill my mother, and you saw how happy I was in the months after. You should feel the same happiness knowing the person who oppressed you is dead."

Angor countered her heat with pure ice. "My malice toward her was juvenile and selfish. I should have worked to improve her; I should have placed her in a rehabilitation center. Instead, I let you throw her in a grave. I took the easiest path, like you want to take the easiest path now. Overthrowing the government might be a simple, effective method for now, but it won't yield long term results. The federal government will retaliate, and your small band of Affinities won't stand a chance. You will spark a civil war, and we will lose."

"We?" she scoffed, throwing her head back to scowl at the sunny sky. "You want no part in this, and we won't force you. You'll be fine in your posh museum, surrounded by all the elite scholars."

"No, I'll be arrested as a terrorist for my appearance," he

said and then snorted at the ridiculousness of it. Olalla lowered her chin but wouldn't look at him, so he took a step closer to her, wishing he could decrease the distance between their minds with such ease. "You'll be amazed by what I've discovered these past few years, Olalla. White matter…it's not nothing. It's what allows the lobes of the brain to interact."

She studied his lab coat, remaining stubbornly silent. He plowed on. "I've been thinking, as I've studied the brain, that we *are* like the lobes of the brain. Aethelred the temporal lobe, where most memories are stored; Casimir the occipital lobe, where vision is translated; me the parietal lobe, where sensation is processed; and you the frontal lobe, where decisions are made."

"And the white matter is what, our love for each other?"

He would have confirmed that if not for the dryness of her tone. In his metaphor, the binds of their friendship were like white matter, allowing them to harmoniously connect, but *love* was perhaps not the right word. "More like our shared ambitions and abilities. The fact that we're all Affinities is our white matter, and our white matter, I believe, is what makes us Affinities—or Mentals, at least. If my thesis is correct, our white matter contains axons that connect not with cell bodies in our gray matter but in *other people's* gray matter through externally transmitting brainwaves. It sounds crazy, I know, but—"

"I must admit, my knowledge on the brain is…dusty," she interrupted, obviously embarrassed. He supposed she should be for not staying current with scientific research, but he wouldn't chastise her.

"That's not a problem—I'll happily explain it to you. I've been eager to share my theories with someone whose mind works quickly enough to understand what I'm talking about. Aethelred listens, but he only ever nods and says '*Interesting*,' so I know he has no idea what any of it means. People's brains function at different frequencies depending on what we're doing. I believe *your* Affinity allows you to alter others' beta waves—the waves active when we make judgements or decisions."

"I know what beta waves are," she mumbled, but in his eagerness, he barely heard her.

"Your ability might be more effective if you could affect alpha waves or theta waves; people are more susceptible when in a meditative or dreamlike state."

One purple eyebrow rose. "Are you inadvertently telling me how I might finally manage to use my Affinity on you?"

"I don't think it'd work. I always know what's a dream and what's reality."

Her narrowed eyes affirmed that she'd comprehended his implication: that their plans to claim Cleveland were an impractical fantasy. "This is wonderful information, Periculy, but what use does the knowledge of brainwaves and white matter have other than to boost your ego with their complexity?"

"You don't understand? With this knowledge, we could create devices to *enhance* your Affinity. If we can determine the right frequency, I could build an antenna of sorts—like a radio that would allow you to control all minds in a vicinity. Using that power, you could make the authorities comply with our terms without violence."

"You want me to wager our future as a species on this theoretical device?" A bitter laugh escaped her lips. "Angor, we need to act *now*. As attractive as that sounds, we can't wait for you to build me some mind controlling helmet. The government is looking for us. We need to have Cleveland as our base—as leverage. We're acting tonight."

He wanted to argue, but the wick of his ecstasy had burned out. If anyone could share his zeal for science, it was Olalla, but her greed for power had suffocated her love of knowledge. Without that shared passion, nothing tethered them; she was a frontal lobe making decisions without a parietal lobe to anchor her to reality.

"All the Affinities are meeting at a house on Forest Ave in Woodland Hills, ten o'clock tonight," she said. "You'll see the vans on the street. You don't have to come—I've always told you that—but know that if you don't join us, we won't help you when the government comes for you."

"Sounds like a cult, Cosmos. You give this threatening little speech to all new recruits?"

"No. We tell other Affinities we'll always be willing to help. It's only *you* I have no interest in babysitting." Despite the harsh words, she puckered her lips in a teasing manner. She believed she'd won this argument, that by entrusting him with this information, she'd earned his allegiance. That was perhaps the saddest part of all this: how completely her intelligence and common sense had dissolved.

"Will you join us, Periculy, or will you be a spineless coward?"

Angor didn't respond, but the intensity of his eyes assured her he would be there.

Oh, he would be there.

After walking from the museum to their car, picking up and driving a few Affinities to different locations throughout the city, and taking a detour to the grocery store, Ephraim drove them to Forest Avenue. The two-story home's neon green exterior practically glowed in the evening darkness, even without streetlights to illuminate it. They'd chosen it for its oddness: a beacon to the weird.

Casimir purposely flew forward into the driver's seat when they stopped behind the line of black vans identical to their own. Usually when he did this, Ephraim grumbled curses and threw fruit at him, but the younger man was silent now, extracting himself from the vehicle without a sound.

The upcoming conflict hung over them, an opaque film of uncertainty. For weeks, Ephraim had been manically optimistic about the plan, and to see his serious, almost somber demeanor now disquieted Olalla. Angor's warnings had not worried her, but a small part of her wondered if his foresight might prove accurate—if they might win this night only to be snuffed out tomorrow.

"Our diversions in each district should be underway as we speak," Ephraim said to Olalla and Casimir as they slipped out of the van. "If our guy in the CDP wasn't lying, the disturbances should be enough to draw out most of the officers on duty. It'll be a lot, but I think we can handle it, especially since everyone else's Physical except us."

"I thought we decided Claramae's diamond Affinity was Natural." Olalla didn't wait for him to answer before hauling a bag of canned goods from their van to one of the others. Their plan, if all their friends throughout the city got arrested, was to take three of their nine minivans and flee the city for a safe house they'd set up near Pittsburg. Sarah had already taken one since Ephraim didn't want her anywhere near Cleveland during this ordeal. She'd probably arrived hours ago with that kid Fraco, safe and secure while the rest of them risked their lives in this mad stunt.

Olalla supposed it wasn't the girl's war to fight, but it still peeved her that the Regg had been spared all danger when her species was the reason they had to do this.

And they did *have* to do this. Perhaps the government had not killed those boys in New York City four years ago, but they had killed Affinities since. In every city they stopped at, they held a peaceful rally for Affinities, trying to draw them out of hiding, and in every city they stopped at, the police aggressively intervened. Granted, one of their group members was typically the one to throw the first punch, but the police didn't mind escalating it.

Despite their losses, they'd accumulated three hundred fifty-seven Affinities to their cause over the years. Many remained in their home cities to gather more Affinities, but fifty-three had ventured to Cleveland with them for this insurrection. Their number was small in comparison to their enemy, but their powers compensated. They'd met so many with extraordinary abilities: a man who could shoot thorns, a girl with fiberglass fists, and even a toddler with a *cereal* Affinity. Angor was not the only one to come across new knowledge since high school.

"It doesn't matter," Ephraim called to her as she deposited her stash of food in the van she would take if the plan failed. "Her Affinity can *physically* damage. Did you convince Periculy to help us? We could really use his Affinity when infiltrating the police departments."

"He'll come," she affirmed, stalking back toward them. She didn't *know* if Angor would come, but her argument had surely convinced him, and if not, then her presence alone had. Though she'd never successfully used her Affinity on him, she knew he had always found her impossible to resist.

Casimir flashed a lazy, spiteful smile. "How'd you manage that? Mind control or smooching?"

"How'd you manage to make innocent Aethelred hate you? Your constant hallucinations or your horrible—" Olalla paused when the low sound of an engine caught her ear. She wouldn't have thought anything of a car passing, except she didn't see any cars. Ephraim and Casimir followed her gaze as she squinted down the street, to where a dark mass rolled toward them—several dark masses.

"Shit, we've been compromised—get in the car!" She grabbed the handle to yank open the door, but then flashing lights swarmed the area, so many more than she'd thought.

The cop cars flowed from every direction, flooding every street to converge on Forest Avenue. Sirens accompanied them, so deafening Olalla almost didn't hear the deep whir of an approaching helicopter.

Ephraim extracted his gun from its holster, eyeing the influx of enemies with a critical eye, but Casimir didn't move, his jaw wound tight as he surveyed the scene. Red and blue flickered over his face, accentuating his cold fury. "Which one of those weak assholes ratted out our location?"

"Probably Luther," Ephraim grunted, rotating back and forth, unsure where to aim. At least ten vehicles had surrounded them, most now stopped, the officers jumping out to engage. "He's always been a wimp."

Olalla kept her mouth clamped shut; she'd compelled everyone who knew of the house to never want to divulge the location. Perhaps she hadn't reinforced it enough; perhaps she was too far now to ensure that determination persisted.

Either way, the blame was on her shoulders. She felt more out of control than she ever had, especially when one of the policemen yelled from behind his door, "Hands in the air!"

Too many minds filled the vicinity for her to determine which had shouted. She supposed it didn't matter; all twenty officers likely had guns trained in their direction. Casimir could plant hallucinations in up to seven people's brains at once, but Olalla had never managed to control more than one mind at a time.

Waiting for Angor's Affinity-enhancing device would have alleviated this problem. Waiting for Angor's Affinity-enhancing device also would have prevented this problem, because as the back door to the nearest car opened, she realized what her denial of his proposal had cost them.

"Periculy?" Casimir rubbed his eyes, probably convinced their former friend was a hallucination. He was not. Olalla saw him clearly in the flashing lights, his face a mask of complacency. "They caught you too? Dude, how'd you convince them not to cuff you? Did you use your mad science to give yourself Olalla's Affinity?"

"No, he didn't," Ephraim growled, training his weapon on their old friend. Olalla should have done something—should have screamed at him—should have tried using her brainwaves to decimate every cell in his body—but she stood motionless in shock.

"These are the leaders of Affinities for Freedom, the ones who have organized terror on your city tonight," Angor told the officers, impassive and authoritative. "Don't shoot. I'll handle this."

Olalla didn't expect an entire police force to heed the words of a twenty-two-year-old, but he didn't give them time to contradict his commands. Within the span of five seconds, Ephraim dropped his gun to clutch his hand, moaning, and Casimir took a step forward only to drop to his knees, seething.

Pain surged from Olalla's toes up her body, infecting every nociceptor from her superficial flesh to her deep organs. When it reached her spinal cord, she nearly collapsed, but she refused to react—refused to let Angor win. Even as black spots blurred her vision, she kept her aching muscles active and braced.

The police rushed forward, most guns trained on Olalla since she was the only one left standing. Through the agony, she wondered if Angor had inflicted less pain on her or if Casimir and Ephraim simply had never learned to block out physical torture the way she had.

As a group of officers handcuffed the writhing Affinities, Angor sauntered toward Olalla, pausing once he stood a foot from her. She clenched her fists until blood pooled beneath her fingernails, wishing she could unleash her rage on the perpetrator of her suffering, but every tendon felt torn, every joint dislocated.

Sighing, his eyes softened with patronizing pity. "You should have listened to me."

"You shouldn't have *tattled on us*," she snarled.

"I didn't want to, but you were being foolish, and I couldn't let you doom us all."

"Screw you—screw…all of this. No cell will hold me. I can…bend anyone's will," she vowed through labored breaths.

"Anyone except me." Slowly, he began to circle her, and the intensity of her pain shifted to different parts of her body, following him like a magnet. "I've been studying antioxidants, you know, along with various other compounds and nutrients. It appears antioxidants help cognitive function—make it easier to think clearly. I won't entirely credit my mental resistance to my love for walnuts, but they helped guard my mind against you." He stopped on her left side to whisper in her ear. "You should have listened to me, Olalla. I could have told you about all my discoveries—about the various scientific methods I've found to combat you. All the substances I've concocted to inhibit your brainwaves; all the substances I've concocted to suppress one's own Affinity from use…"

He slipped in front of her, standing so close she could have felt his heat if her body didn't already feel aflame. His expression turned sad, and when he caressed her jaw, she swore the bone broke. "Maybe one day I'll break you out," he said, "but for now, this is what you deserve."

As he stepped back, all the pain congealed in her chest, so intense it forced a cry from her mouth. Still, she did not fall, not until the magnitude of her tormented cells overwhelmed her brain and stole her last fragment of control.

15

Escapes and Excuses

After experiencing the activation of every nociceptor in her body, Olalla had thought no other pain would compare.

She had been wrong.

Her life became a blur of white walls, bright lights, and needles. She did not know her exact location, but she had once been a researcher, and she knew this was a research facility.

"Fuck me," Casimir groaned every time the masked experimenters rolled him back to their shared cell and carelessly deposited him on his cot. To Ephraim he would add, "Not you," to Olalla he would add, "and *definitely* not you," and then he would burst into hysterical cackles that ended in sobs.

They all returned in a state of hysteria after each bout of dissection—or rather, since they were still alive, vivisection. Painkillers were pumped into their veins, along with other drugs that made them loopy, but they never fully went unconscious. Perhaps the researchers didn't think they could be traumatized—perhaps the researchers didn't *care* if they were traumatized. In the experimenters' minds, Affinities were the lesser species.

They certainly treated them like animals, keeping them in tiny cells behind metal bars. The crammed space didn't allow any room between their three beds; Olalla often awoke with Ephraim's cuffed hands on her face or Casimir's green curls nestled in the crook of her neck. She didn't mind because she didn't feel like she had a mind.

Before, she had sensed other consciousnesses without effort, but now she couldn't detect any thoughts except her own. They slithered through her head like vipers, cold and venomous. She did not know what substances her tormentors injected to suppress her Affinity, but if they ever forgot a dose, she would not hesitate to make every one of these Reggs gouge out their own eyes.

Then she would hunt down Angor Periculy and impose an even worse fate.

What hurt the worst was the image of his face etched on the inside of her eyelids, that self-righteous gleam to his expression before he'd stolen her freedom. She should have known Periculy would never join a group he had not founded—a group he could not control. His lust for power burned as strong as hers, and he had stooped to the lowest low not to acquire it but to ensure she *didn't* acquire it.

For once, she was thankful for her Cosmos genes, her unwillingness to forgive or forget. She would traverse every inch of this Earth until she found him, and once she did, she would traverse it again, this time painting the world in his blood. Angor Periculy would not exist when she was through with him. First, she just had to survive *this*.

And she assumed she *would* survive it until they witnessed the researchers roll a body bag down the hall on a gurney. Sapphire blue hair poked from the top—Luther.

"Can't say I'm sad to see him go." Ephraim sighed,

staring at the ceiling. "Can say I don't like what it means for us."

Olalla didn't like it, either, but the death reignited her will to live. After that, she refused to resign to the drug-induced stupor. Even as chemicals barraged her brain, she forced herself to remain alert, forced herself to retain some information about the facility outside their cell.

That proved impossible while she was starving and malnourished and Affinity-less and *angry*. All she remembered was one scientist saying, "I think we may have found a permanent immunity to her Affinity," which enraged her more.

One day, the researchers opened their cell without a gurney waiting in the hall. Olalla's perception of time was skewed, but she imagined it had been weeks, if not months, since their incarceration began. None of the experimenters looked familiar to her since they all wore lab coats and full head coverings, but this one's voice indicated him as the one who'd discovered the permanent immunity to her Affinity.

"Get up," he barked. They'd never *commanded* the Affinities to do anything; they'd always dragged them from their cells and electrically shocked them if they didn't comply. When the three tentatively stood now, the man waved a dismissive hand at Olalla and Casimir. "Not you two. Just him."

Cautious, she sat at the end of her cot but didn't lie back down. "What's going on?"

In response, the researcher yanked on Ephraim's manacles and *unlocked* them. Olalla's and Casimir's mouths fell open, but their friend did not look surprised. With a contented sigh, he rubbed his wrists and nodded to the experimenters in gratitude.

"You're—you're letting him go?" Olalla jumped from her cot but paused when the researcher in the hall raised his stungun. Physical combat had never been her strength, and considering she could barely stand on her atrophying legs, she did not wish to bawl.

Ephraim stopped massaging his blistered wrists to glare at her. "Rich parents can get you places."

"You *bribed* them?" Casimir stumbled off his own cot, ignorant of the weapon buzzing in the researcher's hand. "Oh, thank God they take bribes. Bail us out, man."

Ephraim straightened his back, lengthening to a taller stature than the men in the doorway. Though his body looked like a collection of frail twigs, he exuded sophistication and a hint of sadism as he retrieved his baseball cap from the closer researcher and shoved it on his too-long locks. "I have a family—I have a *wife*. You two have nothing and no one, and your lives don't matter. It's your fault we're here at all—you were both blinded by romance. You trusted the wrong people, and now you'll pay the consequences."

Fury bubbled in Olalla's chest. All desire to avoid a brawl evaporated as she lunged at her old friend, preparing to strangle him with her metal manacles. She didn't even reach him before the researcher kicked her in the abdomen, shoving her backward into Casimir. The two tumbled onto his cot, collapsing it, and watched in a heap of tangled, weak limbs as Ephraim saluted them and disappeared beyond the metal bars.

Casimir didn't try to disentangle himself; he threw his head back against the broken remnants of his cot and laughed. He laughed and laughed and laughed until a different pair of researchers retrieved him for experimentation. Even once the warmth of his body had disappeared, Olalla didn't move. She contemplated life, contemplated death, contemplated Ephraim's parting words.

"You have nothing and no one," she whispered to herself, realizing it was true. "Your life doesn't matter."

What awaited her if they escaped? A world where Affinities were hunted—a world *they* had created. A world where she had no coalition of her species to protect her. A world where Angor Periculy had betrayed her, and she wouldn't have the strength to stop him if he did so again.

Casimir was all she had left; Casimir was the one person who might still love her despite her mistakes; Casimir was her lifeline, and he seemed on the verge of death. She wondered how long until his insanity and sorrow stopped his heart— until she truly had nothing.

Staring at the concrete walls, she remembered Angor comparing their group to a brain, working harmoniously toward the same goal. The individual lobes of the brain could not properly function alone. Severed from one another, each lobe was nothing more than a meaningless clump of cells. That was what Olalla felt like lying on the floor, caged and chained—a meaningless clump of cells.

"I've spoken to the town *and* the state—must I go to the White House simply to create my own town for a marginalized species of superhumans?"

Walking beside Angor, Than Floros worried at his lower lip. "The government *has* become quite complex over the past two millennia. Back in my day, people simply killed each other for land! Well, perhaps not in the Mediterranean region. We were more advanced than the barbarians in the north… I would say the modern method is less brutal, but this mission of ours has been miserably—"

"Did you say *millennia*?" Angor interrupted, halting his strides before they reached the sidewalk. They'd just exited Columbus City Hall after a long conversation with the governor, and the setting sun bathed the normally white building in hues of orange.

A breeze from the Scioto River blew Than's brown hair in his face. He brushed it aside before hastily asking, "Did I say millennia? Oh, I meant *centuries*. My English is still…mad after only a hundred years of speaking it."

Angor arched an eyebrow as he continued toward his blood red car, parked on the side of the road. "*Bad*, you mean?"

"Oh, yes, I meant *bad*. See, Angor, you really should not take my diction so seriously, especially not when I ramble about ancient Greece or anything of the sort."

On another day, Angor might have found this behavior odd—although, Than generally *was* very odd—but now his thoughts spun solely around the failures of their escapade. After the *incident* in Cleveland, he'd decided real action needed to be taken not only in the science of Affinities but in the *society* of Affinities. Years ago, when he'd first entered college, he'd placed some of the money he and Olalla had stolen in the stock market, which had accumulated a startling amount of wealth since. Two months ago, he'd used a portion of that money to buy a massive plot of farmland in southern Ohio, where he planned to erect *Periculand*.

The problem was not funding the project but *legalizing* the project. Angor's plot of land was already *in* a town, they argued; why must he declare his own town, and why should it be exclusively for a fictional group of people?

Because, they claimed, *Affinities* did not exist. According to them, Angor had dyed his hair and used contact lenses in his eyes; *superpowers* were a comic book myth. To counter this, he had *proven* his ability, first by alleviating pain and then by inflicting pain. Each time he attempted this, the government officials remained stone-faced, insisting they felt nothing.

That was when Angor realized they knew all about Affinities but they wanted the issue to disappear. They didn't want the public to catch on; the Affinities for Freedom stunt in Cleveland had spurred too much panic. This definitely created a new obstacle for the government—and made Angor wonder what they might have done with Olalla, Casimir, and Ephraim.

He'd told the authorities they possessed superpowers, as well as given the police his Affinity-suppressing serum, but he hadn't suspected they would believe him. Frankly, he'd expected them to discard the serum; he'd expected Olalla to use her Affinity to break out once she awoke; he'd expected the whole affair to be more of a warning to his friends than an eternal punishment. If the government *knew* what they were capable of, though, would they have thrown his friends in a normal prison?

Considering he hadn't "committed suicide" in the past three months, he suspected not. Likely they'd been brought to a very high level detainment center, one even Olalla might never escape.

That was why Aethelred had thrown a tantrum.

Angor had returned to their apartment the morning after the incident to find Aethelred sitting on their leather couch, staring numbly at the television. The footage had shown destruction throughout Cleveland, along with a montage of terrorists with oddly-colored hair being arrested.

"Fifty-one suspects have been apprehended by the CDP due to the mayhem that unfolded in Cleveland last night. Officials have declared this the end of the terrorist group, Affinities for Freedom. Citizens are to report sightings of people with strange hair and eyes to the local authorities…"

"Good morning," Angor greeted tentatively, closing the door behind him. He wore the same pink button up shirt and dark khakis from the previous night, since the police had kept him for hours of questioning, but Aethelred didn't need to see his haggard appearance to know what had happened.

"It's not a *good morning*. Angor"—he stood, tears glossing his red eyes—"you *tattled* on them, didn't you?"

Rolling his eyes, he paced to their kitchen to make a cup of coffee. "It would be my luck that, in Olalla's last effort to irk me, she instilled silly beliefs in your mind from an impossible distance."

Aethelred spun to slap his hands on the countertop between them. In an embarrassing display of nerves, Angor *jumped*. Nothing ever startled him—especially not *Aethelred*. In the past four years, his friend had become a rational, stoic individual, the kind of calm that made Angor proud. In that moment, every emotion he'd bottled up unleashed in an unprecedented outburst.

"This is not a *joke*. You've ruined their lives—you've ruined *everything*. We'll never see them again—they're probably *dead*."

With a dismissive wave, Angor returned to brewing his coffee. "They aren't *dead*, Aethelred; they're in *prison*. I only gave the cops enough of my serum to last a few days. Olalla will be at our doorstep by next weekend, hashing out her plan to murder me and take over the world. I don't know why you *care*. We haven't been friends with them for longer than we ever were friends with them."

"I *care* because it's the *government*! Do you think they won't use this opportunity to experiment on criminals? We're a different *species*. They're going to dissect them!"

Angor refused to glance back at his friend's wrathful expression, mostly because he didn't want to believe his prediction could be true. "They don't need to dissect them. I've already discovered the 24th chromosome."

"And have you published that discovery?"

"Well…no. I feared…" He'd feared this—exactly this: government experimentation. He shook his head, refusing to consider it. "No, *no*. If they were experimenting on humans, I think I would know about it."

"Because you'd be in charge of the experiments, I'm sure," Aethelred scoffed. Sighing, Angor spun to face his friend's bloodshot eyes and tear-stained cheeks. Though he'd never been much of a crier, Aethelred had always been the emotional one, the anxious one who over-exaggerated every dilemma. This was no different. Olalla, Casimir, and Ephraim were *not* being dissected, firstly because they weren't dead, and secondly because *vivisection* was highly illegal.

"Look, if you'd like, we can—"

"No, Angor—there is no *we* anymore. I've dutifully followed you for twelve years, but I won't anymore. Not if you'll lead us down this path of betrayal and corruption and distrust. How *can* I trust you now? Will you kick me out of this apartment if I don't want to watch science documentaries with you? Will you convince the school to kick me out if I disagree with your thesis on white matter?"

Angor stopped pouring his coffee to narrow his eyes at his friend. "*Do* you disagree with my thesis on white matter?"

In an uncharacteristic fit of aggression, Aethelred grabbed

the science magazine on the counter and threw it at Angor. It missed, instead hitting the half-poured cup of coffee, which sprayed dark brown droplets all over the wallpaper.

"It doesn't matter what I think. I'm dropping out of school. I'm done with this place. I'm done with *you*." Then, without gathering more than his wallet, he'd stormed from the apartment and never returned.

Angor had not seen him since, not in Cleveland nor Columbus nor anywhere in Ohio. He wouldn't have been surprised if his former friend had rejoined the circus or traveled across the world simply to displace himself as far from Angor as possible.

"You know," Than said as they neared the car. A black minivan had parked close behind, wedging Angor's vehicle between it and a school bus. He exhaled wearily, knowing he would spend the next ten minutes extricating his car and listening to whatever knowledge Than *knew*. "We could make it a *school* instead of a *town*—a private school, where we only accept Affinities. That might bypass the government regula—"

Angor threw a hand against Than's chest, halting his speech and his movements as a figure emerged from behind the minivan, wielding a black rifle.

At least, Angor thought it was a rifle. His understanding of firearms was woefully limited. He'd listened to Ephraim gush about them every lunch period in high school, but he hadn't retained the information. Now, as the boy in the baseball cap stood before him with the weapon trained on him, he wished he'd listened more carefully.

"Well, Periculy, don't you look spiffy." Ephraim ran his lime green eyes over Angor's dark fuchsia suit, a spiteful smile on his lips. "And *healthy*, huh? Been eating three square meals a day these past months? Been sleeping peacefully? Been a free man and not a science experiment who was slapped on a table every day to be poked and prodded by a bunch of twisted creeps?"

Angor maintained an impassive façade, but his heart rate had elevated to an uncommon high. Beneath his black jeans and leather jacket, Ephraim appeared deathly thin, his skin sallow and his cheeks sunken. Aethelred, it seemed, had not overreacted.

After assessing how he might avoid a bullet to the head, Angor cleared his throat. "Did they discover anything useful about your Affinity, at least?"

"Did they—" Ephraim let out a dark laugh, shifting the gun in his hands. "You probably *told* them to experiment on us, didn't you? Probably told them we're some genetic anomaly that they'd love to study and exploit."

"Technically, we're a chromosomal anomoly..." Angor shut his mouth when the man stepped forward. Slowly, he lifted his hands in a sign of surrender. "I don't wish to fight, Ephraim—nor to argue. I didn't know where you would be detained. My goal was to prevent you from inflicting irreparable damage on the city and on our species. I realize my actions might have been extreme—"

"Really, you think?"

Angor moistened his lips, disregarding the sarcasm. "But your actions were extreme, too. We should not be enemies; we are *allies*. I have made plans these past months—plans that will help Affinities in a nonviolent way. You have served your punishment for the chaos you created. Now you can join me—join my mission to create a whole town where our kind can be free."

"I don't want a *town*." Ephraim spat on the sidewalk. "I

want *anywhere* in this country to be free for Affinities. You aim too low, Periculy. You want to contain us, but we can't be contained."

"You don't understand—this will be our first step to greater freedom. If we organize ourselves in a peaceful manner, the government will see we aren't a threat. Work with me on this. We'll convince Casimir and Olalla to join, as well."

"Oh, will we? *How* will we when they're still rats in a lab?"

All hope died in Angor's chest. He'd thought the other two were behind the tinted windows of the minivan, cursing him but not killing him. He'd assumed the fact that Olalla had yet to manipulate Ephraim into shooting him was a sign of their possible alliance. She was still imprisoned, though, still suffering.

"You escaped...but they didn't?"

"My parents bailed me out," Ephraim huffed, seeming a little self-conscious about it. "Looks like *you* have enough wealth to bail them out. Do it, Periculy. Then all three of us can kill you together."

Angor's jaw shifted as he contemplated this predicament. He probably *did* have the funds to bail them out, depending on the magnitude of the price. For unintentionally placing them in such a hell, he should have sacrificed his dreams for Periculand to free them. But...then what? Then they would kill him. Casimir, despite his nonchalance, possessed an untamed rage, and Olalla *was* rage—she was chaos and vengeance and the epitome of unforgiving. She would kill anyone who tried to stop her from killing Angor.

Or anyone who tried to kill him first.

"I'm an impatient man, though," Ephraim said, "so let's get this over with now, shall we?"

Angor wouldn't have had time to react if he hadn't seen this coming, if he hadn't felt the slight pressure in the nociceptors on Ephraim's fingertips as he prepared to pull the trigger. With his Affinity, he sparked debilitating pain in the gunman's hands, and with his body, he launched to the side, tackling Than with him.

The gun fired, provoking screams from afar. City Hall's doors flew open, and within a minute, the police would arrive. Honestly, Angor was surprised no one had noticed the guy with the massive gun before now.

Lying on the ground with groaning Than, he peeked up to see Ephraim's scowling eyes darting around. They landed on Angor, two green flames to match the tattoos on his forearms. "We're enemies now, Periculy. Make a town, and I'll destroy it. Join the government, and I'll execute you along with all the other political assholes. Just because you can't immediately feel the pain I inflict doesn't mean it's not there."

Then he jogged around his vehicle to jump in the driver's seat and speed away. Sirens blared seconds later, and one police cruiser followed the minivan, but Angor knew they wouldn't catch him. He would probably throw watermelons out the window at them.

Sitting upright, Angor beheld the meaning of Ephraim's last words. From a tear in his pink pants, blood oozed, painting the concrete red. The bullet had grazed his outer thigh, and he had not felt it. Even now, sensation was null. Not until he pried away the veil of his Affinity did the pain hit his mind, searing and almost unbearable to someone who had avoided the inconvenience of physical aches for years.

He supposed the feud between him and Ephraim would reflect this flesh wound. The man knew him—knew what would hurt him worst. If Angor created Periculand, the

Affinities for Freedom leader could easily infiltrate his town with spies and tear it apart from the inside without Angor noticing until it was too late.

And if Ephraim freed Olalla and Casimir, all hell would break loose.

For now, Angor wouldn't fret about it. His focus steadied on this moment, on the government officials running down the steps to his aid, on the police officers surrounding him and calling for an ambulance.

Angor didn't need an ambulance; he needed *sympathy*. Though he'd inhibited his nociceptors once again, he screwed his face in pain and looked up at the men who had denied him his town. How could they deny him now when his species was so obviously a target?

"Have you erased my memory?" Casimir tilted his head toward Olalla, a deliriously accusatory look in his eyes. "I feel like I can't remember a life before this."

A long time ago, she would have retreated from his touch—retreated from his *stench*—but they'd grown accustomed to cuddling on their cots for warmth in their chilly cell. Their clothing was threadbare and sullied, but she had become used to the cold and lack of sanitation. This *was* their life now. Sometimes even for her, remembering the past proved difficult.

Then she recalled her everlasting hatred for Angor Periculy, and all the memories returned.

A moss-like shadow coated Casimir's jaw since the researchers hadn't shaved his face in a few days. Olalla's hair probably would have extended past her hips by now if they didn't periodically cut it into a short, uneven mess. Her hair's growth was the only way she could judge time. If her calculations were correct, they'd been here over three years now.

Three years—as long as they'd been friends with Angor and Aethelred; almost as long as they'd taken to form Affinities for Freedom. So many of the Affinities they'd recruited for the Cleveland chaos had since been rolled out in body bags, dead. Most of the time it was difficult to discern who it was, but if the hair was visible, they knew.

She wondered if Ephraim had continued the movement once he'd left, rallying the Affinities from other states to riot over the injustice of these research facilities. Given they'd yet to be broken out, he'd probably decided to have a nice, quiet life with his wife.

Olalla hoped Sarah had assumed her husband dead and found a new partner during his three months of imprisonment. Even that was less than he deserved for leaving them here to rot.

"No, I didn't make you forget the past." Olalla stared beyond Casimir at the darkened walls. At night, the lights turned off in the cells, but a guard still roamed the halls, his shadow flickering over the metal bars. "I *could* make you forget the past…or the now. I could probably erase your entire mind."

Casimir shifted away from her, suspicious.

"I *won't*." Olalla released one laugh, then two more. "I *can't*, Casimir. I can't do anything."

"Right, right," he mumbled, scooting closer again. "Sometimes…I feel like I remember too much, actually. Remember what real food tastes like, not whatever cardboard shit they give us here. Pepperoni—I remember pepperoni!

God, what I would give... I remember driving my car—good old Willy's car, ha. I remember *stealing* that car, remember Red running like a wounded lamb to—"

"*Don't* talk about them," Olalla snarled, more aggressive than she'd felt in months. "Don't even think about them. They put us in here, Casimir."

His entire body froze, like he thought she would slap him. The fearless boy had become so fearful during their years of vivisection, startling at every noise. *He* seemed like the wounded lamb now, and the amount of sympathy she felt for him unsettled her. His assumption that she would slap him also unsettled her. She was *not* her mother. No matter how much the world ripped her apart, she would not become her mother.

"I...remember when life was interesting," he tried again, this time speaking slower to gauge her reaction. When she said nothing, he added, "I remember when my brain always gave you a witch's hat."

She snorted. "I remember when I felt like a witch—powerful, intimidating, ambitious."

Once, Casimir might have made a joke about her being the nerdiest witch alive, but humor had become as unfamiliar to them as the sun. "Everything here looks...weird—dull—normal, I guess. My world was much more vibrant than this one. Can't decide if I like knowing what's real or hate to know that this is real."

With her cuffed hands, she reached toward his cuffed hands, brushing their fingers together but not intertwining them. In his fraying t-shirt, all the tattoos on his arms were visible. None were quite as *clean* as the microscope he'd inked on her thigh. Jagged dragons and dinosaurs riddled his skin, splattered with random colors. He'd used his own flesh to practice drawing with the needle, which was probably why his left arm looked even messier than his right.

Olalla closed her eyes and recalled all their years on the road, all the cities they'd visited and people they'd met. Since her parents were poor, they'd never vacationed, so witnessing beaches and deserts had been novel experiences, the kind she would never enjoy again.

A scream echoed from beyond their cell, but she didn't even flinch. During the day, wails from the lab were common, and during the night, wails from their fellow prisoners' nightmares were common. Perhaps she should have felt empathy, but only frustration and fury surfaced.

"I'm sorry," she whispered, words she had never uttered before. When she squinted her eyes open, Casimir had adopted an expression of absolute disbelief.

"For...what?"

Her eyes squeezed shut again. "For trusting Angor."

"Hey..." His knuckles brushed against hers, then his thumb caressed her hand. "I invited Aethelred along that day. If he hadn't been such a stubborn bastard, I would have gladly given him all our plans. He would have told Angor, like the little sycophant he is, and we'd be in this same shithole. It's not—"

The sound of metal jangling interrupted his speech and pried Olalla's eyes open. Internally, she cursed the researchers for never sleeping, but she supposed she had been that insanely driven once. Exhaling in resignation, she sat upright on her cot to see a middle-aged woman had unlocked their cell—a middle-aged woman wearing tattered clothes, her hair and eyes like sulfur.

She held up her fingers, each one in the shape of a different key. "You kids want those cuffs off, or what?"

With a speed that made her broken muscles ache, Olalla hurried off her cot to present her wrists to the woman. Casimir approached with less fervor, his demeanor guarded.

"Who are you?" he asked. "We…thought we knew all the Affinities here."

"I'm new here—always getting stuck in prisons, always breaking out. The *needles* are new, though. Guess they figured they'd have to sedate me this time. I tripped the asshole before he could administer any drugs, then plunged my fingers into his eyes." After unlocking Olalla's cuffs, she morphed her left hand into an array of tiny drills. "Had to do the same to a few others."

She nodded toward the hall, and when Olalla poked her head through the threshold, she found a guard dead on the floor, two pockets of red instead of eyes. The drill fingers must have been long enough to shred his brain. So, that was where the scream had come from.

About fifteen cells lined one side of the hall; the other was the blank wall of white they'd stared at through their bars. To their right dwelled two cells, from which six Affinities she recognized had emerged. Five had been part of the failed Cleveland mission, and one was the leader of their cell in Cincinnati.

"Olalla!" The largest of them barreled toward her and scooped her into a hug.

"Trevor," she grunted, legs dangling above the ground, "what did we say about physical affection?"

"It's for babies," Casimir chimed in as he stumbled into the hallway. Trevor immediately dropped Olalla to wrap the green-haired man in a suffocating embrace. "Hey, Trev, we're in the same room and I'm not hearing that awful screeching sound of yours. That's nice."

Olalla straightened her shirt as much as the wrinkled fabric would allow. "It's because we've all been regularly injected with an Affinity-suppressing serum." *Angor's Affinity-suppressing serum*, she did not add. For a fleeting moment, she almost wished she had listened to him brag about his inventions, if only so she knew how long until the effects wore off.

"Where's Ephraim?" Trevor asked upon releasing Casimir. "Is he…"

"Dead? No. I wish," Olalla muttered. The big man must have heard, because his teal blue eyes widened.

"Did he… Is he the reason we were arrested in Cleveland?"

She could have confessed to her own naivety and cleared Ephraim's name amongst these Affinities. Instead, she said, "He's not here, is he?"

The group at the end of the hall exchanged outraged looks. Poor Trevor's face drooped with heartbreak. They'd spotted him at his high school graduation about four years ago, and he'd happily thrown off his cap and gown to join their cause. Since then, he and Ephraim had formed a strong friendship. Olalla didn't feel remorse for crushing it now. She wanted to crush everything Ephraim Mayer held dear.

The woman with the key fingers finished unlocking all the cells, but Olalla didn't turn to see who else had survived. Her gaze had fixed on the door at the closer end of the hall, ajar and leaking light. It was the research room, where the Reggs had treated her species like lab rats for three years.

"Trevor," Olalla prompted quietly. His blue eyes found hers, haunted and broken. "Make sure everyone escapes safely—especially Casimir, okay?"

"Wh-what about you?"

"I'll meet you outside. I just have to…do something first." She nodded toward the lab, and his confusion morphed into understanding.

"Right. Make 'em pay, boss."

She projected every unpleasant thought into her smile. "Oh Key Fingers," she sang, her voice carrying down the hall.

Spinning around, the yellow-haired woman pursed her lips. "My name's Bethel."

"I require your assistance for a moment. The rest of you can leave."

No one argued her command to flee this place, not even those she didn't recognize. Casimir shot her a questioning glance, but she shooed him onward, and he was too tired to object.

As the others filed through the door on the opposite end of the corridor, Key Fingers approached Olalla, normally figured hands hanging at her sides. "What do you want? I don't have endless amounts of time, you know. They've already wasted an entire night of thievery for me."

"I need your help in there." She gestured toward the lab, and Key Fingers rolled her eyes.

"I already killed those dimwits."

A simper unfurled on Olalla's lips. "I assumed. I need your help opening some cabinets."

Some cabinets she'd noticed when she'd tried with all her might to remain lucid and understand her surroundings. She knew the experimenters logged all their data and discoveries, and she wanted to know what, exactly, they had uncovered about her Affinity. After all, if there was a way to suppress, there must also be a way to enhance.

16

Another Thieving Stromer Pt. 3

Olalla hopped down the front steps of the Stromers' mobile home, wrapping a scarf tight around her head. To some extent, three years in a chilly cell had accustomed her to the cold, but her thin limbs didn't provide much cushion against the December wind. At least her winter gear hid her malnourished body—and her gradually growing violet hair.

Civilian Reggs had mostly forgotten about the strange occurrences in Cleveland three and a half years ago, but the government had not. Though they claimed to know nothing of humans with superpowers, Olalla had heard many rumors of Affinities mysteriously disappearing. She'd been there, done that, and she did not wish to do it again.

Snow fell on Hastings Street, draping all the little houses in white. Since Casimir's car was the only working vehicle in the trailer park, no tire marks had marred the street. Olalla was grateful for this pristine, peaceful moment; after today, her life would become a series of strategy and mental assassinations.

"Do you feel ready to drive?" she asked Casimir as she approached his car. His legs hung out the open doorway as he lay on the backseat, scrubbing the seats with an ink-stained cloth. Since they'd returned four months ago, Casimir had refused to look at his car, but this morning he'd awoken with a newfound determination to rid the vehicle of all ridiculous drawings.

He sat up to look at her, ink staining his cheeks. "Ready as I was the day we stole this piece of junk from Willy."

Ten years had passed, but Olalla still remembered that night. She and Casimir had decimated Artemis and her jocks. Never mind the other three fools who'd helped them—the three she'd vowed to decimate, as well.

Casimir patted the driver's headrest and then frowned at the mess on the back of the seats.

"We can paint over it, if that'll make you feel better," she offered, since she didn't much want to see drawings of Angor or Aethelred, either.

Pushing out of the car, Casimir threw the dirty rag in the snow and steadied himself by grabbing the roof. "You know what would make me feel better? Killing your ex-boyfriend."

Olalla's eyes slid past him to the Periculy home at the other end of Hastings Street. When they'd first peeked in, they'd found it absent of accents but not *empty*. The couch and the recliner remained, along with Angor's walnut pedestal: the coffee table. They sometimes spent time in the bedrooms, Olalla researching in hers and Casimir doing God-knows-what in his, but neither had the desire to permanently live there.

The Cosmos home was less of an option. Olalla's father still lived there, and he seemed to be doing *well*. Guests frequently visited, and the few times she'd watched from afar with her binoculars, she noticed him *smiling*. She'd never seen her father smile; she'd been convinced his facial muscles didn't know how. The nice Christians had cured his alcoholism—disgusting.

Though she was tempted to march over there and end him, she'd settled for erasing his entire memory of her instead. She feared killing her only remaining parent would offend Casimir. When they'd returned from the research facility, they'd found both of his parents had died, his father of cancer and his mother by suicide. His grief seemed foreign and unnecessary to her, but she possessed enough common sense to know not to aggravate the emotional wound.

"I agree with you on that," she said in reference to murdering Angor. "Although, I believe I have an even better idea. You'll never believe who works at the East Mintle supermarket."

The East Mintle supermarket had undergone a renovation since they'd graduated. Fancy posters of food hung from the ceiling, and everything was red—everything except Aethelred Certior, who now wore a brown wig to hide his oddness.

She hadn't recognized him until her fourth visit here, and then she had ground her teeth but said nothing. In the three years since they'd seen him, his stature had filled out, erasing all hints of his boyishness. He kept his red eyes aimed downward, even when customers asked him questions, and he must have requested not to work at the register, because she only ever saw him stacking shelves.

A vindictive part of her wanted to mock him for his lowly job, but she didn't feel it was her place to insult him. This portion of their revenge was reserved for Casimir, which was why she had him drive them to the supermarket that snowy afternoon.

Confronting Aethelred in public was risky, especially given the volatility of Casimir's moods. One moment he was his calm self, the next he was impaling drawings of Aethelred with butter knives, and the next he was barricading the door with chairs to stop the researchers from finding them. It was sad. It was also burdensome to Olalla, who needed a reliable partner with which to enact her plans.

That was why she'd explained who they were going to see before they'd departed, to gauge his reaction on Hastings Street and abort the mission prior to its start if he proved unstable. Fortunately, he'd barely reacted at all. His eyes had narrowed, his jaw had shifted, and then he'd nodded before sliding into the driver's seat.

Now he exuded the same level of focus as they wove through the aisles, searching for a ridiculous bush of brown hair. They found their target at the back of the store, shelving meats.

"Excuse me, kind sir," Olalla beckoned. As expected, Aethelred refused to make eye contact, instead staring at their shoes. Apparently, wearing sneakers in a snowstorm was a level of idiocy only they were capable of, because his head snapped upward at the sight, red eyes bulging with incredulity. "Can you tell us where to find the spineless traitors, please?"

His vision darted between them, petrified. Olalla maintained her smugness until she noticed Casimir's rigid posture had wilted. The open, tired expression on his face implied he wanted to do nothing more than melt into Aethelred and build a cozy nest in his heart.

She cleared her throat, drawing their attention. "Bet you didn't think you'd see us again, hm? It was clever of you and

Angor to toy with our emotions—sounds like something I would do. I never thought *you* would sink so low, though."

"I-I didn't. I didn't know Angor's plan—I swear. Did they…" He trailed off as he surveyed their jutting cheekbones and wan skin.

"Oh, I'm sure you know exactly what they did," Olalla said, conspicuously pushing up her coat sleeves to display her blistered wrists. Infection and continuous reopening had delayed the healing process. It was possible she had purposely picked at the lacerations to ensure they remained, to ensure she could display them to her enemies as proof of their transgressions. "Didn't Angor gloat to you about all the *science* the researchers unearthed?"

"N-no." He stumbled forward, genuinely appalled. "I…haven't talked to Angor since you two disappeared."

Olalla's smile faltered at that information; she had thought nothing would tear the two apart, but Angor's choice had. Her intention for this encounter had been to convince him to end himself, but even when forming the plan she'd known she would never follow through with it. Killing her mother had been easy, but Aethelred—sweet Aethelred? He had not wanted to join their cause, but neither had he wanted to join Angor's self-indulgent lunacy. He was the same lost boy he'd always been, forever doomed to choose between his immorally ambitious friends.

"Haven't talked to Angor?" Casimir challenged, stepping closer to the other man. His previous shock at seeing Aethelred had faded, paving the way for barely-contained indignation. "Not even to ask him where the research facility was?"

Aethelred swallowed, backing away. "He…told me he thought you were going to prison."

"But you didn't think so?" With a trembling hand, Casimir grabbed their old friend's red employee shirt to stop his retreat. "You knew what was happening, and you didn't try to stop it? You—you...I can't even think of an insult to suit you."

"Coward?"

"Coward doesn't even scratch the surface of what you are," Casimir snarled, pushing him back into the meat shelves. Steaks and chicken tumbled to the floor, but the shorter man didn't relent even when an entire shelf collapsed. "You're a disgrace to your own memory. You're not even *you*. You're a cheap replica of the Aethelred I knew—the boy who fought a tiger with a cotton candy stick and a popcorn bucket for a helmet. What the fuck happened to him?"

"Casimir," Olalla prompted when a woman reached the end of a nearby aisle, spotted them, and then darted toward the front of the store.

"No, Olalla, I won't be nice to him. I won't let him pretend everything's okay. *Nothing* is—"

His words halted when Olalla dug thoughts into his mind, convincing him to shut up. Her mental strength had significantly decreased after the research facility, but Casimir's will was so weary and defeated that it barely took any effort to overhaul. Robotically, he released Aethelred and created a few feet of space between them. Olalla might have liked to see how far he went with his rage, but the last thing they needed was to be arrested.

"I think you understand, don't you, Aethelred?" She sidled next to Casimir, looping her arm through his. The red-haired man hadn't moved from where he lay in a bed of packaged meats, chest heaving beneath his name-tag. "Casimir doesn't love you anymore. You lost his love—his respect—when you sided with Angor all those years ago. It's time you pay for your mistakes."

A store employee sprinted from one of the aisles, panting, but Aethelred held up a reassuring hand. "I fell," he lied, pushing to his feet. "I'm fine."

After a skeptical glance at Olalla and Casimir, the man disappeared, leaving them in relative privacy once more. An audience wouldn't matter now, though; Olalla's next move was purely psychological.

Aethelred straightened his shirt and furrowed his brow at their linked arms. "I don't understand."

"No?" Her free arm reached toward Casimir's face, possessively pulling him closer. "He's mine now, Aethelred—don't you see? Three years in a cell together is truly the perfect incubator for romance, wouldn't you say?"

Aethelred's hands twisted in his own shirt, clearly nauseated. "You...two..."

"Well, we would be together, but he's all hung up on this *ex-boyfriend* of his." She laughed lightly, nuzzling her head into Casimir's chest. "Don't worry, though—I'm erasing his memory as we speak. Every little recollection of that pesky ex will disappear; it'll be like he never even existed."

"Olalla," Aethelred choked, "don't—"

"Don't what?" she questioned as Casimir blinked. His face went from blank to befuddled as he beheld the scene.

"You made this mess, didn't you, Cosmos?" he asked upon surveying the fallen meats. "Are you trying to get this random store employee in trouble? You sly bitch. Why'd you choose him? 'Cus of his weird-ass hair?"

"It's a wig, honey. Don't be rude," she said behind her hand. "I was actually just telling him how we're recently engaged but you haven't bought me a ring. You were just *so eager* to ask that you didn't bother to buy one first."

When Casimir rolled his eyes but didn't refute this truth, Aethelred tried to steady himself on one of the shelves and knocked it over.

"So clumsy!" Olalla declared as Casimir snickered. "I'll help him clean up. Go get us some ice cream, dearest."

"I'm getting pepperoni, too," he said, disentangling himself from her arms. Once he'd vanished into one of the aisles, Olalla fixed Aethelred with a triumphant smile.

"That was...an act," he decided, as if the reality where they'd played a prank on him was the only one in which he could prevent himself from fainting.

"I'll let you think that for another"—she consulted her invisible watch—"fifteen seconds, then it's your turn."

"My..."

"You thought I'd let you keep your memories? That *would* be unusually cruel and very much like me, but alas, I can't risk it. Casimir and I *will* get married—what else are we supposed to do after you've ruined all our dreams? And if we're to be happy, we can't worry about you turning us over to the authorities at any moment. I won't erase the heartbreak—that would be too generous—but after I'm through with your mind, you won't remember anything from Hastings Street."

Tears dripped down his cheeks, and she felt him rehearsing all the highlights of their friendship. "You said you'd never use your Affinity on me."

"Did I?" she hissed before slashing that conversation from his mental apparatus. Confusion swept over his face, increasing with every memory she blocked. As she dammed the flow of certain recollections, she wove a duller history into his brain: Aethelred Certior was an orphan, an outcast—utterly alone. He went to East Mintle High School, and he knew of Angor Periculy and his two close friends, but they never accepted him into their group. They always labeled him a *freak*.

He did not quite remember Angor's two friends—Olalla did not want him to recognize them—but he had formed an unreciprocated crush on one, a crush that would never fully dissolve.

Once her work was done, she allowed Aethelred to return to the present, the lens of her lies distorting his view.

"Thanks so much for your help"—she squinted at his name-tag—"Aethelred. What a *strange* name. So many *freaks* in this town…"

He wiped his cheeks and averted his gaze, which was how she knew she'd succeeded in altering history—in altering fate.

She would marry Casimir as Aethelred should have, stealing his happiness as he had stolen her dreams. Frankly, the worst part of this was that she'd had to make Casimir's love for her shift from platonic to romantic. She had never wanted to manipulate him, and she did not want to use him for her own happiness, but she could not think of anyone else to marry, to have children with.

Marriage and children… Those were not things she'd thought she was capable of having—capable of *wanting*—but she needed them; she needed stability; she needed a purpose; she needed to not feel like every cell in her body was disintegrating all the time.

She also needed to spite Aethelred for hurting Casimir, for not trying to rescue them, and for tilting Angor's morality and ideals too far away from her own.

"Thanks again to Angor Periculy for his tremendous contribution to science!" a voice boomed from the stage. At her vantage point, Olalla couldn't see the speaker, but she did see Angor when he strolled off stage, award in hand. He passed where she stood in the shadows without noticing her, joining his handsome friend before the two disappeared into one of the dressing rooms.

Disregarding every other person swarming around backstage, she stalked after him.

Six months had passed since she'd erased Aethelred's memory—and Casimir's. Six months for her to muster the courage to face Angor. She'd spent that time practicing her Affinity on her husband and gaining a healthy amount of weight. Her mind and body had to be at peak performance if she wished to accomplish the impossible.

The information she'd gathered from the research facility had helped her understand more about brainwaves and white matter, but it hadn't given her all the information she needed to enhance her Affinity. She had a few projects in the works, but she couldn't risk putting this off. With her luck, Angor would randomly decide to rekindle his friendship with Aethelred and unravel all her hard work.

"It's irrelevant," Angor's voice emanated from the dressing room. The door had been left slightly ajar, and through the mirrors within, she saw him packing his briefcase while the brown-haired man examined a broken lightbulb. She recognized him from the medical history museum; his appearance hadn't changed in the slightest. Angor, however, had grown since their last encounter. Broader, leaner, filling out his magenta suit instead of looking like a boy playing world leader. She wished he wore that ugly ponytail so she could at least pretend she didn't find him appealing.

"They'll praise me for discovering dogs have Affinities but not humans—the absurdity! If only they would accept that some humans also have an extra chromosome… Imagine the award I'd receive for *that*! No, no, they'll deny me forever, subjugating me to the research of animals—"

"Oh, poor baby," Olalla cooed as she kicked open the door. The scent of cologne hit her nostrils, expensive but laced with the familiar nutty scent she'd always associated with Angor. That, paired with his unguarded surprise, was almost enough to deteriorate her resolve.

Apprehensive, he straightened and examined her appearance. For the funeral of his memories, she'd stolen a black gown that hugged her curves and displayed enough cleavage to raise those meat-pink eyebrows.

She smirked in his friend's direction. "Who's this handsome devil?"

The man cleared his throat. "In my humble opinion, the devil is a knock-off of Hades."

Resuming his aura of sophistication, Angor said, "As much as I'm sure this stranger would love to hear you talk about Greek mythology, we don't have the time." To Olalla, he curtly added, "If you'd like my autograph, ask my agent."

"Your agent!" An unintended laugh exploded from her lips. "How posh, Periculy."

With wrinkled brows, the man looked between them, and Angor rubbed his forehead. "Fine. Than, give us a minute."

After an awkward bow, Than departed the room, careful not to brush Olalla in the process. She slipped past him to approach Angor, noting the small bowl of walnuts on the vanity with an unwanted tinge of nostalgia.

"I'll spare you the diabolical speech, Periculy. You know why I'm here."

"To make me stab myself to death?"

She peeked around him toward his briefcase. "Do you have any knives?"

His face remained taut. "Spare us both this embarrassment instead, Cosmos. We both know you can't effectively control my mind. I don't know where you've been hiding these years, but I doubt the time away from me has improved your skill."

"My *time away* was illuminating, actually. All my hours in that cell allowed me to form a perfect plan of how I'll enact my revenge. The way they cut my flesh and prodded my brain instilled so much inspiration."

Angor had always been a master at concealing his emotions, therefore the horror that flashed in his eyes was certainly sincere. He didn't seem *shocked*, necessarily, but the thought didn't pleasure him, as she'd assumed. "Ephraim... told me," he managed. "He confronted me... Before that, I didn't know."

"But you *have* known for three years and have done nothing? I shouldn't be surprised, I suppose. People always find a way to let you down." He opened his mouth, but she held up a silencing hand. "Don't make excuses for allowing us to rot, Angor. Groveling is unbecoming. Besides, I've heard enough of it from Aethelred already."

This time he did a better job of hiding his unease, but the bob of his throat betrayed him. "What did you do to Aethelred?"

Her lips spread into a smirk as she prowled toward him. "Stole his boyfriend, stole his memory—the routine procedure when it comes to dealing with traitors."

"Shame I don't have a boyfriend," he mused, cool and careless. The way his eyes followed her every move told a different story. As she began to circle him, his head snapped back and forth to watch her, body and mind braced.

"No, but you had *me*." She stopped before him and ran her finger along the underside of his chin. "You could have had the world, but instead you've settled for this society where they don't acknowledge the full breadth of your work. We could have been a team, you and I." She touched her own face, brandishing the wedding band on her left ring finger. "But it's too late now."

"You actually…"

"Married Casimir? Of course I did. You once told me he had no interest in me—well, I *made* him have an interest in me. Do you doubt my abilities now?" When he said nothing, she tsked. "How disappointing—you didn't even see this coming. You probably thought you were safe from me forever, didn't you? Well, I've returned to exact my revenge, and your lack of foresight annuls all my hesitation."

"Olalla," he tried, but she clutched his chin, physically bending him to her will. Then she crawled into his mind.

Her imagination had envisioned so many ways of murdering Angor that none would actually satisfy her. All forms of revenge had previously occurred in her mind, all except this. She had not considered simply wiping his memory; that was not a just punishment for his unforgivable atrocities.

Oh, but it *was*. Angor could not die as quickly as her mother had—no, no, Angor was her enemy now, and if she was going to have an enemy, she didn't want him to know her strengths; she didn't want him to know her at all. She wanted to slowly tear at every fiber of his white matter until his brain became undone.

It was easier to creep through the cracks of his mind now,

not because anything had changed in him but because everything had changed in her. She no longer craved his approval. She no longer wanted him to believe her beliefs by his own volition. She had stopped considering him an equal long ago, and she had no problem compelling her inferiors.

Casimir stood in a lightless hallway of a thousand doors. He was not sure how he knew there were exactly a thousand, or how he knew there were any doors at all considering he couldn't see *anything*, but he sensed their presence. Every time he attempted to open one, the handles fell off. Then he reached the last door—the open door.

A man stood within it—no, a boy. A boy with gangly limbs, unkempt hair, and blood red eyes. He wore a bowl as a hat, and his lips twisted as he tried very hard not to laugh.

"Not funny, Casimir," his voice warbled through the corridor. "Angor's walnuts are sacred. Olalla, can you compel him to stop dumping food on my head?"

With careful footsteps, Casimir approached the open door, but when he reached the threshold, the boy had lost his bowl-hat, and he had become a man. The laughter had left his eyes, and the innocence had left his face. A ghostly quality overtook his red irises, like fatal wounds on a corpse.

"Red," Casimir said, which seemed a dumb thing to say; yeah, his features were red. Was that really the most intelligent way to greet someone?

The man, wisely, didn't respond. Rather, he slammed shut the door, drenching Casimir in eternal darkness.

Something hit his head, and he jolted upright.

"You missed the ultrasound," Olalla said as she sat on the

edge of their bed putting pressure on his shins. He didn't want to call her *overweight*, but the pregnancy *had* made her rather heavy. He massaged his temple, and she nodded toward the source of the cut on his forehead: a pack of cigarettes lying on the pillow beside him. "There you go. Now, can you stop fidgeting all night? You don't want little baby Avner to be born with an insomnia Affinity."

Casimir retrieved the cigarettes and grumbled, "Wouldn't it be an anti-insomnia Affinity? Wouldn't that make him sleep better? Shouldn't we *hope* for that?"

What he really wanted to ask was, "Can't we name him Aethelred?" but that conversation never went anywhere. He wasn't sure why she was so adamantly against the name. Probably because they didn't live in the thirteen hundreds.

"We should hope he's born with a *useful* Affinity," she said, "like the ability to control nociceptors."

"Noci-what?"

"Pain neurons."

"That sounds evil."

"I am evil."

"No, you're weird."

Smirking, she stood from the bed and rubbed her rotund belly. "Weird breeds weird." He rolled his eyes at her freaky mantra but didn't mock her because a worried gleam had consumed her face. "What if he *doesn't* have an Affinity? I don't know if I'll be able to gain access to the proper equipment to figure out if he has the chromosome…"

"Does it matter?" Casimir asked with a dramatic sigh. "It's not like you can insert him with the chromosome if he doesn't have it."

"Can I not?" she countered so conspiratorially that he wondered if she actually had concocted a drug to alter one's species.

Still, these creepy musings were common for his wife, so he cocked his head against the pillow and gave her a sassy, "Well, what are you gonna do with him if he doesn't have the chromosome?"

She shrugged. "Sell him and make a new baby."

His eyes darted around their bedroom. It was bigger than the one in his parents' trailer, but it made him feel small—empty. Olalla didn't like to decorate, and his hallucinogenic mind had been pitifully dormant these past years. "I don't think you're joking," he finally said, "and it's freaking me out a little."

A fake laugh ensued. He knew it was fake because all of Olalla's laughs were fake. Everything about her was fake, except when she said psychotic things like "I'll sell my baby and make a new one."

She bent down to kiss him on the forehead; it felt worse than the cigarette pack hitting him. "Maybe you're hallucinating this whole conversation, darling."

After ruffling his hair, she waltzed out of the room, her movements too smooth for a woman due with a baby in less than a month.

That scared him, too—a *baby*. If anything was worse than Olalla Stromer raising a child, it was Olalla Stromer and Casimir Stromer raising a child *together*.

No matter what weird name they gave him, the kid was screwed.

Casimir extracted a cigarette, reveling in how the little stick reminded him of a reality he'd always wanted but never had. As he puffed smoke toward the ceiling, he muttered, "I hope I'm hallucinating this whole life."

Bonus Scene

Tattoos and Teleportation

This scene takes place between Chapter 10 and Chapter 11.

It took Casimir less than a week of knowing Ephraim Mayer to discover his outlandish tattoos and decide he wanted some for himself. He was seventeen and therefore could not acquire one legally. Instead of waiting until his birthday in June, like a normal person, he thought it would be smarter to request Ephraim, the fifteen-year-old, ink him now.

Angor didn't particularly care what Casimir did with his body, except that the hallucinator demanded the whole weird hair gang be involved in the process.

"Periculy," Olalla greeted after opening the door to the Cosmoses' home. She wore jeans and a loose fitting sweatshirt, as she always did whenever they spent hours studying or researching. That had been their plan for this chilly Saturday until Casimir had jarringly woken Angor by banging metal pots beside his ears. "Are we going somewhere?"

With a sigh, Angor glanced over his shoulder to where the poorly-painted pine green car idled. "Apparently. Casimir declared, 'We're taking my car to go get me a tattoo,' and so that's what we're doing."

Olalla leaned against the door frame, eyebrows perked. "Is that really what he said?"

"I might have removed some of the expletives."

The front passenger's side window rolled down, revealing Aethelred's alarmed face as Casimir leaned over him to shout, "Hey, Cosmos! Get your ass out here. We're taking my fucking car to go get me a fucking tattoo."

Smirking, Olalla strolled past Angor to heed the command. "That sounds right."

Once the two slipped into the backseat, Casimir sped from Hastings Street, following directions from Aethelred, who held a giant map of East Mintle. Fifteen minutes later, they arrived in the wealthiest neighborhood of the town, where the yards spanned more acreage than the entire trailer park. Only ten homes rested along the winding road, some with driveways so long the houses weren't visible as they drove by.

Ephraim's was number eight, a lavish brick mansion that towered above the surrounding trees. With the leaves glistening bright autumn hues, the estate looked like it belonged on a postcard.

"Are we sure this is the right address?" Angor asked as Casimir drove the car around the driveway's circular bend and parked it right before the front steps.

"Nope." The hallucinator hopped out of the car and jogged up the stairs, entering the mansion without knocking.

"Let's hope it is…and that Ephraim left the front door unlocked purposely," Aethelred muttered as he, too, exited the car. Angor and Olalla slowly followed, their attention honed on the grandness of the house rather than the act of entering it.

"One day, we'll have a house this big," Olalla stated, her wistful gaze morphing to awkwardness when she peeked in Angor's direction. "The four of us, I mean. It'll be our sanctuary of science."

"I thought we were planning to build a town?"

"We'll need our own house within the town, won't we?" Without waiting for a response, she ascended the stairs, running a hand along the bronze railing. "I'm not a fan of this design, though. It feels too...*old*. Our town will be a gateway to the future. Geometric architecture, glass walls...and definitely no shag rugs," she added when she reached the open doorway.

Joining her, Angor balked at the sight of the room within. A hideous squash orange shag carpet hugged a giant indoor pool that diffused the air with the scent of chlorine. He suspected the pool and carpet combination would lead to mold or mildew, but he supposed this rich of a family likely had systems in place to avoid such issues. Along the right wall spanned a lengthy bar, above which shelves of alcohol climbed toward the high ceiling. Three separate televisions were mounted to the wood-paneled walls throughout the room, the discordant sounds of three different programs drowning out Casimir's impressed whistling.

"Am I hallucinating, or is there a pool in this joint?"

Before any of the teens could answer, a woman appeared in an open archway on the opposite end of the room, blinking behind her green-tinted glasses. "Oh my," she said, probably to the oddity of Casimir dipping his sneaker-covered foot into the pool.

"Yup, that's real," he declared, wiping his soaking shoe on the carpet.

"Who—"

"Is that a sculpture of a human heart?" Angor inquired as he paced toward the glass display against the left wall. Hundreds of ceramic art pieces decorated the shelves, but he only had eyes for the life-sized replication of a heart.

"Oh, I don't know." The woman appeared beside him, twirling the tail of the scarf wrapped around her head. "I only bought it because it was expensive, and I like expensive things."

"Clearly," Casimir said from the other side of the room, where he examined the liquor bottles.

"Do you like the sculpture?" she asked Angor, still self-consciously fiddling with her scarf.

"Oh, I love it. You don't happen to have a brain sculpture, do you?"

The woman bit her pink glossed lip. "Um…what would that look like?"

Behind them, Olalla let out a loud, distinctive sigh that was reserved for the least competent this world had to offer. Angor, too, was disheartened that someone with such little intellect could acquire so much wealth.

"*Ima*," Ephraim whined as he materialized in the archway, sporting a leather jacket and black jeans with far too many zippers. The belt he wore appeared to be composed of actual bullets, and he'd spiked his lime green hair in all directions. "Why didn't you tell me my friends were here?"

"*Friends* is a little presumptuous," Olalla teased, now resting her head on Aethelred's shoulder, probably from boredom. The only reason he allowed it was because he wore a thick striped sweater, per usual.

"Oh, are these your friends?" the woman asked, genuinely unsure.

Ephraim arched his green eyebrows, which he hadn't

bothered cosmetically darkening today. To Angor, who looked in the mirror at pinkish eyebrows every day, they seemed more natural than unnatural. "You let them in, Ma. Who did you think they were?"

"I didn't let them in," she stated matter-of-factly. "I just found them in here."

"So they broke in? What did I tell you about intruders?" He waited a moment for her response, and when she gave none beyond a puzzled look, he expelled an exasperated breath. "Sound the alarm so I can come in guns blazing."

"Thank the devil she didn't sound the alarm this time," Casimir said from where he stood atop the bar, analyzing bottles on the higher shelves.

"I didn't feel threatened, Ephy," his mother reasoned, and Olalla snickered behind her hand at the nickname. "I really like this one, actually." Angor stood a little straighter when the woman turned to him with adoring eyes. "He seems very *studious*. Why can't you be more like him?"

Rolling his eyes, Ephraim rounded the pool toward them. "Sorry about my mom—"

"You can call me Ruth—or even Ima, if you want. It's Hebrew for 'Mom,' and I can already tell you'll be like a son to me." She smiled at Angor before spinning toward her son. "Ephraim, you really can't leave the house dressed like that. The cops will think you're a criminal."

"They wouldn't be *wrong*," he mumbled, readjusting his spiked bracelet. "We're not going out, Ma. They came over to hang here."

"Oh. Wonderful! I'll go get some chips and make a cheese plate. Feel free to use the pool and anything else you'd like!" On that cheery note, she scurried from the room, disappearing into the hall beyond the archway.

"Well, then, I'll make use of this." Casimir snatched a bottle from the topmost shelf and then hopped off the bar. "Now, Eph, what was all that about 'guns blazing?' You have *guns*? Why didn't I know about this?"

Olalla lazily tapped her finger in Angor's direction. "Periculy gave us strict orders to prevent the knowledge from reaching your awareness."

Even with a large bottle in one hand, Casimir managed to throw up two middle fingers. "Thanks, Periculy. Let's go see these guns."

With both arms, Ephraim gestured grandly toward the archway. "Right this way."

Grudgingly, Angor followed him and the others from the pool room into the house beyond. The shag carpet continued through the labyrinth of hallways, each wall marked with professional family portraits. After a series of four turns, they descended a staircase into a well-lit metallic bunker swathed in weapons, none of which Angor could identify beyond "gun." Embarrassingly, he knew very little about the subject, and when Ephraim began showing off his firearms, most of the terminology went right over Angor's head.

"Are your parents prepping for World War III, or what?" Casimir questioned as he admired one of the larger guns.

"Nah, this is *my* collection." Ephraim ran a hand along one weapon as if caressing a lover. "I ask for a new one each holiday, and I've really perfected the 'spoiled rotten kid' tantrum if I don't get my way. I just wanna be ready if the government comes knocking about my *weird hair*. Besides, they add to my badassery."

Olalla eyed one of the handguns a little too intently. "Would you teach us how to use them?"

"Sure. I have a whole setup in the back. I'll show you

when I'm done tattooing Stromer."

"Mm," Casimir hummed, "good idea not to let Reddy touch any of these before then. He might shoot me to stop me from getting the tat."

Aethelred blanched. "I wouldn't do that."

Ignoring him, Ephraim ushered them toward the exit like a police officer directing traffic. "Let's go before the red-head gets any ideas."

"I wouldn't—" Aethelred tried again, but his voice was drowned out by Casimir's boisterous laughter.

The rebellious two talked guns the entire walk from the weapon room to Ephraim's bedroom. Aethelred hugged himself, eyes darting around guiltily, while Olalla glared at every family portrait with contempt.

"Any specific reason you wish to improve your shooting skills?" Angor ventured, half goading, half accusatory.

Olalla placed her pointer finger on the wall, tracing waves on the blank whiteness as they walked. "Since Artemis can sometimes resist my ability, the skill might prove advantageous."

"Having sororicidal thoughts?"

Dropping her hand, Olalla set her dark gaze forward. "Always."

When they reached Ephraim's bedroom on the second floor, Angor was surprised to find it was only about twice the size of his bedroom in the mobile home. Unsurprising were the punk rock posters obscuring the walls, the baseball caps hanging like constellations from the ceiling, and the stench of rotting fruit emanating from the pile in the far corner. Olalla scrunched her nose at it before lounging on the unmade bed, which Angor sat at the foot of once Casimir plopped into one of the several bean bag chairs.

"Take a seat, Certior." Ephraim kicked one of the vacant chairs before rummaging through the open drawers of his dresser. "This is gonna take a while."

Aethelred seemed disinclined to move until Ruth appeared in the doorway with her promised snacks; then he hurried to the chair farthest from Casimir and closest to the fruit pile.

"Knock knock," the woman said without knocking. "I have cheese and chips!" Placing the plate and bowl on the desk, she smiled at the teens until her expression soured. "Ephraim, you really need to clean this room. It smells like a garden perished in here."

"Thanks. Now leave. We're busy." Without looking at her, he threw an orange over his shoulder, pelting her stocking-covered shin. She yelped, huffed, and pouted before ultimately departing the bedroom, offendedly but gently shutting the door behind her.

"Your mom's a hot young thing, huh?" Casimir drawled as he unscrewed the cap on his liquor bottle.

Ephraim snorted. "I'm so glad you're gay."

"Better watch out for Periculy."

"Angor won't get any ideas I don't want him to have." Olalla nudged his thigh with her shoe and smiled in a way that could have been joking or threatening.

Extracting an overripe banana from his drawer, Ephraim said, "Isn't there a rule about us not using our superpowers on each other? That's the only reason I haven't squeezed lemons in any of your eyes."

Mid-chug on alcohol, Casimir choked. "Are lemons even a fruit?"

"Besides," Ephraim continued as if the hallucinator hadn't spoken, "I thought Olalla's power didn't work on

Angor?" Her duplicitous grin faded, but he evaded her wrath when he pulled his small tattoo machine from the drawer. "Aha! And here's one of my favorite guns. Convinced my rents to get it for me last Hanukkah. They don't know what the hell it does—probably think it's some kinda firearm, since that's somehow less dangerous."

With a tight jaw, Angor watched Ephraim half shut his drawer and approach a shelf of inks. He wasn't jealous of the younger boy's capabilities with tattoos but simply of his wealth. Though he did understand the plight of their weird hair, he would never understand the hardships within which they'd all grown. Ephraim's parents gave him everything, while the rest of them would give everything—and in Angor's and Aethelred's cases, *had* given everything—to get rid of their parents entirely.

"What do you want me to ink on you, anyway?" Ephraim asked.

Licking his lips, Casimir side-glanced Aethelred. "I want a portrait of Red's face."

The presumptive model coughed. "You…what?"

"Oh, don't act surprised," Olalla chided as she twirled her sweatshirt's string. "We all knew this was coming."

"Frankly, I thought it'd be something more crude. Count yourself lucky," Angor added to his old friend, whose face had paled with nausea.

"Don't look so distraught." Ephraim picked a bright red bottle of ink from the shelf. "Unless you want that ridiculous expression immortalized on Cas's…where? Arm?"

"I was thinking thigh." Slapping his left leg, Casimir stood. "That way I have a nice view when I'm taking a shit. I want it to be upside down, too, so it's facing me." Without warning, he unbuckled his belt and unbuttoned his jeans, dropping them to the floor and exposing his tight polka-dotted briefs. Instantly, Aethelred buried his face in his hands.

"Really, Stromer?" Olalla complained, averting her attention to the ceiling.

"Really, Cosmos," he countered in a sassy impersonation of her voice. Plopping back into the bean bag chair, he patted his thigh. "C'mon over, Ephy."

"I'm gonna need to shave the hair—let me go get a razor."

As he darted from the room, Casimir shrugged and drank from the liquor bottle.

"I don't think alcohol and tattooing are a good combination," Angor commented.

"Interesting opinion." Casimir took a sip and then tauntingly smacked his lips.

"Alcohol thins your blood," Olalla explained, as Ephraim returned to the room with a metal razor in hand, "which will lead to excess bleeding and make it harder for the ink to saturate your skin."

"Interesting opinion." Casimir took another swig, to which Aethelred loudly sighed.

"I think those were facts."

"*Another* interesting opinion—"

"It's gonna look like shit either way, so I'm not concerned," Ephraim chimed in as he knelt beside Casimir's leg. After only one pass with the razor, a tiny nick opened in his skin, sending a slow stream of red down the side of his thigh.

"Owww-y," Casimir whined unconvincingly. "Red, come kiss it, make it better."

Aethelred did not kiss it; his face remained in his hands

for the next several minutes as Ephraim shaved clean a large area on Casimir's left thigh. Once the tattooing began and the hum of the machine dulled the energy in the room, Aethelred nestled deeper into his bean bag chair and took a nap while Angor and Olalla retrieved books from a stack near the closet and read about fondue recipes and the English language's strangest words, respectively.

As Angor's interest in cheese sauce diminished, Casimir's delirium increased. He kept jabbering about the dolphins on the ceiling, which wasn't particularly odd for someone with frequent hallucinations. But then he started raving about what beautiful babies Angor and Olalla would someday create, and that was when they all knew he'd had too much alcohol.

"If you think either of us want children, you've gone *far* over the edge," Olalla said without glancing up from her book.

"Children are necessary to the cycle of life, but they're a duty meant for those with far less ambition," Angor agreed as he slammed shut his fondue book. "If you were in your right mind, Casimir, you would know this."

Uncurling from his fetal position, Aethelred reached across the two vacant bean bag chairs in an attempt to grab the half-empty bottle. Casimir hugged it to his chest defensively, nearly elbowing Ephraim in the forehead.

"Leaveth me, Sir Reddington, or I'll call for the king to taketh your head!"

"Stop moving," Ephraim grumbled, immune to Casimir's atrocious accent. Angor was about to comment on it when the bedroom door swung open.

"Do you kids want more—" Ruth began to ask, but the moment she spotted her son tattooing Casimir's naked, bleeding leg, her eyes widened behind her tinted glasses.

"What are you *doing*?"

"Don't *worry*, Ruthie." Casimir tried to wave with the hand holding the bottle, causing the liquid to slosh within. "I'm almost eighteen. It's all good."

Angor hopped to his feet when the woman swayed as if about to faint, but instead of collapsing into the hallway behind her, she completely vanished.

Olalla's book dropped to the ground as she scrambled to stand. "What the..."

Ephraim resumed tattooing as if nothing strange had occurred. "She does that when she gets stressed—ignore her."

Dumbfounded, Angor stared at the empty doorway. "She... Did she just teleport?"

"No, her molecules disintegrated over there and reintegrated somewhere else. Is that proper Angorian English?"

Slowly, Angor inched toward the door and peered into the corridor. Ruth was nowhere in sight. She'd *teleported*, a supernatural ability greatly surpassing anything they'd assumed within the realm of biology, chemistry, or physics. Certainly it seemed beyond the capability of one's *mind*, deeming *Mental* the incorrect classification for this power. "Where is our notebook when we need to take notes?" he wondered aloud.

"I thought you brought it," Olalla said, thoughts swirling behind her unfocused purple eyes.

"I thought *you* brought it."

"You know my pants are too tight."

"And Angor's not complaining," Casimir jeered as he threw his head back against the bean bag.

"You can get away with carrying around a purse," Angor

reasoned to Olalla. "I can't."

Casimir chortled so hard that he began to hiccup. "Periculy *so* wants to carry around a purse."

"I call dibs on buying him a purse for his birthday," Ephraim sang as he finished off a line on Casimir's tattoo. From this angle, Angor couldn't tell what it was, but *red* was definitely the primary color.

"So," Olalla said as she closed the door with her pointer finger, "are you going to tell us about your mom's superpower willingly, or should I make you?"

Shifting on his knees, Ephraim refused to tear his focus from the tattoo. "She can teleport—it's not that wild. She…well, she doesn't like to talk about it, but she told me that when she was young, her family lived in Poland during World War II. There were bombings, you know, and when her village was being bombed, she somehow managed to teleport her entire family to a field in the middle of Ohio. She says she doesn't know how it happened. One minute she was wishing they were on the other side of the world, and then they were. That's the first time she remembers doing it. Now she only does it when she's irrationally upset with me. Don't tell my dad—he'll flip."

Angor stroked his chin in contemplation. This confirmed his theory that their abilities manifested as a survival mechanism, but displacing one's body from one location to the next seemed crazier than activating nociceptors or manipulating one's brainwaves. "Does your mother have weirdly colored hair?"

"Mint green."

Brow furrowed, Olalla tilted her head to face him. "How has your father not noticed her *mint green* hair?"

"Did you? She *always* wears a scarf and glasses. 'Sides, my parents aren't really *close*. Dad's rarely around, and I think the only time they've ever had sex was to make me."

"That's one advantage the gays have," Casimir said, one arm stretched beyond his tilted-back head to finger-doodle on the wall behind him. "When they do the dirty deed, you know they don't have any yucky ulterior motives like *making kids*."

With a weary laugh, Ephraim rocked back onto his feet and stood. "Okay, it's done. You're welcome. Give me a sec and I'll wash it off."

"Let's see it," Olalla said, pacing toward them as Aethelred discreetly peeked in the tattoo's direction.

Casimir sprang up and hastily pulled on his jeans, simultaneously shielding his fresh skin art with his leather jacket. "Ah, ah, ah"—he wiggled his finger at them—"you're gonna have to seduce me a little better than that if you wanna see my private parts. I'll be waiting for you to up your game." Winking at Aethelred, he limped from the bedroom, chugging the remaining liquor as he went.

Ephraim released the sigh of frustration they all felt from various sources. "He better not give me shit when that thing gets infected."

Thank you for reading!

If you enjoyed this "novella" (or full length novel in disguise), please consider leaving a review on Amazon and Goodreads, and make sure to check out the other novels and novellas in
The Affinities Series!

www.ingramcontent.com/pod-product-compliance
Lightning Source LLC
Chambersburg PA
CBHW030556180626
46816CB00005B/1564